UNWANTED MEMORIES

Roxy's heart was still pounding. Being so close to Tanner after all these years, feeling the heat of his whip-lean body, she had lost all composure.

But as she watched for him, all the pain and heartache he had caused her came rushing back. Standing there, she remembered all the insults she had endured, the contemptuous looks, being shunned by the women of Denver society, and her hostility toward the man she had once loved returned full force.

What was his game? she wondered. What did he mean that there was a misunderstanding about his going off to war? Did he hope to resume their old relationship? Did he think he could smooth talk her into making a daily trip to his cabin and spending a couple hours making love like they used to do? Would he talk of marriage again, all the while having no intention of ever standing in front of a preacher to say those two little words, "I do"?

A soft sigh feathered through her lips. She wished he hadn't returned. The same old magnetism was still there between them. She was thoroughly disgusted with herself, for even now she could remember the feel of his arms around her, holding her softness close to his hard body.

Other *Leisure* books by Norah Hess:

BLAZE
JADE
WILLOW
FOREVER THE FLAME
FANCY
WINTER LOVE
LACEY
TENNESSEE MOON
DEVIL IN SPURS
HAWKE'S PRIDE
KENTUCKY BRIDE
MOUNTAIN ROSE
KENTUCKY WOMAN
SAGE
STORM
WILDFIRE

TANNER

Norah Hess

LEISURE BOOKS NEW YORK CITY

A LEISURE BOOK®

September 1998

Published by

Dorchester Publishing Co., Inc.
276 Fifth Avenue
New York, NY 10001

ISBN 0-8439-4424-2

The name "Leisure Books" and the stylized "L" with design are trademarks of Dorchester Publishing Co., Inc.

Printed in the United States of America.

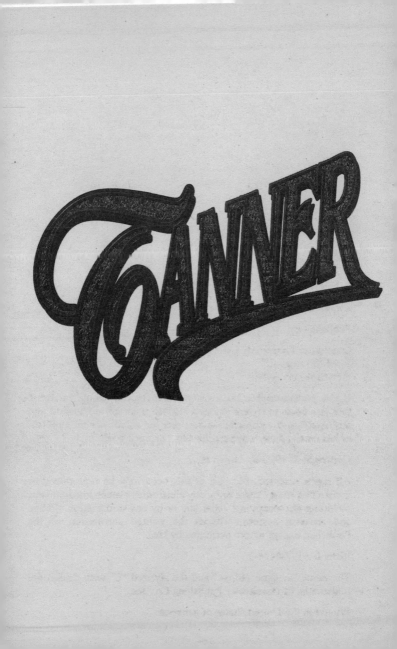

Chapter One

Colorado, 1868

His face was hard-boned and weather-worn from years of exposure to sun and wind. But now the war with the Apaches was over and Tanner Graylord was on the long trail home to Colorado. He had skirted all towns, anxious to arrive at the ranch he hadn't seen in seven years. He should arrive sometime the following day.

For the last two days he had ridden in a drizzly rain, and he was wet, hungry and tired. The previous night he had come upon a Catholic church and had stepped inside to warm up and to sleep. It was crudely constructed, but the stations of the cross were very beautiful. The smell of the incense was sweet and he had breathed deeply of it as he sat in the last pew, in the shadows. He'd had a good night's rest, free of war nightmares.

Dusk was approaching now and the air was growing cool. It was time he looked for a spot to make camp. It was already growing dark when he came upon a bench where pines and aspens dotted a gentle slope. He stopped there to make his night camp.

There was a weariness in his face as he searched for dry limbs beneath a wide pine with low, sweeping branches. When he had gathered enough wood to last him through the night he scooped up a pile of pine needles and placed some of the wood on top them. When he struck a match to the pile, it caught readily, and he soon had a crackling blaze going.

Tanner unsaddled his stallion, Brave, and ran a gentle hand over the long puckered scar on the animal's rump. The big horse also wore a reminder of the war.

He next pegged Brave out at the fringe of the wide branches. The rope was long enough for the horse to graze on the new green grass or to come under the sheltering tree when he chose to get out of the rain.

Tanner's rumbling stomach told him it was time to prepare the evening meal. He spread out his bedroll and, dumping his camp gear onto it, picked from the jumble the battered coffee pot that had served him in the two years of fighting Indians. Taking up his canteen, he poured enough water into the pot to make two cups of coffee. When he had added grounds to the water, he placed the pot on the fire.

After he had set aside a skillet that had seen the same rough treatment as the coffee pot, he set to plucking the feathers off a fat quail he had shot.

When he had it dressed and cut up, he put a dollop of lard, the last he had, in the skillet and set it on the fire alongside the now brewing coffee. When the lard had melted from the heat, he laid the meat on top of it and heaped red coals up around the frying pan to hurry along the cooking process.

As the meat began to sizzle, Tanner took off his slicker and hung it on a branch so that the water would drip off the garment. His clothing was only damp from shoulders to mid-thigh, but from there on he was soaked all the way to his boots. By now the coffee had brewed. Pouring himself a tin cup of it, he sat in front of the fire, his clothing steaming and drying as his body took comfort from the hot drink.

As the cooking meat began to send forth a mouth-watering aroma and the rain pattered on the ground, Tanner stared into the flames while his mind went back through the years.

Roxy. Beautiful, vibrant Roxy with her coal black hair and sparkling eyes the color of new moss. Effortlessly, his mind conjured up an image of the seventeen-year-old that he had loved with all his heart, a heart she had carelessly smashed beneath her small feet.

He would have sworn on his dead parents' graves that Roxy loved him as deeply as he cared for her. He recalled the long hours spent together when he had taught her all about lovemaking. She had readily accepted his proposal of marriage and had made as many plans as he did for the cabin he was building, where they would start their married life together. The place was small, only three rooms, but they told each other that it would be fine until they could afford to build the fine clapboard house they dreamed of. He had worked his rear end off, spending eight to ten hours a day gathering a herd, getting the ranch off the ground in order to give her that dream house.

Tanner still couldn't pinpoint just when things began to go wrong between them. He had always felt that her father, Seth Bartel, was behind it. The big, blustery man owned the largest and fanciest saloon in Denver and when Roxy turned sixteen he had her working in the place. Actually, Roxy didn't really work. It had been his opinion that her father only wanted her there because her beauty drew the men to the Lady Chance and then to his gambling tables. Seth claimed that he wanted Roxy to know all about running the place, that one day, when he retired, he would turn the saloon over to her.

At any rate, it was evident the wily man didn't have plans for his daughter to marry a penniless rancher just starting out. He wanted her under his eye and thumb.

Tanner recalled that suddenly Roxy began to break dates with him. Seth always had some trumped-up reason why her presence was needed at the Lady Chance. When he had mentioned his suspicions that her father was trying to keep them apart, Roxy always protested that he was mistaken, that she had truly been needed at those times.

Three months had passed with him and Roxy seeing less and less of each other. Then one day when he could take it no longer, he took time off from the ranch and rode into town. He intended to have a serious talk with Roxy, bring things to a head. He was going to give her a choice. Either they got married within the month, or they would break things off between them.

Pain flashed in Tanner's eyes as he remembered riding down the rutted street, heading for the Lady Chance. He was approaching Denver's sole hotel when a coach pulled up in front of it. He noticed that Roxy and her father were standing on the boardwalk in front of the building. He knew by the excited smiles on their faces that they were there to meet a passenger in the big vehicle.

He reined in to see whom they would greet. The driver opened the coach door and assisted a middle-aged woman to the dusty street. A teenage boy followed her. Then a handsome, impeccably dressed man in a black suit and white shirt stood in the doorway, smiling at Roxy and Seth. When he stepped to the ground, Roxy threw herself at him with a glad cry. The stranger laughingly caught her by the waist and, hugging her, swung her around and around. He released her then, but kept an arm around her waist as he stepped up on the sidewalk to shake hands with Seth. The three stood there a minute, talking and laughing. Then Roxy and the stranger left Seth and walked toward the Lady Chance arm in arm.

Tanner stared after the pair. He was so stunned by what he had just witnessed, he wasn't aware that Seth had walked over to where he sat the stallion until the saloon keeper spoke.

"Well, Graylord," Seth said with a sly smile, "there goes my future son-in-law."

Every muscle in Tanner's body stiffened and for a moment he couldn't speak. His shock was too great. He gathered his wits then and said coolly, "I wasn't aware that you had another daughter."

"That's very funny, Graylord." Seth took a step back from the icy light in Tanner's eyes. "Roxy and the man she just greeted so warmly have had an

11

Norah Hess

understanding for close to two years. Those trips she made to Utah to visit her Aunt Nell were only an excuse to be with Ace Brandon. He had business to take care of there, but now that it is finished, he is here to tie the knot with Roxy."

When Tanner's eyes continued to shoot ice at him, Seth backed farther away. But before he turned to follow his daughter and the man whose waist she hugged, Seth made a parting shot. "I'm sorry if my little girl led you on, cowboy."

It was all Tanner could do to keep from jumping off the stallion's back and beating Seth until he admitted that he lied. He kept his seat when it occurred to him that maybe Seth wasn't lying. The girl was young, perhaps a little flighty. Maybe she had led him on.

I can't believe that, Tanner thought as he kneed the stallion around and headed back home. Roxy was as honest as she was beautiful. He couldn't believe that she had made love with him while engaged to another man.

Tanner stewed all day about what Seth had said. He saw the same scene over and over, how joyfully Roxy had greeted the man Seth had called Ace. When it grew dark he resaddled Brave and headed for town. He wasn't going to take Seth's word for it; he was going to face Roxy and ask her straight out if what her father had said was true.

When he entered the Lady Chance there was no sign of Roxy. One of the dancers walked past him, giving him a coy look, and he asked her the whereabouts of Roxy. When she answered that Roxy was upstairs in her quarters, he took the stairs two at a time.

Tanner stood in front of her door a minute, collecting his thoughts, planning just what he wanted

12

to say to her. He raised his hand to knock, then held his fist in midair. Roxy had company. Laughter came from inside, Roxy's and a man's. As he stood listening, there followed some conversation he couldn't make out. Then Roxy's words came clearly to him.

"Oh, Ace," her excited voice rang out, "I can't believe that at last our dream is coming true, that we will be together from now on."

Tanner staggered a bit and had to hold on to the railing as he made his blind way down the stairs and out the saloon door. He hadn't been aware of the ride back to his ranch, he was only cognizant of one thing. Roxy had led him on, made a fool of him. Her fiery little body had needed the use of his until she could marry the man she really loved, the one called Ace.

As the stallion raced on, his pain turned into a blinding anger. Roxy had used him like a man used a whore. He felt degraded. She had turned him into a male prostitute.

After a night of restless half-sleep, he had ridden to a neighboring ranch to talk to his longtime friend Rock Brady. Rock was his elder by several years and knew every aspect of running a ranch. When Tanner asked the gray-haired man if he would move into his cabin and take over the running of his ranch, it took his friend a matter of two minutes to agree.

"But where will you be?" the older cowboy asked. "I thought you and that little Roxy was going to get married."

"Well, you thought wrong," Tanner answered shortly. "I'm riding south tomorrow to join General Grant and his men."

"Are you out of your mind?" Rock stared at him.

13

"Why do you want to do a damn fool thing like that?"

"I'd be a fool to stay here right now. There's no telling what I might do."

His friend hadn't asked him to explain. He only said with doubt in his tone, "I reckon you know best," then added, "I'll take care of the place as if it was my own. How long do you think you'll be gone?"

"I don't know." Tanner shrugged a shoulder. "As long as it takes is all I can tell you."

"When do you want me to take over the reins?"

"I'm leaving in the morning, so you might as well come home with me now. . . ."

Tanner stopped his dour reminiscing to turn the meat in the skillet, then sat back down and soon resumed his trip back into the past.

The sun was just coming up the next morning when he and Rock walked to the barn. As he saddled Brave and fastened his camp gear and grub sack on the back of the cantle, he asked Rock to let him know through letters how things were going at the ranch.

"It might take a while for them to get to me, but eventually your letters will get through." He and Rock shook hands then, and as he swung into the saddle he said, "If I should catch a fatal bullet, the ranch is yours."

"Don't say that, Tanner." Rock's gruff protest followed him as Brave cantered away, headed south.

Tanner remembered it had taken him close to a month to catch up with Grant and his men. He had liked the burly general right off, even if he was drunk half the time. Regardless of his drinking, the general was a good campaigner and they won most of the battles they entered into.

Tanner had received two letters from Rock during the time he fought with General Grant. In the first one his friend had written that the ranch was coming along fine, that his cattle were multiplying like rabbits. He wrote that he had made a cattle drive and that he had deposited a check to his friend's bank account. Before signing off, he wrote, "Take care of yourself, Tanner, and come home sound in mind and body."

The second letter arrived six months later, the envelope creased and smudged from much handling. This one was about the same as the first one, telling how Rock had made another cattle drive and that his bank account was growing steadily. There was a postscript he'd just as soon not have read. Roxy had given birth to a son. Rock hadn't bothered to date his letters, so there wasn't any way of knowing when this had happened.

Tanner had gone through a rough patch then. His mind had been swamped with old memories.

He had been able to put Roxy out of his mind somewhat when late one morning, as Grant was leading his troop toward Vicksburg, they were suddenly attacked. Tanner had just dismounted and was about to take cover behind a large oak when a Johnny Reb stepped from behind it. Simultaneously they drew their pistols and took aim. Tanner felt a bullet hit him in the left shoulder as he squeezed the trigger of his own firearm. As he dropped to the ground, blood oozing from his wound, he saw the reb fall, shot through the heart.

He always hated to remember what had happened next. He was lying on his back in excruciating pain, the smoking pistol in his limp hand when he saw two of the enemy standing over him, their rifles aimed at his chest.

He had been taken prisoner and had spent a hellish year in a Confederate prison. His wound managed to heal despite the filthy conditions and the near starvation diet he and the other prisoners were fed. Then, on July fourth, 1863, Vicksburg surrendered to the north. The beginning of the end. He had been freed and had continued to fight under Grant until the war ended in 1865. He could go home now, but he wasn't ready to run into Roxy and her husband and the son that should have been his.

So, instead of returning to his ranch, he signed on to fight the Apaches. After 35 battles, the war with the Indians was over. Seven years had passed since Tanner left Colorado, and whether he was ready or not, he must go home. There were no more wars to be fought. Only the one inside him.

Tanner sighed, stood up, and forked the cooked meat onto a tin plate. Pouring another cup of coffee, he sat down before the fire and ate his supper.

Later, rolled up in his blankets, a twinge of excitement fluttered through his chest. Sometime tomorrow he would see his ranch again.

Chapter Two

Roxy Bartel thought she had never seen a more beautiful sight as she sat her mare on a grassy hill and looked down at the sloping valley of pines and aspens. She had lived in the vicinity of these hills and valleys all her life, yet they still had the power to move her deeply.

A cool spring wind blew up, tossing her black curls around her face when she turned her head to look to her right. A flicker of pain flashed in her eyes as she gazed down at the cabin sitting in a grove of pines at the foot of the valley. There had been a time, years ago, when she'd dreamed of living in that neat, sturdy little building. A time when Tanner Graylord had talked in glowing terms of how he was going to build his ranch into one of the largest in the area. She had assumed his plans included her.

And why shouldn't I have thought that? she asked herself. Hadn't he taught her all about love-making, showing her things that she had never dreamed went on between a man and a woman? Every time she saw his tall, lean person, even at a distance, or heard the low timbre of his voice, she wanted him to make love to her.

The night he proposed to her down by the river, shortly after they had made love to each other for a couple of hours, she could hardly contain her happiness.

The glow of her elation was still on her face when she told her father that she was going to marry Tanner Graylord. When he frowned at her news and cautioned, "Give a lot of thought before you hitch yourself to a penniless, down-at-the-heels cowboy," it was the first time she realized he didn't like her intended. Her father had gone on to say that Tanner would never have more than a scrub ranch and that she would grow old before her time slaving on it. "I have better dreams for you, little girl."

"But, Dad," she had protested, "I love Tanner, and he won't always be poor. He has plans for his ranch, and he's a hard worker. He'll succeed, I know he will."

Her father had shaken his head and scoffed, "What do you know about men? You are only seventeen and blinded by his soft words, and probably hot kisses. I hear the talk in the saloon and what Belle's girls have to say about him. He's a womanizer, Roxy, and always will be. He will lead you on and in the end break your heart. Give yourself a chance to meet other young men who can give you a good life."

"Tanner might have chased women before,"

Roxy said, angrily defending the man she loved. "Half the single men in the area do the same thing. But since Tanner has been seeing me, he hasn't looked at another woman that way."

When Seth gave her a look that said she was a foolish young girl, she made one last attempt to reason with her father. "When you and Ma got married, you had nothing but some change in your pocket and a dream to own the fanciest saloon in Denver. But because you loved each other, you still went ahead and got married."

As Roxy continued going back in her mind, she recalled the nights she and her mother would sit in their living quarters above the saloon while her father was downstairs greeting the patrons, laughing and joking and smoking his big cigars. Her mother would sit in the light of the kerosene lamp, her blonde head bent over a sampler she was embroidering. Sometimes she would lift her head and her soft brown eyes would be filled with tears. Then Roxy would urge the gentle Ruth to put on a fancy dress and go downstairs and join her husband, to become part of the chatter and laughter that floated up to their rooms.

Her mother's answer had always been the same. "I can't do that, dear. Seth doesn't want me to be around the kind of people who visit the Lady Chance."

Roxy had thought at the time that her father was probably right. There were a lot of sleazy looking characters who patronized the saloon, and that was not counting the women from Belle Lang's Pleasure House who dropped in to drum up business.

She had approved of her father's wish to keep his wife away from the kind of people her mother

wasn't used to, until one night when she was supposed to be sleeping, she began to doubt that her
father had ever loved his wife.

While her mother slept, Roxy had sat in the dark
gazing out the window, looking down on the alley
below. She had thought nothing of it when one of
Belle's girls left the saloon by the side door that
led to the alley. They often used that shortcut
when going home. The backyard of the Pleasure
House was directly across from the tavern. She
gave a start when her father came out the same
door the woman had used and joined her. She
watched in shock as the pair embraced and kissed
before opening the gate to the Pleasure House and
passing on into the house.

Roxy's eyes grew moist as she remembered that
her mother had passed away shortly after that.
The doctor was stumped at the cause of her death
and couldn't determine why she had died. When
her father, a couple of months after laying his wife
to rest, started seeing other women openly, she
had told herself that her mother had died of a broken heart. She had never felt the same about her
father after that.

She did, however, like Belle Lang. Strangely, it
was she who had comforted the broken-hearted
girl. She had cradled her in gentle arms and let
her cry the many times grief had overtaken her.

It had also been the madam who had guided her
through her adolescent years, warned her against
teenage boys and their hot, fumbling hands. She
had made the motherless daughter go to church
every Sunday, something her father never thought
of.

And later, when her father was pushing her not
to see Tanner anymore, Belle had encouraged her

to stick by her cowboy. "He's a good man, Roxy, and regardless of what Seth thinks, Tanner Graylord will amount to something some day."

Then one day, without a word of goodbye to her, Tanner was gone. She remembered that time with bitterness in her eyes. When three days had passed and Tanner hadn't ridden in to see her, she had ridden out to the cabin. It had occurred to her that maybe he was ill, or he'd had an accident. He lived alone and there wouldn't be anybody around to know if he was laid up in bed.

Rock Brady had hailed her from the half-finished barn when she rode up to the cabin. "Tanner's not here, Roxy," he said gruffly, walking toward her. Up close she saw a glimmer of pity in Rock's eyes and had a premonition that all was not well.

"I expect he's out with the cattle," she said, trying to smile.

"Well, no, he's not." The big man took off his hat and ran uneasy fingers through his hair before settling it back in place. "The thing is, honey, Tanner rode off to join the war three days ago."

Roxy remembered how her throat had closed and how she could only stare at the uncomfortable man who plainly wished he was somewhere else. After swallowing a couple of times she managed to croak, "He never said anything to me about going to war. Did he leave me a message, or a letter?"

Rock shook his head and looked away from the hurt and confusion that must have shown in her eyes. "He just hinted that he was restless and asked if I would mind his ranch while he was gone."

"Did he say how long he would be away?"

"He only said that he'd be gone as long as it took."

Roxy sat a moment, blinking back tears. Then wordlessly she kneed the mare around and rode away, giving her tears free rein. She couldn't believe that her father had been right about Tanner. She couldn't believe that when Tanner had said he loved her, he wasn't being sincere. She recalled all those nights of lovemaking when it seemed he couldn't get enough of her.

The pines and valleys faded as with bitterness Roxy recalled how fate hadn't been finished with her yet. A month after Tanner left, she'd had to face up to the fact that she was expecting his child. Gladness and panic warred within her. At first there was the elation that she was going to have his child. Then came the dismaying thought that Tanner might not be happy at all about becoming a father. She had learned that she didn't know him as well as she thought she did. Maybe the thought of being saddled with a family would keep him from ever returning to his ranch.

She had finally decided that however he might feel about it, Tanner had the right to know that he would become a father this coming winter.

She had gone straight to Belle then, and the caring woman had held her as she sobbed out the story. When she had cried herself out, Belle handed her a handkerchief and said gently, "Everything will be all right, honey. Write your letter to Tanner and he'll come home as fast as that stallion of his can bring him. I don't know what sent him away, but your news will bring him back. I still believe that Tanner loves you deeply."

Her father, however, took a different view when she got up the nerve to tell him that he was to become a grandfather. When he had finished ranting and raving, calling Tanner every vile name he could think of, he advised her to go to the local midwife and get rid of the baby.

She had stared at him aghast. "I would never do such a thing," she cried out. "It would be murder."

When Seth saw that he wasn't going to sway her to his way of thinking, he finally gave in. "Go ahead and have the brat," he growled, "but don't go calling the bastard back to marry you. You don't need him."

"But, Pa, he has a right to know about the baby. He must have the chance to make up his mind about what he wants to do. I won't beg him, if that's what you're thinking."

Seth stomped over to the window and stared out, his back stiff with anger. Roxy watched him as she nervously twisted a handkerchief between her fingers. It wouldn't surprise her if her father threw her out onto the street.

Her chest heaved in relief when he turned around and said as if in defeat, "Go ahead and write your letter. I'll mail it for you in the morning."

She had ridden out to the ranch that afternoon to ask Rock where she could send a letter to Tanner. He had answered that Tanner was with General Grant's division somewhere in Virginia.

That night she composed her letter.

"Dear Tanner. I hope all is well with you. This is just a short note to let you know that you will become a father sometime in December. Roxy."

She had wanted to write more, to pour out her heartache, to ask why he had left her. She had wanted to beg him to return to her, but the pride Belle had instilled in her wouldn't let her do it. It was up to Tanner to make his own decision without any urging from her.

The next morning her father took her letter and went up the street to mail it.

The waiting began then. The days grew into weeks, then months. Finally, she could no longer deny it. She had her answer. Tanner wasn't coming home.

As the baby grew inside her, Roxy didn't know how she could have borne her grief if not for Belle and her cousin Ace. Ace had been a bulwark of support and comfort through those days. Every time she cried, he threatened to find Tanner and shoot him between the eyes.

Ace was her first cousin, the son of her mother's sister Nell. She had adored her handsome twenty-year-old relative from the first time she met him when she and her mother had visited Aunt Nell in Utah. He was always kind to her, never seemed to mind when she dogged his footsteps. His many lady friends hadn't appreciated her company and childish chatter, though. But even then, he ignored their pouting and sullen looks. He had always been sure of himself with the ladies.

Still reminiscing, Roxy recalled the last time she went to visit their relatives in Utah, after her mother's death. Her aunt had been upset that Ace had chosen gambling as his profession. "It can be a very dangerous thing, playing poker against drunks and all kinds of riffraff," she had said worriedly.

Ace, however, loved pitting his wits against other players and was very good at it. She remembered how she had begged him to come to Denver and deal for her father in the Lady Chance.

He had given her curls a gentle tug and said with a smile, "Maybe I will someday."

24

She and Ace had corresponded sporadically as the years passed, but she hadn't seen him since her mother's death. Then one day, she received a letter from him that made her heart leap in alarm, but also in joy. Her cousin wrote that he had caught a man cheating at cards, and that when he called the player on it, the man had drawn a gun. In defense of his life Ace had grabbed up the Colt he always kept handy, and they had both shot at the same time. Ace wrote that he had only received a grazed arm, but that his bullet had hit his opponent in the heart. "It grieves me, Roxy, that I have taken a human being's life, even though I was fighting for my own. For sanity's sake I must get away from here. Do you think Uncle Seth would let me be a dealer at one of his tables? Let me know as soon as possible. Your loving cousin, Ace."

Her father had said yes, and Ace arrived in Denver two weeks later. It had been a joyous reunion, and she couldn't wait for Tanner to meet her beloved relative.

That had never happened. Tanner had left Colorado two days after Ace's arrival.

Roxy never liked to remember the months that followed. By her fifth month she could no longer hide her pregnancy, and tongues began to wag. Rumor being a tireless worker, all kinds of stories flew back and forth. Belle heard from her girls, who had got it from their customers, that the consensus was the gambler had fathered her baby, that Tanner Graylord would never go off and leave a woman pregnant.

She had tried to ignore the condemning looks, the slights from the women she had known all her life. When Ace learned that leering men had been making suggestive remarks to her, he took them out in the alley and beat them into near unconsciousness. He only had to do that three times. One look at the men's battered faces had stopped others from making the same mistake.

The women, however, had continued with their sneers and contemptuous looks. Ace could hardly invite them to accompany him into the alley.

There had been one woman who had not abandoned her, Roxy thought with a soft smile. Christy Allen. She and the blue-eyed blonde had grown up together and were as close as sisters. Christy had stood by her all through her pregnancy, and still did. Only once had she come right out and asked who the father of her baby was, but Roxy hadn't confided in her friend. Christy might tell her husband, and then John would write Tanner, which would shame him into coming home and marrying her. That she did not want to happen.

She had answered, "What does it matter who put me in this condition? The baby growing inside me is mine alone."

Christy never brought the subject up again, but Roxy felt that her friend thought Ace was the father.

It had never been mentioned to anyone that Ace was a relative. Her cousin thought it best that way. If it ever came out that he had killed a man over cards, it wouldn't look good to the patrons of the Lady Chance.

Then, one night in December, during a blizzard, she had given birth to a healthy baby boy. From the moment Belle put him to Roxy's breast she had loved the little mite with all her heart. From that time on she had put Tanner and everything else from her mind. Her whole being was concentrated on the child she named Jory. Jory Bartel. Roxy's bastard, he was called by most of Denver.

Ace had again stepped in to give her support. Something her father hadn't done. He had chosen to completely ignore the child. So it had been Ace who wheeled the baby carriage around town, his dark eyes daring anyone to make a degrading remark. When Jory grew older, his second cousin took him out for walks. Jory had the same coloring as Ace, and everyone felt sure now that the gambler was the boy's father. And now the question on everyone's tongue was why he didn't marry Roxy and give his son a name.

As the mare stamped impatiently, eager to move on, Roxy's thoughts turned to another event that had changed her life. One sizzling hot day after Jory's sixth birthday, her father had been bitten by a rattlesnake in the Arizona desert.

Seth had gone to that state to look at some property he was interested in buying, to open up another saloon. He had been out in the desert alone, and the snake's venom had spread quickly through his body. He was dead when the search party found him. Due to the hundred-degree heat, and the time it took to find an address in her father's belongings, he had been buried in a cemetery on the outskirts of a town called Mesa.

No one had really grieved for Seth Bartel. Roxy had never been close to her father to begin with, and his attitude toward his grandson had pushed them further apart. Ace hadn't liked Seth for the same reason. As for Jory, the child only knew him as the man who always had gruff words for him.

My poor little son, Roxy thought now. He was only seven years old, but when someone called him *bastard*, he knew what the word meant. He had become a moody, sullen youngster who was pulling away from her. She dreaded the day when he would ask her who his father was. In the meantime, luckily, Ace's company was enough for him.

Every time she looked at her son's small, troubled face, she hated his father a little more. She didn't realize it, but her friends could have told her that she had grown into a hard, bitter woman over the years.

Roxy roused herself from her memories when she saw that the sky was darkening. Also, the drizzle that had fallen off and on all day now threatened to become a full-fledged rain. She shivered in the cooling air and thought of the warmth inside the Lady Chance. She picked up the reins and urged Beauty down the hill.

Chapter Three

Tanner crossed a grassy valley, then began to climb a knoll. At its top he cut across country, urging the stallion into a gallop. His ranch was only a few miles away.

He had not ridden far when he reined Brave in and sat staring in disbelief. In the shelter of a deep, wide valley was a herd of at least 700 cattle. Could they be his? he asked himself in awe.

He lifted the reins and sent the stallion down the gentle slope until he was close enough to read the brands on the longhorns' hips. "By the Almighty," he exclaimed, his dark eyes hardly able to take it all in, "they wear the T-Box brand." It didn't seem possible, but the animals were his. Rock had written that the animals were multiplying like rabbits, and it looked as though his friend was right. After all, there had been over seven years for the herd to increase.

With a smile that was seldom seen on his face these days, Tanner wheeled the stallion around and guided him back up the hill. A mile later he hit the much-trodden trail that would take him to his ranch. After ten minutes he drew rein again and looked down on the place he had ridden away from seven and a half years before.

But how it had changed, he thought. It didn't even resemble the picture he'd had in his mind during the war years. Only the cabin was recognizable. The barn he'd started to build before he left had been finished. And that wasn't the only thing that had him staring in wonderment. Midway between the cabin and barn was a long, plain building that could only be a bunkhouse. And to confuse him more, close by to the right of it was a building with smoke coming out of a stove-pipe chimney. A cook house, he thought and shook his head, completely bewildered.

A frown gathered between his eyes. Had somebody moved in, taken over his ranch? He hadn't heard from Rock since he was taken prisoner by the rebs. Many things could have happened in the meantime.

He touched his spurs to the stallion and sent him galloping toward the buildings. The look on his face said that he was ready to do battle if necessary.

When Tanner brought Brave to a rearing halt in front of the barn, the biggest dog he had ever seen came bounding toward him from behind the cabin. Ready to dismount, he kept his seat. A barking dog he could handle, but this great yellow beast was snarling a warning that if he stepped to the ground he would find its long fangs in his throat.

Now what? he asked himself. He couldn't sit here all day, and it didn't look as if there was anyone around to call the mean-looking brute off. He pulled his Colt from its holster. Maybe if he put a bullet in front of those big paws, scattered some gravel on its legs and chest, it would scare him away.

He aimed the firearm at a spot about a foot from the animal, and had curled his finger around the trigger when Rock Brady burst from the cabin, yelling, "Don't shoot, Tanner. I'll call Gus off."

Tanner watched his old friend hurrying toward him. He's aged, he thought. His hair is totally gray now and I don't remember his face having so many wrinkles. But hell, he realized, it's been over seven years. No doubt he'll see some changes in my face as well.

Rock spoke an order to the dog and it turned and went back behind the cabin. Then with a wide smile splitting his face, Rock exclaimed, "I knew you would come home some day! I just knew it."

"I was a long time doing it, friend." Tanner climbed out of the saddle and held out his hand.

After they shook hands and slapped each other on the back, Rock said, "I guess you see a lot of changes around here, Tanner. I hope you don't think I overstepped myself. But the cattle kept multiplying so fast I had to do something."

"I sure can't complain, Rock, but a bunkhouse and a cook shack?"

"You don't know it, Tanner, but you've got the biggest spread within three hundred miles. Three years ago I had to hire ten men to help me run the place, and that meant I had to have a bunkhouse built to house them. And since I can't cook any-thing worth eating, I had to hire a cook, and—"

"I know." Tanner held up a hand. "You had to have a cook house built so he'd have some place to cook."

"Yeah." Rock grinned. "That's about the size of it."

"Tell me, Rock," Tanner joked, "with all this building and hiring going on, do I have any money lying around?"

"Ain't much lyin' around. Maybe fifty dollars in an empty jelly jar. But you sure got a bunch of greenbacks in at Bradford Savings and Loan. Every time I drove a herd to Kansas I added a hefty check to your account."

"You mean you've made cattle drives?"

"Hell, yes. Every spring and fall for the past seven years. Come on up to the cabin and I'll show you. I've kept strict books on how many cattle have been sold, what they brought, and what I had to lay out."

"I was only joshing you, Rock, you know that," Tanner said as they walked side by side up the neat path to the cabin.

"I know that, Tanner, but things got so big I had to start putting everything down on paper."

As they climbed the two steps to the porch, the dog came from around the cabin, this time wag-ging his tail. "Who does he belong to?" Tanner asked, still not quite at ease around the animal, even though it now seemed friendly enough.

"I guess he belongs to the ranch. I bought him from a man in Denver. Wolves had been killing the cattle, so he's been riding night herd on the longhorns. Ain't lost a head since."

When Tanner stepped into the cabin he was

struck with unwanted nostalgia. The first thing that caught his eye was two pot holders that Roxy had made and hung on a peg next to the kitchen range. He looked at the curtains she had hung at the window, now faded and limp with dust. He glanced through to the main room. The big colorful Mexican rug that he and Roxy had chosen together still lay in front of the fireplace.

He shook his head as though to dislodge all the bittersweet memories that raced through his mind.

"Sit down, Tanner," Rock said. "I'll get the ledger from the bedroom."

"If you don't mind, let's go over everything at the cook house. I'd like a bite to eat and a cup of coffee. I haven't had anything to eat or drink since early this morning."

"Sure thing. I'll be right there."

Tanner couldn't leave the cabin fast enough. Roxy's presence there was too strong for him to bear. There was no way he could sleep in his bed tonight either. Until he could hire some woman to come in and remove all evidence that Roxy had ever been there, he would sleep in the bunkhouse.

When he stepped off the porch Gus followed him, his thick, wagging tail slapping him on the leg. Tanner ventured to drop a hand on the yellow head and scratch the silky ears. When the dog closed his eyes in pleasure, Tanner said, "Good, fellow. You and I are going to be good friends." He pushed open the door to the unpainted two-room building, and Gus flopped down in the grass, his big head lying between his paws.

The savory smell of roasting beef coming from the oven made Tanner's mouth water. He could count on one hand the times he'd had a tasty meal since joining the army. Three pies were cooling on a shelf. He sniffed the air and decided that from their spicy scent they were apple.

Before sitting down at the table, Tanner walked over to the stove and felt the blue speckled coffee pot. It was half full and hot. He was looking for a cup when a cracked voice demanded, "What do you think you're doin' in my kitchen, grub liner?"

Tanner withheld a grin as he looked down into the wizened face of a small man. From the condition of his sparse, rumpled hair, he had just awakened from a nap.

"I'm getting myself a cup of coffee, and maybe a wedge of that good-smelling pie," Tanner answered.

"Like hell you are," the bantam-sized cook shrilled at him. "Them pies are for hard-workin' cowboys and not for a no-account grub liner. Just who do you think you are, sneakin' in here and makin' yourself at home?"

"Well," Tanner drawled, sitting down at the table and pushing his hat to the back of his head, "I own this cook house and everything in it."

"The hell you do, mister," the cook blustered, not sure that the stranger wasn't speaking the truth. "Rock Brady hired me, so I reckon the place is his."

"If that's the way you've figured it out, I hired Rock Brady, so that makes the place mine."

The little man narrowed gimlet eyes at Tanner and asked uncertainly, "Do you be Tanner Graylord?"

"That's who I be," Tanner answered with an amused grin.

"Well, fry me up and feed me to the hogs." The

shocked cook stepped forward and offered his hand. "I'm called Pee Wee."

Tanner stood up and shook the small, though strong, hand. "Glad to meet you, Pee Wee. Do you think you could spare me a wedge of that pie? I haven't had anything sweet in a long time."

"Sure thing. A cup of coffee, too." Pee Wee picked up a knife and sliced into the juicy dessert. When he placed it in front of Tanner, he said, "I'll bet Rock will be happy to see you. He always claimed that you'd be back someday, but me and the men could tell a couple years ago he was beginnin' to have doubts. Seven years is a long time for a man to leave his property."

Tanner was saved from having to make an answer by the appearance of Rock with a big, thin ledger under his arm. He said to the excited cook, "I know Tanner is home, Pee Wee. I'll have a slice of that pie to go with my coffee, too. Then you can make yourself scarce. Me and Tanner got some business to discuss."

Tanner wolfed down his pie, then sipped at his coffee while Rock spread open the ledger and began explaining all the entries he had made in it.

Half an hour later Tanner sat back and said with awe in his voice, "I'm a wealthy man, Rock."

"You are that, my friend. Now you can build that big fancy house you used to yammer about all the time. As for that, you can do anything else you want to do, too."

"The first thing I'm going to do is make you a partner." Tanner tapped the ledger. "All this wouldn't be mine if not for you."

"I couldn't take half this ranch, Tanner," Rock protested. "You could have done the same thing I did if you'd been here. When the war ended, the

35

people back East was starving for beef. We ranchers couldn't keep up with the demand. As you saw, we've been gettin' top price for our beeves."

"I'm going to town one day next week and deed over half this ranch to you and that's the end of it," Tanner said as he pushed away from the table. "Let's go look at the herd."

When they arrived at the barn, with Gus at Tanner's heels, Rock looked into the stall where Brave was munching oats from a pail. "I see you still have the stallion."

"Yes. I almost lost him once, though. See that long scar on his rump?"

"What about you, Tanner? You got any scars?"

"One. Up near my shoulder blade."

Rock dropped the subject at Tanner's terse answer. It was clear he had no intention of discussing the years he had been away. Maybe he only had one scar on his body, Rock thought to himself, but he felt sure his friend had many inside. It showed on his face. He looked much older than his thirty years. He was thinner, his features almost hawkish, and his sideburns were gray. Rock wondered if he had nightmares when he slept.

When they passed Brave's stall, Tanner said, "I'm taking a fresh mount. The stallion has traveled many miles and deserves a long rest." A few minutes later he led a big black from the barn. Swinging into the saddle, he asked, "How many cattle do you usually lose during our bitter winters?"

"Hardly any," Rock answered, riding a chestnut-colored horse. "I hired a couple hay-waddies. They're teenage brothers. Good steady workers. Their parents are homesteaders, and can use the money they bring in. All they do all summer is cut the tall grass in the meadows, haul it in and scatter it on the ground to dry out. When it's all cured they stack it to the height of a tall man, then cover it with a tarp. By the time the first snow falls they have over two hundred piles placed about.

"The men keep a wagon road cleared through the snow so they can haul the hay to different spots out of the wind. The cattle soon learn that there will be feed for them at those places. They don't get fat on that diet, but they stay alive until spring when the grass turns green and begins to grow."

"You're a smart old renegade, Rock Brady," Tanner said, admiration in his voice. "I wouldn't have thought to do that."

Rock ducked his head, hiding his pleasure at the compliment. "I would have told you to do it," he said.

When they had ridden around one large herd, Tanner was well pleased with the condition of the longhorns busily cropping the new tender grass. "They look in excellent shape, Rock," he said.

"That's because whenever we make a drive to Kansas, I keep back the best of the cows and bulls to start a new herd. When calving time comes you get big, healthy calves.

"A lot of ranchers make the mistake of sendin' off their best stock and keep back the scrubs for breeding. They never have good strong herds."

Tanner and Rock turned their horses homeward. "It looks like the sky has finally run out of water," Rock said, glancing up as they neared the bunkhouse, where the cowhands were gathered outside waiting to be called to dinner.

"It's about time," Tanner said. "I haven't been completely dry for a week."

37

When they dismounted, a young wrangler came forward and took charge of the horses, and then it was time for Tanner to meet the men who helped run his place.

The ranch hands gave Tanner a cursory look as he and Rock approached them, then dropped their gaze to the cartridge-studded belt that encircled his lean waist, sagging at his right hip with the weight of a Colt. Tanner hid his amusement when they quickly looked away. They thought he was a gunfighter.

The men's curiosity turned to surprise when Rock introduced their boss. Most were open-faced and met his eyes squarely and gave him a firm handshake. There were a couple, however, who wore a half furtive look. They would need to have an eye kept on them. Rock might know cattle inside and out, but he was an expert at reading men's faces. The war years had taught him that.

He was thinking that it would take a few days to place names with faces when Pee Wee came to the kitchen door and shouted, "Grub's on the table, come get it!"

The men trooped into the cook house, and much bantering and good-natured taunting went on among them as steaming bowls of food were passed around. When everyone's plate had been heaped high with slices of beef, mashed potatoes, string beans and hot biscuits, the only sound in the kitchen was the clinking of knives and forks and an occasional "Pass the biscuits."

Tanner ate until he became embarrassed to fill his plate again. Pee Wee was a fine cook, and his stomach hadn't known what it felt like to be full for a long time.

When everyone sat back, sated, the cook poured

coffee around and the men built cigarettes. Tanner drank his coffee, then stepped outside to enjoy his smoke as he walked off some of his meal.

It had grown dark while supper was being eaten and the sky was ablaze with a million shimmering stars as Tanner leaned on the top rail of the corral that held the cowboys' work horses. He felt at peace in the familiar surroundings. He didn't have to fear that a reb, or an Indian, was lurking in the shadows, waiting to kill him.

But something was missing and he didn't lie to himself that he didn't know what it was. Black-haired, laughing-eyed Roxy. Not the Roxy who had betrayed his love, but the one who had pretended to share his dreams, the one who left him drained and half witless from her lovemaking.

Tanner recalled the faceless women he had used on occasion when fighting the Indian war. But although his body had achieved a sort of relief, his mind had continued to ask for something more. He had missed the soft, loving arms, the sweet, clinging kisses, the whispered love-words.

With an angry jerk of his shoulders Tanner forced his thoughts away from how it used to be with Roxy. He was remembering how it had all ended when Rock walked up and leaned beside him on the corral.

"I guess you're about ready to turn in, Tanner. It will only take me a minute to move my duds down to the bunkhouse."

"No need to do that. I'll bunk with the men."

"But that's not—"

"Just for tonight, Rock. Do you know of a woman who would come in and clean the place?"

"Yes," Rock said after a pause. "The hay-waddies' mother would do it." Then, with grievance in his tone, he added, "I've always tried to keep the place neat and clean."

"I meant you no insult, Rock," Tanner quickly apologized. "You've kept the place in good order." He dropped his smoke in the dirt and ground it out beneath his heel. "I might as well tell you the truth. I can't bring myself to sleep in the cabin until all evidence that Roxy was ever there is removed. I want everything cleared out. The pot holders, the curtains, the quilt, the pictures, and especially the rug in front of the fireplace."

Rock was silent for a minute as he turned over in his mind the day a confused young girl had come looking for the bitter man leaning against the corral fence. Should he tell Tanner about Roxy's visit, ask him straight out what the girl had done to him that had sent him off in a rage to fight in a war?

He decided that the time wasn't right. His young friend had a lot of things to think through. So all he said was, "I'll ride over to the Sheldon farm right now and ask Bertha to come clear out the place tomorrow."

Chapter Four

Roxy smiled and nodded to the old swamper as she walked through the gambling room off the saloon proper. "Why don't you open the windows, Paddy?" she asked as she stepped around his mop pail. "Get some clean air in here, clear out the odor of smoke and stale spirits."

The gambling had been fierce last night. Well-to-do ranchers had rubbed elbows with bankers, high society figures, rough-clad cowboys and even a few miners, who had ridden in from the silver mines in Cripple Creek. Monte, faro and fortune had been played, but the poker table, as usual, had been the most crowded.

A crooked smile lifted the corners of Roxy's lips. Cousin Ace had looked as if he'd been wrung out and hung up to dry by four o'clock this morning when the place closed.

Every professional gambler within a radius of a hundred miles had heard of Ace Brandon's skill at cards and had come to test him. Another thing that drew the gamblers to the Lady Chance was her cousin's reputation of being an honest dealer who never cheated at cards.

Ace had another reputation. He was known as a lady's man. His handsome good looks and gentlemanly ways with women got him most any woman he went after. He stayed clear of the so-called decent women, those under twenty years old, and married women. All the others he looked upon as fair game. Many had tried to lure him into marriage, including some of Denver's elite. He always managed somehow to elude their nets.

As she walked through the door to the kitchen, Roxy wondered which of the dancers Ace had chosen to relax with this morning. When it came right down to it, he preferred the worldly dancers to the spoiled, calculating daughters of the wealthy. He had confided to her once that those society women didn't know spit when it came to making love.

Roxy's son, Jory, looked up from the breakfast of bacon and eggs and home fries that he was pushing around in his plate. "How are you this morning, honey?" She ruffled his black curls as she walked past him to take a seat at the table. When her fat cook, called Skinny, had poured her a cup of coffee, she asked, "Did you do your homework last night?"

"No I didn't." Jory's answer was sullen.

"Why not?" Roxy frowned. "I don't want to be called to school again because you haven't done your lessons."

"For pete's sake, Ma," Jory said impatiently, "today is Saturday. I'll do that dumb stuff tomorrow night."

"So it is. I forgot." Roxy smiled sheepishly. "So, what are you going to do today? Look up your friends?"

Jory looked at his mother as though she were senile. "I ain't got no friends, you know that."

"Don't say ain't, honey. And of course you have friends."

Jory's answer was to leave the table and stamp out of the room.

Roxy stared at the shuddering door her son had slammed behind him. Tears sprang to her eyes. It was true. Her little boy didn't have any friends his age, only a few adult ones. There was Ace, Belle, her friend Christy, and the people who worked at the Lady Chance. Although all good friends, they weren't her son's peers. The poor little fellow had been ostracized from children his own age.

Oh, how she hated his father!

Roxy pushed away her empty cup and left the table. Her friend Christy would be arriving in about an hour to take their usual Saturday ride. She looked forward to those outings. It was the only time she got away from the Lady Chance for any length of time. The rest of the week was taken up with saloon duties. She had to keep tabs on which spirits to order each week, see that the saloon and gambling rooms were kept clean, settle disputes among the dancers, and do book work every afternoon.

Then, starting at six she had to be downstairs watching for customers who were drinking too much, becoming quarrelsome and rowdy. She would signal Ace and he would escort the trouble-makers outside.

She also had to keep an eye on the dancers. She had a strict rule that they were not to take men to their rooms between acts. Her living quarters were upstairs also, and she didn't want Jory to see a parade of men coming and going from the entertainers' rooms. Most of the girls abided by her wishes, but there were two or three who tried to sneak customers upstairs.

With Ace it was different. He had three rooms back of the bar that had an exit to the alley. His quarters were also off limits to Jory.

Roxy climbed the stairs to her three-room apartment. She unlocked a heavy door and stepped into a room so opulent it could rival the grandest house in Denver.

Her high-heeled mules sank into the thick nap of the blue carpet that covered the floor. Closing the door, she slid the bolt that locked it. Where she and Jory resided was strictly private. No one came into her quarters unless invited.

Her daily maid, Matty, was almost finished straightening up the bedroom and Roxy sat down in her favorite chair to wait until the girl had finished. She looked around her parlor with pride. Two weeks after receiving word that her father was dead and buried and the Lady Chance was now hers, she began the rejuvenation of the dreary, drab three rooms.

She had given away the plain, serviceable pieces of furniture her mother had lived with ever since the saloon was built, and she and Jory had bunked in with Ace while wallpaper was hung and carpet laid throughout. While all this was going on, she and her cousin had spent hours choosing the new furniture and window dressings to replace the old worn-out lace and faded drapes.

When the day came for the new pieces to be put in place, her home took on the soft and elegant beauty she had hoped for. The shades of blue and soft gray were restful to the eye as well as to the spirit. No matter how sad she felt some days, she had only to step into her rooms to start to feel better.

Usually, she added. There were some days when nothing seemed to chase away the darkness of her mind.

Matty came from Jory's room. It had no frills, but was furnished with good heavy pieces that could take a young boy's abuse and still retain their good looks. She smiled at the sixteen-year-old and stood up. Walking across the room to a dainty rosewood desk, she opened a drawer and took two silver dollars from it. "Thank you, Matty," she said, handing over the silver. "I'll see you Monday morning."

"Yes, ma'am." The young girl smiled and departed, taking her mop and dust rags with her.

Roxy had already taken her bath this morning so all she had to do was change into day clothes. She took off her pink, frilly robe and silk gown and laid them across the foot of the four-poster. Crossing the floor to a very feminine-looking dresser with roses carved on the drawers, she took from it a fine lawn camisole with matching thigh-high, narrow pantalettes. When she had pulled her underclothing on, she opened the double doors to the wardrobe that matched the dresser and took from it a dark blue riding skirt and a white long-sleeved shirt. When she was dressed, she tied a light blue neckerchief around her throat.

She had just finished brushing her black curls

45

and was tying them back with a blue ribbon when a light knock sounded on the back door. Christy had arrived. Her little friend was the only one who climbed the back stairs when she came visiting. Decent women never entered the saloon.

"All ready?" Christy asked with a wide smile when Roxy opened the door.

"All set. Just let me put my vest on and get my gloves," Roxy said, excitement in her voice.

Christy had tethered her horse in the alley, and he trailed after the two young women as they walked to the livery stable where Roxy kept her mare, Beauty. The teenager who cleaned the stable and tended to the horses knew the time and day the two friends went riding. He had Beauty saddled and waiting outside the livery.

It was a cool, crisp morning with the sun just beginning to burn off the fog that hovered over the valleys when Roxy and Christy hit the open range. When the rain-darkened buildings of Denver were no longer visible, they lifted their horses into a smart canter.

Roxy breathed deeply of the pure, fresh air, wishing that she didn't have to return to the smell of tobacco smoke and stale whiskey and beer.

Neither woman spoke as they traveled at a comfortable, rocking gait down a long grassy valley. Once, they startled a small herd of deer, sending them bounding for the protection of a distant foothill. Another time, they saw a band of grazing horses on a knoll a hundred yards away. The stallion, a beautiful chestnut color, sent out a clear clarion call that made Beauty prick her ears and shake her head uneasily.

Roxy and Christy smiled knowingly at each other. If Beauty had been in heat, her reaction would have been quite different. Roxy would have a hard time of it, keeping the mare from joining the stallion's harem. Both women knew it was unwise to ride out on the range at that particular time. There were too many wild stallions in the area always looking for new mares.

They had been riding close to an hour when they hit the river trail. Coming to a patch of willows shading the river, as was their habit, they reined in to let their horses blow, and then drink from the flowing water.

"This spot always brings back memories," Christy said, looking around. "Remember when we used to come here with John and Tanner?" A soft smile curved her lips. "It was here one Saturday evening that John proposed to me."

Roxy remembered with bitterness that Tanner had asked her to be his wife here also. And the first time they had made love one hot summer night had been beside these waters.

She recalled then that it was here she had cried out her heartache when a few months later Tanner rode off to fight in a war he didn't believe in. It was here she cried again when she discovered she was to bear him a child in shame.

"I wonder what ever happened to Tanner," Christy said, breaking the short silence. "He's been gone close to eight years now. Do you suppose he was killed in the war? His friend Rock Brady used to hear from him occasionally when he first left, but the last time I talked to Rock he said he hadn't heard from him for over five years."

"I'm sure we'd have heard if he had been killed," Roxy said, a strange little flutter in her heart.

"I expect so. It's said that his spread now runs more cattle than all the other ranchers combined.

If he only knew it, Tanner Graylord is a very wealthy man."

Just what he always wanted, Roxy thought, staring moodily into the slow-moving water. He had shared his dreams with her, talked in glowing terms about the big house he was going to build for her some day.

What had happened to change all that? she wondered. Why had he changed his mind about marrying her? Hadn't he had any intention of ever marrying her? Had he whispered empty promises so she would continue making love with him?

As confused today as she was when Tanner disappeared without a word to her, Roxy lifted the reins and pulled Beauty's muzzle out of the water. "We'd better get started back to town, Christy. It's time I checked on Jory."

As they cantered homeward, Christy was sorry she had brought up Tanner Graylord's name. It had caused her friend to go into a blue funk. Did she still have feelings for the rancher after all this time? Didn't her long relationship with Ace Brandon mean anything? It was clear that Roxy loved the gambler, and that he returned the feeling. She wondered, as did the rest of the community, why they didn't get married and give little Jory a name.

"This part of the country has a long way to go before it's tamed," Pee Wee said as he fed wood into the big black stove.

"According to Rock, Denver is pretty well tamed these days," Tanner said, standing in front of a small wall mirror shaving off the heavy stubble of whiskers covering his jaws.

"On the face of it it looks that way, but keep out of the alleys at night. There are still as many killin's there as ever. And when you see some rough-lookin' characters sittin' at a table with their heads together, you can bet they are plotting somethin' they wouldn't want the sheriff to know about."

"Just so they leave my cattle alone." Tanner rinsed his face, then dried it with a clean towel the cook had put out for him.

"You're up early." Pee Wee placed a plate of flapjacks in front of Tanner when he sat down at the table. "Did all the snorin' in the bunkhouse keep you awake?"

Tanner's grin said that Pee Wee was right. But in reality it was his own tormented thoughts that had kept him from going back to sleep. It always happened in the middle of the night. The war and every bad thing that had ever happened to him filled his mind then and kept him from resting.

"I have some business to take care of in town and I want to get an early start."

"You sure look better in your civilian clothes than you did in those ragged army issues. Did you lose some weight in the army? Your Levi's are kinda loose."

"Yes, I guess I did," Tanner answered, slathering butter on his flapjacks, then pouring syrup over them. "Army cooks aren't the best in the world to begin with. Then there were times when we'd be caught in a battle and maybe wouldn't eat for close to two days." He grinned up at his cook as he forked a piece of his breakfast toward his mouth. "I'm sure I'll gain it all back in a short time eating the good food you dish out."

"I do my best." The little man looked down, trying to hide the pleasure his boss's praise gave him.

After a second cup of coffee, Tanner rose and, taking his gun belt from the back of his chair, buckled it on. As he left the cook house he said, "See you later, Pee Wee."

As Tanner rode down the valley toward town, everywhere he looked he saw cattle wearing his brand. Vexation creased his brow. He had survived two wars, now had all the money he would ever need, was still young and healthy. So why, he asked himself, wasn't he more content?

"Maybe I just have to get used to living a normal life again," he told himself when the sprawling town of Denver appeared in the distance. Once he saw his old friend John Allen again, raised a little hell, visited the girls at Belle's place, he'd be his old self again.

Riding down Denver's main street, Tanner was amazed at how the town had grown in his absence. Where before there had been wide spaces between buildings, now every foot of land had a business of some sort on it.

There was now a barber shop and two doctor's offices; the cafe where he and Roxy had once had coffee had been expanded and spruced up with paint and a large window. He passed two new hotels, each two stories high, with brightly painted false fronts and wide porches where customers could sit and watch what was going on in the street. There were two new saloons, a fancy restaurant, a lawyer's office, three mercantiles, and a dress and hat shop.

Tanner's heart beat a little faster when he rode past the Lady Chance and glanced up at the window he knew used to be Roxy's bedroom. He imagined she probably didn't live over the saloon these days. Now that she owned the Lady Chance and was married to the man he had seen her greet so warmly that long-ago day, she probably lived in a fancy house somewhere on the outskirts of town.

He came to the end of the street and pulled up in front of the Bradford Savings and Loan, still the only bank in town. As he dismounted and tied Brave to a hitching post in front of the solid-looking brick building, he remembered coming here over eight years ago to ask for a loan. Climbing the steps to the big heavy door, he recalled that day.

After a wait of twenty minutes or so he had finally been shown in to Enos Bradford's office. The paunchy banker hadn't offered his hand in greeting, nor had Tanner been invited to sit down. He had been left standing to state his business. After the five minutes he had been allowed, Bradford had shook his head and said coolly, "Money is too tight these days for me to take a gamble on a shoe-string ranch."

How Tanner had wanted to lunge across the heavy desk, put his hands around the arrogant man's fat neck and squeeze the life out of him. While he stood there contemplating how good it would feel to carry out his wish, Enos Bradford had looked up at him and said rudely, "You can go now, Graylord. I'm a busy man."

He had turned on his heel then and walked out of the room, his boot heels coming down hard on the shiny floor. As he slammed the door shut behind him, he hoped that his spurs had gouged deep grooves in the hardwood.

What would his reception be today? he wondered, pushing open the heavy door that was supposed to be protecting his money.

The bank was empty of customers this early in the morning. The only person in evidence was a thin young man behind a barred cage who peered at him through wire-framed spectacles. When Tanner got close enough to be recognized, the teller slid off his high stool and hurried to knock at Enos Bradford's door.

Tanner could hardly keep from laughing aloud his amusement when Bradford rushed from his office, grabbed his hand and pumped it as if he were greeting an old friend he hadn't seen for a long time.

"Tanner, it's good to see you." A smile stretched from ear to ear on the fat face. "Come into my office. I expect you're here to learn how well off you are financially."

This time, his second visit to the big office, Tanner not only was invited to sit down but was offered whiskey and a cigar. He refused both. "I'm a busy man," he said, repeating the words Enos Bradford had said to him years ago. "Let's get down to business."

Half an hour later, Tanner learned that he stood very well financially. He was probably wealthier than the banker. His business finished, he stood up, ready to leave. Just then, the office door opened and a young woman stepped through it. Julia Bradford, he thought, recognizing the banker's daughter. Before he left Denver he had seen the blonde beauty around town, her nose in the air as if she owned all of Denver. He remembered that Roxy and Christy couldn't stand the spoiled, snobbish teenage girl they had gone to school with. As for himself and his friends, they didn't spare the haughty miss a glance.

He picked up the large envelope that contained all the bank transactions Rock had made over the years and wordlessly walked past Miss Bradford and out the door.

Back in his office, Bradford sat with tented fingers, a thoughtful look on his face. He finally turned to his daughter, who stood at the window looking discontentedly at the street. "There goes a good catch for you, Julia. You ought to latch onto him. I know he's rough around the edges, part puma and part wolf, but he's the wealthiest man in Denver, maybe in all of Colorado."

Julia made no response to her father's advice.

Tanner stood outside, wondering what to do next. The saloons weren't open yet and Belle's girls were probably still sleeping.

Actually, he didn't feel like visiting either establishment. He struck off down the street, headed for the store whose sign read Denver's Mercantile. He needed some Levi's that fit him, some shirts, a new Stetson, underclothing and new boots. The ones he wore now were scuffed and run down at the heels.

If I'm the wealthiest man in the area, I shouldn't go around looking like the grub liner Pee Wee mistook me for, he thought wryly.

He was almost at the store where he had done business most of his adult life when he heard shouting coming from young voices. When he came to the end of the block and looked down the alley, he saw two youngsters grappling together on the ground. The yelling came from five voices that shouted encouragement to one of the pair mixing it up. He noted that one of the fighters was much bigger and older than the other.

But the younger, black-haired boy was holding his own for all his smaller size, so Tanner stood and watched, remembering the battles he had lost and won in his youth.

He soon learned that the catcalls were directed at the younger youth. He frowned when two of the watching boys darted in and kicked the small one. It wasn't a fair fight to begin with, he thought, but three against one was downright unfair.

When the tough little fellow was wrestled onto his back and his opponent began jabbing him in the groin with his bent knee, Tanner jumped into the fray.

He reached the pair in a second, and grabbing the bigger boy, who looked around twelve, he yanked him away. The bully went sprawling on his back, and the young audience took one look at Tanner's angry face and lit off down the alley. Their friend scrambled to his feet and ran after them.

"Are you in much pain, kid?" Tanner helped the boy to stand up.

"A little," came the choked answer.

"Lean against the wall here until you cool off and catch your breath. The pain will go away after a while."

When the boy thankfully rested his back against the bricks, Tanner handed him a handkerchief and asked, "What's your name, button?"

"Jory." The boy swiped at his bloody nose.

"You're going to have a shiner on your left eye."

Jory shrugged. "It won't be the first time."

"You got in some good licks on the other fellow."

"I did, didn't I?" Jory grinned, pleased that the tall man had noticed.

"Yeah, you did. You're a tough fellow." Tanner

ruffled the black curls. "Are you feeling better now?"

"Yes." The boy straightened up from the wall.

"You'd better go home now and take care of that eye," Tanner said, and after a moment walked on down the sidewalk and entered the mercantile.

It didn't take him long to purchase what he had come to town for. The old man who used to wait on him had been replaced by a younger man full of questions. Tanner had answered with grunts and as few words as possible. As soon as everything had been packaged up, he grabbed the bundle and hurried out of the store, telling himself he'd never shop in that store again.

Tanner was surprised to see the boy leaning against the building as though waiting for him. "What are you doing here, Jory?"

"I thought I'd just trail along with you. If you don't mind."

"Don't you have anything to do at home?"

"Naw. There's nothing to do there."

"What about your mother and father? Won't they be worried about you?"

Jory shook his head. "My mom is always busy, and I don't have a dad."

Poor little kid, Tanner thought. His father dead and his mother has to work to support them. "All right then." He smiled down at the dirty, earnest face lifted to him. "Come along. But I'm only going to the livery stable to get my horse. Then I'm going home."

"I wish I had a horse," Jory said, walking alongside Tanner.

"Did you ever tell your mother that you'd like one?"

"Yeah. I told her three times. She always said

no. She's afraid something will happen to me."

Tanner remembered that he'd had his own horse when he was around this button's age. Riding was part of a youngster's growing up. One thing for sure, the mother was coddling her son too much. It wasn't good for a boy to be raised without a father.

He didn't speak his thoughts aloud. It wasn't his place to go against the mother's wishes. He said instead, "A lot of things can happen out on the range alone. Your horse could step in a gopher hole and throw you and you could end up with a broken bone; you could be attacked by a mad bull or bitten by a rattlesnake." Tanner went on to explain some of the other dangers of the open range.

"It ain't likely anything like that would happen," Jory protested.

"Don't say ain't."

Jory grinned. "My mom always says that." After a short silence he said, "Would you like to meet my mom? She's awfully pretty."

"Maybe, one of these days," Tanner said after a slight hesitation. He didn't want to get too involved with this youngster, who was hungry for a man's attention. And it would be easy to do, for already he was drawn to the lonely boy.

Tanner pushed away the soft feelings for the boy and said gruffly as they came to the livery, "Shouldn't you be getting home now?"

"I guess so." Jory shrugged indifferently. "My mom will be looking for me pretty soon." He started walking back uptown, then stopped and called to Tanner, "When will you be coming back to town?"

"Not for a while. I've got a ranch to run."

"I'll be looking for you." Jory smiled and walked on.

Chapter Five

Roxy pushed her chair away from the big heavy desk, wiggled her stiff shoulders and stretched her fingers. She had been working on the saloon books since returning home from her ride with Christy.

She glanced out the window, where dusk was settling in. Closing the heavy ledger, she stood up. She hadn't seen Jory all afternoon. It was time she went looking for him.

Her son was so secretive these days . . . and unhappy. If only we could get away from here, she thought.

Roxy left her office, next to the kitchen, and locking the door behind her, she started walking toward the saloon's bat-wing doors. She stopped in mid stride when she heard Jory's laughing voice coming from Ace's room. She smiled. She hadn't heard her son laugh like that in a long time. She crossed the room, gave a rap on Ace's door and entered his quarters.

Her cousin and son lifted their dark heads and gave her startled looks. "What's wrong?" she exclaimed, looking at the wet cloth Ace was holding to Jory's eye.

"It's nothing, Ma." Jory grinned at her as Roxy hurried to inspect his bruise. "It's only a shiner," he explained proudly.

"A shiner? Where did you pick that word up? That's cowboy talk."

"I guess I heard it from some cowpoke."

Roxy and Ace looked at each other with raised eyebrows and mouthed, "Cowpoke?"

"Well, Jory, that's about all I can do for your shiner," Ace said, tossing the cloth into a basin of water.

"Go along now and get washed up and change out of those dirty clothes." Roxy pushed Jory toward the door. "It's almost supper time."

When the door closed behind her son, Roxy sighed and said, "He's been fighting again. What am I going to do, Ace? I can't keep him in when he's not in school, and if he goes out, the town boys pick on him."

"I don't know what to tell you, honey. I guess you could send him to a boarding school where nobody knows his background."

"You mean where nobody knows he's a bastard," Roxy said bitterly.

"I don't like that word, Roxy," Ace said coldly.

"I don't either, but it's true where my son is concerned."

"There's a well-known boarding school in Utah.

Why don't I write to them and get the particulars for you?"

"I don't know, Ace. I'd miss him so. He's still a baby, not even nine yet. He still needs his mother."

He needs his father, too, Ace thought as he looked at his cousin's unhappy face. He cleared his throat and said, "An old friend of yours has come home."

"A friend?" Roxy gave a short laugh. "I didn't know I had a friend outside of Christy and Belle."

"Let's say an acquaintance then."

"All right," Roxy said impatiently, "who is this acquaintance?"

"Tanner Graylord."

Roxy could only gape at Ace, too stunned to speak. She finally got her wits together to ask, "How do you know?"

"Our swamper saw him go into the bank this morning shortly after you and Christy rode off."

"Oh dear Lord, Ace, Jory mustn't see him." Roxy fumbled for a chair and sat down. "And Tanner mustn't see Jory."

"I think it's too late for that, Roxy. I'm pretty sure it was Graylord who broke up the fight that Jory was in. All the boy talked about while I was taking care of his bruises was this cowboy who wore a Colt and knew all about horses. I imagine he picked up the word *shiner* from Graylord."

Roxy sat rubbing her temples, trying to ward off the headache that was threatening to pounce on her. "I thought that after all these years I'd never see the man again, never have to worry that he would learn some day that Jory was his and take him away from me."

"He couldn't take the boy away from you," Ace scoffed gently.

"Oh, but he could if he wanted to. He could go to court and claim that I'm an unfit mother. That I run a saloon and live with my son in rooms above the saloon."

"Aw, honey, that's not likely to happen." Ace took her trembling hands in his and held them.

"I can't take that chance, Ace. You have my permission to write to that school. As soon as possible."

"I'll do it tonight. And, Roxy, you might think about selling the Lady Chance and moving to Utah yourself."

"I don't know, Ace," Roxy said wearily. "Let me take care of one thing at a time."

Pity and love were in the gambler's eyes as he watched his cousin leave his room.

When Roxy climbed the stairs and entered her parlor, a forced smile on her lips, she found Jory waiting for her. He had washed up and dressed in clean clothes, and wore a wide smile on his still babyish face. Her heart felt as if it had turned over. She hadn't seen him smile like that for a long time.

"Does your eye still hurt?" she asked, sitting down on the sofa beside him.

"Naw, I'm a tough fellow."

"Are you now?" Roxy teased. "Who told you that?"

"A big cowboy. He's a tough fellow too. You should have seen the boys run when he pulled the big kid off me. I walked with him a piece on his way to the livery to get his horse. I told him how much I wanted a horse of my own and he said a lot of bad things could happen to a fellow out on the range alone. I guess I ought to wait awhile before I get a horse."

"Did this cowboy say what his name is?"

Jory shook his head. "And durn it, I forgot to ask him."

"It's just as well that you didn't. It's not polite to ask a stranger his name. If you ever see him again, wait until he gives you his name on his own. But don't pester the man by forcing your company on him."

Roxy failed to notice that her son didn't make her that promise. He looked alarmed when she asked, "How would you like to go away to a boarding school where you could make new friends, and not fight all the time?"

"I wouldn't like that, Ma! I wouldn't like it at all. I'd miss you and Ace and . . ."

Roxy felt sure Jory was about to add that he would also miss seeing his new friend again but had sensed from their earlier talk that she didn't fully approve of his new acquaintance.

"You'd come home for the holidays, and of course spend the summers with me. You'd be with boys your age who wouldn't pick on you."

"I don't believe that the boys around here will pick on me anymore. They'll be afraid my cowboy friend will get after them."

"Jory," Roxy said impatiently, "you may not see him again for weeks, maybe months. Cowhands usually only come to town at night."

His face set in stubborn lines, he declared, "He'll come to town in the daytime."

"We'll talk some more about boarding school later." Roxy stood up. "Let's go downstairs and see what Skinny has made us for supper."

Jory jumped to his feet, his small hands clenched into fists and his lower lip trembling. "I won't like it, Ma!" he burst out. "I won't like it at all."

When Roxy made as if to put her arm around his narrow shoulders, he jerked away from her and rushed to the door. When he yanked it open he almost knocked over a young woman who stood there, ready to knock. "Sorry, miss," he muttered and went stamping down the stairs.

"Are you all right?" Roxy asked with concern. "My son doesn't usually leave a room in such fashion."

"I saw by the scowl on his face that he was upset," the woman said softly, "but no harm has been done. I'm fine."

All the time Roxy had been wondering who the stranger was and why she had come knocking on her door. Certainly she wasn't the type to look for employment in a saloon. Her serene features and soft brown eyes would be out of place in the Lady Chance. The men who came here would never approach a woman who resembled a sister or mother and invite her to sit at their table and share a drink with them.

"Please come in and tell me what I can do for you," Roxy invited.

"My name is Michelle LaBlanc," the young woman said when they were both seated on the sofa. "I'm a singer and I'm looking for employment." Long, slender fingers nervously smoothed the folds of her green taffeta skirt. "I was told that the Lady Chance is the most popular saloon in Denver and that you might be interested in hiring a singer."

Startled, Roxy paused before saying, "It's an interesting thought, but do you realize you would be singing to a pretty rough bunch of men who are usually full of spirits of some kind? It wouldn't be like singing in a church choir."

Michelle's tinkling laugh sounded softly. "I know that. Until recently I sang in a saloon in St. Louis. There were all sorts of men who came to listen to me. I promise, my presence won't cause you any problems, Miss Bartel."

Roxy knew that Michelle LaBlanc sincerely believed that, but something told her that this young lady would cause a problem of some sort. But maybe it wasn't a bad idea to have a singer in the place. None of the other saloons had one. "Well," she joked, "I'll take a chance that you can carry a tune. When do you want to start?"

"Is tomorrow night all right? I have a room at the boardinghouse but I'd like to find more comfortable quarters. I'll spend tomorrow looking for a little house to rent."

"You may be in luck. The woman who runs the boardinghouse also has a couple cottages that she rents out. They're at the edge of town, easy walking distance to the Lady Chance."

"Great. I'll go talk to her right now."

"I'll see you around nine o'clock tomorrow night then," Roxy said as they descended the stairs together.

"I'll be here," Michelle said, then laughingly added, "By the way, I can carry a tune, Miss Bartel."

"Please call me Roxy. Everyone else does."

"Thank you, Roxy." Michelle smiled, then turned to leave. She was jolted to a halt when she walked headlong into Ace. He grabbed her shoulders to steady her, and as he looked into her upturned face his smile faded and his pupils widened. Roxy had never before seen her cousin at a loss for words.

"Michelle," she said, "meet my friend, Ace. Ace, meet the singer I just hired. Michelle LaBlanc."

When a couple of seconds passed and Ace continued to silently gaze down at Michelle, Roxy smiled with wry amusement and said, "Michelle was just on her way home, Ace. You can turn her loose now."

"Oh. Yes, of course." The handsome gambler, who was usually so at ease with the ladies, blushed as he stepped away from the young woman. "I look forward to hearing you sing, Michelle," he stammered like a greenhorn teenager.

Michelle dimpled at him and departed. When she went through the bat-wing doors, Roxy had to jiggle Ace's arm to bring him back to the present. "Shall we go eat supper now?" she suggested.

"Yes. Supper," Ace answered absentmindedly, his mind still on the singer.

"She's lovely, isn't she?" Roxy remarked as they walked toward the kitchen.

"Yes. Lovely."

Michelle drew much male attention as she hurried along to the boardinghouse. But none of the men made rude remarks or invitations to her. Her inner beauty overshadowed her outer beauty, keeping crass thoughts from forming in men's minds.

She wasn't aware of the admiring looks sent her way. Michelle was busy counting her blessings that things had turned out so well for her. The sheaf of greenbacks in her wrist purse was getting pretty thin. She hoped she had enough money left to rent a small house.

She had left St. Louis in such a hurry, she had only taken the time to pack her clothes and personal belongings. At the station the train was about to pull out and she'd barely had time to check her bags and purchase a ticket before boarding the long passenger car that would start her journey westward.

As her father had lain dying on a barroom floor, shot for cheating at cards, he'd gripped her hands and said with labored breath, "Leave this sinful town, honey. Go west to Denver. My old friend Seth Bartel has a saloon there. He will give you a job."

When her father had decided to become a professional gambler, Michelle had soon learned that he didn't have the skill or the knowledge to be good at poker. He lost more often than he won. The money she earned at singing in the same saloon kept them afloat. She'd had no idea how that was affecting her father's pride. Finally it had driven him to cheat at cards.

He had, of course, failed miserably at it. He had been caught trying to slip an ace up his sleeve. A drunken merchant had pulled a derringer out of his pocket and shot Nat LaBlanc on the spot.

A muttering crowd had gathered around the table, staring angrily at the man who lay dying. Cheating at cards was almost a hanging offense. Afraid that the irate mob might turn their anger on her, Michelle had jumped to her feet and sped away as soon as her father breathed his last.

On first arriving in Denver, her hopes for a job had been dashed when she learned that Seth Bartel was dead. While she was wondering what to do now, alone in a strange town, she was told that Bartel's daughter ran the Lady Chance. She hadn't had much hope of being hired, though. For some reason women were seldom friendly to her.

It had been a pleasant surprise to meet Roxy. The beautiful woman with the sad eyes couldn't have been nicer.

As Michelle opened the door to the boarding-house, the handsome face of the man called Ace flashed before her. A gambler if ever she'd seen one, she thought, and she had seen plenty. She did not need another gambler in her life.

Chapter Six

Childish voices and laughter sounded in the vicinity of the cabin as Brave loped up to the barn. When Tanner swung to the ground and handed the stallion over to a stable hand, a young boy and a little girl came running from behind the cook house. The tow-headed boy was around Jory's age, he thought, and the girl about six. They came to an abrupt halt when they saw him approaching the cabin.

"Well, now," he said, a smile softening his hard features, "it looks like I've got company."

The alarm faded out of the boy's eyes, but his sister still looked a little frightened as she tried to hide behind her brother. "We ain't company," the boy said. "We're here with our ma. She's cleaning your cabin."

"I see. I take it Paul and Aaron are your brothers."

"Yes, they are." Pride was in the boy's voice. "They cut hay for you."

"So you know who I am."

"I figure you must be Mr. Graylord since I know all the rest of the help around here. Besides, Mr. Brady said that the owner of the spread was a tall galoot. I reckon you be over six foot tall."

The more the boy talked, the more he reminded Tanner of Jory. Jory also ran off at the mouth. "I guess I'm over six foot tall," he began with an amused grin. He was interrupted when a big-boned woman in her late forties stepped from the cabin and stood on the porch.

"Sonny will talk your arm and leg off if you don't stuff a sock in his mouth," she called out, coming down the two steps.

Tanner walked to meet the smiling woman, who was rolling down the sleeves of her dress. "You must be Mr. Graylord." She held out a work-hardened hand.

As her callused palm met his, Tanner knew he was going to like this genial, open-faced woman. He guessed she was a hard worker, and a good mother from the way her children came to her, the little girl hanging on to her skirt.

He nodded. "I'm Graylord, but call me Tanner."

"All right, Tanner. I'm Bertha Sheldon and this chatterbox is Sonny, and my shy one"—she pulled the little girl forward—"we call Sissy. I had to bring them with me. They would get into too much mischief if I left them home alone."

"That's quite all right, Bertha. Have you finished with the cabin?"

"Yes. I was just about to leave. My man, Ben,

68

will be wanting something to eat before long. Oh, and before I forget, Rock took some things out of the cabin and put them in a box. I don't want you to think that I took it on myself to do that."

"I understand. How much do I owe you, Bertha?" Tanner said, taking some bills from his hip pocket.

"Well . . . is three dollars too much?"

"I'm sure your labor is worth more than that." Tanner handed her a ten-dollar greenback.

"Oh, that's way too much," Bertha exclaimed, pushing the bill back at him.

"No, you keep it. Buy Sonny and Sissy something."

"Yeah, Ma." The boy's eyes danced with excitement. "You can buy me my own horse."

"Hush up, Sonny," Bertha ordered. "You've got a horse to ride."

"Yeah, that old plow horse. He can't run more than five minutes without having to stop and blow for another five minutes."

"So you know how to sit a horse, do you?" Tanner studied the sturdy little body and sun-tanned face. "How long have you been riding?"

"For a long time." Sonny pushed out his narrow chest. "I wasn't quite seven when Pa put me on top of the plow horse and told me to ride him to the river for a drink of water."

"All right, stop your bragging," Bertha said. "Let's get along home now." She turned to Tanner. "This money will go a long way this winter when the snow flies and Ben can't find work."

Tanner found himself wanting to help this fine, hardworking family. "Bertha, I've been thinking," he said. "It might help you out, and help us as well, if you could provide us with fresh vegetables and

69

fruit from your garden this summer. And I'm sure my cook would take any canned goods you could spare this winter. As well as eggs and milk. Milk freezes and eggs crack on a trip from town in icy cold conditions."

"We can do all that, Tanner." Bertha clasped her hands to her breast as though in thanksgiving.

"And as for your man finding work when a person is mostly snowed in, we can always use a hardworking man around here to do things a cowhand isn't handy at doing." He grinned. "They're real good at punching cattle, but when it comes to mending something around the ranch, they're like me. Mostly all thumbs."

Hope for a better future, something Bertha Sheldon hadn't had in a long time, glowed in her eyes. "You don't know how relieved and pleased that will make Ben," she said in a choked voice.

Tanner watched with some envy as the big woman left him, Sonny running ahead and the little girl holding her hand. The Sheldons were churchmouse poor, but he felt sure that love abounded in their home.

He walked on to the cabin and with a heavy sigh stepped up on the porch. He hoped that all traces of Roxy had been removed from his home.

It looks so bare, he thought, stepping into the kitchen. The gay red and white checked tablecloth was gone and so was the brightly painted Mexican vase that Roxy used to put wildflowers in. Only a kerosene lamp sat in the middle of the table. The kitchen window had been stripped of curtains. He lifted his gaze to the spot beside the stove where colorful pot holders used to hang. They were gone also.

With a pensive look on his face, Tanner walked

into the main room. It had been stripped also. It had lost the character it once had. The big rug where he and Roxy had made love so many times was gone, the hearth swept clean. The window hangings had been taken away, and the clean, bare panes seemed to mock him. Only a lamp sat on the table beside his favorite chair. The lace doily was gone, as was the little figurine of a man on a horse. The mantel boasted only a big clock and his rifle hung above it. All three pictures of landscapes had been taken off the wall, leaving white squares in their places.

Tanner dreaded what he would find in his bedroom as he walked down the short hall and pushed the door open. Again, as in the other rooms, he found it cold and colorless. This room was on the east side of the cabin and was in semi-gloom even though the window had no drapes. But he could still see that the colorful quilt had been replaced with a dark gray blanket. His gaze dropped to the floor. The Indian rug that used to lie beside the bed had also been taken away. The bedside table held only a lamp.

He walked over to the dresser that now held only his brush and shaving paraphernalia and started opening drawers. He found no reminder of Roxy there.

"Well, Rock," he thought out loud, a husky note in his voice, "you've done a thorough job of erasing all traces of Roxy."

As Tanner walked back down the hall, he paused in front of the other bedroom. This room had never been used and he told himself there was no reason to inspect it. Nevertheless, he found himself pushing the door open.

A bedstead, minus a mattress, sat against one

wall, and a narrow wardrobe sat opposite it. He and Roxy had planned to finish this room when their first baby came along. He remembered the day they bought the wardrobe as he opened its door.

The breath caught in his throat. Hanging there alone was a blue shirt of Roxy's. He remembered they had been caught in a rain shower one day and that Roxy had used the spare room to exchange her soaked shirt for one of his. Her slender body had been lost in the big garment, but when she walked into the main room and he looked at her, he had never wanted her more. They had spent the rest of the afternoon making love on the rug before the fire.

He reached out a hand to stroke the shirt sleeve, then jerked it back as if he would be burned if he touched the material. Disgusted with himself for having a flashing moment of longing for the black-haired beauty who had played him for a fool, he rushed out of the room, slamming the door behind him.

The sun had gone down and the air was nippy when Tanner left the cabin. The only sound in the deep dusk was the rasp of his boot soles in the gravel as he walked toward the cook house.

Near the long building, he made out the dim figure of a man coming from the bunkhouse. He squinted in the uncertain light and recognized the sturdy form of Rock. He sat down on the bench alongside the building and waited for his longtime friend to join him.

"Well, did you go to town? To the bank?" Rock asked, sitting down and pulling out tobacco and paper.

"Yes, I did." Tanner stretched his long legs out in front of him.

"And did you find yourself in pretty good shape at the bank?"

"I found that both of us are in good shape moneywise."

"I want you to forget that partnership nonsense," Rock said gruffly as he tapped tobacco into a thin white piece of paper.

"I want you to stop arguing about it. I'm going into town next week and have a lawyer draw up the papers that will make you my equal partner."

"I won't take it," Rock declared stubbornly, sliding his tongue over one edge of the paper and deftly rolling it into a thin cylinder.

"We'll see, you old goat," Tanner said affectionately. "I'm not going to pay you any wages, and after a while you'll get tired of going around with empty pockets."

Silence grew between them as Rock struck a match against the sole of his boot and held it to his cigarette. When a thin spiral of fragrant smoke feathered through his lips and nostrils, he asked, "How did Bradford treat you this time? I imagine quite different from the other time you ventured into his bank."

Tanner gave a short, sardonic laugh. "Like I was a long lost son he had been pining for. He shook my hand so long and so hard I thought my arm was going to fall off. You can be sure I was offered a seat this time. There was no standing with my hat in my hand while I asked for a loan."

"What did you expect? Everybody knows that money is Bradford's god."

"Yeah. I hope he chokes on it someday."

"Did you run into any of your old pals?"

Tanner shook his head. "I guess it was too early for any of them to be out and about."

"So you didn't see anyone, then?"

"No, not really. Nobody that I knew. I saw the clerk at the mercantile when I went to buy some duds. Then there was this young boy who followed me around, talking two to the minute.

"Oh, and I saw Bradford's daughter for a second. She came into the bank just as I was about to leave."

"I bet her attitude toward you was different from what it used to be."

A wry smile curved Tanner's lips. "Let's just say she looked at me. That never happened before. A poor cowpoke was too far beneath her to even give him a glance."

"Stay clear of that one, Tanner. If she finds out that you have more money than her father, she'll pretend to be something that she's not just to get her claws on your money. That cold-eyed bitch is just as hard and grasping as her father is."

In the darkness Tanner's lips twisted into a bitter smile. Could Julia Bradford be any worse than Roxy Bartel?

"What have you got planned for tomorrow?" Tanner asked, changing the subject.

"We've got about a couple hundred mavericks to be branded. I figure to get started early tomorrow morning." Rock looked at Tanner, his teeth flashing in a smile. "After being away so long, do you think you're up to puttin' your brand on a longhorn's rump?"

"You won't be able to keep up with me," Tanner retorted, his own teeth shining in a grin.

"We'll see," Rock said as he dropped the cigarette butt and kicked dirt over it.

"Rock." Tanner drew his legs up and rested his elbows on his knees. "It's been my dream for a long time to interbreed my longhorns with some Herefords. The resulting stock would produce more meat than our existing herd."

"That's a right good idea, but there's one thing you ain't took into consideration. Herefords have short legs. A bull wouldn't be able to mount a long-legged longhorn."

"Do you think I'm so dumb I never thought of that?" Tanner growled. "I'd only buy cows, of course. Then that problem would be solved."

Rock grinned sheepishly. "I got to admit you're one step ahead of me. When do you plan on gettin' them stubby-legged critters?"

"Early this fall maybe. After the roundup. I'd want to get them used to our cold weather before the first snowfall."

"That's a good idea. We'll have to watch that they don't get caught in snowdrifts, too. With them short legs, their bellies would drag in the snow."

"I've been thinking about that," Tanner said.

There was a moment of silence, then Rock asked, "Did Miz Sheldon clean out the cabin all right?"

"Yes. Everything is clean as a whistle. The place looks bare, though. I've got to get some window hangings up."

"I packed all the things you wanted cleared out. If you ever feel you want them, they're in a box up in the hayloft."

"I'll not be wanting them. You might as well throw them away."

Rock made no response to the bitter remark, but he was hoping that Tanner was wrong.

75

Both men stood up when they saw the men leaving the bunkhouse. Rock laughed. "Their stomachs are telling them that Pee Wee will be using his striker against the triangle any minute, calling them to supper."

Tanner only listened with half his attention to the bantering going on between the men as they drank their coffee after the evening meal. He was thinking, with some dread, of going to bed in the cabin, which was so silent now, so lacking in warmth.

Finally, with a heavy sigh he rose from the table, said good night to the men and walked to the dark cabin. Inside he fumbled his way through the kitchen and main room before entering his bedroom and lighting the lamp there.

In the dim light the bare walls seemed to mock him. He could almost hear them whispering, "Foolish man. Do you think that soap and water and the removal of a quilt will keep the memory of Roxy's soft body from haunting you?"

"Go to hell," Tanner muttered and quickly stripped down to his underwear. He blew out the lamp and slid between the covers.

He had no sooner stretched out and laid his head down when it started. His pillow still held the delicate odor of the rose-scented soap Roxy used on her hair and in her bath. He told himself to ignore the well-remembered fragrance, that he was probably only imagining it anyway.

But as his head warmed the feathers, the scent of flowers became stronger, wrapping around him like a soft cloud.

Finally, in desperation, he rose, and taking the blanket from the bed felt his way back to the kitchen. Rolling himself in the cover, he lay down on the bare floor

The last thing that went through his mind before he fell asleep was that he would never get used to living in the cabin again. There were too many memories. Memories that he must forget.

Chapter Seven

Roxy stepped out of Suzy's Dress Shop. The package she carried contained a flamboyant dressing gown for Belle's fiftieth birthday. She and the madam always celebrated each other's birthdays. She was very fond of Belle and there was seldom a day when she didn't see the woman who had become a second mother. They shopped together regularly, or had lunch at the cafe.

Which hasn't helped my reputation, Roxy thought wryly. But then, anything she did was fodder for the gossip mongers. If she so much as smiled and spoke to a man she had grown up with, the tongues started wagging.

She sighed and started walking down the boardwalk. She wondered who the gossipers would turn their tongues on if she moved away. "I pity the woman, whoever she might be," she muttered to herself.

Roxy was about to cross the street to enter the Lady Chance when she heard her name called. She turned around and smiled at the big woman who supplied her cook with fresh vegetables and milk. "Good morning, Mrs. Sheldon," she said when the farm lady caught up with her. "It's going to be a beautiful day, isn't it?"

"Yes, it is." Bertha puffed slightly. "Time for a person to get her garden started. I just bought some packets of seeds from the General Store. I made a deal with Tanner Graylord to supply his cook with fresh vegetables this summer. My man Ben is plowing up extra ground right now. I'll be busy all day, sowing the extra seeds."

"I always thought I'd like to raise a small garden. A person must get a lot of satisfaction putting seeds into the ground and watching them grow and produce nourishing food. I grow a few flowers," she continued with a smile, "but I'd like to try vegetables, too, one day."

"It takes a lot of hard work." Bertha looked at Roxy's smooth hands, then back at her own red, chapped ones.

"Yes, I expect so," Roxy said weakly, suddenly wanting to hide her white hands and clean, polished nails. "I'd better be getting along," she said, smiling at Bertha, "and see what my son is up to. He took off early this morning when I wasn't looking."

"Jory is with my Sonny and Sissy down at the livery. He's the reason I called to you," Bertha explained. "He would like to go home with us, spend the day with the children."

79

"Oh, I don't know, Mrs. Sheldon." Roxy's brow wrinkled. "Wouldn't that be a lot of trouble for you, with your garden work and all?"

"He won't be no trouble at all for me. One of my older sons will be keeping an eye on the younguns. Probably Paul. He's fifteen and very dependable. Besides, Sonny and Jory get along fine together. There won't be any fighting between them."

So, Roxy thought bitterly, even the homesteaders know of Jory's fights with the town boys. How nice it was of this kind woman to offer her son a day free of taunts and punishing blows from hard little fists.

But what did farm boys play at? she worried. Did they play rough games where Jory could be hurt? Were they around a lot of animals? Especially horses.

When she saw that Bertha was waiting for her answer, a frown on her brow now, she said reluctantly, "I don't see why Jory can't spend the day with Sonny. Tell him that I said he's to behave himself, and to do whatever you tell him."

"That's not necessary, Roxy. I wish my Sonny was as well behaved as your boy is."

"Thank you." Roxy's eyes shone at the compliment. "I don't know if I can find the way to your place when it's time to pick him up."

"You don't have to come after him. Paul or Aaron will bring him home. Maybe after supper, if that's all right with you."

"That will be fine, and thank you very much for your kindness," Roxy said sincerely.

"No thanks needed." Bertha smiled and turning around, walked toward the livery, clutching the cloth bag of seeds as though they were gold nuggets.

Roxy entered the Lady Chance and laid her package on the bar. "So, what have you bought from Miss Suzy's Dress Shop?" Ace asked, coming from his rooms.

"It's a birthday gift for Belle. She turned fifty today."

"I'd better get over there and buy her something, too. What do you suggest?"

"I saw a bright red petticoat. Belle would love that."

"I'll get over there later and buy it," Ace said, then started fidgeting with his cuff links.

Roxy watched him. He always worried the diamond studs when he had something on his mind. She wasn't surprised when he brought up Michelle LaBlanc's name. She had seen yesterday how taken he had been with the young singer.

"I've been wondering how our new singer will dress for her debut tonight," Ace said finally. "What she had on yesterday wasn't very eye-catching."

Roxy hid her amusement. It wasn't what Michelle would wear tonight that was on her cousin's mind. He was probably wondering how soon he could get her clothing off. "I'm sure she'll dress the part of a saloon singer," she said. "After all, she was dressed for the street yesterday. I feel, though, that however she dresses it will be in good taste. I have a feeling Miss Michelle LaBlanc is pretty much a lady."

"You do, do you?" Ace said, a look in his eyes that wasn't very gentlemanly. "I hope she's not too much a lady."

"Look, Ace," Roxy said impatiently. "If Michelle sings well and the men like her, I want you to leave her alone. I don't want you to romance the young woman, then drop her when you tire of the relationship. If she's good for business, I want to keep her. So I'm warning you, keep your hands to yourself."

"Don't get your bustle ruffled up, Cousin," Ace said, grinning. "I think it would be a long time before I tired of this one. For one thing, it would take me a while to melt the ice she's encased in."

"She is a little aloof, isn't she?"

"Yeah, but the right man can change that."

"And of course you think you're that man. Just remember what I told you."

Ace grinned, then said, "I haven't seen Jory around. Where is he, out looking for his cowboy?"

"I gave him permission to spend the day at the Sheldon farm. He gets along fine with the young son there. There are no fights or name-calling between them."

"That's what the button needs. Fresh air, a place where he can rip around, whoop and yell, kick up his heels a little. I used to spend the summers with my grandparents on my father's side. I couldn't wait for school to be out so I could go to their farm. There I could go barefoot, climb trees, go fishing."

"Do you think they'll be climbing trees today or playing along the river?" Alarm sounded in Roxy's voice. "Jory doesn't know how to swim."

"No, I don't think he'll be climbing trees, for pete's sake," Ace said disgustedly. "You're like an old mother hen with one chick. You smother the boy. If you had your way, he'd never grow up."

"I don't mean to be that way, Ace. It's just that he's all I've got. He's my life. I don't know what I'd do if I ever lost him."

"You're not going to lose him, honey. Just ease

up on him a little. Let him enjoy his childhood. What Jory really needs is a father. Aren't any of those men who pant after you good father material?"

"Really, Ace." Roxy gave him an impatient look. "That's a poor reason to get married. Anyway, I like it fine the way things are. Jory and I don't need a man in our lives."

"Speak for yourself, cousin. Why do you think Jory is so excited about his cowboy? The kid might not know it, but he's looking for a father figure. And if I'm not mistaken, you need a husband. You have become too hard and brittle over the years. You're beginning to act like a dried-up old maid."

When Ace saw the angry, hurt look on Roxy's face, he wished he could recall his words. He didn't want to fight with her. God knew she had enough on her slender shoulders.

Gathering up her packages, Roxy said. "I'm going to go wish Belle happy birthday, then take a little nap. I was awakened twice last night by those two dancers who are always squabbling. If it keeps up I'll have to let one of them go."

"Get rid of the redhead," Ace advised, half serious, half joking. "She's awful in bed, and she follows me around like a lovesick puppy."

"Oh sure, Ace. That's a good reason to fire someone," Roxy shot back scornfully as she walked toward the stairs.

As Roxy had hoped, Belle loved the brilliant robe. Her eyes sparkling her appreciation of the garment, she pulled it on and wore it as she served Roxy tea and a slice of the birthday cake her "girls" had baked for her. They reminisced about past birthdays, some happy, some sad. After Roxy yawned a couple of times, Belle sent her home with the order to take a nap.

Half asleep, Roxy tried to brush away something that was tickling her nose and lips. She turned over on her side, and a split second later the tickling was back at the corner of her lip. A smothered giggle alerted her to what was happening.

Aha, she thought, keeping her eyes closed, my son is having a little fun at his mother's expense. When the tickling started again, she opened her eyes and caught Jory's wrist.

"Gotcha!" she said in a threatening voice, then laughed at the startled look in her son's eyes.

"You really thought it was a bug crawling over your face, didn't you?" Jory said, quickly composing his features.

"Yes, I did. But my goodness, what time is it?" Roxy exclaimed when she saw that her bedside lamp had been lit.

Jory turned the small, fancy clock around until he could read the hands. "Quarter to six."

"When did you get home?"

"Just now. Paul brought me home."

"Did you have a good time playing with Sonny?" Roxy raised herself on an elbow and ran her gaze over her grubby looking son. His face was dirt smudged with sweat lines running down his cheeks, and there was a dirt line around his neck. A button was missing from his shirt, and there was a large tear in the knee of his Levi's.

"Ma, I had the best time of my life," Jory said, interrupting her inspection. "There's so much to do on a farm."

"I hope you didn't sit down at Mrs. Sheldon's table with such a dirty face."

Jory shook his head. "Everybody except Mrs. Sheldon and Sissy washed up on the back porch. It was a lot of fun. You could splash all you wanted to. I didn't have to be careful like I do in the water closet. I got dirty again helping Sonny with his chores after supper."

Roxy sat up and swung her feet to the floor. "I've got to freshen up and change my dress. When I'm finished you can wash again." She gave Jory's curls a gentle tug when he groaned at her order.

Ace was at his table, pitting his wits against two players, when Roxy descended the stairs and began mingling with the customers. The piano player was hammering out a rollicking tune, and the dancers, in a line on the stage, were high-kicking to the delight of the men gathered round, avidly ogling the bare flesh of shoulders and legs. Three waitresses weaved their way around crowded tables, trying to elude the male hands that sought to slide up their short skirts as they delivered drinks.

In half an hour Roxy's head began to ache. When Belle's girls came laughing through the bat-wing doors wearing their gaudy dresses, their eyes searching for men they could lure to their rooms, Roxy thought with a sigh, *What I wouldn't give to be rid of this place.*

In a small house on the other side of town, where places of business gave way to the residential section, Michelle LaBlanc sat in front of a vanity mirror with kerosene lamps flanking each side of it. She had turned up the wicks as high as she dared to give her as much light as possible to apply paint to her face.

Luck had smiled on her twice now, she thought, sorting through the bottles, fancy boxes and small pots that held the tools of her trade.

She had found a job and this darling little house. It had only three rooms but they were large and not too badly furnished. She had lived in much worse. Her landlady had agreed to wait for the rent until she drew her first pay from the Lady Chance.

Michelle's spirits were high as she began to deftly and expertly apply her stage makeup. As she worked, her mind ticked off the groceries she would need to cook her meals in the kitchen adjacent to the parlor.

Her fingers moved quickly over her face as she brushed on powder and rouge, for she was an old hand at painting her face. She had been singing in saloons and barrooms since she was fourteen years old.

She had inherited her mother's singing voice and when Mona LaBlanc was alive, Michelle had sung with her in the church choir every Sunday. Then her beautiful mother came down with pneumonia one cold winter, and in two days' time she was gone.

She and her father had been devastated. Their home was so empty without Mona's gay laughter floating through the house. A short time later Michelle and her father started dropping in at some saloon or other just to be around people and to hear laughter again.

One night in one of the saloons, the piano player was running his fingers softly over the keys, picking out the tune of "Beale Street Blues." Michelle

knew the song well. It had been a favorite of her
mother's, who sang it often.

Without really being aware of it, she walked
over to the scarred piano and slid onto the seat
beside the handsome young man who played so
beautifully. She started humming the words to the
song, then before she realized it, she was softly
singing the sad, sweet words. The man sitting next
to her gave her a startled look, then began to
stroke the keys with a force that made her raise
her voice.

As her pure, clear voice carried through the
room, the raucous din gradually died down and
finally ended altogether as the patrons left off
whatever had been holding their attention and
leaned forward to listen intently to the song that
brought back memories of other days.

The women, and some of the men, had tears in
their eyes when the last notes of voice and piano
faded into silence. There followed a roaring cheer
and clapping hands. Michelle stood up, and when
she smiled her thanks she was greeted with a
shower of silver dollars falling around her feet.

When she would have bent over to pick up the
silver, the young man held her back, whispering,
"You must never scramble around on the floor
picking up coins. You are above that. Always let
somebody else do it for you." He had scooped up
the money and tied it in his handkerchief before
handing it to her.

Before she and her father left the saloon that
night, the bar owner had hired her to sing five
nights a week. She had performed there until she
was sixteen, until her father got the wanderlust.
Two years followed in which they traveled from
state to state, from town to town.

Then Nat LaBlanc got it into his head that he was good at cards. However, he was woefully bad at it, and had finally lost his life trying to cheat at poker.

Michelle sighed and pushed away the memory of that night as she rose and walked into the bedroom to select a dress to wear. She riffled through the gowns she had hung in the narrow wardrobe and chose a blue satin and chiffon creation. The bodice was cut just low enough to reveal a hint of cleavage and had short cap sleeves that showed off her arms and shoulders. Its bodice was of shimmering satin, as was the underskirt. But there was a top layer of full, filmy chiffon that would twirl around her feet as she walked. It made her look innocent and worldly at the same time.

She sat back down before the mirror and began grooming her hair. When she had pinned it in curls on top of her head, she fastened dangling rhinestone ear-bobs in her ears, then pulled on sheer elbow-length gloves.

It was eight-thirty when she took up a lacy stole and arranged it over her shoulders, then picked up her wrist purse. She turned down the lamp and left the little rented house. She wanted to get to the Lady Chance early, since this was her first night to sing there. She wanted to check out where she would sing, meet the piano player.

Michelle received many interested looks as she hurried along. None of the men accosted her, however. She looked too much the lady. The Lady Chance was in full swing when she stepped through the bat-wing doors. She stood a moment, looking around, trying to spot Roxy. Her gaze fell on Ace, his handsome face serious as he studied the cards in his hand.

She saw Roxy then, standing at the end of the long, shiny bar as though waiting for her. My new boss is truly a beautiful woman, she thought as she gazed at the black-haired beauty whose expression said she was a hundred miles away.

Roxy's face came alive when she saw Michelle making her way through the milling crowd of men, dancers and ladies of the night. "You're early," she said, giving the singer a genial look.

Michelle nodded. "I wanted to see where I would be singing, and meet the man who will be accompanying me on the piano."

"You'll perform there." Roxy nodded toward the stage that had been erected about three feet above the saloon floor. A railing went across the front of it. The railing had been added after some of the rowdier customers climbed up on the platform to join the dancers.

Michelle inspected the stage with a quick glance. It was bare of anything that might draw the spectators' attention away from the performance. A tall stool, the only furnishing, had been placed directly beneath the bright light of three kerosene lamps suspended from the ceiling. She was pleased with the setting.

"Come along and I'll introduce you to Zack." Roxy took Michelle's arm.

They were walking toward the piano when Michelle pulled loose from Roxy's light grip on her arm. With a cry of surprise and joy, she rushed to meet the slender blond man coming toward them. "Zack," she said softly as she went into his open arms.

When she and Zack stepped apart, smiling at each other, Roxy laughed and said, "I guess no introductions are necessary between the two of you."

"I should say not," Michelle said, happy excitement dancing in her eyes. "Zack and I go back a long way. He and I used to work together."

"Yes, we do. And, Roxy, if you haven't heard Michelle sing yet, you're in for a great treat. She sings like an angel."

"Oh, Zack, that's not true," Michelle protested, embarrassed.

"Well, let's see if he's right." Roxy urged the blushing singer to one side of the platform, where three steps led up to it. "Get up there on that stool and let me hear you."

Michelle settled herself upon the padded seat and smoothed her skirts. The kerosene lamplight struck golden glints off her hair as she and Zack exchanged a knowing look. Her long-ago friend lifted his hands, and his fingers began to move lightly over the keys.

The notes of "Beale Street Blues," the first piece they had ever done together, lifted into the air. The bell-like quality of Michelle's voice reached every corner of the room.

Almost immediately the noise in the room began to hush; then the roulette wheel stopped spinning and the little ball stopped its whirling. The room grew completely quiet then as everyone left off what they were doing to listen intently to the song that brought back memories of happier times.

Ace, in the act of dealing a new hand, paused, then rose to his feet. As stirred as everyone else, he crossed the room to stand beside Roxy. "Damn," he whispered, "but she can sing. Why is she wasting her time here? She should be performing in San Francisco in a theater."

"I was thinking the same thing. I feel there is a mystery about Michelle LaBlanc. . . ."

The song ended with a loud burst of approval. Hands were clapped together, and as silver dollars rained around Michelle's feet, voices begged, "More! More!"

Michelle smiled her thanks and Zack began a rollicking cowboy song. The men cheered and stamped their feet in time with the tune.

"She knows how to work the crowd, doesn't she?" Roxy said.

"She does indeed," Ace agreed, then added in disgruntled tones, "She seems to be getting on well with Zack."

"Yes. They're old friends. They've worked together before."

"Is that so?" Ace half growled.

"You sound displeased about that." Roxy's lips twitched in amusement as she looked at Ace's frowning brow.

"You're loco. Why should I care who she's known in the past?"

When Michelle's first performance of the evening ended, however, and she stepped off the stage and sat down beside Zack, Ace knew he cared a lot about her past. Otherwise he wouldn't be thinking how satisfying it would be to blacken the piano player's eye.

Chapter Eight

Tanner stood up and loosened the rope from around the yearling's feet. As it ran bawling away, he put the branding iron back on the red glowing coals of the fire. He wiped his sweating face on the corner of the bandana tied around his throat, then took a long swallow from the canteen he had placed in the shade of some aspens.

He hadn't realized he was so out of shape. He supposed that one didn't use many muscles fighting Indians. Also, he had been up since the crack of dawn, and his bones and muscles were aching from sleeping on the floor as usual.

As Tanner hunkered down beneath the trees for a short rest before resuming the task of branding more stock, he told himself that he must do something about his sleeping arrangements. He hadn't had a good night's rest for a week and it was beginning to tell on him. He knew he was short-tempered and that the men were beginning to stay clear of him when they could.

But what with the branding and the dozen other things that came up on a ranch, he hadn't found the time to go into town and purchase the pillows that he hoped would let him sleep in bed. He didn't want to ask Rock to run the errand for him. He would have to explain that Roxy's scent in the old pillows was keeping him awake. His friend would pooh-pooh such a thought. He would say that it was all in his head.

Tanner picked a blade of grass growing between his feet. As his fingers worried it, he asked himself if he was just imagining that her scent was in the pillows; like he imagined that he could feel her presence in the cabin, that when he looked out the kitchen window he could see her riding away among the pine and aspens, the way he had seen her do so many times.

Nobody ever mentions Roxy's name, he thought, then allowed that wasn't really surprising. Most likely none of the men working on the ranch were aware that he'd had plans to marry her, and that he had practically been stood up at the altar. Rock never brought her name up, whether because he was afraid her name might be hurtful to his friend or because he no longer gave the past engagement a thought. Rock was no romantic.

Tanner rose to his feet, stretched his stiff back and prepared to brand the maverick that had just been dragged over to the fire. The thunder of galloping hooves on the gravelly wagon road made him pause and look over his shoulder. A handsome white stallion with flecks of foam on his chest and shoulders was coming toward the branding camp at breakneck speed.

"Who in the hell is riding a horse like that?" he muttered, then thought that maybe someone was in trouble.

That idea was quickly aborted when a smiling Julia Bradford brought the animal to a rearing halt only feet from where he stood. "Good morning, Tanner," she called gaily.

A black frown on his face, Tanner ignored her greeting as he walked over to the heaving animal. His anger grew when he saw that the bit had sawed the horse's mouth so cruelly that it was oozing blood. A glance at the horse's shoulder and rump showed long welts made by the whip being laid on him.

"Didn't anyone ever teach you how to treat fine horse flesh?" he demanded in a voice that made Miss Bradford flinch. "Someone should put a bit in your mouth and saw on it while a whip is put to your rump."

"But, Tanner," Julia was quick to whine, "I don't ride a horse like this unless it's absolutely necessary. I ran into a pack of wolves and raced to get away from them."

Tanner wasn't taken in by her lie. Some of the lash marks on the beautiful hide were old. They had bled, scabbed over and left a scar.

"What are you doing so far away from town, and alone at that? If you had run into a bunch of renegade Indians, you wouldn't have outrun them."

Julia's face paled. "I thought all the Indians had been put on a reservation after the Indian War."

"Most are, but there are always young renegades who didn't like the peace treaty and have drawn away from their tribes."

"I guess my father didn't think of that when he sent me to your ranch to invite you to supper Saturday night."

Tanner gave her a startled look, then his eyes glittered with suppressed amusement. Was the old banker pushing his daughter at the now wealthy rancher? Was he hoping that along the way they could merge their wealth through marriage between him and his spoiled daughter?

Tanner had to put some effort into keeping a sober face as he said, "I'm not one for social gatherings. Besides, we are at a busy time at the ranch right now. At the end of the day all I think about is eating supper and going to bed. Thank your father for me, but tell him I can't accept his invitation."

Miss Bradford wasn't as adept at keeping her emotions hidden as Tanner was. Anger darkened her eyes, and her lips drew into such a tight line they almost disappeared. As Tanner watched her, however, she composed her features and asked sweetly, "I wonder if you would ride back to town with me? Those wolves are still out there."

Tanner suspected that she hadn't seen any wolves in the first place. The swearing men and the bawling cattle were making so much noise, no wolf or any other critter would come within miles of the area.

"I'm sorry," he said, "I don't have the time. But I'll send young Paul Sheldon with you." He pointed to the teenager, who sat his plow horse watching the branding of the cattle with interest.

"But he's just a boy," Julia snapped. "He'd be no help if we were set upon by wolves."

"He can shoot a gun as well as any of my men,"

Tanner said coolly. "I can't spare any of the others."

"I'll go by myself then." The irate woman's eyes shot blue sparks. When she raised her arm to bring her riding crop down on the hapless stallion, Tanner grabbed her wrist. "There are no wolves here, Miss Bradford. You have no cause to lash the animal."

Julia dropped her hand, but it was plain in her cold blue eyes that as soon as she was out of sight, she would take her anger out on the stallion.

Seething in frustration, Julia brought her riding crop down on the stallion's rump, making him lunge forward.

"I can't believe that that churlish, unpolished boor, that nobody, turned down my invitation," she gritted out. Back East in New York, men fought over who would dance with her, who would ride with her in the park on Sunday afternoons.

Oh, but I miss the city, she thought. She missed the excitement there: the playhouses, the parties, the dances. And she missed her friend Jenny. Jenny with her boyish figure and her short-cropped hair.

She and Jenny had planned to go abroad this spring, to be free of all who knew them, to live as they pleased in gay Paris. But dear *Papa* had smashed that dream.

She had cried for an hour after receiving his answer to her letter informing him of her plan and requesting money for her tour of Europe.

"My dearest daughter, Julia," the letter had begun, "it grieves me deeply that I cannot afford your trip, but I have fallen on hard times. I have made some unwise investments with bank money and live in dread of being found out. If several of my customers should make large withdrawals, the bank would run short of funds. There would be such a run on the bank, I would have to close the door.

"I'm sorry also that I can no longer afford to let you stay on with your friend Jenny. But I know that you understand the trouble I'm in and that you want to be with me in this trying time. Please come home as soon as you can. Your loving father."

Julia's lips drew back in a sneering smile. The old fool, she would have ignored his whining letter except that pride kept her from imposing on Jenny's parents. She'd had only enough money to buy her fare back to Denver.

So here I am, she thought bitterly, lowering myself by asking a crude cowboy to dinner. A pleased smile curved her thin lips. Papa wouldn't like it that Tanner Graylord had turned down her invitation.

Julia's smile faded. Her father would only heckle and nag her until she tried again to get the rude rancher interested in her. But there was one thing she would never do, she vowed, and that was to marry the man. To marry any man, for that matter.

The sun was going down as Denver loomed ahead. Julia sighed. Another long, boring evening stretched ahead of her. "Oh, Jenny, I miss you so." Tears glimmered in her eyes.

Tanner opened his mouth in a wide yawn as he watched Julia ride away. I've got to get a good night's rest, he thought, and decided on the spot that he could no longer put off purchasing new pillows.

When Rock finished branding the yearling hog-tied at his feet, Tanner walked up to him. "I've got an errand to run in town. The men look pretty beat. When you finish with that couple in the holding pen, why don't you call it a day."

Rock nodded, then as he set the young cow loose, he asked, "What did Miss Uppity want? The way she was laying the whip on that poor stallion, I felt like jerking it out of her hand and giving her a taste of it."

There was amused irony in Tanner's voice when he answered, "Can you believe that she brought me an invite from her father to have supper with them? The man who wouldn't invite me to sit down in his bank eight years ago."

"Oh, I believe it all right. That old scoundrel wants to get his hands on your money. He's plotting a marriage between you and his daughter."

"Fat chance of that ever happening," Tanner hooted. "I'd no more marry that cold bitch than I would Fat Nellie, the cook at the cafe. That's an insult to the cook, though. Fat Nellie has more tenderness in her little finger than Julia Bradford has in her whole body."

"You just watch it, though. Both of the Bradfords are as slick as foxes. Given a chance, they'll get you in a corner you might not get out of."

"I'm used to getting out of corners, friend. It would be no effort at all, escaping a trap they might set for me."

Tanner mounted the little quarter horse he used when working cattle and cantered away. Using a shortcut across country, he arrived in Denver twenty minutes ahead of Julia.

Covered with dust from his Stetson to his boots, a darkening stubble on his jaw, Tanner rode straight to the general store. He would buy his pillows and ride straight back home.

When he arrived at the store, he dismounted, leaving the reins hanging loose. The sturdy little horse had been trained to stand in place. Tanner took off his hat and slapped it against his thigh, dislodging some of the dust. Placing it back on his head, he turned to go inside and walked headlong into a soft feminine body.

His hands automatically reached out to keep the woman from falling. He was about to apologize when he looked into her face. A cold paralysis seized him.

Roxy, more beautiful than ever, gazed up at him. All normal thought left him. He could only think how he wanted to grab her up in his arms and kiss her red, tender lips.

He jerked himself out of the strange spell when Roxy said in a cold, hostile voice, "I see you've finally come home."

He released her arm and answered in a harsh, flat voice, "Yes, I've come home."

Giving him a cool, impersonal look, Roxy said after a moment, "Welcome home," and walked on.

Tanner stared after her, anger growing inside him at the lack of warmth in her voice. She was acting as though it was his fault that he had ridden off to war. She knew damn well that it was her actions that had driven him away.

He strode after her and, taking hold of her arm, turned her around to face him. "I think we need to talk," he said roughly.

Roxy was sweating with impatience to get away from him. Paul Sheldon would be bringing Jory home any minute and she didn't want her son to see her talking to his cowboy friend. She stared up at Tanner and demanded in a tight voice, "What is there to talk about?"

"I think there's some misunderstanding about why I left here eight years ago."

"There's no need to talk about that. I understand perfectly why you went away."

"If you understand, why your cold attitude?"

Roxy stared up at him, astonishment in her eyes. "You're really something, Tanner Graylord," she ground out. And jerking her arm free, she turned and hurried away.

Tanner stared after her as she made her way to the Lady Chance. *After all she's put me through, I still want to make love with her,* he thought with self-disgust.

Roxy walked with her head up, her back straight, until she entered the Lady Chance. There, she gathered up the folds of her skirts and ran up the stairs to her quarters. She entered her parlor and rushed to the window that looked down on the street. Parting the curtains just enough to see the store across the street, she waited for Tanner to finish his business there and step back outside.

Her heart was still pounding. Being so close to Tanner after all these years, feeling the heat of his whip-lean body, she had lost all composure.

But as she watched for him, all the pain and heartache he had caused her came rushing back. Standing there she remembered all the insults she had endured, the contemptuous looks, being shunned by the women of Denver society, and her hostility toward the man she had once loved returned full force.

What was his game? she wondered. What did he mean that there was a misunderstanding about his going off to war? Did he hope to resume their old relationship? Did he think he could smooth talk her into making a daily trip to his cabin and spending a couple hours making love like they used to do? Would he talk of marriage again, all the while having no intention of ever standing in front of a preacher to say those two little words, "I do"?

Well, he'd be in for a big surprise when she didn't fall a second time for his soft, empty words. She was far from being the lovesick teenager he had known then. No man had fooled her since.

At last Tanner stepped from the store, a large package under his arm. He stood a minute on the narrow porch as if making up his mind about something. Roxy's body went still when he looked up at her window. She prayed that he couldn't see her standing there, peering down at him.

As she continued to watch, Tanner stepped onto the street, fastened the package to the back of the saddle, then swung onto the horse's back. He leaned forward, picked up the reins, nudged the animal with his knees and rode off down the street. She stared after him until he reached the end of town and hit the open range, riding out of her sight.

A soft sigh feathered through her lips. She wished he hadn't returned. The same old magnetism was still there between them. She was thoroughly disgusted with herself, for even now she could remember the feel of his arms around her, holding her softness close to his hard body.

The air had been hot and close that summer day when she and Tanner rode to their favorite spot beside the river. It would be cool there, beneath the willows whose branches hung out over the water. Tanner had spread a blanket under the large tree, and she laid out the beef sandwiches she had brought from the Lady Chance. They didn't talk too much as they ate. They let their eyes do all the talking.

Then, the last of their lunch eaten, Tanner reached for her as usual and they fell back onto the blanket, wrapped in each other's arms. Tanner began to kiss her as his hands moved restlessly over her body. His palms skimmed across her shirt front, slid down her midriff and molded her hips.

But today it was different. There seemed to be an urgency in his touch, a trembling in his hands. When he began to undo the buttons of her shirt, something he had never done before, her body went still and she held her breath.

She had dreamed of Tanner doing this, wanted it to happen. Still, she was a little nervous about it. Besides, it was broad daylight. What if someone came upon them?

Nevertheless, she lay quietly as his lean fingers undid the buttons one by one and spread the edges of the shirt apart. There remained only her camisole to cover her. She closed her eyes shyly as Tanner gazed down at her heaving bosom.

Her breasts felt suddenly cool when he pulled the camisole down. A moment later her breasts was quite warm as hot lips closed over the nipple. "Ahhh," she cried out as Tanner drew the puckered areola deep into his mouth and suckled it in slow rhythm. A tingling warmth spread from her breast to the core of her; she'd never dreamed anything could feel so wonderful.

Lost in a fog of desire and a need she hardly understood, Roxy wasn't aware that Tanner had raised her shoulders high enough to get her out of the shirt and camisole. She slowly became cognizant of his kneeling over her and pulling off her boots, then sliding her riding skirt and underpants down over her body.

"No, Tanner," she protested weakly, feeling so vulnerable lying naked on the blanket, with the birds singing in the branches and the lap of water on the river bank reminding her they were out in the open.

Tanner gently took her wrist when her hand came down to cover herself. "Please let me, Roxy," he said hoarsely, "let me look at you. I've wanted to for so long."

Roxy slowly relaxed at the pleading in Tanner's voice. She loved him so much it was hard to deny him anything.

She soon stiffened again, though, when he stretched out beside her and started trailing hot kisses over her midriff, then across her stomach and finally coming to the patch of soft curls in the vee of her thighs.

She grabbed his head and stopped him there. Breathing fast, Tanner pulled himself up until he lay even with her. "Roxy," he whispered huskily, "I want you so badly I hurt all over. Don't you want me, just a little?"

"Of course I do, Tanner," Roxy said, stroking his hot, flushed face, "but I'm a little afraid."

The glide of his tongue on her swollen nipples caused the warmth to flow through Roxy again, and gazing into Tanner's desire-ridden eyes she whispered, "I'm not afraid anymore."

It took Tanner half a minute to tug off his boots

and strip off his clothes. Roxy withheld a gasp as she stared at the male part of him. It was so long, so thick. Her body would never take it.

Tanner saw the alarm in her eyes and whispered huskily, "You'll stretch for it, honey."

Roxy doubted it, but didn't resist when he gently pulled her legs apart and knelt between them.

"Relax, Roxy," he coaxed, and taking his throbbing self in his hand began to slowly enter her.

It doesn't hurt, Roxy thought in surprise. A moment later when he broke through her virginity, a gasping cry of pain fluttered through her lips.

Tanner stopped his progress, but didn't remove himself from her. Instead, he bent his head and began to slowly suckle a breast. With each draw of his lips, Roxy forgot her pain as desire raged through her again. She pressed her hips against his. She saw Tanner smile. Then he pushed himself all the way inside her, paused a moment, and with slow rhythm rose and fell in the well of her hips.

Roxy didn't know what was happening to her when suddenly a tingling started in her breasts and traveled all the way to where Tanner's manhood stroked her. She grasped his shoulders and cried out as she soared upward.

Tanner knew what was happening to Roxy and he slid his hands beneath her hips and lifted her to fit more tightly against him and increased his pace. She hung awhile in the clouds of desire, then started tumbling back to earth, calling Tanner's name as her body jerked and trembled.

Roxy remembered how Tanner had slumped against her a moment later, his breathing fast and harsh in her ear as he lay with his head in the curve of her shoulder.

When they were both breathing normally again, Tanner lifted his head and, smiling down at Roxy, asked, "That didn't seem to hurt you too much, now did it?"

"No," she answered shyly, then giving him a roguish grin asked, "Do you want to show me again how painless it is?"

"I'd love to," Tanner said, brushing the sweat-damp curls off her forehead, "but you're tender inside now and I don't want to damage you. I want you to heal, be ready and eager for me the next time."

And she had been eager for him the next day and all the days that followed. Roxy sighed for that young, trusting girl who had so willingly given herself to a man who had taken her love too lightly.

She shook her head and let the curtain fall back in place. The sun was ready to go down and it was time she went downstairs to have a word with Ace, and wait for her son, who should be getting home any minute. She was thankful he hadn't returned while she was talking to Tanner. He wouldn't have understood the tension and bad feelings between them.

Chapter Nine

A short time later Roxy learned that Jory had seen Tanner after all. When the boy burst into the saloon, his grubby face was drooping with disappointment.

"What's wrong, honey?" She put an arm around his narrow shoulders. "Did you and Sonny have a disagreement?"

"Naw. We always get along fine. Just as me and Paul rode into town I saw my cowboy friend riding away. I called to him, but I guess he couldn't hear me over the noise of the galloping hooves."

Roxy looked up at Ace, who had joined them. Her eyes were full of torment. How many times would her son feel the pain of not being a part of his father's life?

Ace smoothed the damp curls off Jory's forehead. "You'll see your friend again, button," he said softly. "He probably rides into town at least once a week."

"But maybe I'll miss him just like I did today because I'll be at the farm." A worried frown marred his smooth forehead. "Maybe I'd better not go there anymore."

"You mustn't give that up, Jory," Roxy exclaimed. That was the last thing she wanted the boy to do. "You have so much fun playing with Sonny. You'll run into your friend again."

"I'll have to think about it," Jory said with a sigh, his slender body sagging a bit.

"Yes, you do that while you're washing up," Roxy said as she turned Jory in the direction of the stairs. "I'll be up in a minute and you can tell me all about your day."

When her son disappeared into their quarters, Roxy looked up at Ace, tears in her eyes. "What am I going to do about this fascination Jory has for Tanner? Is it true that blood always tells? Do you think Tanner has the same feeling for Jory?"

She dabbed at her eyes with a little lacy handkerchief she took from inside her sleeve. "I have this awful feeling that Tanner's return is going to bring me more heartache. If he ever learns that Jory is his son, he will take him away from me. I couldn't bear losing him, Ace."

"Roxy girl," Ace soothed, "he's not going to take your son. I'll see to that."

"I don't know how you could stop him." Roxy was near tears again.

"I'll find a way. Now stop crying. Your nose will get all red and your eyes will get puffy. You won't look like the most beautiful woman in Denver then," Ace teased gently.

"The way you were ogling Michelle last night, I

got the feeling you thought she was the most beautiful woman around." Roxy wiped her eyes and blew her nose.

"Michelle has another kind of beauty, a quiet kind. There's an innocence about her that tempts a man."

"Ace, I warned you. Don't go messing with Michelle's mind and emotions," Roxy said sharply. "I think she's had enough sadness in her life without you adding to it."

Ace made no response to his cousin's warning, but asked instead, "Have you found out what her relationship is to Zack?"

"No, I haven't and I'm not going to ask Michelle. Her personal life is her own business. I know that Zack walked her home when the saloon closed."

"Yeah. I saw them leave together," Ace said sourly. "I offered to walk with her but she turned me down."

"She's a wise young woman," Roxy said, a heaviness in her voice. "She won't be taken in by empty words." She looked at Ace and asked on a lighter note, "By the way, which of the dancers did you invite into your room when the saloon closed?"

Ace shrugged. "I wasn't in the mood for feminine company. I had the bed all to myself."

"That must be a first." Roxy pretended shock. "Age must be catching up with you. Or could it be you're saving yourself in the hope you can lure the lovely singer into your bed?"

From the way Ace's face reddened, Roxy suspected that her teasing words had come close to the truth. Was it possible her handsome cousin was finally falling in love? She considered that idea a moment, then shook her head. Right now he was captivated with a new type of woman. A lady. But maybe this time he would be the one to get hurt. It was high time some woman jerked him off his high horse.

When Roxy left Ace and went upstairs to her apartment, she found Jory still in his bathwater. As she had expected, his face was shiny clean but his neck was still grimy, as were his ears.

"Well, young man," she said, kneeling beside the tub and taking the washcloth out of his hand, "I see you still have an aversion to soap and water on your neck."

"Ah, Ma, I washed there," Jory complained as Roxy lathered his dirty skin.

"And I suppose you rinsed the soup out of your hair, too."

"Yes, I did. I ducked my head under the water."

"I see that. And all you did was rinse the front part of your head. The back part is still full of dirty soap suds." Roxy picked up a pitcher of water from the washstand and saying, "Cover your eyes," poured it over his head.

As the dirt and soap washed down over his shoulders, Jory let out a squeal. "That water is cold, Ma."

"From now on rinse your hair properly and I won't have to help you. I'll bring you your night-shirt and when you've dried off and got into it, you can tell me all about what you and Sonny did this afternoon."

A few minutes later Jory joined Roxy on her comfortable sofa. But instead of his usual glowing report of how he and Sonny spent their time on the farm, Jory brought up his cowboy friend.

"Do you really think I'll see my friend again, Ma?" He looked earnestly at her.

I'm scared to death that you will, Roxy thought;

it is my worst nightmare. Instead of answering his question, she asked Jory one. "Why do you call him your friend when you only saw him that one time?"

"I don't know. He talked to me like I was a grownup, not a dumb little kid that nobody listens to. When he broke up the fight I was having with the town bully, he handed me his handkerchief to wipe my bloody nose, and he told me that I was a scrapper."

Jory gave Roxy an accusing look and added, "You would have scolded me for fighting. And another thing, he understood that I would like to have a horse. But he did point out all the things that could happen to a boy if he was out on the range alone. Like what could happen if a person got thrown from his horse. He said it was bad business to get caught afoot in cattle country. A man could be in danger from thirst and starvation, wild beasts, renegade Indians, the elements and cattle. He said that cattle have no fear of a man who's walking. And he said that maybe I should wait awhile before you got me a horse."

Roxy didn't say anything for a long while. Why hadn't she taken the time to explain all those dangers to Jory instead of just saying she was afraid he'd get hurt? Maybe he did feel like a dumb little boy that no one would listen to.

Jory tugged at her arm and said in a small, longing voice, "He called me 'son' one time, Ma."

Roxy turned her head to hide the tears that jumped into her eyes. Jory didn't realize that "son" was commonly used by older people when speaking to a youngster.

What could she say to this little boy who was her whole world? She had heard the poignancy in his voice and hadn't realized until now his longing for a father. Jory was an intelligent child and the day would come when he would question her about his father. A year or so ago Ace had told him that his father had gone off to war and hadn't come back. That had seemed to satify him at the time, but now he knew the meaning of the word "bastard" and would want answers about that.

She turned back to her son and, giving him a kiss on the cheek, said, "You'd better get started on your lessons now."

As Roxy walked back downstairs to start her nightly routine, she faced the fact that the time was drawing near when Tanner and Jory would learn they were father and son.

Unless, she thought, pausing on a step, she took Jory and moved far away.

Chapter Ten

As Tanner rode homeward he felt a stirring of guilt. He had heard the boy calling his name, but his emotions were in such a turmoil he was in no condition to carry on a light conversation with a youngster. He'd make it up to the lonely little fellow the next time he saw him.

A crooked smile lifted the corners of his lips. If he could sneak him away from that mother who held the apron strings so tightly, he'd take him fishing. And later, he dreamed on, he would take the boy to his ranch and teach him how to ride—starting him out on a gentle mare, of course. The kid musn't come to any harm. That mother of his would skin Tanner alive if Jory should take a spill on his rump.

I should have a son of my own by now, Tanner thought as the horse hit the river trail. A son like the kid, one he could teach all about the range. A son who would take over the reins of running the ranch when he retired. A son who would give him grandchildren that he could also teach.

"Damn you to hell, Roxy Bartel, or whatever your name is now." Tanner's fingers tightened angrily on the reins. "I could have a couple sons by now if you hadn't played me false."

The horse snorted and paused when the trail ended at the river crossing. Tanner knew he was thristy and he let the reins lie loose. As the animal snuffled the water, he told himself to stop thinking of the past. It couldn't be changed.

When the horse lifted his head, water dripping from his muzzle, Tanner kneed him into motion and he splashed across the shallow, slow-moving stream.

Up ahead, through the pines and aspens, glimmering lights shone from the cook house and bunkhouse. Tanner hoped that the men would be at supper, especially Rock. His friend would want to know what was in the package, and he wasn't about to tell him that it contained new pillows, or to explain why the purchase had been necessary.

He made a disgruntled sound when he arrived at the barn and saw that the hands were still standing around the cook house waiting for Pee Wee to call them inside. Rock came toward him as he dismounted.

"What you got there, Tanner?" His friend eyed the package tied to the saddle. "More new duds?"

Tanner jumped on the answer Rock had unwittingly given him. "Yeah," he said, and with his purchase under his arm, he turned the horse over to a stable hand.

An hour later, after a hearty meal of beef stew

and hot biscuits, Tanner was almost falling asleep in the tub of bathwater he had prepared in the kitchen. He stepped out of the tub, toweled himself off, then walked naked into his bedroom. By the light of the moon shining through the window he turned back the covers, pressed his fingers on the new pillows with their clean cases. It was time to test them.

He climbed under the sheet, laid his head down and waited for Roxy's scent to engulf him. His stiff body relaxed when all he smelled was the fragrance of clean linens.

The mantel clock in the main room ticked softly and the quiet of the bedroom closed in on Tanner. He slept.

However, even with the new pillows, his rest was fitful. Roxy insisted on entering his dreams. She slid her soft palms over his body; her slim fingers fondled and stroked him until he groaned her name. In the end, as she persisted, he parted her legs, entered her, and they made long, sweet love the way they had years ago.

When Tanner awakened the next morning he was sticky from spent passion. He was thoroughly disgusted with himself as he washed his private parts before getting dressed.

The sun was up when Roxy awakened and gazed through the window at a cloudless sky. It promises to be a nice morning, she thought, and rolled over on her back. Staring up at the ceiling, she planned her day.

It was Saturday, the day she usually went riding with Christy. But her friend had sent word that she wasn't feeling well and that they would get together the following Saturday.

Jory would be spending the day at the Sheldon farm, and after young Paul picked him up she would go shopping. She needed a new bonnet. The sun was getting brighter these days and she must protect her skin against its rays. If she didn't, her face would become a mass of freckles.

Also, there was shopping to do for Jory. Lately, he was growing out of his clothes. Those few pieces that he could still wear were torn at the knees, or had pockets and buttons ripped off. The games he and Sonny played were rough on clothing.

But her son had never looked so healthy and happy. His eyes were bright and sparkling, his skin taking on a tan. It was true he often came home bruised and scratched, but he had come by hurts through play, not from the young bullies in town. He was still thrown into their company at school, but Aaron Sheldon, who attended eighth grade, kept an eye out for him. Consequently, no more fights had occurred.

Roxy wondered sadly if the name-calling still went on, though. Sonny had been begging her to let Jory spend a whole weekend at the farm. "Mom says it's fine with her." He had grinned and added, "She said she can use an extra hand weeding the garden. And we've got the room. I have my own bed up in the attic."

She could still see the hopeful look in Jory's eyes as he waited for her answer. She had temporized by saying she would think about it. And now that she had mulled it over, she decided that next week she would let Jory spend the two nights and days with his friend.

Roxy lay a moment longer in bed, gathering her courage to leave the warmth of the covers. The

115

spring mornings were still pretty nippy, and the fire had gone out of her small stove.

She took a deep breath, pushed aside the feather comforter and stood up. Shivering, she hurriedly pulled on her robe and tied its belt tightly around her waist. When she had slid her feet into the slippers lying where she had kicked them off the night before, she looked in on her son. He was sound asleep, hunched under the blankets, only the top of his head showing. She touched his curls lightly, then hurried down the stairs, heading for the warmth of the kitchen and a cup of coffee.

She said good morning to the old swamper mopping up the saloon floor. He was nearly finished; only a corner of the large room remained to be done. Ace and three men were just finishing up an all-night poker game there.

She looked at them and shook her head. All four had red-rimmed eyes and dark emerging whiskers on their jaws. She sat down at the end of the bar and waited for her cousin to join her.

"You look awful," she said when Ace pushed open the kitchen door and held it for her to precede him into the cook's domain.

"The way I look is only half as bad as I feel," Ace said, yawning. "But it was a lucrative night for the house. After I eat breakfast I'm going to bed and sleep for a week."

Roxy only laughed at his remark. She knew her cousin. After six or eight hours of sleep he would be up, rested and bright-eyed, eager to get a deck of cards in his hands once night had fallen. He was a born gambler.

"Which of the dancers will keep you company

in that big bed of yours?" Roxy asked slyly as she sat down at the table across from him.

"There will be no dancer in my bed." Ace reached across the table and gave her tangled curls a yank. He patted the pocket of his red satin vest. "I've got the keys to my rooms right here."

"Humm, that makes another night of no bed partner. You're not ill, are you?" Her pretense of being serious was spoiled when she burst out laughing. Her cousin looked as healthy as a horse. "Skinny"—Ace looked up at the cook as he came toward the table, two steaming cups in his hands—"pour Roxy's coffee over her head. Maybe it will take the sharp edge off her tongue."

Skinny only smiled. He was used to these two sniping at each other.

Roxy took a sip of her coffee, then asked, "Did you get to talk to Michelle last night?"

Ace snorted a short laugh. "I spoke to her when she came in, but before I could get a conversation started, Zack came swooping down on us and took her off to the piano."

"I suppose he walked her home as usual."

Ace nodded, staring into his cup. "I wish I knew how long he stays with her," he said, then grew silent, a sour look on his face.

"He might not even go inside with her," Roxy pointed out, trying to cheer up her cousin. "It's possible they are only good friends."

"Ha!" Ace snorted. "It would be impossible for a man to only be good friends with Michelle LaBlanc."

"You're mistaken, Ace. Have you ever tried being friends with a woman?"

"Now, why would I want to be friends with a woman?" Ace laughed.

"You might learn something about us females:

how we feel, what we think about, what we like and don't like. You might discover that there's more to a woman than just her body." There was bitterness in Roxy's voice as she finished talking.

Ace looked at Roxy, then glanced away. He knew she had been thinking about the rancher as she spoke. No more was said on the subject when Skinny brought bacon and eggs and hot biscuits to the table. They ate in silence until Ace finished and left the table. He touched Roxy's shoulder and said quietly, "I'll see you later."

Roxy sat on at the table, her chin propped on the heel of her hand, staring unseeingly through the grimy kitchen window. Tanner had slept with her last night . . . in her dreams. It had been wonderful. They had made love just as they had in the years past, eager to come together. He had been a silent lover, though. There had been no softly spoken love words as before. When they were both sated and exhausted, she had laid her head on Tanner's shoulder and whispered, "Do you love me, Tanner?"

In the quiet darkness of the room he had given a contemptuous snort and shoved her head away. As she lay in heartbroken silence, he rose, got dressed and left her without a word.

When she had awakened, tears were rolling down her cheeks. She had brushed them away, thinking angrily that even in her dreams Tanner Graylord could still hurt her.

The closing of the oven door brought Roxy back to the kitchen and her seat at the table. When Skinny asked her if she wanted more coffee, she shook her head. "No, thank you, Skinny. I've got to get Jory up. One of the Sheldon boys will be picking him up before long."

When Roxy left the kitchen, the cook went back to his bowl of dough and started shaping another loaf to go into the oven. His mind was in a deep study as he worked the sour dough. He couldn't understand Roxy and Ace. They were both fine people; he couldn't figure out why they hadn't married each other so that their son could have his father's name. Ace was very fond of the boy. It showed in the way he treated him. And the gambler cared very much for Roxy. He knew that the citizens of Denver were just as puzzled about them as he was. Everyone was aware that Roxy never showed any interest in the men who eyed her longingly. They also knew, however, that Ace consorted with other women. The strange thing about that was Roxy didn't seem to care how many women he took up with.

Poor little Jory, he was the one suffering. The cook shook his head. Upstairs, Jory was awake and already dressed.

"I'm going outside to wait for Aaron," Jory said, edging toward the door.

"Wait a minute or two and I'll go down with you," Roxy said, pinning her curls on top of her head.

"You don't have to come with me, Ma," Jory said in petulant tones. "I'm not a baby."

"I know that, honey. The thing is, I'm going to Miss Newheart's shop to purchase a new bonnet. I might as well leave when you do."

Jory gave in reluctantly, and when he and Roxy stepped out of the Lady Chance, Aaron was riding up on the big plow horse. The fourteen-year-old was at the gawkish stage, with big feet and hands. He blushed uncomfortably when Roxy smiled at him and said, "Good morning, Aaron. It looks like we're going to have a lovely day."

His Adam's apple bobbing, the teenager answered, "Yes, ma'am," and reached down to help Jory climb up behind him.

When the old horse went plodding away, Roxy stepped off the porch and walked briskly across the street. Miss Newheart had just raised the shade of her shop and put in the window the cardboard that had "Open" printed on it. Roxy wanted to get her business finished before the ladies of Denver started coming into the store to visit with each other, catch up on the latest gossip.

Miss Aggie Newheart, an old maid in her late thirties, gave Roxy a genial smile when she stepped into the shop, and the little bell over the door tinkled gaily. Besides liking Roxy and feeling sorry for her, Aggie knew that the young woman had come to purchase something. She was not one to stand around and talk about her neighbors as most of her customers did.

"Good morning, Roxy," she said, thinking to herself that the young mother seemed more beautiful every time she saw her. She felt sure that Roxy's exceptional good looks caused fifty percent of the mean talk that went on about her. If she were flat-chested and cross-eyed, the women would be more lenient about the unwed mother.

"How can I help you this morning, dear?"

"I need a new bonnet." Roxy advanced to the counter. "Have you had any deliveries this spring yet?"

"You're just in time for the latest styles in bonnets. I got in an order from Chicago yesterday. I haven't finished putting them all out yet, but there is one I've put aside for you. It is the loveliest of the lot and I wanted you to have first choice. I knew if the banker's daughter saw it, she would grab it right up. Come in the back with me and try it on. I have it in my bedroom."

Roxy always felt honored to be invited into Miss Aggie's living quarters. None of her other customers had that privilege. As she perched on the edge of a sofa that held so many different shapes and sizes of fancy pillows there wasn't room enough to sit back, she viewed the room. The walls were papered with a rose floral print, knickknacks covered every inch of the two side tables, and the walls held framed pictures of relatives. It was definitely the sort of room that would give an old maid comfort, she thought. Including Teeny, the black and gray striped cat that came and jumped into her lap.

"Here it is," Miss Aggie said as she carried a hat box into the room. She opened it up and asked, "What do you think?" as she lifted out a bonnet that took Roxy's breath away. "Come sit in front of the mirror and I'll put it on you."

Roxy gasped her delight when Aggie set the beautiful creation on top of her coal black hair. It was fashioned from stiff white lace with a narrow, perky brim that dipped down on the right side of her face to shade one eye. A dark green, plumy feather, the color of her eyes, curled gracefully down beside her right cheek.

"You look absolutely stunning, Roxy," Miss Aggie exclaimed, her hands clasped to her breast. "It's like it was made especially for you. Julia Bradford will have a conniption fit when she sees it on your head."

The corners of Roxy's lips twitched in a small

smile. It was plain that Julia wasn't a favorite of Miss Newheart.

"I love it, Miss Aggie," Roxy said, her eyes sparkling. "I think I'll wear it home."

"You do that. It's too lovely to be hidden in a box."

When Roxy handed over the price of the bonnet, Miss Aggie asked, "Would you mind taking this package over to Belle Lang? It's a couple of hats for one of her girls. I don't mind when the young prostitutes come into my shop, but most of my ladies put up a fuss when they come in."

"I understand, Miss Aggie. I'll take it to Belle right now."

Roxy stepped out of the shop and right into Julia Bradford's path. "Excuse me," she said automatically, but the haughty Miss Bradford didn't even hear her. Her hard blue eyes were fastened on the perky bonnet sitting rakishly on top of Roxy's curls.

"Did you get that bonnet from Miss Aggie's shop?" she demanded.

"Yes, I did, and good morning to you, too."

"I didn't see it in her shop yesterday," Julia snapped, ignoring Roxy's hinted rebuke.

"She's still unpacking her new merchandise. You'll probably find one that you like."

"I like that one. I'll buy it from you."

"No, you won't. I like it, too."

"I'll give you more than you paid for it," Julia pressed. "I'll give you an additional ten dollars."

"I wouldn't sell it to you for an extra hundred dollars," Roxy said sharply. When she started to walk around the irate woman, Julia stopped her by grabbing her arm.

"Why would you want such a beautiful bonnet?

122

Where would you wear it? You don't go to church, you don't go out walking with a gentleman friend. All you'll do is parade around in that saloon of yours, showing off in front of drunks and riffraff."

"Take your hands off me," Roxy demanded.

"Hey, ladies," an amused male voice said, "am I going to see a cat fight here on Main Street?"

While Roxy stood rooted to the ground, Julia dropped her hand and turned to smile at Tanner Graylord. "We've been discussing Miss Bartel's new bonnet," Julia explained, then added insolently, "I've been trying to buy it from her. After all, I will have more occasion to wear it than she will. As I just told her, who's going to see it on her except the drunks in her saloon? She never goes anywhere."

Tanner shot a hooded glance at Roxy and hid a pleased smile. Far back in her green eyes, not quite hidden by her anger, he caught a glimmer of what used to be there when she looked at him. If only a thread of what had been remained in her mind and heart, he was going to play on it. Maybe in a small way he could make her suffer as he had.

With a desire for revenge that his smile camouflaged, he took Julia's arm and placing it in the crook of his, said softly, "Why don't we stop in the cafe and talk about a bonnet especially for you?"

Julia nodded eagerly, and they turned gloating eyes on Roxy. Roxy wasn't there, however. She was halfway down the block, and Tanner, disappointed, knew she hadn't heard a word he had said.

He watched the graceful sway of her hips as she crossed the street, irritation in his expression. He had failed to elicit her jealousy this time, but there would be other times when she couldn't miss seeing Miss Bradford and him together. He would see to that.

But as he and Julia entered the cafe, he wondered if maybe he had misread what he had seen in Roxy's eyes. Maybe she wouldn't give a damn if he courted the woman who clutched his arm.

Chapter Eleven

Roxy looked straight ahead as she made her way to the Lady Chance. She made no eye contact with anyone she passed. It had shaken her, seeing Tanner so soon after her passionate dream of him. For a split second her eyes had stripped away his clothes and she saw his powerful body as she had seen it last night. When he ignored her, as if she wasn't even there, giving all his attention to Julia, she had turned and walked away, filled with self-disgust that for an instant she had been stirred by the man who had ruined her life. To this day he made her life a misery.

Roxy was about to enter the Lady Chance when she remembered the package under her arm. She turned and walked down the alley to the gate that led to the Pleasure House's back door.

The irritated frown on Belle's face changed into

a wide smile when she answered Roxy's knock.

"Roxy!" she exclaimed happily. "I was afraid you were some drunk wanting the company of one of the girls. Sober gents know not to come around in the daytime. Come on in. I just finished making a pot of tea. We'll have a cup while we chat."

Roxy followed the curvaceous figure clad in a red, ruffled robe into a kitchen that was as familiar as home. Its brightness and warmth cheered her some. This room had always comforted her when she came here as a youngster. She had sat in this kitchen with Belle when she was a teenager full of questions about life, love and boyfriend. Here she had come to her friend to announce that Tanner had asked her to marry him.

Then later, she had brought her broken heart to draw comfort from Belle's warm arms.

Roxy sat down and laid the package on the table that was covered with a floral cloth. The shaft of sun coming through the window shone on Belle's unbrushed frizzy hair as she carried a tray to the table. She transferred from it a teapot, two cups with saucers, two spoons and a sugar bowl.

"I love your bonnet, Roxy," Belle said as she sat down and lifted the pot and filled the two delicate cups with steaming tea. "It's new, isn't it?"

"Yes. I just bought it from Miss Aggie." She pushed the package toward Belle. "She asked me to bring you this. It has two bonnets in it for one of the girls."

"They would be for Irene," Belle said, amused. "I never saw a woman so crazy about hats. She spends most of her money on them."

Belle took a sip of tea, then placing the cup back in its saucer, said, "Now tell me what's bothering you. And don't say nothing is wrong. I know you too well, Roxy Bartel. You're on the verge of crying any minute."

"I never have been able to fool you, have I, Belle?" Roxy looked fondly at her longtime friend.

"Maybe a couple times," Belle answered, half joking, half serious. "Tanner Graylord is back. Does he have anything to do with that upset look in your eyes?"

"Partly. He and that Julia Bradford. I saw them both outside Miss Aggie's shop. Julia was determined to buy this bonnet right off my head. We were having quite an argument about it when Tanner showed up." Roxy paused a moment, then with hurt and anger in her voice, she burst out, "He totally ignored me, Belle. I felt like I wasn't even there as he gave all his attention to Julia."

The withheld tears rolled down Roxy's cheeks, hot and bitter. "I hate him so," she sobbed. "He ruined my life, and now he's got the gall to pretend it was my fault that he left Denver."

Belle laid her hand on Roxy's clenched fist. "Tanner ruined your life only because you let him. You could have married some other man years ago. By now you could have a home and a father for Jory. There are a lot of good men here in Denver who would jump at the chance to marry you if you'd just turn loose your hatred for Tanner and give them a chance. You could even tame that rascal Ace. Everyone knows how fond he is of you and Jory. I guess you know that half of Denver believes he's Jory's father."

Roxy wiped her eyes, then looked at Belle. "I'm well aware of what people think, Belle, but I could never marry Ace. You see, Ace is my first cousin."

"Your cousin!" Belle's cup clattered back in its

saucer. "Seth never said anything about him being a relative."

"It was Ace's suggestion that no one know of our relationship. Back in Utah he killed a man over cards and he didn't want the stigma of that to rub off on the Lady Chance." Roxy laughed shortly. "Of course Pa agreed with him."

"Yes, he would." Belle nodded sadly. "Seth was always self-serving. He was a man who used people."

Neither woman spoke for a minute; the muted sounds of people on the street were the only sounds in the room.

Roxy broke the silence. "Belle, I'm scared to death that Tanner will realize he's Jory's father and take my son away from me. And Jory might want to go with him. He has gotten to know Tanner and he adores the man."

"Roxy, I can't see that happening. Tanner wouldn't do that to you."

"Wouldn't he though? You haven't seen the contempt in his eyes when he looks at me."

"I thought you said he ignored you."

"I ran into him once before today. It was awful. That's when he hinted that it was my fault he went away. Belle, I'm seriously thinking of selling the Lady Chance and leaving Denver. Jory and I will go someplace where we'll never see Tanner Graylord again."

"Roxy, you mustn't do that!" Belle exclaimed, alarmed. "A young woman alone with a child in a strange town would have a rough go of it. That is not the answer."

"But don't you see, Belle, that would be the beauty of it. Nobody would know me either. I would change my name, pass myself off as a young widow with a child. Finally Jory and I would be shown respect."

"How would you make your living? Whatever money you'd get from the sale of the Lady Chance wouldn't last forever. You're young with a lot of years stretching ahead of you. Would you buy another saloon?"

"Never that," Roxy said vehemently. "I hate the saloon business. I've hated it all my life. I hated not having a place to play as a child. I hated living over a saloon where I couldn't invite girlfriends to visit.

"And I'm sure Jory feels the same way." Roxy made herself calm down before adding, "And the poor little fellow has to put up with mean name-calling besides."

"Honey, I never knew you felt that way about the saloon. You never mentioned it before."

"I used to tell Tanner," Roxy said bitterly. "The snake pretended to be sympathetic, let me think that I would share the cabin he was building. I so loved that little place when it was finished. While I waited for us to get married, I hung curtains, put up pictures and placed little knickknacks in the family room. And all the while he was laughing behind my back."

"I'm sure he never laughed at you, Roxy," Belle said gently. "I still think he cared for you then."

"Are you so sure, Belle? Does a woman ever know what a man is thinking?"

"I can't answer that, but I do know that Tanner should be told that he's a father."

"Really? What if I told you I wrote a letter telling him that I was expecting, and that he didn't even bother to answer it? Are you sure now that he loved me?"

Belle made no response. Roxy was too upset to listen to anything she would say. When Roxy left, Belle watched her walk across the alley and enter the Lady Chance through the kitchen door. Belle turned back into the kitchen, a thoughtful, troubled look on her face.

Tanner sat across the table from Julia in the small cafe, cursing himself for a fool. What had ever made him invite this snappish woman to have coffee with him? So far she had only talked about herself, or had complained about Roxy. If he heard her whine one more time "She wouldn't sell me the bonnet out of spite," he just might walk out of the place and leave her sitting alone.

He was thinking of ways he could get away from the annoying female when she said, "You and Roxy were quite friendly at one time, weren't you?"

He brought his hand up to his mouth to hide an amused smile. He had been waiting for such a remark. "I guess you could say that." He removed his hand, in control again.

"I was just wondering if she would let me have the bonnet if you spoke to her about it."

Tanner couldn't hide his amusement this time. He threw back his head and gave a bark of laughter. "Believe me, Miss Bradford, we were never that friendly."

"I guess the gossip about your relationship is wrong then."

"Gossip usually is."

"I suppose the gambler is the one I should talk to. I imagine he would have more persuasive power with her than you would. I don't think the gossipers are wrong when they say that he is the father of Roxy's child. It's said, however, that he's quite a womanizer and that Roxy turns a blind eye to his cheating."

Tanner couldn't believe that he had felt a moment of sympathy for Roxy. He should be glad that she was hurting now as he had hurt when she tossed him aside for another man.

"I'd say it would be worth your while to talk to him anyway," he said, picking his hat off the floor and settling it on his head. "He'll probably be able to convince her to give up the hat. I've got to get going now. I've got a lot of work to do at the ranch."

"Oh . . . yes . . . well, thank you for the coffee," Julia managed to say, flustered that she was going to be left sitting alone at the table. Her angry gaze stabbed him in the back as he went through the door.

"I'm surprised the boor left money to pay for our coffee." She fingered a silver dollar.

Tanner was almost at the end of town when his stallion approached the saloon where he and his friend John Allen used to carouse, a hundred years ago, it seemed. He could hear the shrill and false laughter of the saloon girls and a tinny-sounding piano. Three horses were tied to the hitching rail, one wearing the Allen brand on his hip. On the spur of the moment, Tanner reined Brave in. Maybe John had ridden into town and stopped off for a drink before going home. Tanner had been meaning to ride out to his place but had been too busy at the ranch.

When Tanner walked into the dim interior of the Red Dog saloon, the first person to greet him was his longtime friend. "Hey, you ole' tomcat!"

John swung away from the bar and came to meet him. "It's about time you came home."

Wide smiles were exchanged, hands shaken and backs pummeled. "Where have you been all this time while you're getting rich?" John asked as they lined up at the bar.

"Last two years were spent fighting the Indians," Tanner answered as the bartender, new to him, poured him a glass of whiskey. "I got a hankering for the ranch then and headed for Colorado. What's new with you?"

"Nothing much. My spread is coming along pretty good and me and Christy got married. Don't have any younguns yet. We feel bad about that."

"Maybe you're trying too hard." Tanner grinned, tossing back half his glass of whiskey.

"Do you reckon?" John looked serious as though considering that possibility.

When Tanner answered, "I reckon," they both burst out laughing.

They talked ranching and cows for a while, then Tanner said slowly, "I suppose Christy and Roxy are still friends."

"Oh yeah. Nothing could ever break up that friendship. I guess Christy and Belle Lang are about the only women friends Roxy has these days."

"Why is that?" Tanner asked blankly. He couldn't understand why the women had turned on Roxy.

"Well, the simple truth is Roxy had a baby, but no husband."

"What?" Tanner reared back and stared at John. "Are you saying that she didn't marry that gent from Utah?"

"You mean the gambler. No, she never married

him. They're thick as thieves, though. He plays poker for the saloon, and lives there. Now, I'm not saying that they live together, but everyone thinks so. Except for Christy, that is. She's in Roxy's quarters most every Saturday and she says that she has never seen a sign of a man living there."

After a short pause, John said, "Christy thinks that Roxy still cares for you."

"What a laugh that is." Tanner snorted. "Christy had better have her head examined, or stop smoking loco weed."

"I don't know about that. Christy blames Seth Bartel for what happened between you two. She thinks the old bastard pushed Roxy at Ace Brandon."

"If she had really loved me, no one could have changed her mind." Tanner's eyes were hard and cold.

"She was only seventeen, Tanner. Hardly a woman yet. Seth could have heckled her into it." John took a swallow of his drink, then said, "Damn, but Roxy is a beauty. If I didn't love Christy so, I'd make a play for her. Me and half the men in town," he laughingly added.

"How does she feel about that?" Tanner asked, trying to speak casually.

"She doesn't even see the hungry looks that follow her when she walks down the street. I'll say one thing for the gambler, his hard fists ensure that every man who comes into the Lady Chance treats Roxy with respect. The word spread fast that it was hands off Roxy Bartel. And he's good to the boy, in his cavalier way."

But he doesn't care enough for his son to give him his name, Tanner thought, and wished he could get his hands on the gambler. Suddenly he

133

Norah Hess

didn't want to hear any more about Roxy.

"I've got to be going," he said, finishing his drink. "We've been branding mavericks and every man is needed."

"Christy would love to see you, Tanner. Come to dinner some Sunday."

"I'd like that, John. Let me know when."

As he rode out of town, Tanner had second thoughts about visiting John and Christy. He and Roxy had been friends with John and Christy in the old days, and a lot of memories were bound to surface in the Allens' company. He didn't need that.

As the stallion loped along, he wondered if he could stomach Julia Bradford long enough to make Roxy jealous. He decided that he would wait a couple weeks, then call on the waspish female. He'd test himself to see if he could tolerate her company for an hour.

"I'll make myself put up with her," he muttered.

Chapter Twelve

"Here they come now," Ace said, nudging Roxy. They had been standing on the porch of the Lady Chance for about ten minutes watching for Jory to come home from his weekend visit at the Sheldon farm.

"It seems like he's been gone for a week," Roxy said, her eyes shining at the sight of her son sitting behind Aaron on the big plow horse, his legs sticking straight out.

When Jory slid to the ground and climbed the steps, a wide smile on his face, Roxy remembered in time that her son would be embarrassed if she hugged and kissed him in public.

Ace, however, was allowed to slap him affectionately on the back and ask, "How did things go on the farm, fellow?"

"They went great. I can't wait to tell you about it."

After they said goodbye to Aaron and stepped inside the saloon, it was Roxy's turn for attention. As they climbed the stairs to their rooms, Jory put his arm around her waist and said, "I missed you, Ma. Especially at bedtime."

"Well, I like that," Roxy said, pretending to be insulted. "I missed you all the time."

"No, you didn't." An impish grin spread across Jory's dirty face. "You had all your work to do."

"Yes, I did." Roxy grabbed a handful of black curls and gave them a tug. "But I still missed you all the time." They entered the parlor, giggling together.

"Now. Tell me everything about your visit with Sonny," Roxy said, then bit her tongue not to scold Jory for sitting on her lovely sofa in his dirty Levi's.

"It was just great, Ma. Did you know that on a farm you get up before daylight? It was still dark outside when me and Sonny drove the milch cows in from the pasture to be milked. Everybody works on a farm. Mr. Sheldon said it's earning your keep. Even little Sissy has her job. She feeds the chickens and gathers their eggs. Me and Sonny had to keep the woodbox filled for Mrs. Sheldon and shovel out the stalls in the barn.

"Every morning after breakfast, me and Sonny and Sissy and Mrs. Sheldon went to their big garden and started weeding. Sonny explained that their garden is larger this year because they're raising vegetables to sell to a nearby rancher."

"When did you get to play? It sounds like you worked all the time."

"After lunch me and Sonny could do anything we wanted to. I'm talking about playing, of course.

We mostly just horsed around." He laughed and added, "We spent a lot of time hiding from Sissy. She always wanted to tag along with us."

"I'm glad you had a good time, honey." Roxy gave Jory an affectionate squeeze. "But it's time now to get to your homework."

"Yeah," Jory groaned. "Thank goodness this is the last week of school until next fall. Me and Sonny have some big plans made for this summer."

"You do? Like what?"

"Me and Sonny talked it over with Mrs. Sheldon first to get her permission. She said it was all right that when school lets out me and Sonny can spend the weekdays at the farm, then come back here for the weekends. It would be like a vacation for Sonny.

"What do you think?"

"I don't know, Jory." Roxy frowned. "I'd miss you terribly."

"I'd miss you too, Ma." Jory took her hand and, squeezing it, added, "But I wouldn't miss being teased and beat up every day by the hoodlums here in town."

Roxy's eyes grew moist. Her young son had suffered more than she had realized. Had she been wrong not to have married one of the men who had tried to court her when Jory was still very young? If she had he would have a father now. He would not have to suffer taunts and name-calling. She wouldn't let her mind dwell on the reason she had found fault with every man who tried to court her.

"I'll talk to Uncle Ace about it." She blinked back the tears in her eyes.

Norah Hess

"Great!" She received a bear hug from tight little arms. "He'll say yes, I know he will."

When Jory left to wash up, Roxy sat on, staring down at her clasped hands. She also knew that her cousin would agree with her son. Ever since Jory had started school, Ace had nagged her to either get married or take Jory and leave Denver.

For some reason, and she refused to think why, she had balked at that idea until recently. She had two reasons now to act. She must put an end to Jory's unhappiness, and get him away before Tanner learned of their kinship.

But if I were to marry, she thought, both of my worries would be solved. Jory's tormentors would let up on him if there was a father figure behind him, and Tanner would have less chance of taking Jory from her if it ever came to that.

All the time Jory splashed around in his bath, Roxy mentally reviewed every eligible man she knew. By the time Jory went to his room to tackle his school assignment, she had found fault with every man she had considered. I don't have to make a decision until fall, she thought. I'll talk it over with Christy.

She and Christy had gone horseback riding as they usually did on Saturday mornings. As they walked their horses, Christy had said in an off-hand manner, "John saw Tanner in town the other day. They had a drink at the Red Dog saloon."

Although her heart began to beat in hard thuds, Roxy made no response.

"John says he's changed a lot," Christy continued. "He looks old for his age. He's got a lot of gray in his hair, and he's grown hard and bitter. John thinks the war did that to him.

"Anyway, when John invited him to dinner

138

some Sunday, Tanner said he'd be happy to come." She glanced at Roxy. "I don't suppose you'd come too."

"You suppose right. I wouldn't come."

"I just thought it would be nice . . . like old times when we used to do things together."

"The old times are gone and forgotten, Christy."

Christy said no more on the subject of a Sunday dinner, but Roxy's mind lingered on what Christy's husband had said about Tanner. She, too, had noticed the changes in him and wondered about them. The war years must have been very hard.

She wondered a bit what it would be like, spending some time with him and Christy and John, as they had done so long ago. Could they recapture those days of fun and laughter when the world was sweet and without a care? She shook her head.

Those golden days are no more, she thought with a catch in her throat as she stood up and called to Jory, "I'm going downstairs for a while. I'll be up before you go to bed."

When Ace didn't answer Roxy's knock on his door, she went out onto the saloon's porch and found him sitting there. With his feet propped up on the railing, he looked at her and asked with a grin, "Did the kid finally run down?"

"Some. He's got it in his head that he wants to spend the summer weekdays with the Sheldons and come home for the weekends. What do you think?"

"I think it's a fine idea. Have you noticed the change in him since he's been spending time on the farm? He's losing some of his baby fat, he's got color in his cheeks, and most of all, he no longer wears that sullen look."

"I guess I'll let him go then," Roxy began, then closed her mouth. Julia Bradford was coming across the street, headed for the Lady Chance. As she climbed the steps she smiled at Ace, but ignored Roxy.

"Mr. Brandon, I'd like to talk to you," she said in a commanding voice; then looking pointedly at Roxy she added, "Alone."

Ace brought his feet down and, giving her a wicked smile, said, "Make yourself scarce, Roxy. I think I'm about to be propositioned by the lovely Miss Bradford."

Roxy stood up, hiding an amused smile. Did the proud Julia realize the implications of Cousin Ace's words? She somehow doubted it. She was too wrapped up in her own importance to think that anyone would dare poke fun at her.

Roxy was wrong, though. Just before she walked into the saloon, she glanced over her shoulder at Julia and saw that she had blushed a fiery red. I've got to hear this, Roxy thought, and unashamedly sat down in a chair close to the door.

"So, Miss Julia"—Ace's voice was low and seductive—"what can I do for you this lovely evening? Shall I take you to supper, go for a moonlight walk, or"—his voice dropped to a whisper—"would you like for me to show you my rooms? You would find them very comfortable. Especially the—"

"You can stop right there, you insufferable cad." Julia's eyes glared hate at him. "I should have known that you're just as low as Roxy Bartel. No wonder Tanner Graylord had to leave town to get away from her."

"If that remark is true, it's the luckiest day Roxy ever had," Ace said lazily, though his eyes were as cold and hard as ice. "Roxy is much too good for the likes of that one.

"And a piece of advice, Miss Bradford. Don't set your sights on Tanner Graylord. Roxy might decide that she wants him back. He'd come running, you know."

"Oh!" Julia actually stamped her foot in her rage. "You make me sick," she flung at Ace. As she tapped her way down the boardwalk, Ace chuckled and propped his feet back on the railing.

"Did you get all that, Roxy?" he called.

Roxy hadn't felt so good in a long time as she climbed the stairs to check on her son. Ace had certainly knocked Miss High and Mighty off her high horse.

When Roxy had checked that Jory had finished his school work and was in bed, she walked back down the stairs and into the racket of loud male voices, maudlin feminine laughter, and the ring of silver dollars on the bar.

She made her way through the crowd, stopping to speak to a customer, listen a minute to a sad drunken tale. When she finally got to Zack, he had just finished pounding out "Camptown Races" on the yellowed piano keys. He gave her a boyish smile and slid across the bench, making room for her to sit down.

"I don't know why I bother to play when Michelle is not here to sing. I can't even be heard over this din."

"They do settle down when she sings, don't they?"

"They sure do. It's always been that way. Even when she was just a kid, everyone stopped to hear her. No reflection on the Lady Chance, but Michelle should be singing in some fancy place in San Francisco."

"I wonder why she hasn't gone there," Roxy thought out loud.

"I don't think she realizes how good she is. Her father, as much as he loved her, always downplayed her talent. She was his meal ticket. When I heard that he had been killed over a poker game, I imagined that she would go to some large city to sing in a night club there. I couldn't believe it when she turned out to be your new singer."

"Do you love her, Zack?"

"Only in a way I would love a sister if I had one."

"Ace is quite taken with her. I've never seen him so hard hit by a woman before."

"I've noticed," Zack laughed. "I get a lot of dirty looks from him. But he'll be wasting his time, chasing after Michelle. She's down on gamblers. If he was a store clerk, or even a cowboy, he might have a chance."

"Well," Roxy sighed, "I guess I should start mixing with that crowd. It's expected of me."

"Roxy," Zack began hesitantly when she started to get up, "I was wondering . . . would you have supper with me some night? On one of my nights off?"

For a moment Roxy could only stare into his soft brown eyes in the thin handsome face. She had not been out with a man socially since Tanner had deserted her. She doubted if she would know how to act, make small talk.

But Zack looked so earnest, so hopeful, she

142

found herself smiling at him and answering, "I think that would be very nice."

"Great. I'm off tomorrow night. Would that suit you?"

"That will be fine." Roxy felt a little breathless. Things were moving too fast. She must let Zack know from the beginning that she could only offer him friendship. When she saw Ace standing at the end of the bar she said, "Excuse me, Zack. I want to have a few words with Ace before he starts work."

Ace was having a cup of coffee when she reached him. "I saw you talking with the piano thumper," he said with a sneer.

"You don't have to use that tone about Zack," Roxy scolded. "I just found out that there's no romance between him and Michelle. They are old friends from way back."

"Did he say that?" Ace's eyes lit up.

"Don't look so excited. You're not going to like what else I discovered. Michelle has no time for gamblers. You might as well go back to your woman chasing."

"Like hell I will." There was a determined glint in Ace's eyes. "I'll wear her down, see if I don't."

"Good luck. But I'm afraid you've met your Waterloo at last."

Chapter Thirteen

It was the first day of summer, hot and muggy. "It's going to rain before I get home," Tanner muttered as he rode along.

Anyhow, he added to himself, I'm looking forward to seeing Christy again.

He had run into his friend John Allen on the street yesterday and before they parted John had invited him to drop by and have a piece of Christy's birthday cake today. "We might have a little party later in the week, but I'd like for just the three of us to sit around and chat," John had said.

I'd like that better too, Tanner thought. Roxy was bound to be at the party and he didn't know how he might react to her presence. The pillows he'd bought to get rid of her scent in his bed had worked. One problem had remained, however.

Most times after he retired he caught himself listening for light footsteps approaching the bed. That in turn would keep him awake for hours as he relived the hot, steamy lovemaking that used to take place in the bedroom.

He had told himself countless times that this mustn't continue. It was driving him out of his mind. He was ashamed that he was still haunted by the lovemaking of a woman who had chosen another man over him.

To date, no solution had come to mind, unless he had a house built in which Roxy had never set foot. He didn't know why he was dragging his heels about doing it. God knew he could afford it.

As he approached the Allens' neat little ranch house, Tanner promised himself that as soon as he got caught up with the work around his own ranch, he would make arrangements for his dream home to be built.

When Roxy had ridden out of town, with Christy's birthday gift tied to her saddle, the angry looking clouds warned of an impending storm.

She had been a bit surprised when a teenager had brought her a note from Christy. It was short, saying only, "Stop by the ranch tomorrow night and have some of my birthday cake with me and John."

Two days ago when she and Christy had taken their usual Saturday ride, her friend hadn't mentioned anything about a birthday cake. But that was like her impulsive little friend. She was always doing things on the spur of the moment.

Roxy often envied her friend. She was married to a good man who loved her, had a snug little home and a growing ranch. What did she herself have? A saloon that she hated, no husband and a little boy who carried no man's name.

The sky was dark when Roxy rode into the Allen yard. Christy had seen her coming and was standing on the porch to greet her.

"Beauty is in heat," Roxy said. "I think I'd better put her in the barn." Christy nodded agreement and went back inside.

John was in the barn when Roxy led Beauty inside its dim interior. "Hiya, Roxy." He smiled at her as he closed the half-door to a stable he had just put his horse in. "I'm afraid we're in for a storm."

Beauty and the stallion sniffed the air and began acting up, each wanting to get to the other. "I see your mare is horsin'." John grinned. "Hand her over and I'll put her in the last stall of the barn. Maybe a little distance between them will cool them down."

"I probably shouldn't have ridden Beauty over here. A wild stallion might have caught her scent and come after her."

"There's no denying that," John agreed. "And a rider on her back wouldn't have deterred him. Go on up to the house," he said, leading the mare away. "I'll be up as soon as I get Beauty settled."

Roxy walked into Christy's cozy little parlor and then into the kitchen where she heard the clinking of china.

"Here you are, birthday girl," she said, grinning as she shoved the wrapped package at Christy.

"Oh, Roxy, you shouldn't have," Christy exclaimed as she set a stack of dessert plates next to a three-layer cake covered with white icing.

"Hah!" Roxy snorted. "Who are you trying to

hoodwink? You would never forgive me if I forgot your birthday."

"Would too."

"Would not."

They were both giggling when John walked into the kitchen. "What's so funny?" he asked, going to the sink and working the hand pump for water to wash his hands.

"Nothing really," Christy said, laughter still in her eyes. "Roxy and I were engaged in the same kind of squabble we used to engage in when we were children."

Christy was standing with a knife poised over the cake when a male voice called from the parlor, "Anybody at home?"

Roxy frowned when John called back, "We're in the kitchen." She knew that voice, but she still couldn't believe it when he appeared in the doorway.

As she and Tanner glared at each other, an embarrassed, sheepish look came over the Allens' faces.

"I don't appreciate this, Christy," Roxy exclaimed. She jumped to her feet, her chair scraping backwards.

When she started toward the door, Christy begged, "Don't go, Roxy. Stay long enough to have a piece of my cake."

"Yes, Roxy, stay. I'm not going to bite you," Tanner sneered. "I hope we're both adult enough to enjoy Christy's culinary effort for ten minutes."

Tanner's taunt was all it took for Roxy to rethink her plans for leaving. If he could endure her company for a short time, she guessed she could put up with his. She pulled her chair back to the table and sat down, her stiffly held body saying that she wasn't happy with the way the evening was turning out.

As Christy cut the cake and passed it around, Tanner and John started talking about the approaching storm, each agreeing that a good, heavy rain was needed, that the grass was beginning to dry up.

Roxy and Christy made no attempt at conversation. Roxy sat stony-faced while Christy gave her apologetic looks.

The cake had been eaten and the coffee poured when a flash of lightning lit up the yard. The ominous roll of thunder that followed made both women jump.

"I've got to get started home before it begins to rain," Roxy said nervously as she stood up.

"Me, too." Tanner pushed his chair away from the table. "When the storm hits, it's going to spook the cattle and all hands will be needed to keep them calm."

"I hate to see you go, but I'm glad you're leaving together," Christy said anxiously, following them out of the kitchen. "I don't like the idea of Roxy riding alone in a storm."

"I'll be all right, Christy," Roxy said. "I've ridden in storms before."

"But not alone," Tanner growled. "And stop acting like you've been put upon."

As Roxy glared at Tanner, John muttered, "I'll go get Beauty."

When Tanner slapped his hat on his head and followed John, Christy, near tears, said, "I'm sorry, Roxy. I just wanted the four of us to be together again like old times. It was my dearest birthday wish."

"I'm sorry it turned out such a failure," Roxy

said, softening a bit, "but as you just saw, those days will never happen again."

"I know that now," Christy said sadly. "Thank you for whatever you brought me."

"Beauty is waiting for you, Roxy," John called from outside.

With a quick goodbye, Roxy hurried outside and John boosted her into the saddle. Tanner, astride his stallion, sat waiting for her. As they rode off together, another flash of lightning lit up the sky.

Tanner set as fast a pace as was safe in the darkness. They hadn't traveled more than a quarter of a mile when the heat lightning turned into zigzag streaks, followed by thunder that cracked and rolled.

The rain came then, slicing unmercifully at anything in its path. In seconds Roxy and Tanner were drenched, and the horses highly agitated.

They were approaching the dark shape of a wooded area when an uneasiness gripped Tanner. He knew how dangerous it was to be beneath a tree during a storm. But what could they do? Where could they go?

He remembered then a high, steep, cliff-like face of rock somewhere in the area. Over the years the wind had hollowed out an overhang. It was deep enough for him and Roxy to find shelter and safety there.

He slowed Brave down to a walk to get his bearings in the storm. Finally satisfied in which direction to go, he grabbed the mare's bridle and struck off to the right.

In a fierce crackle of lightning Tanner saw the big stone formation, the dark opening in it. He spurred Brave toward it, dragging Beauty behind him. Reaching safety, he slid to the ground and, pulling a shivering Roxy into his arms, sprinted toward the dark hole. Gaining the dry shelter, he dropped to his knees and laid Roxy down, her back against the inside wall. He took off his hat then and stretched out beside her, his back to the storm outside.

They lay quietly, catching their breath from the wild dash to safety. Then, when lightning struck a nearby tree, splitting it down the middle, Roxy gave a frightened cry and reached for Tanner. He automatically pulled her into his arms and settled her head on his shoulder.

The storm raged on, and somewhere in its fury Roxy's and Tanner's lips met with hot, clinging desire as strong as the storm that raged outside their shelter.

Mindlessly they tore at the buttons of their shirts, stripping them off their bodies. With a groan of hunger, Tanner lowered his head and fastened his mouth over the puckered nipple of her firm breast. Roxy cried out her pleasure as his lips drew and nibbled, and soon her hands were tugging at his belt buckle.

Switching his mouth to the other yearning breast, Tanner reached down between their bodies and undid the buckle. When he had done the same to his fly, he waited, holding his breath for Roxy's soft hand to stroke him as he remembered.

When her hand found its way beneath his underwear and her fingers curled around his throbbing arousal, he groaned deep in his throat and thrust himself against the hand that was stroking up and down his thick length.

It felt to Tanner as though Roxy had caressed him like this only yesterday, not eight years ago.

He hated to take the time to take off their boots so that their clothes could be removed. But he wanted this time to be just like it used to be, whether they were in bed or on a blanket beside the river.

Roxy was of the same mind, and sitting up she yanked off her boots and struggled out of her wet Levi's and underpants. She pulled the wet, cling ing camisole over her head and lay back down.

Tanner went through the same motions, ridding himself of his clothes moments before Roxy had finished. In the darkness, occasionally lit by lightning, Roxy lifted her arms to receive him as he gazed down at her. With a sigh from the depths of his body he came down between her legs. He hung over her a moment in anticipation. He lifted her legs then to cross over his back, and in a tempest of need, slid himself inside her.

They both groaned their ecstasy at being joined together. Then Tanner, as he had in the old days, slid his hands under Roxy's small rear and began to work over her.

They had yearned and dreamed of this coming together for so long, it only took a few thrusts of Tanner's hips and they were adding their cries to the clamor of the storm that still raged outside.

Roxy supported Tanner's shuddering body, her palms stroking his back. When his breathing calmed down, he rested on his elbows, taking part of his weight off her as he settled his mouth on hers.

As his lips moved slowly, ever deepening the kiss, Roxy felt him growing hard inside her. She lifted her arms to wind around his shoulders and bucked her hips at him.

Tanner caught his breath, and moving his

mouth to fasten on a swollen nipple, he took her hips in his hands and lifted them to take his thrusts again.

His stroking was slow and deep, setting a fire in Roxy that begged to be put out. She caught his easy rhythm and eagerly rose to meet each of his thrusts.

Neither had an awareness of how long they rocked together, but when finally they reached the crest and soared away, both were wet with sweat.

When Tanner had the strength to move, he withdrew himself and rolled over on his back. They rested then, even napped a moment. Then their hunger for each other returned, demanding to be fed again.

Roxy welcomed Tanner between her legs again and endless moments passed as they rose and fell together.

Completely exhausted this time, they lay side by side, willing their breathing to slow down. Roxy hadn't felt so happy and contented in a long time. She had just learned that the same old fire burned between them, and that, for the time being, would be enough. The important thing was that Jory would know who his father was. Wouldn't he be surprised that his cowboy was that man?

Tanner wasn't experiencing any contentment in his mind. Although his body hadn't known such relief in eight long years, he was furious at himself. He cursed himself for not being strong enough to reject what Roxy's soft arms had offered. He only knew that he must possess her.

His face hardened. What was done, was done, and it wouldn't happen again. He sat up and as he began to get dressed, he said gruffly, "The storm is over. You can go on home now."

Tanner's cold dismissal of her shocked and cut Roxy to the heart. She experienced the same pain she had known when learning that he had gone off without a word to her eight years ago. She felt the same abandonment she had experienced on learning that she was carrying his baby.

As she watched the dim outline of Tanner getting dressed, she remembered something that chilled her blood. Tanner had spilled his seed inside her three times tonight. Was she again to bear his bastard child? She knew that if she had a gun she would shoot him through his rotten heart. He had used her again, vented his lust on her.

She lay quietly, hating the man she had been unable to resist, hating herself, as Tanner slapped on his hat and wordlessly walked away.

"You will pay for this," she vowed furiously, bitter tears in her eyes. "You will not get away with treating me like a whore."

Chapter Fourteen

Tanner leaned against the cook house wall and yawned as he watched his men ride away with Rock.

It had started again.

For three nights after being with Roxy he had slept like a baby. There had been no dreams of Roxy, no nightmares of the wars he had fought. Then last night, near daybreak, he had awakened, his desire for Roxy so strong his body wore a sheen of sweat.

In his sleep he had been reliving their lovemaking during the storm. He had been loving her, ready to reach the crest of his passion when suddenly, with a cool laugh she pushed him away and said, "You can go on home now." She had spoken the same words he had said to her before leaving her that night. It had taken him hours to fall back to sleep.

He hadn't ridden away from Roxy five minutes before he was sorry for his harsh words, his cold departure. It was true she had treated him badly in the past, and he didn't want to get involved with her again; nevertheless she didn't deserve to be treated like a common whore.

Tanner pushed himself away from the wall when a young wrangler approached, leading Tanner's stallion. "Thanks, kid," he said and swung into the saddle.

He rode steadily across country, heading toward the ranch of his elderly neighbor. As he neared his neighbor's spread, Tanner pulled the stallion to a halt.

While Brave chomped on green tender grass, Tanner leaned forward, his arms crossed on the saddle. Below him in a long, wide valley, sparsely populated with aspen and pine, was the Henderson ranch house. Oliver Henderson had sent word to him yesterday that he wanted a word with him.

Tanner knew the old man well, liked and respected him. He had worked for the rancher before he started his own spread. Oliver had given him ten cows and a bull to start his herd with. He would never forget Mr. Henderson's generosity.

Gazing down at the big house, badly in need of paint, Tanner remembered that it was there he had begun dreaming of owning one like it some day. As he started Brave down the gentle slope, he wondered what the old fellow wanted to see him about. Rock had mentioned that Mrs. Henderson had passed away a couple years ago, and that Mr.

Henderson, having no children to give him comfort, was lost without his wife.

Up close, Tanner saw that the big house was in more disrepair than he had seen at a distance. Two of the tall window shutters were missing, the porch steps needed some boards replaced, and the flower beds that Mrs. Henderson had been so proud of had long ago given way to weeds and saw grass.

Reining the stallion in, Tanner climbed out of the saddle and, avoiding the loose boards, stepped up on the porch that ran the width of the house. His hand was in midair to knock on the door when it swung open.

"Good morning, Tanner," Oliver Henderson said, greeting him with a smile and a handshake. "It's good to see you back safe and sound. Come on in."

Tanner stepped into a large parlor that hadn't changed since the days he had come here to get his orders for each workday. It had a musty odor from being shut up and the drapes pulled all the time, Tanner imagined. In the semi-gloom he could see that the furniture was badly in need of polishing.

"Will you have something to drink, Tanner?" Henderson asked. "I can have the girl bring us some coffee. Or would you rather have a glass of whiskey?"

"Nothing, Mr. Henderson, thanks. I had breakfast not long ago and rode right over to see what you've got on your mind. If I can help you in any way, just let me know."

Henderson took a seat a few feet away from Tanner and sat silent for a moment, as though getting his thoughts together. Finally he spoke. "I've got myself in a bad bind, Tanner. I've fallen on really bad times. My dear wife was sick for over a year before she passed away. During that time I spent all my days and nights with her, leaving the running of the ranch to my foreman."

The old man paused and sighed. "He took advantage of my never being around to sell off most of my cattle, a few at a time. After Janie passed away I discovered what had been going on. I only had about a hundred head left. Of course, he'd taken off by then and it was too late to sic the sheriff on him. Anyway, the doctor visits, medicine and paying for a woman to help me care for Janie came to an overwhelming amount of money. Short of cash, I went to the Bradford Bank and mortgaged the ranch. It was only for a small amount, a figure I thought I could easily pay back after my next cattle drive.

"Last week," Oliver continued at the end of a heavy sigh, "I received a letter from that polecat Bradford, stating that if I don't pay off my loan tomorrow he's going to foreclose."

Tanner sat forward in his chair, anger and sympathy warring in his eyes. "Look, Mr. Henderson, let me loan you the money to pay off that bloodsucking Bradford," he said heatedly. "You can take all the time you need to pay me back."

"No, Tanner." Henderson shook his white head. "That's not what I want from you. I have lost all interest in the ranch since Janie's passing. Besides, I'm too old to start building a herd again. What I want from you, son, is this. Give me what I owe Bradford, plus a couple thousand and the spread is yours."

"Are you sure, Mr. Henderson?" Tanner looked earnestly at the rancher, disbelief in his eyes.

"Your spread is worth way more than that."

"I've given it a lot of thought, Tanner. I don't want Bradford getting it for a fraction of its worth. If you agree, it will give me great pleasure to walk into his bank tomorrow and see the look on his face when I plunk down the money I owe him. He is going to be one angry, disgruntled man."

"He will that." Tanner grinned, then asked with a worried frown, "Where will you go?"

"I haven't given that much thought. But if you don't mind, maybe I'll move into one of the better line-shacks."

"I don't know if that's a good idea. Even the best of those buildings isn't very comfortable, especially in the winter. You could easily get snowed in. I have a better thought. You can move into my cabin. Everything you'll need is there."

"I couldn't do that, Tanner."

"Of course you can. I'd appreciate it if you did, to keep an eye on things. You know what can happen to a place when it's left empty."

"If you're sure"—Henderson's lips parted with a relieved smile—"I'll take you up on your offer."

"I'm sure. Now, what time do you want to go to town?"

"I guess we should go early. We'll have to go to the bank, then see a lawyer about getting the deed changed over to you."

"All right, I'll be here tomorrow morning at eight o'clock." Tanner stood up, offering his hand. A minute later he was back in the saddle and riding toward his ranch, his mind spinning at this turn of events.

He wanted to shout aloud his elation. He wanted the hills and valleys to ring with the sound of it. Tomorrow the biggest and fanciest house outside Denver would be his. A house that Roxy had never entered He wouldn't see her ghost in any of the rooms, or imagine he heard her light laughter. And he needed to tell someone of his good fortune.

Bertha Sheldon came to mind. He needed to see her anyway. He was going to need more of her produce now that he would have more hands to feed.

It was near noon when he drew rein in front of the large, unpainted farmhouse. There didn't seem to be anyone around: all was quiet in the vicinity of the house and barn. He heard the scratching of a hoe and, dismounting, flipped the reins over a bush at the end of the porch and followed the sound to the back of the house.

He found Bertha, dressed in a pair of her husband's trousers with a slatted bonnet on her head, busily wielding a hoe between two rows of corn. At the far end of the garden patch he saw Aaron and Paul doing the same to a row of vegetables he couldn't make out.

When he cleared his throat, Bertha looked up, then pushed the bonnet off her head to hang by the ties on her neck. "Good morning, Tanner." She smiled at him as she took a white rag from her sleeve and mopped at her sweating face. "I was just telling myself it was time I stop hoeing long enough to have a glass of cold buttermilk from the spring house. Will you join me?"

"I sure will," Tanner heartily agreed, then asked with a grin, "Do you have cornbread to go with it?"

"Half a pan left over from breakfast. Let's go to the kitchen."

In the kitchen, Bertha filled a basin with water

from a tin pitcher. As she washed her hands she asked, "How are things at the ranch?"

"Fine. Everything is fine." Tanner couldn't hold back his excitement any longer and burst out, "Bertha, I'm buying the Henderson place tomorrow."

Bertha gaped at him for several seconds before exclaiming, "You're not!"

"I sure am!"

"Are you going to live in it?"

"You betcha. It needs a good cleaning inside. Do you think you'd have the time to tackle the job for me? Maybe your boys could help you. I'd pay them wages, of course."

"We can do it," Bertha agreed as she filled a glass with buttermilk from a stone pitcher. Placing it with a plate of cornbread in front of Tanner, and sitting down with her own glass of milk, she asked, "When do you want us to get started?"

"I think the middle of next week. I'm real excited about living in it, Bertha. I've dreamed of having a house like that ever since I worked for Mr. Henderson."

When Tanner put his empty glass down a few minutes later, he remarked, "I'll be needing more produce from your garden, plus milk, butter and eggs. I'll have another five men to feed. Do you think you can handle it?"

"Sure, nothing to it. I'll just plant more seeds," Bertha said, grinning.

Their joined laughter was interrupted when the screen door banged open and two grubby looking boys seemed to erupt into the room. They both stopped and stared when they saw Tanner sitting at the table. After a moment the curly-headed one exclaimed, "I knew I would see you again."

"You did, did you?" Tanner's eyes grew soft as he smiled at Jory. "I told you I'd see you later, didn't I?"

"Yes, but I was afraid you'd forget. Grownups do that a lot," Jory said as he dragged a chair as close as he could get it to Tanner. "I sure never expected to see you here, though."

"Mr. Graylord is our neighbor, Jory," Bertha explained. "He has a ranch a few miles from here."

"You do?" Jory's eyes shimmered with excitement. "Could I come see it someday?"

"I don't know why not." Tanner restrained himself from brushing the damp curls off the dirt-smudged brow. He couldn't understand his attraction to this little boy with the hungry eyes. "Maybe you and Sonny can come to the ranch one afternoon next week. I'll show you around the place."

When the boys began talking excitedly about the coming visit, Bertha shooed them out of the kitchen. "Go help Aaron and Paul in the garden."

When the door slammed behind them, she said, "Poor little Jory has sure taken a liking to you, Tanner."

"He told me he doesn't have a father. Maybe that's why he's taken a shine to me."

"Well, the child doesn't have a father who will claim him," Bertha said sadly, then on a brighter note added, "But I think Roxy is doing a fine job raising Jory on her own."

Tanner felt as if he'd been kicked in the stomach by a mule. Jory was Roxy's son! Why hadn't he realized that before? The boy looked like her. Was that why he had been drawn to the child so strongly?

Finally he managed to ask, "Who is this man

161

who doesn't want to claim such a fine little boy?"

"Roxy has never said who the father is, but the speculation is that the poor little fellow belongs to the gambler, Ace Brandon. Why they've never married, I don't know. I do know that Roxy Bartel is a fine young woman, and doesn't deserve the mean gossip that goes on about her."

Tanner told himself that Roxy deserved everything that was said about her. Hadn't she taken eight years of his life away from him?

Later, however, riding home, Tanner went back in his memory to the young girl he had loved. He would have staked his life that she was sweet and loving, her character beyond reproach. How wrong he had been. He had one consolation, though. The man she had chosen over him was paying her back in spades.

What about the boy, Jory, though? It wasn't fair that he should suffer for his mother's mistake. What was to become of him, growing up with the stigma of being a bastard? He was such a fine little fellow. Would name-calling finally break his spirit, make him a bitter, troubled teenager who would later in life drift into the company of men who ran on the wrong side of the law?

An angry glint came into his eyes. The next time he saw Roxy, she would get a piece of his mind that she wouldn't want to hear. But first, he was going to have words with the gambler, demand why he would let his son be known as a bastard.

Chapter Fifteen

Roxy folded the last piece of clothing, a small boy's shirt, and placed it on top of the other clothing in the carpetbag. Today was the last day of school. The bell on top of the small building at the edge of town wouldn't ring again until next September, and her son couldn't wait for vacation to begin.

A sad little smile lifted the corners of her lips. Jory would come bounding up the stairs any minute, eager to spend the weekdays of summer at the Sheldon farm. He was growing up so fast, drawing away from her more and more. Sometimes she wished that he was a girl. Girls were seldom anxious to leave their mothers.

She was thankful for one thing. Since Jory had been spending so much time at the farm, he seemed to have forgotten his cowboy friend. Once he had been full of talk about his hero, but he never mentioned him anymore.

As Roxy sat by the window, watching for her son to come running down the street, she wondered idly if her cousin Ace was making any headway with Michelle. The singer had allowed him to walk her home a couple of times, but he never got beyond her front door. Being around him these days was like being penned up with a wounded bear. She was beginning to feel a little sorry for him. She had never before seen him go after a woman with such determination, or be so unsuccessful. Had he really fallen so hard for Michelle, or was he just being stubborn, refusing to accept that there was a woman he couldn't get?

Roxy left off thinking of Ace and his woman problem when she saw a familiar figure riding down the street. She would know that erect carriage, those broad shoulders anywhere. She had clung to them in passion only a short time ago. Much to her regret.

Where's he going? she asked herself. To the bank to count his money, or to visit the proud Julia?

Tanner mostly socialized with a different set of people these days, all the bigwigs in Denver. He had joined several clubs, as well as the Cattlemen's Association. It was claimed that he was the wealthiest man in all of northern Colorado, and she guessed it was only natural that he would fraternize with other monied people. Also, he had to live up to that big fancy house he had purchased. Rumor had it that he was going to marry Julia Bradford. He would naturally want a woman like her to run his fancy home.

"But, damn you, Tanner Graylord," Roxy whispered bitterly, "she'll never give you sons like the one you already have."

She fell to thinking of those Graylord sons yet to be born, and grew more bitter. As they grew up in an atmosphere of idleness and wealth, their half-brother would be working hard for anything he achieved. At least she could afford to send Jory to college, to get a good education. She didn't want him working in the Lady Chance. Maybe he could become a lawyer or a doctor.

Roxy suddenly sat forward, frowning anxiously. Tanner was tying his horse to the hitching rack in front of the general store, and Jory was running down the street, calling his name. She held her breath as they smiled and talked to each other. She wished that she could read lips. Jory looked excited about something Tanner was saying, grinning and nodding his head. Tanner ruffled his hair, looked up at her window, then walked on into the store, and Jory came running across the street.

She moved away from the window. She didn't want the boy to think she had been spying on him. When he burst into the room, breathless, she waited for him to start talking about his cowboy friend.

Although his eyes were sparkling, Jory didn't say a word about meeting Tanner. All he talked about was the fun he was going to have on the farm this summer.

"What will you do with your days on the farm?" Roxy asked as she laid out clean, everyday clothes for him to change into.

"Oh, Sonny and I will"—he paused slightly— "do kid stuff. You know, play hide and seek, roll our hoops. And there will be chores for us to do.

Like Mr. Sheldon says, 'There's always something to do on a farm.' "

When Roxy went into the parlor to give Jory privacy while he changed his clothes, there was guilt in his eyes as he watched her leave. He and Sonny wouldn't be playing the games he had told her they would, but he didn't dare tell her that they would be climbing trees, going fishing, swimming in the creek back of the barn. His mother would never let him go to the Sheldon farm again if she knew he had been doing those things right along. And heaven forbid she ever learn that his friend Tanner was going to show him around his ranch, on horseback, at that. He could hardly wait to sit in a saddle instead of on a blanket, and on a horse that was not an old farm animal.

When Roxy called that Aaron was waiting for him, they walked downstairs and joined Ace, who stood on the porch to see Jory off. "Have a good time, kid," he said, ruffling the boy's black curls.

Her eyes wet with suppressed tears, Roxy only dared to give her son a brief hug; then she stepped away from him. Hardly able to contain his excitement, Jory hopped off the porch and scrambled up behind Aaron.

Ace looked at Roxy's trembling lips when the old horse went jogging down the street, two pairs of bare, skinny legs flapping in time with its gait, and said, "He'll be fine, honey."

"But he's going to be gone for a week," Roxy wailed softly. "I'll miss him so."

Ace put an arm around her waist and she laid her head on his shoulder. She was dabbing at her wet eyes when she saw Tanner step out of the store. He stood a moment, his gaze traveling across the street to home in on them.

The cold contempt in his eyes made Roxy straighten away from Ace as though she had been caught in a shameful act. "Don't let that bastard know he can upset you," Ace growled and pulled her back to lean snugly against him.

Coming to the same conclusion, Roxy smiled up at Ace and pretended not to see Tanner. But from the corner of her eye she saw him swing into the saddle, gather up the reins and give her a condemning look before riding off down the street. She stared after his retreating back, wondering out loud at his look of condemnation. "It's as if he's blaming me for something bad I have done."

"It's clear to me," Ace said thoughtfully as they walked back into the saloon. "He was jealous as hell, seeing my arm around you. The damn fool will never admit it, but he's still in love with you. He probably won't even admit it to himself."

"You're crazy." Roxy gave a short laugh. "How can he *still* be in love with me when he never loved me in the first place?"

"Don't be too sure about that. There's something about Graylord's behavior I haven't been able to figure out yet."

"What's that?"

"Why is he squiring Julia Bradford around, for instance? According to John Allen, Tanner wouldn't have looked at her in the old days. And there's the company he keeps lately. John claims that most of his new associates aren't the type of people Tanner would be comfortable with.

"Now, think about it. Why would he do all these things that are so wholly against his nature? Why suddenly start seeing a woman he never had any use for before? Because he wants to make you jealous. Why has he involved himself with men of importance? To impress you. It's his way of saying, 'Hey, look at me. See what you've missed.' "

"You're forgetting one thing, Ace. He's the one who broke off our relationship."

"I haven't forgotten, but I haven't figured out why he did it."

"I haven't figured it out either, but I'm getting sick and tired of his black, accusing looks," Roxy said, and left Ace chewing thoughtfully on his mustache.

Tanner was still seething as he rode across the range. He asked himself how Roxy and that gambler could stand in plain view of anyone passing by, their arms around each other's waists, and let their fine little son be called a bastard. He'd give half his ranch to have such a son.

It's time I started thinking about having a family, Tanner thought. I need to have sons to inherit my ranch and holdings, a wife to live out my old age with.

But not Julia Bradford. He shook his head. He couldn't imagine babies at that one's flat chest. Nor could he imagine sitting in front of a fire in the winter, remembering and talking about their youth. Julia was too wrapped up in herself to give anyone else a thought.

Julia was a very strange woman, he mused as the hot sun bore down on his head and thighs. She chased him shamefully, but grew cold and stiff if she thought he was about to embrace or kiss her. Something he had no real urge to do.

It was that coldness of hers that had enabled him to continue calling on her occasionally. He knew his kisses weren't welcome, so he was excused from making the effort. He had no desire to feel those thin lips beneath his own. There would be no fire in them. Not like the heat that scorched him when he kissed Roxy.

He fell to wondering why Enos Bradford made it plain that he would welcome him into his home as a son-in-law. Could it be his new wealth, as Rock claimed? But surely the banker had enough money of his own.

Maybe he just wants to get rid of his brittle, waspish daughter, Tanner thought, grinning wryly. He wouldn't, however, want her to marry just any man. His future son-in-law must be wealthy.

Half an hour later as the stallion approached the lovely home where he now resided, Tanner came to the decision that it was time he break off with Julia Bradford. He didn't even like her; he could never consider making her his wife.

As he dismounted at the long stable building and handed the reins over to fifteen-year-old Paul Sheldon, who now worked full time for him, Tanner refused to admit to himself that he had only given Julia attention to make Roxy jealous. If he admitted to that, he'd have to acknowledge that his ploy hadn't worked.

He stood a moment, pride of ownership in his eyes as he gazed at the newly painted house he had been living in for the past two weeks. He remembered with pleasure the stunned look on the banker's face when Mr. Henderson handed Bradford a check for the amount owed him.

"Are you sure you want to do this?" Bradford had asked, fingering the check. "You musn't make yourself short of money."

"I haven't done that," Oliver said. "I've sold my

ranch to Tanner here, so I'm in good shape money-wise."

The look Bradford shot Tanner wasn't friendly. There was barely concealed anger in his pale blue eyes. Tanner knew in that instant that his buying the Henderson spread had spoiled some scheme of the banker's. Enos had wanted the place for himself.

He watched Bradford fight to control his features and smiled inwardly when the man said with forced heartiness, "Congratulations, Tanner. You have bought yourself a fine ranch. How about coming to dinner tonight to celebrate? Julia will be excited to hear your news."

"Thanks, but I've got to turn you down. Mr. Henderson and I have made plans for this evening," Tanner lied.

"Maybe we can get together later in the week then." Bradford's smile didn't reach his eyes.

"I'll let you know." Tanner stood up and looking at Oliver asked, "You ready to go?"

Bradford gave them both a limp handshake and watched with narrowed eyes as they left his office.

After a hearty laugh at the banker's expense, Tanner and Oliver stopped in at the Red Dog saloon for a drink, to celebrate the transaction.

"When should we switch homes?" Oliver asked after the bartender poured them each a glass of whiskey and moved on down the bar.

"How about tomorrow?" Tanner asked.

"Sounds good. I just have a few personal things to pack up: pictures and letters and some mementoes of my life with Janie."

"Take anything that will make you happy, friend." Tanner laid a friendly hand on the old man's shoulder. "I intend to leave the cabin as it

170

was when I lived in it. It's not fancy, but I think it's got everything you'll need."

"I'm sure it will, Tanner."

They had raised their glasses, toasted each other and left shortly after that.

Tanner went back to studying his new home. The pale leaf-green of the repaired shutters, and the window trim of the same color, contrasted beautifully with the white clapboard walls. The yard area was beginning to need its first mowing, but the laid-out flower beds and shrub patches still waited to be filled in.

He had been putting off that task simply because he knew nothing about flowers and such, and had no idea where to begin. He had thought about asking Bertha Sheldon for advice, but decided against it when he realized she had no color in her yard, and very little grass.

As he stepped up on the porch that wrapped around three sides of the house, he remembered that Belle Lang always had flowers blooming in her back yard. He would make another trip to town and get her advice on his yard.

It was time he visited Belle's Pleasure House anyway, he thought wryly, opening the wide door and stepping into a large foyer. He was damned if he'd seek comfort in Roxy's arms again.

Tanner bent over and removed his spurs before walking on the dark, slate-tiled floor. The spurs would scratch the tile and cut into the beautiful Indian rugs that were scattered down the hall's middle. Only in the kitchen he kept his spurs on. The floor there was fitted with narrow bricks, so old and scratched already that a few more scratches wouldn't make any difference. But the old brick lent a warm and inviting aura to the big room with its woodwork of knotty pine, big black range, and sink with a bright red pump installed on its apron.

He walked down a long hall, passing four doors that opened into bedrooms. At the end of the hall he entered a large parlor.

This room was neither feminine nor masculine, but a mixture of both. The walls were paneled in knotty pine with pictures of flowers and landscapes adorning them. There was a deer's head over the mantel and beneath it were a clock and several delicate little figurines. Against one wall was a liquor cabinet; next to it was a dainty little cabinet of shelves which still held skeins of yarn from Mrs. Henderson's day.

A dark brown leather couch had been placed between a matching chair and a small rocking chair covered in a floral material. There was a sturdy masculine table next to the big chair and a dainty little one next to the rocker. Plain matching lamps sat on the tables.

The bright rays of the noonday sun striking though the curtains of the tall double windows seemed to welcome Tanner. He walked over to the liquor cabinet, pulled out a bottle and filled a glass with smooth bourbon. Replacing the bottle, he picked up the glass and sat down in the big chair. As he sipped at the golden liquid, he noticed that the furniture was in need of a good dusting. He must take the time to find a housekeeper. Besides, he was in need of some clean clothes and he was growing short of bed linens and towels. He couldn't continue depending on Bertha to do his washing. Although he paid her, she had enough work to do as it was.

Maybe Christy Allen could direct him to some

woman he could hire. When a slender figure with coal black hair and sparkling green eyes swam before him, he swore under his breath and hurried from the house.

Chapter Sixteen

Tanner awakened to the soft patter of rain on the window. "Will this infernal rain never stop," he grunted.

The coming of summer had brought drought again, and the earth was parched, the grass turning brown. So when the sky opened up and sent water flowing over the land, it had been welcomed with wide smiles and words of thanksgiving.

But it had been raining for four straight days now, and everyone was as edgy as they had been when all you could see were dust devils on the range. The cowhands, soaked from the time they left the bunkhouse until they returned at the end of the day, were growing short-tempered and quarrelsome.

Tanner threw back the sheet, and walked naked into the main room to look out the window to the river. It had flooded its banks yesterday and if it didn't crest pretty soon it would reach the pen where he kept his prize breeding steers. He didn't want them running loose, mounting any available cow. They were meant to breed with the new stock he intended to buy. He saw with relief that the river had crested; the rain had let up to a drizzle and the sky was lightening up. He saw, too, that the grass had been revitalized, standing straight and tall, its green color beginning to return. Now if only the sun could break through, the range would return to normal.

Tanner went back to his bedroom. As he pulled his last set of clean clothes from the chest of drawers, he reminded himself that he couldn't put off much longer hiring a housekeeper. After he had breakfast he would ride over to the Sheldon farm and ask Bertha if she knew of any farm woman who would be interested in the job. A recommendation from her would probably be better than anyone Belle might suggest.

Pee Wee was as grouchy as everyone else when Tanner stepped into the new cook house where the cook now worked. "It feels like I've got rheumatiz in all my joints," he complained as he set a plate of bacon and eggs and flapjacks in front of Tanner.

Tanner hurried through his meal to get away from his grouchy cook. When he stepped outside, his eyes crinkled at the corners in amusement. Jory and Sonny were waiting for him in the stable yard, the old work horse tied to a tree. He had forgotten that he had promised to take them horseback riding today, and the impatient look on their faces told him that they had been waiting for quite a while.

175

They must have got here at the crack of dawn, he thought as the two boys spied him and came splashing their way through the mud puddles toward him. How ironic, he thought, that Roxy's son had become so attached to him. She wouldn't like it at all if she knew how much time the boy spent with him: that he had taken Jory fishing, taught him how to swim, even taken him and Sonny camping overnight one time. A tight smile curved his lips. She would have a hissie if she ever learned that he had been teaching her son how to ride one of his gentle mares.

"We were beginning to think that you weren't going to leave the house today." Jory's eyes sparkled as he looked up at Tanner. "But I knew you would. Like you told me, a man should never break his word."

"You thought that, did you?" Deep affection softened Tanner's hard features. "I didn't know you would remember that."

"Oh, yes. I remember everything you say."

Well, Tanner thought ruefully, *I'd better watch what I say around this youngster from now on.*

With his hand on Jory's shoulder, he said, "Let's get our horses saddled and mount up. We'll ride along the river, see how badly it has flooded."

A stable hand lifted the heavy saddles onto the backs of two gentle mares; then the boys finished saddling the animals.

With Tanner in front, they led the three horses outside and were about to mount up when a feminine voice called out, "Good morning, Tanner."

"What does she want?" Jory grumbled.

"I don't know, son." Tanner frowned, watching Julia Bradford approaching. "I'm sure we'll find out soon enough." Julia reined in beside them, and paying no attention to the two boys, she gave Tanner a bright smile and said, "When I woke up this morning and saw that the rain had let up some, I decided that it was a good day for you and me to go riding. You must have read my mind, for here you are, all saddled up."

Tanner nodded and said curtly, "The boys and I are going to take a ride, check out the river."

"Oh well, you can do that anytime." She gave Jory and Sonny a false smile. "I'm sure they won't mind if I take you away from them."

Jory's answer to her cool assumption was to scramble onto his mare and to sit there, glaring down at her.

Tanner was struck by the way the boy's defiant face resembled his mother's when she used to get angry with him.

When Sonny hung back, intimidated by the haughty lady, Tanner said in a firm voice as he climbed into the saddle, "We'll have to do it another day. I've already promised Jory and his friend that I would take them riding today."

Julia looked at him in angry disbelief. "Surely," she exploded, "you're not turning down my company for that of Roxy Bartel's bastard son."

Tanner couldn't remember ever being so incensed as he was now. How dare this arrogant bitch say such a mean thing in front of the boy!

"Mount up, Sonny," he ordered, then giving Miss Bradford a chilling look, snapped, "As you see, I prefer the boys' company." He touched spurs to Brave, and the two boys, after shooting the furious Julia triumphant looks, rode after him.

As Tanner and the boys rode along at a walk, he tried to control the anger raging inside him. How many times, he asked himself, had the boy heard himself referred to as Roxy's bastard son?

They had ridden but a short time when Jory rode up beside Tanner. "Tanner," he said, looking earnestly at him, "what is a bastard son?"

Tanner gazed mutely at the confusion in the boy's dark eyes. He had always been truthful with Jory, but how could he be that way with him this time? He couldn't tell him that his father hadn't cared enough to marry his mother.

He pushed back the emotions that threatened to overcome him and managed to say casually, "It doesn't mean anything. It's just a word."

"Oh, I see." Jory grinned up at him. "I've been called that a lot."

Tears sprang to Tanner's eyes at the innocent remark. Before this day was over, he was going to confront the gambler and demand some answers.

Roxy stood at the window watching the raindrops roll off the gutter and hit the top of the porch roof with a splash. A glance across the street showed the unpainted boards of the buildings now dark from the rain that had fallen for four days.

It crossed her mind to wonder if the flowers she had set out in Tanner's flower beds had been flattened to the ground, or if they were sturdy enough to stand up to the force of the weather.

Her lips curved in a crooked smile. Tanner had no idea that it was she who had come to his place with boxes of tender plants, extras from Belle's yard. She hadn't made the trip out to the big fancy house until she was sure he was out on the range somewhere.

She hadn't wanted to do it in the first place, but Belle had talked her into it. She had pointed out what a big joke it would be on Tanner when he discovered that he'd accepted help from the woman he had so much contempt for.

Belle hadn't let on to Tanner that she knew nothing about flowers except that they smelled good and were pretty to look at. She hadn't told him that it was Roxy who planted her flower garden every spring, had done so since she was around ten years old.

When Tanner approached her about help with his yard, the fun-loving woman had immediately seen the humorous side of the situation: the joke that could be played on the rancher. She had promised him solemnly that by midsummer his flower beds would look exactly like hers.

Roxy remembered how she had hurried through the yard work. She hadn't wanted Tanner to catch her there. Also, it was painful to work at beautifying Tanner's home. She and Tanner had once dreamed of how nice it would be to own a place like it some day.

Roxy pushed such painful thoughts out of her mind and peered down the street, looking for the Sheldon plow horse to come jogging along. It would be bringing Jory home to spend the weekend with her. She couldn't wait to see his little sun-tanned face again, to hear his excited account of the past week. Although she was happy that he was enjoying himself so, she still felt a little jab of hurt that he could find so much pleasure away from her.

A softness came into her eyes. At bedtime, though, when she sat on the edge of the bed to kiss him good night, and his thin boy's arms hugged her around the neck and he whispered, "I missed you a lot, Ma," her hurt was replaced with overwhelming happiness.

Because of the rain, most of the men in the area were in town. All up and down the boardwalk the clomping sound of boot heels and the jangle of spurs could be heard. As she looked down on the bobbing heads, some bare, some wearing Stetsons, others the shapeless hats of farmers, her heart leapt.

She recognized one male figure that was a head taller than most of the others. He came striding across the street, splashing heedlessly through puddles of water.

What has put that black look on his face? she wondered, then gripped the windowsill with suddenly nervous fingers. It looked as if Tanner was going to enter the Lady Chance. But why would he be coming here?

Ace had picked up the cards, squared the deck, riffled them, then started to deal to the three men at the table when the bat-wing doors were flung open. A tall man with a pair of Colts dangling from the ammunition belt around his waist strode toward him.

There was an unspoken promise of violence in Tanner Graylord's eyes. Ace laid the cards down and waited.

"I want a few words with you . . . privately," Tanner said, his voice harsh as he stopped behind one of the seated players.

Ace stared back at him a moment, then motioned the men to leave the table. When they had gone to the bar at the other end of the room, Tanner pulled up a chair and sat down.

"So, what are the words you want to say to me?" Ace asked coolly.

"I want some answers to a question that has been bothering me."

"I'll answer if I can."

"You can answer all right."

"Okay, shoot."

"Why haven't you married Jory's mother and given him your name?"

Ace was silent for a moment; then he looked at Tanner and asked, "Have you talked to Roxy about this?"

"No, I haven't. I figured I'd go to the man who let his son be called a bastard."

"So you think I'm the kid's father?" Ace fingered the deck of cards.

"I do. Me and the rest of Denver."

"I see. They could be wrong, you know."

"Not hardly. They see you with the boy all the time, they know you live with his mother."

Ace jerked up his hand. "Whoa there, Graylord. Roxy and I live under the same roof, but we don't *live* together."

"Hah!" Tanner snorted. "Is there a difference?"

"You're damn well right there is. Roxy and I have different quarters."

Tanner made a disbelieving noise. "Next you'll be telling me that you have no feelings for Roxy."

"I feel very deeply for Roxy. She's a fine young woman."

"Well then—"

"I don't care for her in a way that would make me want to marry her."

"But you care enough for her to sleep with her, to ruin her reputation." Tanner bit the words out savagely.

"Look, Graylord, you'd better simmer down a bit. It's none of your affair what goes on in Roxy's life. You lost that right when you went off to war without a word to her. As for the boy, don't worry about him. Roxy and I will take care of him."

"But you won't give him your name?" Tanner's fingers clenched into fists as he glared at Ace.

"No, I won't be doing that."

"I ought to kick your ass out of the country." Tanner stood up and leaned across the table, his eyes burning.

"Maybe you ought to try." Ace glared back at him.

For a few seconds the men eyed each other like two cougars ready to spring. Then Tanner straightened up and walked away, kicking chairs out of his path.

Ace stared after him, muttering, "You poor dumb bastard."

Chapter Seventeen

Roxy let the breath she had been holding feather through her lips as she stood in the shadows at the head of the stairs.

At least they hadn't come to blows, she thought, but she knew that Ace and Tanner had come close to it. What had set Tanner off? she wondered. Why was he suddenly so concerned about Jory's welfare? To her knowledge he had only seen the boy twice.

She walked downstairs and found Ace still sitting at the table, muttering to himself. "I heard the two of you," she said quietly, taking a seat across from him. "I'm proud of the way you stood up to him, that you didn't give my secret away."

"You don't know how I wanted to punch him in his arrogant face, though."

"I'm glad you didn't. He's been fighting a war

and Indians for the last eight years and he's probably as tough as a piece of rawhide. And all this time you have been sitting at a table dealing cards. He could have beaten you badly."

"I agree, but it would be worth it just to smash his handsome face."

"Well, one thing is for sure," Roxy said with a deep sigh, "if he ever learns that Jory is his son, he'll go to any lengths to take him away from me."

"I know it looks that way, honey, but let's don't panic unless it comes to that. I don't know how he'd ever find out. I won't tell, and certainly Belle won't."

"I hope you're right." A worried frown continued to mar Roxy's brow as she left the table and started to go back upstairs.

She paused when she heard someone call from the bar, "Hey, Roxy girl." She turned around and smiled when she saw white-haired Elisha Roundtree, a seventy-year-old miner whom she had known all her life. She crossed the floor and searched his pale blue eyes as she shook his bony, gnarled hand.

"I haven't seen you around for a while. Where have you been?"

"Down in Cripple Creek the past six months. Besides the silver strike, some gold has been discovered as well. I've got me a real good claim there, a good show of color."

"What are you doing here then? Shouldn't you be panning for those yellow nuggets?" Roxy teased.

"You're right there, Roxy girl, but I had to leave my spot by the river for a spell. One day when I was up river pannin', out of sight of my tent, some lowlife sneaked into it. He not only took all my grub, he found my pouch of gold. It took me four months of hard work gettin' it out of the coldest water you ever stepped foot in."

"That's awful, Elisha. Did you report it to the authorities?"

"What authorities? Ain't no law in Cripple Creek. A man has to take care of himself."

With concern in her eyes, Roxy asked, "What are you going to do now?"

"Well"—Elisha began to nervously finger his short, white beard—"I'll go right back to my claim if you will stake me again. I know you'll probably think it's like pouring money down a deep hole, but there's gold to be found there, and I promise I'll be careful this time," he finished earnestly.

"Of course I'll stake you, old friend." Roxy gave his thin arm a gentle squeeze. "When you're ready, go to the mercantile and get what you need. Tell the clerk to put everything on my bill."

"You won't be sorry, Roxy." Elisha reached into his vest pocket and pulled out a folded piece of paper. "This is my registered claim. It shows the location of the land. And see at the top of the page, it's in both our names."

Touched, Roxy said softly, "You didn't have to do that, Elisha. I trust you completely."

"I know you do, girl, but I wanted to do it. I named our holdin's Lady Chance after the saloon. If you ever get the time, I wish you'd come visit it."

"Maybe I will. Maybe I'll do a little panning and find a big nugget." Roxy's eyes sparkled in fun.

"Wouldn't that be somethin'." Elisha grinned, then finishing his glass of whiskey, he stepped away from the bar. "I'm gonna go get my supplies now and head back to Cripple Creek."

"You be careful now, and keep your gold on your person from now on."

"That's my intention," the old man said, giving her shoulder a squeeze as he walked away.

Roxy watched him go through the door, a fond smile on her face. She hoped for his sake that he would find enough gold to take care of himself when he grew too old to wade the cold streams searching for it.

She left the bar and went to her office to do some book work.

Two weeks had passed since Tanner's altercation with Ace Brandon. He still fumed every time he thought about it. And the rain that had decided to visit them again didn't help lighten his dark mood.

He'd gotten no satisfaction from Brandon that day. The gambler had sat there and bluntly told him that Jory was none of his business, that he and Roxy were taking good care of the boy.

Dammit, he thought, swiping at the rain hitting him in the face, as far as he was concerned, they were doing a poor job of it. But as the gambler had said, the boy wasn't any concern of his. It was just that the youngster was such a fine little fellow who didn't deserve the name a lot of people called him. He was innocent of his mother's reckless behavior.

Tanner was about to pass by the muddy cutoff to the Sheldon farm when he remembered why he was out in the rain. He still hadn't gotten around to asking Bertha Sheldon to recommend some woman to keep house for him.

The big farmhouse was a dismal sight, its unpainted clapboards dark and dreary-looking from

186

the rain. There was no one out in the yard, which was unusual. On a fine day youngsters would be running around, whooping and yelling at some game. Especially now that Jory was spending most of his summer vacation with the Sheldons.

When Bertha opened the door to his knock, she looked so rattled from having all the children underfoot, Tanner decided that now wasn't a good time to ask her about hiring a housekeeper.

When Jory spotted him and came running, the corners of Tanner's eyes crinkled with affection. The boy was the bright spot in his life these days. He knew he might be letting himself in for possible heartache. Roxy might very well put an end to the boy's visits to the farm, could even forbid her old lover to have any association with him.

He decided that he would handle that problem when, and if, it arose, and asked, "Anybody here want to go horseback riding? The rain has almost stopped."

"We do. We do," Jory and Sonny chorused together.

Tanner looked at Bertha for permission and she exclaimed, "Thank you, Tanner. Take them for a long ride. Their roughhousing is driving me crazy."

The boys pulled on slickers that were two sizes too big for them and waited impatiently for Tanner to say goodbye to Bertha.

The three took off for the Graylord ranch, Jory and Sonny riding bareback on the old plow horse. When they reached the ranch, Tanner saddled the two gentle mares the boys always rode. When he boosted Jory into the saddle, he asked, his tone serious, "Do you still remember everything I told you about handling a horse?"

"Yes I do, Tanner," Jory answered, equally serious, although his eyes sparkled with excitement.

When Tanner had helped Sonny to mount his mare, he swung into his own saddle and led out.

Tanner kept the horses at a walk at first. When they hit the river road, where the water lapped within a foot of the trail, he loosened the reins and set the pace at a safe, comfortable canter. He glanced at Jory and saw that the youngster was having no trouble with the increased pace. By the end of summer the boy was going to be a fine rider.

He and Jory had just exchanged wide grins when a snake came out of the river and slithered across the stallion's path. The big horse let loose a terrified snort, rose up on his hind legs and rammed into Jory's mare. She in turn reared up, pawing the air with her front hooves. Jory went sailing over her head.

With a savage curse Tanner fought the stallion's head down and leaped from the saddle.

Jory lay from his waist down in the water, his head and shoulders on land. His head, however, had hit a large rock. He lay so still, Tanner's breath caught in his throat. He flung himself down beside Jory and felt for a pulse in the boy's wrist.

He breathed again when he felt it beating. Gathering the small, limp body in his arms, he looked at Sonny's anxious face and ordered, "Go get Doc Evans, son, and hurry."

Tanner managed somehow to struggle into the saddle, then holding Jory against his chest, he rode as fast as he dared. He didn't know how hard Jory's head had hit the rock, but he felt he shouldn't be jarred more than necessary.

When Tanner reached the ranch house and

carefully slid out of the saddle, he was so upset it didn't enter his mind that his spurs would scratch the tiles in his large hall. Jory's condition was all that was on his mind.

As he laid Jory on the bed and straightened out his limbs, Pee Wee stepped into the room. "What's wrong with the boy?" he asked, peering over Tanner's shoulder.

"The mare spooked and threw him. Bring me some warm water, will you?"

By the time Tanner found a clean towel and washcloth Pee Wee entered the bedroom with a basin of warm water he had dipped from the stove reservoir.

Jory hadn't changed his position since Tanner had put him down. The freckles on his nose stood out starkly against the paleness of his face. With gentle fingers, Tanner began to wash the spattered mud off the small features. He found a good-sized lump on the back of Jory's head when he mopped at the pieces of mud in the black curls.

"Oh, Lord," he whispered, "he's got a concussion." Would the boy die? he asked himself, feeling as if a giant hand were squeezing his heart.

Close to an hour later, when Sonny showed Dr. Evans into the bedroom, Jory still hadn't moved. "What have we got here, Graylord?" The short, stocky man motioned him to move away from the bed.

"His horse threw him and he hit his head on a rock. He's got a lump on the back of his head."

"Let me take a look at him." The doctor sat down on the spot that Tanner had vacated.

While he lifted Jory's lids, peered into his eyes, examined his inner ears, then probed gently at the

189

lump, Tanner and Sonny stood at the foot of the bed barely breathing.

Finally the doctor finished his examination and stood up. "The boy has a slight concussion, Graylord. He's going to be coming around soon, and he's going to have one hell of a headache." He rummaged in his black doctor's bag and pulled out a small brown bottle. As he placed it on the bedside table, he said, "Keep him quiet, and give him a few drops of this laudanum in a glass of water every two hours for the pain. Keep him in bed for at least a week."

"Thanks, Doc," Tanner said, relief in his voice. "What do I owe you?"

"I'll send you a bill," Evans said on his way to the door.

Tanner and Sonny smiled at each other. Jory was going to be all right.

"Would you go get one of Jory's nightshirts, Sonny?"

"Sure, Tanner. I'll go fetch one right now."

Sonny had barely left when Jory stirred, groaned and cried out, "Ma, where are you? My head hurts."

"It's all right, son." Tanner took hold of the grubby-looking hands that were trying to rub his head and held them. "Do you remember the mare throwing you?"

"Yes," Jory answered impatiently. "I want my ma."

Tanner saw that the boy was becoming upset, and remembered that the doctor had said he shouldn't. He hurried to calm him. "Your mother isn't here, Jory, but I'll go get her right now. Will you lie quietly while I'm gone? I'll have Pee Wee come give you something for your headache."

190

"Thank you, Tanner." Jory smiled weakly. "I'll lie real still."

"That's a good boy," Tanner said, smiling back, then rushed out of the house.

On his way to the barn he stopped long enough at the cook house to ask Pee Wee to give him the laudanum. "I'm going after his mother," he explained.

Within five minutes he was on Brave's back and racing toward the Lady Chance. He would rather face a firing squad than tell Roxy that her son had had an accident.

Roxy happened to glance out her bedroom window and saw Tanner hurrying across the street. When he stepped up on the saloon's porch, she muttered, "What does he want this time?"

Should she go downstairs to give Ace support? she wondered. She walked to the door and jerked it open, then stood there. Tanner was standing only feet away, a harried look on his face. A tingling prickled her skin. "What do you want?" Her hand went to her throat.

"Jory has been hurt."

All the color drained from Roxy's face at the brutal words flung at her. "Hurt? How?" she managed to cry out.

"He fell off a horse and bumped his head. Nothing serious."

"I can't believe the Sheldons would let him get on a horse. They know I wouldn't like that."

"The Sheldons had nothing to do with it. I put him on a horse."

"You did!" Roxy's fingers clenched into fists. "Who are you to be putting my son on a horse, endangering his life?"

191

"I agree that I didn't have that right and I'm sorry as hell it happened. But right now, get dressed for riding. I'll go get your mare saddled."

Tanner wheeled and started down the stairs. Still in shock, Roxy was about to close the door behind him, but she stopped. Ace was coming up the stairs, concern on his face. Both men paused as they came abreast of each other, and she held her breath. Would they have words? Would they fight?

Her breath came out in a relieved whoosh when they only exchanged hard looks before each continued on.

As Roxy changed into a shirt and riding skirt, she told Ace what little she knew of Jory's condition. "I may be gone all night. You'll have to keep an eye on the place."

Chapter Eighteen

As the mare galloped along behind the stallion, Roxy hunched against the drizzle that had started up again. Up ahead Tanner's slicker shone wet and she wished that she had taken the time to pull one on before leaving the saloon.

But she had been so upset, she hadn't thought to do it. She had only been able to think that her son was hurt, and that he needed her.

Tanner hadn't spoken a word to her since they'd started out and she still didn't know the extent of Jory's injuries. Tanner had only said that a horse had thrown him and that his head had hit a rock when he landed. A hit on the head could be very dangerous. Jory could have a concussion, even a skull fracture. Dear Lord, she thought, almost hysterically, her son could die.

When at last the big house and outbuildings

came into sight, Roxy was soaked to the skin and her teeth were chattering. When they pulled rein in front of the barn, a teenager and Rock Brady stepped outside. Without a word or glance at her, Tanner slid out of the saddle and hurried toward the house.

Rock stared after him, displeasure on his craggy face. He walked over to the mare, and reaching up to help Roxy dismount, he said in dismay, "You're soaked to the skin, Roxy." As she leaned forward and practically fell into his arms, he added, "We'll stop at the cook house and borrow something of Pee Wee's for you to change into. You can't be around the boy dripping water like this."

"How is Jory, Rock? Tanner didn't tell me anything except that a horse threw him."

The gray-haired, middle-aged man frowned. Tanner was wrong, making Roxy ride all this way without telling her everything the doctor had said. He was carrying his bitterness too far.

"He's fine, Roxy," he said gently as he took her arm and guided her to the cook house. "He has a slight concussion, and of course a headache." He laughed lightly. "Doc Evans left something that will take care of that."

Roxy's mind was more at ease when she walked into the warmth of the long building. And though she looked like a drowned chicken, Pee Wee thought to himself that he had never seen a more beautiful woman. He could only nod when Rock said, "Pee Wee, this is Roxy, the boy's mother. Could you scare up some of your clothes for her to change into?"

The cook nodded again, and when he disappeared into his living quarters, Rock pushed Roxy into a chair and poured her a cup of coffee. The expression in her eyes said thank you as with cold, shaking fingers she brought it to her lips. As she sipped the strong brew, Rock took a towel from a hook on the wall and began drying her hair.

"I hope Pee Wee hurries," Roxy said as the towel was rubbed briskly over her head. "I want to get to Jory."

Her wish was granted almost immediately as the small man spoke from the curtained doorway. "I laid some clothes out on my bed."

Roxy nodded, and a few minutes later when she stepped back into the kitchen area, she wore a pair of Levi's and a bright plaid shirt. The Levi's were snug against her hips and bottom, and the shirt strained the buttons across her full breasts. She had tied her damp hair back with a neckerchief of Pee Wee's she found lying on his dresser.

Rock hid a grin behind his hand. Tanner's eyes were going to pop out of his head when he saw her in this rig. He would forget for a moment that he was supposed to hate her.

"Hold my slicker over your head," Pee Wee said and handed her the black garment when she headed toward the door.

Roxy barely glanced at the splendor of Tanner's new home as Rock led her down the large entry hall, through a parlor room, then down another hall before coming to the room where Jory lay.

"It's about time you got here . . ." Tanner rose from the chair pulled up to the bed, his words trailing off. His eyes had dilated as they fastened on the curves he had once known so well. He pulled himself back from those long-ago days when with a small cry Roxy rushed to her son, who lay so quietly, whose face was so pale.

Rock gave Tanner a sour look and said in a hard

voice, "We stopped at the cook house long enough for her to change into some of Pee Wee's clothes. She was soaking wet. It wouldn't have done for her to drip water all over your grand house."

Tanner heard the disapproval in Rock's voice, but only scowled as he sat back down.

"How is the boy?" Rock moved to stand behind Roxy and to look down at the sleeping Jory.

"He's got a hell of a headache." Tanner glanced at Roxy and could tell by the way she was holding her body so still that she was listening intently to what he was saying. For a moment he was tempted to say no more, let her wonder and worry about her son's condition. He realized then how distraught she was and he relented. Whether he hated her or not, she was a mother concerned about her child.

"Doc left some laudanum for him if the pain gets bad," he said. "Other than that he's fine. No broken bones or bruises."

"That's good news, ain't it, Roxy?" Rock said. "He'll be up and rarin' to play with his friend Sonny this time tomorrow."

"He'll not be up and running around for at least a week," Tanner said coolly. "Doctor's orders."

Rock stayed a moment longer, then muttered, "I've got some things to do at the barn."

When Roxy and Tanner were left alone, the silence in the room became so intense that Roxy's head began to ache. A restless movement and a small groan brought them both leaning anxiously over Jory. Tears leapt into Roxy's eyes when he complained, "Mama, where are you? My head hurts." Jory hadn't called her Mama since he was six years old.

She took his hand and said softly, "Mama is here, honey, right beside you."

Jory's heavy lids lifted, and his pain-filled eyes cleared when he saw Roxy bending over him. "Ma." He smiled weakly. "I thought you were never going to get here."

"Well, I'm here now." She stroked his cheek, then gently brushed the hair off his forehead. "Does your head hurt a lot?"

"Yes, but not as bad as it did." He turned his cheek into her palm. "I knew that when you got here I would feel better."

"Are you hungry or thirsty? I was in the cook house before and it smelled like Pee Wee was stewing a chicken. Would you like a bowl of soup? And could I make you some tea?"

"The kind we have at home?"

"The same kind we have with the ginger cookies Skinny bakes for you."

"I am a little hungry, and the tea sounds good. A lot of sugar in it, all right?"

"Yes, a lot of sugar." Roxy leaned forward and kissed him lightly on his forehead. "I'll go get it now."

"I'll go," Tanner said gruffly, scraping his chair away from the bed.

"Tanner!" Jory turned his head to look at the dark-browed man. "I didn't see you there. Ma, this is my cowboy friend I told you about. Tanner, this is my mom. Don't you think she's pretty like I told you?"

"Calm down, son, before your headache gets worse," Tanner warned, ignoring the question about Roxy's looks.

"Do you know how to brew tea, Tanner?" Roxy asked.

"No, but I expect Pee Wee knows how."

"It's not like making a pot of coffee. There's different steps you have to take to make it right."

"You'd better let Ma do it, Tanner," Jory said. "She does it real good."

Tanner sat back down with a shrug and waved Roxy out of the room.

When Roxy stepped outside, the sun was going down and the drizzle had stopped. Lamplight shone from the cook house, and she could see through the window that the ranch hands were just sitting down to eat supper.

All the faces were familiar. The men were regulars at the Lady Chance. When she pushed the door open, she was greeted warmly by a dozen voices.

"How's your boy?" one of the men asked.

"He's hungry, so I guess he's coming along," Roxy laughed lightly. She looked at Pee Wee and said, "I'd like to bring him a bowl of your chicken soup, and do you have any tea leaves?"

The men looked at each other with raised eyebrows. *Tea?* they seemed to say in astonishment. *Cowboys don't drink that sissy stuff.*

Pee Wee saw the looks, and though he knew he would never hear the end of it, admitted that he had a tin of fine tea leaves that had come from England. The look on his bony, wizened face dared the men to laugh.

"If you'll get it for me I'll start it to brewing," Roxy said as she walked to the stove to check if the tea kettle had water in it. The big cast-iron pot was full and steaming. When Pee Wee brought out the tin he had kept hidden from the men, and a plain white teapot he had also secreted from the cowhands, Roxy started the ritual of making tea.

Pee Wee watched her from the corner of his eye

and nodded approval when Roxy's first act was to pour hot water into the pot and wait a minute for it to heat up. She next poured out that water, then filled the vessel with hot water again. She measured tea leaves into the steaming water, replaced the lid and let the leaves begin to steep.

Other male eyes watched Roxy also. They weren't interested in how she made tea, though. With the exception of Rock, and maybe the teen-aged wrangler, there wasn't a man among them who hadn't dreamed of making love to Roxy Bartel.

Pee Wee dug out a wooden tray from a bottom cupboard and set a bowl of steaming chicken soup on it. He then placed a thick slice of bread and two cups, two spoons and a sugar bowl beside the soup.

A couple of minutes later Roxy added the pot of finished tea. She picked up the tray and three men jumped to their feet to open the door for her. She smiled her thanks and all three blushed a fiery red.

When she walked into the bedroom, Tanner didn't look up, nor did he clear a spot on the table so she could put the tray down. As she stood there wondering where to put it, Jory chided, "I think Ma needs some help, Tanner."

With a slight frown, Tanner sat forward, pushed aside the glass and water, then leaned back in the chair. He made no effort to take the tray from Roxy and place it on the table.

Roxy was seething, but she didn't let her anger show. To light into the boorish man the way she wanted to would upset Jory. She kept a pleasant look on her face as she placed the soup and tea on the table. When she started to ease Jory up so that he could eat, Tanner got to his feet.

"I'll do that." He elbowed Roxy aside. "You might drop him and jar his head."

Roxy shot him a scalding look, thinking that she would like to jar his head as she stepped around him to prop the two pillows behind Jory's back. Their hands accidentally touched and both jumped as though they had been struck by a bolt of lightning. Tanner sat back down, and Roxy's hands trembled as she lifted the tray onto Jory's lap. "I really like Pee Wee's soup," Jory said as he picked up the spoon and dipped it into the bowl.

As Roxy poured the tea, she wondered how often Jory had eaten at the ranch to have developed a liking for the cook's soup. A lot had been going on that she didn't know anything about.

Tanner stood up suddenly, his hands shoved into his pockets. "I'm going to eat supper now," he muttered. "I won't be gone long."

Roxy breathed a long sigh of relief when the door closed behind him. She didn't know how much longer she could bear to be in his sullen presence. She felt certain that if Jory hadn't asked for her, he wouldn't have bothered to let her know the boy had been hurt. He would have kept Jory here until she came looking for him.

When Jory pushed away the empty bowl and patted his stomach with a grin, Roxy poured them both a cup of tea.

His men had eaten and left when Tanner entered the cook house. "I held some grub from them hogs," Pee Wee said, giving him a gap-toothed grin.

"Thanks, Pee Wee. I'm starved. I almost took Jory's soup away from him," Tanner joked.

"His mother seems like a fine young woman."

200

Pee Wee placed Tanner's supper in front of him. "A looker too. I could have served the men sawdust for all the attention they paid to what they put into their mouths. They were too busy eyein' her tight britches and that shirt that was a little too tight on her in some places, if you get my drift."

Tanner understood his meaning, and his head jerked up. "Did they make any off-color remarks to her?" His eyes glinted dangerously.

"Oh no," Pee Wee denied. "The men have all the respect in the world for her. They only looked."

When Tanner saw the confusion in his cook's eyes, he turned his anger onto himself. Why should he care what the men might have said to the little witch? She was no longer any concern of his. But did Pee Wee think that after his sharp words?

"Miss Bartel is Jory's mother, and I wanted to be sure she wasn't insulted while under my roof," he explained, trying to rationalize his angry reaction to Pee Wee's remark.

"You can rest easy about that," Pee Wee said, but his tone sounded as though he wasn't entirely convinced by his boss's explanation. Tanner had looked like a man in a jealous rage.

He turned back to his basin of soapy water and continued to wash the stack of dirty dishes, pots and skillets. No more was said between them until Tanner pushed his chair away from the table, ready to leave.

Pee Wee dried his hands on his apron and reached up and took a plate of food from the warming oven. "I saved Roxy her supper, too," he said. "You can take it to her."

Tanner paused on his way to the door. He

wasn't about to fetch and carry for the woman who had spurned his love years ago. Then Roxy's small face and haunted eyes swam before him. She had paid and was probably still paying for choosing another man over him. Besides, his cook would think it strange if he refused to take a meal to her.

He nodded, and Pee Wee handed him the cloth-covered tray.

When Tanner entered the bedroom, he found that Roxy had lit the lamp on the bedside table and that Jory was asleep. "How come he's asleep already?" He frowned.

"His head began to ache and I gave him a few drops of laudanum."

"Here." Tanner shoved the tray at her. "Pee Wee made you up a plate."

As Roxy took the tray, she wondered if Tanner had requested the cook to prepare her a plate, or if Pee Wee had done it on his own.

One look at the stony-faced man who had resumed his seat told her that it was Pee Wee's thoughtfulness. Tanner wouldn't care if she ever ate again.

Roxy made short work of her meal, and Tanner, watching her from the corner of his eye, remembered that she always had the appetite of a cowhand.

She never put on weight, though, he thought, his gaze traveling over her trim body, lingering where the shirt's buttons strained across her breasts. They still looked as firm as they had when he used to cradle them in his hands, covered their pink tips with his mouth.

He felt a stirring in his loins, and impatiently shook such memories from his mind. When Roxy set aside her empty plate and stretched her stiff back, he said tersely, "You're probably tired. You can spend the night if you want to. There's a bedroom across the hall."

Roxy said stiffly. "As long as Jory sleeps here, I'll be sleeping here, too. I'm not about to go off and leave him in your care. The reason he's here in the first place is because of the care you took with him today."

Tanner glared at her a minute, then shot back, "You'll not be welcome here for a week."

"Then tomorrow I'll take Jory home."

"You know you can't do that. To ride a horse or travel in a wagon would jar his head."

"Then you're just going to be stuck with me, aren't you?"

Tanner tried to stare her down but she didn't flicker an eyelash. Finally he looked away and growled, "Go on to bed, witch."

"No, I'm spending the night here beside Jory. He'll be waking up off and on all night, and he will want me here beside him."

"I'll be here if he wants anything." Tanner's voice was cold and firm.

Roxy gazed down at Jory's sleeping face thoughtfully. Tanner thought he knew so much about children. Maybe she should go to bed and let him find out that when a youngster was sick, he only wanted his mother doing for him. Besides, she was too spent, mentally and physically, to argue further.

Chapter Nineteen

Entering the bedroom, dimly lit by a pale moon, Roxy walked to the bedside table. She took a match from a jar, struck it on a scratcher and lit the lamp sitting there. In its light she glanced around the large room. Besides the bed and table there was a dresser, a wardrobe, a washstand with basin and pitcher, and a padded rocking chair.

A very nice room, she thought, but it needs to be brought alive with some color. As did Tanner's bedroom. There was no warmth and welcome in his room either. She sniffed the air. It smelled musty, as if the room had been shut up for a long time.

Yawning, Roxy turned back the covers, and sitting down on the edge of the bed she removed her boots, then Pee Wee's Levi's. With a sigh she stretched out between sheets yellowed with age, clad only in the too tight shirt.

"Drat," she muttered when she realized she had left the lamp burning. She flung her arm across her eyes to shut out the light. She was too tired to get up and blow it out.

Somewhere in the dark house a clock ticked, lulling her to sleep.

It was around midnight when Tanner was awakened by a plaintive whimpering. When he stood up to bend over Jory, his back was stiff and he had a crick in his neck from napping in the chair.

"What is it, son?" He sat down on the bed and laid his palm on Jory's forehead.

"My head aches." Jory looked around the room, then whined, "Where's Ma? She said she would stay with me. Has she gone back to town?"

"No, she's still here. She's asleep across the hall."

"I want her here." Jory's voice rose to a wail.

"Let me give you something for your pain." Tanner reached for the laudanum.

"No! Ma will do it," Jory protested loudly. "She always makes my pain go away."

"All right," Tanner gave in, afraid that Jory was working himself up into a state that would make his head hurt worse. "Lie still and I'll go get your mother."

Tanner walked softly into the room and gazed down at Roxy, asleep in the shadow of the lamplight. She still looks so innocent, he thought, shaking his head. Just as she had eight years ago when she would fall asleep down by the river, exhausted from their heated lovemaking.

His gaze traveled down her throat to where the top button had come undone, leaving one firm breast partially bared. His heart began to pound with slow, deep beats. He still wanted her. He wanted her so badly it was driving him crazy. It was all he could do to keep from getting into bed with her, gathering her in his arms and kissing her into submission. To make wild love.

One thing stopped him. Her son waited across the hall for her to come and comfort him.

He carefully pulled the sheet up to cover Roxy's breast, then shook her shoulder. She roused, and gazed up at him with eyes still full of sleep. Her lips curved in a slow, soft smile and her arms reached up to him.

Tanner swallowed back a deep groan. How many times had she done that before. But this time she wasn't going to get his strength inside her, although he was stiff and hard with wanting her. She had probably been dreaming of the gambler anyway.

When Roxy gasped and dropped her arms, he knew that she was fully awake now and cognizant of what she had done in her near sleep state. "What do you want?" she asked, propping herself up on her elbows, her eyes wary.

"I don't want what you're wanting," Tanner sneered, making Roxy blush furiously. "Jory needs you."

"I'll be right there." Roxy was the concerned mother now, forgetting her embarrassment. She threw back the covers and had one bare leg uncovered before she remembered she had nothing on from the waist down.

"Will you leave so I can get dressed!" She glared at Tanner, who leaned in the doorway enjoying her dilemma.

"Why should I leave?" Tanner didn't budge. "I've seen your bare body before, remember. You shouldn't mind me seeing it again."

"I guess you're right." Roxy shrugged a shoulder in pretended indifference and sweeping the covers back, stood up. Tanner tried to act as unconcerned as she, but had to give up as he watched her step into the Levi's. The desire was too strong to push her back onto the bed, lie between her long legs and ease his aching self inside her.

He wheeled around and crossed the hall, leaving Roxy with a wide, pleased smile on her lips. Tanner might hate her, but she could see that he still wanted her in the same way he used to. She was going to get her revenge for the way he had treated the seventeen-year-old girl. Somehow she would bring him to his knees.

Pulling on her Levi's, she hurried to her son. "You promised to stay with me, Ma," Jory complained as soon as he saw her.

"Shhh." Roxy sat down on the edge of the bed and took his hands in hers. "I wanted to get a little sleep. And, Jory, don't whine. Do you want Tanner to think you're a baby?" she chastised gently.

"I'm sorry, Tanner." Jory gave his idol a sheepish smile. "I only wanted Ma to give me the medicine 'cause I'm used to her taking care of me when I'm sick. I'd be pleased if you'd give it to me now."

"I can understand a fellow wanting his ma around when he's feeling poorly." Tanner poured water into a glass, then picked up the small brown bottle of laudanum. As he measured out the drops,

Norah Hess

he wondered how often over the years Roxy had sat alone with her son, tending to him, worrying about him. She had been practically a child herself when Jory was born. He felt a stirring of pity for her. It couldn't have been easy, struggling alone with a baby. Then there was the way the women of Denver had turned on her.

Don't waste your pity on Roxy Bartel, Tanner ordered himself as he lifted Jory's head to drink the pain-relieving mixture.

Within five minutes Jory was yawning. Before he closed his eyes, he tugged at Roxy's hand and whispered, "You're gonna stay with me, aren't you, Ma?"

Roxy nodded and squeezed his hand, and Jory was asleep immediately. She and Tanner exchanged amused glances. The boy hadn't wanted Tanner to know that he still wanted his mother with him.

Roxy smoothed the sheet over Jory, then defended him, saying, "He usually doesn't cling to me so."

"I know that. He's a tough little fellow despite your mollycoddling him the way you do."

"I do not mollycoddle him," Roxy denied sharply. "I'm only careful of his well-being. He has never gotten hurt in my care." She shot Tanner a reproachful look.

"That's right. You wouldn't let him ride a horse for fear he'd get hurt, but you haven't done a damn thing to keep him from being called a bastard. Don't you think that hurts him?"

Roxy had no answer for that and she lapsed into silence.

Tanner broke the silence after a few minutes. "While you were sleeping I gave some thought to

Thrill to the most sensual, adventure-filled Historical Romances on the market today...

FROM ▐▌ LEISURE BOOKS

As a home subscriber to Leisure Romance Book Club, you'll enjoy the best in today's BRAND-NEW Historical Romance fiction. For over twenty-five years, Leisure Books has brought you the award-winning, high-quality authors you know and love to read. Each Leisure Historical Romance will sweep you away to a world of high adventure...and intimate romance. Discover for yourself all the passion and excitement millions of readers thrill to each and every month.

Save $5.⁰⁰ Each Time You Buy!

Each month, the Leisure Romance Book Club brings you four brand-new titles from Leisure Books, America's foremost publisher of Historical Romances. EACH PACKAGE WILL SAVE YOU $5.00 FROM THE BOOKSTORE PRICE! And you'll never miss a new title with our convenient home delivery service.

Here's how we do it. Each package will carry a FREE 10-DAY EXAMINATION privilege. At the end of that time, if you decide to keep your books, simply pay the low invoice price of $16.96, no shipping or handling charges added. HOME DELIVERY IS ALWAYS FREE. With today's top Historical Romance novels selling for $5.99 and higher, our price SAVES YOU $5.00 with each shipment.

AND YOUR FIRST FOUR-BOOK SHIPMENT IS TOTALLY FREE!

IT'S A BARGAIN YOU CAN'T BEAT! A Super $21.96 Value!

▐▌ LEISURE BOOKS A Division of Dorchester Publishing Co., Inc.

Get Four Books Totally FREE – A $21.96 Value!

PLEASE RUSH
MY FOUR FREE
BOOKS TO ME
RIGHT AWAY!

Leisure Romance Book Club
P.O. Box 6613
Edison, NJ 08818-6613

AFFIX
STAMP
HERE

the name-calling Jory has to put up with in town. I have come up with an idea that might work to the boy's benefit. I'm in need of a housekeeper. I had planned on hiring a farm woman, but maybe you could take on the role . . . for a while."

Roxy forgot to breathe. Surely she had misunderstood what Tanner had said. "You want me to be your housekeeper?" she squeaked.

"Yes. Only for a short time."

"How short a time?"

"Not too long. I plan on getting married in a couple months."

Although Tanner's words hit her hard, Roxy steeled her features not to show it. And as though his announcement meant nothing to her, she asked, "Your housekeeper, not your mistress?"

"Yes, my housekeeper," Tanner answered impatiently. "I have no desire to wallow around in bed with you. My tastes are more refined these days. I'm only interested in ladies."

The hell you don't want to wallow around with me, Tanner Graylord, Roxy thought indignantly. *Who brought that bulge to your Levi's? I'll wager thoughts of beanpole Julia didn't put it there.*

She sent Tanner a sly smile. "A lady in your bed would never satisfy you. She would never act the whore for you."

"You know all about acting the whore, do you?" Tanner narrowed a dark look on her.

"Of course. You taught me. Remember when we used to spread a blanket under the willows down by the river? Don't you recall coaxing the little green teenager to follow your lead . . . how before you rode away and left her she was as accomplished in the ways of pleasing a man as any of Belle's girls?"

Tanner did remember those hot nights, the two of them lying bare in the moonlight, the slowly moving river a background to his deep groans, Roxy's soft cries of pleasure when they soared to the sky in a release that left them as weak as kittens.

His only response was a muttered, "I'm sure you've learned new tricks from the gambler."

Roxy wasn't sure, but she thought she heard a tinge of pain in Tanner's words. Recalling those nights of passion was affecting her also, so she switched the subject back to her being his housekeeper.

"If I should decide to take over the care of your house, what would the job entail? I still don't know how to cook."

"We could take our meals in the cook house."

"But not with the hands. Jory and I have always eaten alone together like a family and I would want to continue doing that. We could eat before or after the men have eaten."

"All right, we can do that," Tanner said, inviting himself to take his meals with Roxy and Jory. "As for the housekeeping, I guess it means keeping the house clean and my clothes washed and ironed. I'll hire some farm woman to come in a couple days a week to give you a hand with the heavy work. The place is pretty big."

"It's pretty dreary too," Roxy said. "Do I have your permission to lighten it up some, bring some life to the rooms?"

"I guess so," Tanner agreed reluctantly, remembering how he'd had to have all traces of Roxy's handiwork removed from the cabin. He didn't want to go through that again. "Just don't overdo it," he said gruffly.

"Do you have accounts around town, where I can buy and charge?" When Tanner frowned, she said, "Don't worry, I won't be buying furniture or pricey items, if that's what you're thinking."

"Go ahead then. Get what you want."

"I'll need the weekends off. I still have a business to run. Ace can take care of the place during the week, but he's no good at doing the book work."

Tanner looked at her from under lowered lids and said harshly, "I guess that's as good an excuse as any to check up on your gambler. From what I've heard, he has little self-restraint when it comes to your dancers, or any other willing female, as for that. Doesn't it bother you that your bed isn't the only one he warms?"

"Not particularly." Roxy shrugged off his question. "Ace and I have an understanding. We look the other way when one of us takes a new lover. It's—"

She didn't finish her sentence. The fury that had come over Tanner's face was a little frightening. Although somewhat alarmed, she was also gleeful. Her words had hit a raw nerve in the rancher. She'd had her first taste of revenge.

"You bitch," Tanner hissed, sitting forward. "What kind of mother are you to take a man into your bed when your son is in the next room?"

"Of course I don't do that," Roxy said indignantly. She warmed to the tale she was spinning and began to embroider on it.

"I have a very comfortable cot in my office behind the bar. My gentlemen friends are well known businessmen in Denver, and wouldn't want to be seen climbing the stairs to my quarters. My office has a back door that leads outside. So you see, everything is very discreet."

211

She smiled at Tanner as though proud she had worked out such a perfect scheme. He lunged to his feet, his fingers clenching and unclenching. "You're even worse than I thought. But let me tell you this, and listen hard. I'd better not catch any of your men around my ranch."

"They won't come here. After all, I can see them on the weekends."

"You little whoring bitch," Tanner ground out before striding toward the door.

As he walked through it, Roxy called, "I have to go to the Lady Chance tomorrow to pick up some clothes. Will you stay with Jory while I'm gone?"

She grinned. Tanner hadn't answered her—not that she had expected he would. But she knew he would look after Jory in her absence.

Chapter Twenty

Roxy awakened to her shoulder being shaken. She opened her eyes and gazed into her son's bright, smiling face.

"You're looking perky this morning," she said in a raspy, sleep-filled voice. "How are you feeling?"

"Just like my old self. I think I'll get up in a little while."

"You can think again, young man. You heard what Tanner said. You have to take it easy for the rest of the week. Your head took a hard knock."

Jory turned over on his back and stared up at the ceiling. "Will you be here with me?"

"Yes, I plan to." After a pause she asked, "How would you feel about living on a ranch all the time?"

"I'd like that fine." Jory turned his head to look at her. "Tanner says that a ranch is the best place

213

in the world for a boy to grow up. There is so much a fellow can do on a ranch."

"Do you like Tanner a lot?"

"You know I do, Ma. I like being around him. He teaches me about things."

"He has asked me to be his housekeeper. Do you think I should?"

"Yes, I do! Would it mean we'd be living here all the time?" In his excitement Jory started to sit up.

Roxy pushed him back down. "Yes, we would live here all the time."

"Take him up on it, Ma. It will be a wonderful job for you." Then, as though thinking out loud he said, "And for me, too. There would be no more walking around town trying to find something to do, no more being called names."

Roxy turned over on her back to hide the tears that sprang into her eyes. How long had her innocent little boy been paying for her mistake? When she had control of her emotions, she said, "I've got to go into town for a while. I have to talk to Uncle Ace about running the saloon, then pack us some clothes, then I have some shopping to do."

"Aren't you afraid I'll get out of bed while you're gone?" Jory gave her a mischievous look.

"No, I'm not afraid of that happening." Roxy tweaked his nose as she sat up and swung her feet to the floor. "Tanner is going to sit with you."

"Hey, I like that. He can tell me more about ranch life."

Roxy was looking under the bed for her boots when Tanner entered the room. Ignoring her, he smiled at Jory and said, "I see you're feeling better."

"A lot better. My head hardly hurts at all." His

eyes sparkling, Jory said, "Ma tells me she is going to be your housekeeper, that I'll get to live here all the time."

"How do you feel about that? Do you approve?" Tanner blew out the lamp; its light wasn't necessary any longer.

"I like it a lot," Jory answered as Tanner sat down on the chair that was still pulled up to the bed. "I want to learn how to be a cowboy, just like you."

My son's aspirations aren't too high, Roxy thought with a curl of her lips as she found the boots. As Tanner continued to ignore her, she pulled them on and quietly left the room.

Had she looked back she would have seen Tanner's gaze following her.

As Roxy walked toward the cook house, situated between the house and outbuildings, she breathed deep the scent of fresh pine and wet earth. It was an odor she wasn't used to, but she loved it all the same. The sky was bright blue and the sun warm. It was hard to believe that yesterday it had been gray overhead, with ceaseless rain hiding the sun.

When she entered Pee Wee's domain, he looked up from a basin of dirty dishes in soapy water. "You ready for breakfast?" he asked, grinning at her and drying his hands on the towel tied around his waist.

"Yes, I am. This fresh air makes me ravenous."

The small cook chuckled. "When Tanner told me to fix you some breakfast, he said to make plenty of grub for you, that you have an appetite like a cowhand."

Roxy let Pee Wee's remark pass. "I'm going to change back into my own clothes. I imagine they're dry by now."

"They are. I draped them in front of the stove before I went to bed last night. They're on the bed now."

"Thank you, Pee Wee. That was very thoughtful of you."

A few minutes later, feeling much better in her own clothes, although they were wrinkled, Roxy walked back into the kitchen area. By the time she washed her face and hands in a basin of warm water, the cook had a plate of bacon and eggs and fried potatoes waiting for her.

As she sat down at the table, Pee Wee asked, "How is the button this morning?"

"Much better. Almost his old devilish self."

"Tanner sure was upset when he brought the kid home. The way he carried on, a person would think the boy was his own son."

When Roxy made no response to his remark, Pee Wee asked, "Are you gonna be stayin' on while your boy is laid up?"

Roxy wiped her empty plate clean with a piece of bread before saying, "I'll be a permanent resident here for a while." She picked up her cup of coffee and said before taking a long swallow of it, "I'm going to be Tanner's housekeeper."

The cook looked at her goggle-eyed. "You're joshin' me, ain't you? Why would a good-lookin' city woman like yourself want to keep house for a rough character like Tanner Graylord?"

"Mostly I'm doing it for Jory. It's hard raising a boy in town. There's nothing for him to do there. Besides, I find it very peaceful on the ranch."

"I reckon that makes sense," Pee Wee said after a short silence. "Do you know how to keep house?"

An amused smile twisted Roxy's lips. Evidently the old cook thought she was only capable of running a saloon. Well, he and Tanner would discover that her mother had taught her how to care for a house very well.

"I know how to keep a house clean, Pee Wee," she said dryly. "However, I don't know how to cook except to brew coffee and tea."

He looked at her empty plate and jokingly complained, "I see I'll have to cook a lot more."

They were both laughing at his nonsense when Bertha Sheldon knocked on the net-covered door.

"Come on in, Bertha," Pee Wee invited. "You're three days early with your vegetable delivery."

"I didn't bring any garden truck." Bertha nodded a good morning to Roxy as she placed a cloth-covered plate on the table. "I brought this for Jory. It's a custard pie, his favorite. How is the boy?" She sat down across the table from Roxy.

"He's coming along fine. He wants to get out of bed," Roxy said with a small laugh.

"Best not let him. You can't be too careful after getting a crack on the head. Sonny wanted to come with me, but I made him stay home. He was awfully upset when his friend got hurt."

"Yes, I can understand that." Roxy nodded. "They are very close. Sonny is the first friend Jory has ever had."

"When will you be taking him home, Roxy?" Bertha nodded her thanks to Pee Wee when he placed a cup of coffee in front of her.

"I won't be taking him home, Bertha. Tanner has offered me the job of keeping house for him, and I'm taking it."

"You are? But do you—"

"Yes, I do know how to keep house," Roxy interrupted before Bertha could finish asking the same question the cook had.

"I meant you no insult, Roxy. It's just hard for me to imagine you scrubbing floors and dusting furniture. It's such a big place and all . . ." Bertha's voice trailed off a moment, then she said, "I bet Jory is pleased to be living here."

"Yes, he is. He's the reason I agreed to take the job."

Pee Wee and Bertha exchanged a quick glance that said they didn't think the boy was the main reason the young woman had taken the job as housekeeper for the handsome rancher.

"Well, I've got to leave you folks." Roxy stood up. "I've got some business to take care of in town. Thanks for the pie, Bertha."

"I've got to be getting along, too." Bertha pushed her chair away from the table. "My strawberry patch is ripening and I've got to beat the birds to the fruit."

Two young stable hands rushed to saddle Roxy's mare for her. She frowned in amusement. The two boys got in each other's way so much, she could have done it in half the time herself. She dreaded telling them that she wanted a packhorse readied also.

But finally both horses were ready. Swinging into the saddle before she could be assisted, Roxy galloped off toward town.

As she rode along, Roxy ticked off in her mind what she must buy to brighten up Tanner's home. All the rooms throughout the house needed a new coat of paint, a light color, possibly white, so she must hire a man to do that.

Every window would need new hangings, she felt sure. The same went for pictures. What few she had seen were dark and dreary-looking. And that dreadful deer's head hanging over the mantel must go. She intended to purchase new bed-spreads and rugs and pretty lamps. The plain ones on the tables now did nothing to liven up the rooms even when they were lit.

She would make Tanner's room very masculine looking, but hers would be much like her room upstairs over the saloon. She would need a lot of soap and furniture oil, she remembered. She had noticed when she walked through the parlor this morning that the wood furniture looked dry and dull, in need of a good rubbing.

She didn't know what the china looked like. She would check that out later. What with everything else that needed doing around the house, she would have her hands full for some time.

It was around noon when Roxy tied Beauty and the packhorse to the long hitching post in front of the Lady Chance. As she walked through the bat-wing doors, Belle entered the saloon by the side door. At the same time Ace stepped away from the bar. They all came together at one of the tables.

"How's the kid?" Ace asked as they sat down.

"He's going to be all right. He has a slight concussion and has to stay in bed for a week."

"Is he at the Sheldon farm?" Belle asked.

"No, he's at Tanner's ranch. Tanner took it upon himself to take Jory home with him. Maybe it's just as well, though. It's quiet there. There is always so much noise and activity at the farm. Jory will get more rest there."

"He's going to miss you, Roxy," Belle said with concern.

"No, he won't. I'll be staying with him."

"You're going to spend a week in that man's house?" Belle and Ace asked in unison. "You've gone loco," Ace added.

Roxy didn't make eye contact with them as she said, "I'll be staying there longer than a week."

"What do you mean, you're staying longer?" Ace demanded. "How long?"

Roxy focused her eyes on the bar as she said in a small voice, "I've agreed to hire on as Tanner's housekeeper."

"What!" Ace exploded, followed by Belle's, "Roxy, you didn't!"

"I have my reasons," Roxy said, finally looking up at her cousin and her longtime friend.

"I sure as hell hope they're good ones." Ace looked as though he would like to shake her. "You're laying yourself open for more heartache from that one."

"Ace may be right, Roxy. Unless you're sure you're over Tanner, I don't think it's a good idea for you to live under the same roof with him."

"Don't worry about it, Belle. I'm not the same seventeen-year-old he used before."

"I hope you're right," Belle said as she rose from the table, doubt in her voice. "When will I see you again?"

"I'll be home every weekend. And Belle, would you keep an eye on the dancers for me in my absence?" When Belle nodded that she would, Roxy added, "You'll have to be strict with them. They argue a lot among themselves and there's a couple who like to sneak men up to their rooms."

"You're too easy with them, Roxy. If you'd kick a couple out, the others would straighten up and follow rules." Belle picked up the package she had been holding when she entered the saloon. "They'll step around for me. I've been handling ladies like them for a long time. Those who don't behave won't dance for a week. When they miss the money that is tossed to them every night, they'll rethink their actions. The same thing goes for my girls. A few nights of not making any money makes them get along with each other real good."

Belle left the saloon, and Ace and Roxy's laughter followed her. "Now, why didn't I think of that?" Roxy questioned. When their mirth subsided, Roxy turned to Ace and said, "I'm depending on you to look after the saloon while I'm gone during the week."

"Don't worry about the Lady Chance," Ace said. "Just look after yourself. Don't let that long-legged wolf get within three feet of you."

"I won't. I promise." Roxy prepared to go up to her quarters. "I've got to pack some clothes for Jory and myself, then do some shopping for the ranch. I'll see you this weekend."

The hours had slipped by and the shadows in the valley were deepening when Roxy left Denver and headed for the ranch. She kept Beauty at a walk, for the packhorse would be unable to run with the many packages strapped on his back.

She was pleased with her purchases. She had been able to buy everything on her mental list, and she had made arrangements with a man to come to the ranch tomorrow to start painting the rooms. Also, she had visited the seamstress at the edge of town to choose materials and prints for the windows. All that had taken quite a while and that was why she was late setting out.

Would Tanner be angry that she had been gone all day, she wondered, a little uneasy. Manlike, he wouldn't consider that it took time to choose window material that would complement rugs and bed covers. She doubted if most men paid any attention to what their homes looked like. Certainly her father hadn't noticed how drab and sparsely furnished their living quarters over the saloon had been. Of course, he had only slept there, seldom seeing the old pieces of furniture and threadbare carpet in the light of day.

Roxy pushed away the resentful thoughts of her father and put her mind on how nice Tanner's home would be when she finished with it.

Darkness had settled in when the illumined windows of the ranch came into sight. Roxy's stomach growled. It was supper time and the men were probably sitting down to a hot, hearty meal. When she rode up to the barn, she saw, through the cook-house window, that she had been right. She could see the cowhands sitting at the long table, their heads bent over their plates.

She sighed as she slipped out of the saddle. She would have to strip the packages off the pack-horse.

She had untied one rope when a male figure came from the darkness of the barn. "I'll do that, Roxy," Rock said, walking up to her. "It looks like you bought out all the stores in Denver," he chuckled, eyeing the bundles and packages on the weary horse.

"Not quite," Roxy laughingly agreed. "The house needs a lot of sprucing up."

"Tanner told me that you're gonna be his house-keeper," Rock said as he began unloading the packages. As Roxy waited for him to express the same doubts as the others had, he surprised her by saying, "I think that's a fine idea. It will give the two of you a chance to get to know each other again."

"I thought we knew each other well enough to

last a lifetime before he went off to war," Roxy said bitterly.

"Naw, you were both too young. You were practically a baby at seventeen, and Tanner still had a lot of growing up to do. But you're both mature now. Tanner has fought a war and you have given birth. The way you think and look at things today has changed."

"Tanner has certainly changed," Roxy said as she lifted the last package off the horse. "He's sour and bitter, and so hateful. To me, at least. He's even hinted that it was my fault that he went away."

"Yeah, I know. He's all mixed up, but you just hang in there, girl. Everything will get straightened out."

"Hah! I don't care if it does or not. He has said a lot of cruel things to me. Words that I will probably never forget."

"We'll see. You mustn't get bullheaded like he is. Now, should we go up to the house? His face resembled a storm cloud half an hour ago because you weren't home yet. I don't imagine his temper has improved any."

When Roxy and Rock walked into the parlor, their arms full of packages, they looked at each other and chuckled when they heard Tanner come stomping down the hall. He burst into the room, the look on his face saying that he couldn't wait to pick a fight.

He stopped short when he saw them laying out Roxy's purchases on the sofa. For the time being he contented himself with saying harshly, "It's about time you got home. Jory has been asking for you."

Roxy doubted that. Her son would have enjoyed

every minute spent with his idol. "I'm sorry he's been such a bother to you," she said coolly.

"I didn't say he's been a bother," Tanner snapped back, the black look in his eyes saying that he would have more to say to her later, in private.

It was quite some time before Tanner had the chance to unload his anger on Roxy. They had taken turns going to the cook house for their evening meal, Roxy bringing back Jory's supper with her. Then, after giving him a sponge bath, she decided that he should be moved into a bedroom of his own.

She chose the room next to Tanner's and spent half an hour making up the bed with clean, yellowed linens after she had lit the lamp on the table beside the bed. When all was ready, Tanner carried Jory next door. Roxy followed behind, carrying the laudanum, glass and water pitcher.

When Tanner had laid Jory on the bed, Roxy asked as she arranged everything on the table, "How do you like your new room?"

"Well," Jory began hesitantly, "the mattress is comfortable, but the room isn't cozy like my room in our quarters in Denver."

"It will be later." Roxy sat down on the edge of the bed. "I did a lot of shopping today, and the first room I'm going to tackle will be yours. You won't recognize it when I'm finished."

"Don't worry about it, Ma. I'm just happy to be living here with Tanner."

Roxy glanced at Tanner standing at the foot of the bed and saw by the expression on his face that he was pleased with what Jory had said. She hoped that she would feel the same, living with him, but doubted it.

She leaned over and dropped a kiss on Jory's forehead. "I'll leave our doors open," she said as she turned down the lamp. "My room is across the hall and I'll hear you if you want me during the night."

She left Tanner to say good night to Jory and walked into the parlor, bracing herself to face Tanner alone.

It was only a minute later when he strode into the room, his face hard and tight. While she waited for him to start in on her, he went to the liquor cabinet and poured himself a glass of whiskey. When he sat down in a chair across from her, she steeled herself for his onslaught.

"Now," he began after swallowing half the contents in his glass, "do you want to tell me why you had to be gone all day to do a little shopping?"

"A little shopping!" Roxy cried indignantly. "Do those packages and bundles piled on the couch look like a little shopping?"

"Bah!" Tanner snorted contemptuously, "I could have bought all that in half the time."

"You probably could," Roxy retorted, her voice raised. "You would have handed the clerk the list and let him fill it, taking anything he wanted to give you."

"I would not, but it wouldn't take me forever to pick out what I wanted."

He fixed hard eyes on Roxy. "Why don't you admit that you spent most of the time wallowing around in bed with the gambler."

"Whether I did or not, it's no business of yours, Tanner Graylord," Roxy bristled. "I don't ask you how long you *wallow* around with beanpole Julia."

Tanner was about to deny that he'd spent any time in Julia's bed, then stopped himself. Had he

225

detected a hint of jealousy in Roxy's voice? He said instead, "I don't mind telling you. Sometimes it's only a couple hours, then sometimes it's all night."

He wasn't so sure he heard an undertone of jealousy in Roxy's voice when she threw back her head and derisive laughter rang out. "Miss Bradford couldn't last half an hour with your brand of lovemaking, let alone all night. I bet that frosty woman hasn't gone to bed with you yet."

Tanner jumped to his feet and, glaring down at her, grated out, "That's all you know. Beneath her ladylike ways she could teach you a lot in the bed department."

Roxy knew he was lying, and as he stomped out of the room, the laughter that trilled behind him said clearly that he hadn't fooled her.

Roxy went limp with relief when she heard Tanner's bedroom door snap shut. In another few minutes she would have been in tears.

Chapter Twenty-one

Tanner's expression wasn't happy as he cantered Brave over the well-defined trail to Denver. He was on his way to attend a party at the Bradford home which he had no interest in going to. The guests at the shindig would be all the important people in and around Denver. Some he liked well enough, but they weren't the sort of people he really enjoyed.

It was mid-July and the day was still warm, even though twilight had set in. He pulled at the collar of his white, starched shirt, wondering if he dared remove the string tie that seemed to be choking him. If he had been going to attend a function with his old friends, he would be wearing a shirt rolled up to his elbows with most of the buttons undone. A far cry from the black suit he wore now.

When Julia had brought him the invitation a

couple of days before, he'd had every intention of turning it down. But then he had seen Roxy watching him from the corner of her eye and knew that he must accept if he was to continue pretending that he was courting the banker's daughter. So he had smiled and graciously accepted the invitation.

So here he was, dressed up like a popinjay, pushed into a corner knowing that he would have a miserable evening. And it was all Roxy's fault, he thought unreasonably.

When Tanner entered Denver and rode past the Red Dog saloon and heard the laughter and the piano coming from inside, he grew all the more resentful about attending the party at the other end of town. He would give anything to tie Brave to the hitching post and join his rowdy friends inside.

When he arrived at the Bradford home, light was blazing out of all the windows.

A teenager came to take Brave away, and with the look of a man going to the gallows, Tanner stepped up on the wide porch and lifted the brass knocker. As he waited to be let in, he could hear the low murmur of polite conversation. He smiled wryly as he compared it to the rollicking parties he and Roxy had once attended.

The door opened and a beaming Enos pulled him inside. Tanner knew everyone there and was greeted warmly. He glanced around the room looking for Julia but saw no sign of her.

"Julia will be down in a minute," the banker said. "One of her bad headaches came on her this afternoon, but she took some kind of draught and when I looked in on her half an hour ago she was feeling better and was getting dressed for the party." Tanner nodded his understanding, hoping that Julia wouldn't make an appearance all night.

A short time later, however, she came down the stairs, a strained smile on her lips. When he looked closely at her, he saw traces of tears on her face. Also, there was a puzzling sullenness in her eyes. Who was she angry with? he wondered indifferently. A moment later when he saw her shoot a resentful look at Bradford, he realized that her father had displeased her in some way. The old man must have refused something to his spoiled darling, Tanner thought, and dismissed the pouting Julia from his mind. He took a glass of whiskey from the tray being passed around and joined a group of ranchers in a corner discussing grass, water and beef—the three most important things to a man who ran cattle.

He felt more at ease with these men. Their interests were the same as his. He knew also that in their youth most of them had raised hell and were probably as ill at ease as he was.

An hour later the loud voice of Bradford calling for attention interrupted their conversation. When the room grew quiet and the guests looked at their host and daughter, he called, "Tanner, come over here, son."

Puzzled, Tanner crossed the room and joined them. "Folks," Enos began, "as you know, Tanner and Julia have been keeping company ever since she returned from the East. It is now my pleasure to announce their engagement."

When a rush of people gathered around them, offering congratulations, Julia gave them a weak smile and Tanner stood as though paralyzed, making no response to the well-wishers.

What in the hell did the old bastard think he was

doing? he fumed silently. He had never even hinted to Julia that he had marriage on his mind. And if he wasn't mistaken, Julia had no more desire than he did to become engaged.

The rest of the evening was a blur to him, and Tanner left as soon as he politely could. As he walked to the door, he imagined the company thought it strange that Julia didn't see him out. He hadn't seen her for the past half hour. When Bradford started walking toward him, he sent the man a dark, threatening look that stopped him in his tracks.

As Brave galloped along, carrying him toward town, Tanner's mind raced, trying to figure out a way to escape the trap Enos had put him in. He remembered Rock's warning and realized his friend was more savvy than he was when it came to reading the wily banker.

But why was the man so determined that *he* marry his daughter? Tanner asked himself. Could it possibly be because he was wealthier than any of the other bachelors in town?

Unbidden, the image of Roxy's face floated before Tanner and he received a jolt that shocked him to the toes of his polished boots. If she cared the least bit about him, his engagement would kill her feelings. He knew suddenly that what he most wanted in the world was to resume their old relationship, that it was Roxy he wanted to marry.

He was sunk in a dark depression when he came opposite the Red Dog. He reined in. What he needed tonight was to get roaring drunk, to forget for a while all the painful demons, past and present, that had dogged him.

* * *

After Jory had come up from the river, dried off his body and slipped into his night clothes, Roxy had kissed him good night and walked out onto the porch. It was getting dark and night sounds had begun when she sat down in one of the tree rockers there.

With a push of her foot she started the chair rocking slowly and leaned her head back. She looked up at the sky where a trillion stars turned the Colorado countryside to silver. I love this land, she thought; its tall tree-studded hills, its valleys, its rivers.

But how much longer can I stay here? she wondered, chewing on her lower lip. She had been at the ranch for a month, and daily Jory and Tanner became more attached to each other. The day was bound to come when somehow Tanner would discover that Jory was his son. The thought of losing her child was always nagging at the back of her mind.

For the most part, she and Tanner got along fairly well with each other. Especially when Jory was with them. Tanner had learned that her son didn't like his rude remarks, and she in turn kept a civil tongue in her mouth because Jory was so fond of the brute.

Roxy's mind went back to earlier in the evening when Tanner was getting dressed to attend the party at the Bradfords. He had looked so handsome in his black suit and a shirt that was so white it dazzled her eyes. He had tried to slick back his hair, but the dark, unruly curls wouldn't stay put.

A few of them had straggled onto his forehead in their usual way, giving him a rakish look.

She had been sitting in the parlor when he left, but as he passed by, he paid no more attention to her than if she were another piece of furniture.

And strangely, that had hurt. But why? He had done the same thing numerous times before and she hadn't paid any attention to it. She did the same thing to him all the time and he hadn't seemed to mind it.

She avoided him as much as possible, seeing him mostly at supper time. He never missed joining her and Jory for the evening meal. After the hands had eaten and left the cook house, the three of them would sit at the table, much as a small family would do. He and Jory would talk over the events of the day, often laughing about things they had done together.

She was excluded from their conversation and quietly ate whatever Pee Wee had prepared for them. Many times, though, when she looked up from her plate, she would find Tanner's brooding gaze on her.

When Roxy saw some of the cowhands ride away from the ranch, going in the direction of town, she rose and walked back inside.

It was a pleasure to enter the parlor these days. She had put much thought and work into its present appearance. The bright window dressing of soft blue and ecru lace had brightened the room, but the newly painted walls in a soft cream color, the bright scatter rugs and pretty milk-glass lamps had brought the room to its glory.

Roxy sat down in the smaller chair she had marked as her own and picked up the weekly newspaper Tanner had brought home that day. When she found herself reading every page of it, even the want ads and items for sale, she realized when the clock struck nine that she was waiting for Tanner to return home. She flung the paper on the floor and jumped to her feet, muttering, "Why should I care when he gets home? He can spend the night with Julia for all I care."

Still, as she lay in bed she found herself listening for his footsteps in the house. It was past midnight when she could no longer ward off sleep.

The next morning when she rose and found the lamp still burning in the parlor, she realized that Tanner had not returned home last night. But to make sure, she eased his bedroom door open and looked inside. His bed was still made up, exactly as she had made it yesterday.

Jory's bed, however, was a mass of tangled sheets and blankets when she looked into his room. A small smile hovered on her lips. Her son was an early riser, always afraid that he might miss something.

Low in spirits, Roxy walked into the kitchen to brew a pot of coffee when a wildly sobbing Jory burst into the room, a much concerned Tanner at his heels.

"What's wrong, Jory?" She caught his arm, stopping his mad rush to his room.

"Yes, son, what's wrong?" Tanner echoed. "Has someone said something to you that has upset you?"

"Yes, they did," Jory shouted, tears running down his cheeks. "The men are saying that you're going to marry that awful Julia Bradford."

Tanner swore under his breath. He was ready to vehemently deny that he would ever marry Miss Bradford, then stopped. From his peripheral vision he had seen Roxy's body stiffen and her eyes widen. He hid the elation that made his pulse soar. He knew jealousy when he saw it. Maybe Roxy didn't know it, but she still cared for him.

He decided on the spot that he would not break it off with Julia just now. Roxy would fight any tender feelings she had for him, but he felt, hoped, that she would weaken as he continued to court Julia.

But what about Jory? He ran nervous fingers through his hair. The boy cared deeply that he might marry the spoiled woman, judging from the sobs that shook his narrow shoulders.

He hunkered down beside Jory's chair and laid his hand on the boy's knee. "Let's take a ride, son," he said gently. "I want to talk to you."

"I don't want to talk to you," Jory sobbed and jerked his knee away. "Go talk to skinny ole Julia."

"Hush, Jory," Roxy chastised. "It's no business of yours if Tanner wants to get married, or whom he marries. I'm sure he'll still be your friend."

"That's right, son," Tanner coaxed. "Nothing will ever change how I feel about you."

"Don't call me son. You're not my father." The words came out on a painful wail.

"I think you'd better go." Roxy looked at Tanner, then sniffed the air and added, "You smell awful. A dip in the river with a bar of soap would make you more appealing to be around. You smell like you spent the night in the Red Dog saloon."

"I did," Tanner growled and standing up, stalked off to his room.

Roxy put a comforting hand on Jory's shoulder as she felt the same devastation as she had when Tanner had gone off without a word to her eight years before.

She should have seen this coming, she thought. Tanner had been seeing Julia regularly, and he had told her when she took the job of housekeeper that he was getting married in the near future. She

234

hadn't believed him, especially since they had made love together a few weeks back. He had been so ardent, so intense that night, she had felt sure he would never marry a cold woman like Julia Bradford.

She composed herself with an effort and said soothingly, "Tanner's getting married won't spoil your friendship with him. He will always find time for you."

"It will too spoil it." Jory wiped a hand across his wet eyes. "When she comes here to live, me and you will have to go back to town and I won't hardly ever see him."

Jory's words gave Roxy a start. She hadn't got that far in her thinking. Of course, she and Jory couldn't stay on at the ranch after Tanner brought his bride here.

"They may not get married for months, maybe even a year," Roxy said, trying to console her son, at the same time trying to comfort herself.

"No, Ma. It will be soon, I know it will," Jory insisted and burst into another flood of tears.

Chapter Twenty-two

Julia Bradford sat in the breakfast room of her father's house, nibbling on a sweet bun and sipping coffee as she read the letter that had arrived the day before.

The morning sun striking through the window brought into relief the petulant lines around her lips and on her forehead, robbing her face of any attractiveness as she laid the two pages down and stared blankly out the window.

The letter was from her friend Jenny back East. The young woman had written about all the exciting things going on in her life, the parties and balls she had been attending. On the last page she had written how much she missed her lovely Julia and asked when she was coming back to New York. She had written that she hoped Julia would be able to go to Europe with her in the fall.

A steely determination glittered in Julia's eyes. She was going on that tour, no matter what. Her father had got himself into his financial mess and she wasn't going to pay for it. There was no way she was going to spend the rest of her life in this small, drab town married to a ruffian rancher of no class.

She shuddered, thinking how she would have to share a bed with a husband, respond to his demands on her body. Her father could rot in prison for all she cared. The old fool, playing around with other people's money.

Julia was mentally laying out her plans when Enos walked into the room "How's my little girl this morning?" He dropped a kiss on top of her head before sitting down. When he had called to the cook to bring him bacon and eggs, he looked at his sullen-faced daughter and asked, "What are your plans for today, honey?"

"Nothing exciting, you can bet." Julia shrugged a contemptuous shoulder. "What can one plan in this out-of-date hick town?"

"Now don't go picking on Denver." Enos frowned. "It's an up-and-coming city that is growing every day."

"Bah," Julia snorted. "It will take twenty years before it's halfway as big as New York City."

"That may be, but in time it's going to outdo the Eastern cities in wealth."

"What good is money if the citizens don't know how to enjoy it?"

"They'll know how to enjoy it. There will be big homes built, bigger and better stores will go up, and a theater for the people to attend."

"I can imagine what sort of plays these rustics will want to see," Julia sneered.

Norah Hess

Irritation grew in Enos's eyes. He got very nervous when Julia talked this way, when he heard the unrest in her words and voice. He had hoped that by now she would have forgotten all about big-city life and would settle down where she belonged. He sighed silently. It didn't sound that way this morning.

When the cook had placed his breakfast in front of him and left, Enos looked at Julia and said, "It's been two weeks since I announced your engagement to Tanner. I haven't seen him around here, or in town since. Isn't that strange?"

"Not at all," Julia said indifferently. "He's more interested in his cattle than he is in me."

"I wonder," Enos said thoughtfully. "That Roxy Bartel is keeping house for him. Maybe his interest lies there. She's a looker, so you'd better start warming up to him or you might lose the best catch in town."

Julia was about to retort that that wouldn't bother her in the least, but she thought better of it. She would go along with him for the time being. When the time was right she'd leave all this behind.

She looked at Enos and asked, "What would you have me do? Continue to chase after him?"

"If need be. You know how important it is to me that you marry him."

Julia wanted to lean across the table and hiss in his face that he was a fool if he thought she would sacrifice herself for him, that it made her skin crawl every time Tanner Graylord touched her.

She swallowed back the words and, picking up her coffee, said calmly, "I'll ride out to his ranch this afternoon."

* * *

238

Roxy stretched, yawned and continued to lie in bed another few minutes, thinking back over the two weeks that had passed since Tanner's engagement to Julia was announced. In all that time he hadn't left the ranch; not a good sign that he missed his intended, she thought.

Her mind switched to her son. Jory still hadn't forgiven his idol. When she had tried to reason with him, repeating what she had said the morning he had come crying to her, he had answered with childish logic.

"He should marry you, Ma, because you're so pretty and kind ... and because you're my mother. If he wedded you he would be my father then." He had run off after that outburst, going to the farm to spend the day with Sonny. That had been his habit for the past two weeks.

He's as stubborn as his father, Roxy thought as she slipped out of bed.

Half an hour later she was bathed and dressed, and sitting in the cook house waiting for Tanner to join her. Even though her son wouldn't have anything to do with him anymore, Tanner still came to have breakfast and supper with her. She wished he wouldn't, and wondered why he did. They never talked, hardly looked at each other. His hard eyes and harsh face didn't invite any conversation.

Roxy heard the kitchen door of the house slam and grew tense. It was becoming harder and harder to be in Tanner's presence, especially now that Jory wasn't with them to break the silence that always developed between them.

But she had to talk to Tanner today, to say a few words to him at least. Tomorrow was Friday and she had to remind him that she would be leaving for the weekend. She dreaded it. She would have to listen to his same old arrogant questions. Was she leaving him enough clean clothing, enough towels, and so on and so on.

When Tanner entered Pee Wee's kitchen and sat down at the table without a word to Roxy, she noticed that he looked crosser than usual. Who had put a burr under his tail? she wondered.

When, near the end of the silent meal, she mentioned she was leaving for the weekend the next day, she knew the reason for his stony face. He glared at her and snarled, "I guess I should know that by now."

Of course, she thought, today is Thursday. He always gets this way a couple of days before I leave. "I just thought I would remind you," she said. "And before you ask, your dresser is full of clean clothes and the linen closet is full of towels."

His answer was a sour look and the loud scraping of his chair from the table before he walked wordlessly outside.

"Tanner Graylord can sometimes be the orneriest man I ever worked for," Pee Wee said, clearing the table. "I don't know if it's possible, but he seems to be worse lately. I never say anything to him unless I have to. I'm afraid he'd bite my head off."

"Me, too," Roxy agreed, wondering if Jory's snubbing him had anything to do with his rancor these days.

When Roxy left the cook house, intending to give the house a good going over to make sure there would be nothing for Tanner to complain about, she was surprised to see him still hanging around the barn. It was his habit to ride out as soon as he had finished breakfast.

240

She was more surprised when she took a lunch break around noon and saw that he still hadn't left the ranch. She was about to go to the cook house when she saw a rider approaching. As the roan drew nearer, she recognized Julia Bradford on its back.

So that's why he's still hanging around, she thought, her lips unconsciously firming. He knew she was coming for a visit. But he doesn't seem all that happy to see his intended, she puzzled, watching Tanner take his time to walk over and help Julia dismount.

When they started walking toward the house, Roxy became aware of the kerchief tied around her head and the dirt-smudged apron around her waist. As she hurried to her room, her fingers were busy untying strings. Standing in front of the dresser mirror, she brushed her curls, then smoothed out the creases in her skirt made by the apron. The dress wasn't one of her best, but it was a pretty little blue frock with white ruffles around the low-cut neckline.

Roxy heard Tanner and Julia enter the kitchen, then walk into the parlor. Julia was chattering away in her nasal voice, but Roxy heard nothing from Tanner.

What was expected of her? Roxy wondered. Should she join them or stay in her room? The decision was made for her when Tanner rapped on the door and said through the paneling, "I have company. Is there anything in the house to drink?"

She jerked the door open and hissed, "You know damn well there isn't."

"Couldn't you brew a pot of coffee?" he growled back.

"Yes, I could, but don't you think it's a little hot to drink coffee after a long ride?"

"Hell, I don't know, but she's asked for something to drink."

"I'll go make it," Roxy said sharply and pushed him out of the way. The unexpected action made Tanner step back, off balance. He swore softly as he caught the edge of the door to keep from falling. Roxy grinned at his awkwardness, and eluding the hand he shot out to grab her, she sailed down the hall.

"Good afternoon, Julia," she said pleasantly as she swept through the parlor, not pausing to see if Julia responded.

But as she entered the kitchen, she heard Julia remark irritably, "She acts like she's the lady of the house instead of a lowly housekeeper." Roxy waited to hear whether Tanner would make a demeaning remark about her, but only Julia's words hung in the air.

The fact that Tanner hadn't said anything lifted her spirits and she hummed a little tune as she pumped water into the coffee pot and measured coffee into it. As she set it on the stove, she realized she would have to build a fire to brew it. She stood a moment, then declared under her breath, "I am not going to heat up the kitchen so that bitch can have a cup of coffee." She left the house and walked across the yard to beg Pee Wee for some coffee.

"I dunno," the cook said doubtfully. "It's probably pretty strong by now. I made it this morning."

"That will be just fine." Roxy gave an impish grin. "Is it still hot?"

"Most likely. I've had a fire going for the past two hours, baking pies for them hogs' supper."

When Roxy filled two cups with the very dark liquid, Pee Wee asked with a gap-toothed grin, "You tryin' to pizen Miss Bradford?"

"Naw, just give her stomach a good jolt."

"That'll do it," Pee Wee chuckled as Roxy placed the cups on the wooden tray that had carried Jory's food to him when he was laid up. Still amused, he added a chipped sugar bowl and a glass jar of milk to the tray. "Do you think that will be fancy enough for the boss's guest?" Pee Wee's eyes sparkled with mischief.

"If it's not, Miss Bradford doesn't know good china when she sees it." The cook's laughter followed her out the door.

Tanner and Julia looked up when Roxy entered the parlor, and as she placed the tray on a table near their reach, she met their cold stares with an innocent smile.

Tanner took in the muddy-looking coffee, the chipped sugar bowl and the glass jar of milk, then turned an outraged stare on Roxy. He opened his mouth, then snapped it shut, his expression saying that he would deal with her later.

As Julia picked up the spoon, its handle slightly bent, and dipped it into the sugar bowl, she said disdainfully, "You know, Roxy, I never visualized you as a drab housekeeper, scrubbing floors, washing and ironing clothing, cooking meals over a hot stove. Your poor hands and knees must look a fright."

Roxy controlled the anger that jumped inside her, and light laughter feathered through her lips. She held up her slim white hands, adorned with rings, and said, "My hands are the same as they were when I ran the Lady Chance and my knees are still soft. You see, Tanner hired a woman to come in twice a week to do the heavy work, like scrubbing the floors and doing the washing and ironing. As for cooking over a hot stove, I don't know how to cook. Tanner and I take our meals at the cook house after the men have eaten."

When Roxy silenced her reckless tongue, she looked at Tanner's furious face and realized she had gone too far. But a quick look at Julia's face made her feel that however angry Tanner was, it was worth it. At least she had wiped the smug haughtiness off Julia's face.

With a forced smile, Roxy turned and left the room.

Roxy was thankful that Julia didn't stay long. The closed door of her bedroom shut out the cool breeze coming off the river and the room was growing quite warm. When she heard their foot-steps going down the porch steps, she opened the door and walked into the kitchen. Peering past the edge of the window curtain, she watched Tanner and Julia walk to the hitching rack where Julia's horse was tethered. They don't look very lover-like, she thought, continuing to peer at the couple. You would think that they would at least hold hands.

She shook her head when Tanner, very busi-nesslike, boosted Julia into the saddle, then stepped back. "Not even a kiss on the cheek," Roxy muttered. When the big roan galloped away, she turned from the window, thinking that Tanner would go about ranch business now. She gave a small gasp when she saw him coming toward the house, his stride long and full of purpose. The scowl on his face told her that he couldn't wait to take a piece of her hide.

Gathering up her skirt, she sped to her room

and had just turned the lock on the heavy door when she heard his feet hit the kitchen floor. When his heavy, commanding knock thundered on the door, she looked wildly around the room. There was no place to hide if he should break down the door. He would never strike her, she knew, but he would give her a tongue lashing that would be worse than a beating.

Tanner pounded on the door again and demanded, "Open the door, Roxy, I know you're in there."

A wild idea, born of desperation, came to her. She ran to the window, raised the sash high, then slammed it down. Tanner's savage oath and hurrying footsteps running down the hall told her he had bought her ruse, that he thought she had eluded him by climbing through the window. He would search for her outside.

She was sure of it when she saw him run past the window. She drew a long, shaky breath of relief. With any luck, his anger would wear off during the time he hunted for her.

In the meantime, though, to be on the safe side, she would have to stay holed up in her room, which was growing uncomfortably warm.

Chapter Twenty-three

As Tanner searched the grounds around the house, then the barn and its area, his anger began to cool. He knew it was his fault that Roxy had acted the way she had. Hers was a proud spirit and he should have realized that she would react to Julia's snubs with angry recklessness.

But as Roxy began to number the things she didn't do—she didn't cook, didn't scrub floors or do the laundry—anger grew inside him. He asked himself what kind of damn fool he was. Was he paying her a hefty wage just to dust the furniture?

He rapidly transferred his anger at himself to Roxy. She had taken advantage of him and all this time had secretly been laughing at him. Well, he could take care of that. He would tell Roxy's helper not to come anymore. Miss Roxy could do the scrubbing of floors and dirty clothes herself.

But he knew he would never really do that. Roxy might leave him, and he would miss having her around, hearing her laughter, eating two meals a day with her even though they never talked during that time.

He was a damn fool, he knew. He'd do better to send her packing, he told himself as he saddled Brave. She was another man's woman now. She would only bring him heartache if she stayed on at the ranch.

Tanner shut the words out of his mind as he kicked the stallion into a gallop.

When Roxy saw Tanner ride away, she opened her door and walked into the parlor. As she gathered up the cups and placed them on the tray, along with the sugar bowl and the glass jar of milk, her lips curved in a pleased smile. The cups were still full of bitter black coffee. She imagined that one sip of it had been enough for Tanner and his fiancee.

When she carried the tray to the cook house, Pee Wee looked at the full cups, then, raising questioning eyes to her, he asked innocently, "Didn't they like the coffee?"

When Roxy choked out, "No, they didn't and I can't figure out why," they both broke into peals of laughter.

"I kinda figured that." Pee Wee wiped his wet eyes. "When I saw their stony faces, I knew you'd be in for it."

"I'm afraid I'm still in for it." Roxy smiled weakly. "I haven't faced Tanner yet."

Pee Wee shook his white head. "I don't envy you when you do."

"I'm not looking forward to it," Roxy said as she left the cook house.

Roxy stepped outside just as Bertha Sheldon drove up in her wagon. Jory and Sonny sat in the back, among the baskets of vegetables. "How are you, Bertha?" Roxy asked as the boys climbed out of the wagon. "Is it warm enough for you?"

"Lord, yes." Bertha mopped her red, sweating face with a white rag. "I feel like my very bones are going to melt," she added as she heaved herself off the high wagon seat and climbed to the ground.

"Come in the cook house and have a glass of cool water while Pee Wee picks through your produce."

"There's some fine green beans and tomatoes in the bunch," Bertha said. "I just dropped some off to Mr. Henderson. He seems real comfortable, living in Tanner's cabin."

It always saddened Roxy to think that someone else now lived in the small place that she had once thought would be her home. She shook the thought from her mind when Jory tugged at her arm.

"Where is Tanner working today?" he asked.

"I don't know, honey. Out somewhere with the men, I suppose." When Jory didn't say any more, but still stood beside her, she said gently, "You miss his company, don't you?"

Jory nodded, looking down at the ground and scraping a bare foot in the gravel. "I'm still mad at him, though. I thought he was too smart to marry that stuck-up Bradford woman."

"He hasn't married her yet," Roxy pointed out. "And even if he does, I don't think it will be in the near future."

His mother's words made hope flare inside Jory.

248

It shone in his eyes as he grinned and said, "Maybe I'll start talking to him again."

"You do that. It will make him happy. I can tell he's been missing you."

Pee Wee stepped outside at that moment and Jory took off after Sonny, a happy smile on his face. While the cook scrambled into the wagon, Roxy stepped inside the kitchen to get Bertha her glass of spring water.

The rest of the day dragged for Roxy. Always in the back of her mind was the thought that she still had to face Tanner—this evening at the supper table. Maybe with Pee Wee there, he wouldn't speak too harshly to her.

With that faint hope in mind, an hour before it was time for the men to ride in, she gathered up a bar of soap, washcloth, towel and robe and made her way to the river. There was a small pool formed behind some large boulders and it had been her private, secret bathing place since the first hot day of summer.

Roxy didn't linger in her bath, however. One never knew when one of the men might ride in early. Back at the house, in her room, she pinned her curls on top of her head and, forgoing underwear because of the muggy evening air, slipped into a cool cotton dress. With a sigh of dread, she paused inside the door and prepared herself to face Tanner and his anger.

She took one step onto the porch, then stood stock-still, her pulse racing. Tanner stood at the bottom of the steps, staring up at her like an avenging angel. There will be no Pee Wee to buffer his fury, she thought, her stomach churning.

Well, I'm not going to be cowed by him, she decided, firming her lips and taking one step down. When she took the second one, her toe caught in the hem of her dress and she was suddenly falling straight toward Tanner. She fell into his arms as his hands automatically reached out to steady her.

She gazed up at him, waiting to be released. Instead he pulled her closer, until his chest pressed against her breasts. He gazed back at her, his eyes growing dark; then he lowered his head to her lips. As he kissed her she tried to escape his marauding lips by twisting her head away. His hands came up and cupped her head on either side, keeping it captive as the kiss went on.

She began to feel flutterings of passion grow inside her and unconsciously leaned into him. His hand was immediately at her bodice, undoing it and freeing her breasts. He smoothed a hand over one, then with a deep moan cupped it in his hand. Lowering his face, he sucked her nipple into his mouth. As he tongued and teased it with his teeth, Roxy found her mind and body in conflict. Her mind demanded that she not let him use her, insisting that he didn't love her, that he was going to marry another woman. But the longer Tanner's lips moved on her breast, the more determined her body was to find satisfaction.

Finally passion overcame her and she went limp. With a satisfied sound in his throat, Tanner swept her up in his arms, took one step to reach the porch, then moved through the house, arriving at her bedroom door. He laid her on the bed, and kneeling beside it, he gently removed Roxy's dress. The breath caught in his throat when he gazed down at the white beauty of her body. He lifted a hand and stroked her breasts until the pink nipples grew pebble hard. Then he slid his hand down her midriff and across her stomach.

His hand lingered there. Watching her face, he slowly moved his head down to the thatch of tight curls. When he saw her eyelids flicker and felt a slight stirring of her body, he began to massage her, slowly rubbing his finger against the little nub hidden there. When he realized by the tightening of her body that she was on the verge of reaching the crest of her passion, he hurried out of his clothes. He lay down then and leaned over her until she raised eager, willing arms to him.

With gentle hands he pulled her legs apart and moved his lean, powerful body between them. He hung there a second as though savoring the moment, then with the moan of a man who had hungered for a long time, he took his throbbing arousal in his hand and slid it into Roxy's moistness.

When he was firmly and completely inside her, he hesitated again before moving slowly inside her. Roxy lifted her arms and, wrapping them around his shoulders, raised her hips to meet each thrust of his.

Tanner kept his pace slow. His hunger for the woman lying beneath him was so fierce, he wanted their loving to last for a long time. He did not want to reach his peak in a hurried state, but to make it so good, so satisfying for Roxy that she would never think of another man again.

But when Roxy's body stiffened and jerked beneath him for the second time, he could not hold off any longer. His body bathed in sweat, he slid his hands under her small rear, and lifting it up, he began to thrust hard and fast. The bed squeaked and the bed springs bounced as he climbed the mountain of pleasure, hung there a moment, then fell off. As he spiraled downward, Roxy held him close, stroking his back.

When at last Tanner's body stopped shuddering and his mind returned to normal, he realized what he had done, and not done. Instead of warning Roxy never to pull such a trick as she had earlier, like a damn fool, he had made love to her. The little witch was probably silently laughing at him right now, pleased that she had such a hold on him.

Roxy, listening to Tanner's breathing return to normal, waited for him to tell her that he still loved her and wanted to marry her. She would tell him then all about Jory.

It was like a dash of cold spring water in the face when he lifted himself off her and wordlessly picked his clothes off the floor. Still she waited as he pulled on his shirt and Levi's, and still he was silent.

When he had pulled on his boots and stood up, he spoke. She could only stare at him with anguished eyes as he said harshly, "When you lie in the gambler's arms tomorrow, I dare you to forget what happened here tonight."

He walked out of the room then, leaving her curled up on the bed, deep sobs racking her body. Tanner had used her again. When would she ever learn?

Chapter Twenty-four

The sun was quite high when Roxy awoke the next morning. She looked out the open window and judged it to be around nine o'clock.

She hadn't slept well. The few times she nodded off, she dreamed of Tanner, hearing again his cold, cruel words. Gazing up at the ceiling, she thought, I can't possibly stay on here. I'm too weak when it comes to Tanner. Anytime he decided he wanted me I would be at his mercy. All it would take would be a few hot kisses and his hand stroking my body and I would go up in flames. When she and Jory left today, she would leave him a note saying that she wouldn't be coming back.

Since she had taken a sponge bath last night, after Tanner left, washing away his scent and spent passion, Roxy had only to wash her face this morning. She was getting dressed when she heard

Jory's laughter, then Tanner's deep, rich voice. She hurried to the window and looked out.

They stood outside the cook house, Jory gazing up at Tanner in his old adoring way. Tanner said something and Jory nodded his head, smiling. Tanner laid a hand on his shoulder, then walked away, headed toward the barn.

So, Roxy thought, Jory is talking to the snake again. When she saw her son enter the cook house, she finished dressing and went to have breakfast with the happy boy.

"I saw you talking to Tanner," Roxy said as Jory helped himself from the stack of flapjacks Pee Wee had placed on the table.

"Yeah." Jory nodded his head, his eyes shining. "We're pals again. He's going to take me fishing Monday afternoon."

"You may not be here, honey," Roxy said, helping herself to a flapjack.

"What do you mean? Of course I'll be here." Jory looked at her anxiously.

"The thing is, Uncle Ace is finding it too hard to run the Lady Chance all by himself. I'm afraid we'll have to move back to town."

Roxy thought for a minute that Jory hadn't heard her, he was so quiet. But when she looked at him, she knew she was mistaken. There was a look of panic in his eyes and his bottom lip was quivering. He threw down his fork and his voice trembled as he shouted, "I won't go!"

"Of course you will," Roxy said in a firm voice. "You belong with me. If I have to leave, so do you."

"You're just jealous of Tanner," Jory cried in childish defiance. "You don't care how much I hate living in town. You care more for that old saloon." Jory was openly crying now, big tears running down his cheeks. "I'll run away before I'll go back there to live."

Roxy sat stunned. She had known that Jory hadn't liked living in town, but she hadn't known just how much he hated it, or how deep his feelings were for Tanner. But could she make herself continue living under the same roof with Tanner after last night? Could she control her rebellious body if he caught her unawares like last night? When he made her crazy with his hot kisses and stroking hands?

She sighed in defeat as Jory continued to sob his unhappiness. She placed her hand on his clenched fist and said softly, "If it means that much to you, maybe I can hire someone to help Uncle Ace run the Lady Chance."

"Do you mean it, Ma?" Jory was up and around the table to hug her fiercely. "I really couldn't bear to leave the ranch . . . and Tanner."

It's Tanner you can't bear to leave, Roxy thought, near tears herself as Jory dashed out of the cook house, the screen door slapping behind him.

Dear Lord, how was it going to end?

Tanner was leading Brave out of the barn when Jory came running up. He gave one look at the boy's tear-stained face and asked in concern, "What's wrong, son? Why have you been crying?"

"I got upset when Ma told me just now that we were moving back to town."

"Moving back to town?" Tanner parroted, Jory's words hitting him like hammer blows to the chest.

"Yeah. She said that Uncle Ace needs her help to run the saloon."

That wasn't the reason she was leaving, Tanner knew. What could he expect after the insulting

Norah Hess

words he had flung at her last night? He must do something, say something that would let her know he was sorry for the way he'd spoken to her.

He looked up at the house, then back at Jory. "Maybe she'll change her mind if I talk to her."

"You don't have to do that." Jory grinned at him. "I already have. We'll be staying on."

Relief washed over Tanner, leaving him weak. He didn't know whether to hug Jory or bawl him out for giving him such a fright. He knew one thing for sure, though. If he was to continue having Roxy around, he'd damn well better keep his hands to himself. And that would take all the will power he possessed. Every minute of every day he wanted to make love to her.

It was close to noon by the time Roxy and Jory rode off toward town. Before she got dressed in a split skirt for riding, Roxy had taken the time to make up the beds and straighten the parlor. She would not lay herself open to any criticism from Tanner. He would find everything neat and in order.

The sun shone hot on her thighs as she and Jory rode along, but the breeze off the river was cool. She thought of Denver where the breeze, if any, would be blistering hot. At the moment she felt as resentful as Jory, leaving the ranch to spend a couple of days in town. Besides the heat, she found little peace there.

The moment she walked through the saloon door the dancers would pounce on her, each one complaining about something. Then there would be a backlog of five days' worth of book work to do. And before she could draw a deep breath, she would have to get all dressed up and come back downstairs to smile and chat with the customers. Zack's pounding on the piano would be loud, and the laughter from men and women's throats would be louder. It would all throb in her head until she would want to clap her hands over her ears.

You might as well accept it, she told herself as they rode into town. *It's either the Lady Chance or some other way to earn a living.*

But what other kind of work could she find? Roxy pondered the question as she and Jory turned the horses over to a livery hand. All she knew how to do was run a saloon and see to the running of a house. As for being a housekeeper, that was a laugh. She couldn't cook and she had never scrubbed a floor or washed clothes. By the time she walked into the saloon, she was feeling pretty worthless.

As Roxy had expected, the dancers were sitting at a table, waiting for her. It took at least twenty minutes to hear their grievances, to pacify them, then settle an argument between the two who were always at odds with each other.

When the last one had disappeared upstairs, she looked across the room where Ace leaned against the bar, grinning at her. "You could settle some of their disputes, their whining, their complaints," she said heatedly, walking up to her cousin. "I don't know why it all has to wait until I get here."

"They know better than to come to me with their silliness. They know that I would tell them to straighten out or go look for another job." Ace dismissed the dancers and gave Roxy a close, sharp look. "You don't look so hot, Cousin. What put those dark shadows under your eyes?"

257

"The ride out here, I guess," Roxy said evasively. "It's a very hot day."

"You're sure that's all? You haven't been having trouble with Graylord, have you?"

"Trouble?" Roxy shrugged. "My only trouble with him is having to see him occasionally."

"Same old pleasant fellow, I take it," Ace said, tongue in cheek.

Roxy grinned at his sarcastic discription of Tanner, then said, "I'm going across the alley to say hello to Belle before I get started on the books." She started to walk away, then turned back and asked, "How are things between you and Michelle?"

"Better. I'm hopeful, but I'm getting tired of her holding me at arm's length. I'm going to pin her down tonight. She either lets me into her house and into her bed or I'm going to stop chasing her. I can't live like a monk much longer."

Roxy frowned and gave her handsome cousin a sharp look. "I guess I was mistaken, thinking you had fallen in love with Michelle. It turns out your big interest is bedding her."

"That's not true," Ace denied heatedly. "I have fallen in love with Michelle, and the natural conclusion of that is making love to her. When I sleep with one of the dancers, that is lust, simply to appease the body. My heart has nothing to do with it."

"Hah!" Roxy snorted. "I'll see what Belle has to say about that. She'd know the difference between love and lust if anyone does."

"Go ahead and ask her. She'll tell you the same thing." Ace caught Roxy's chin and turned her head so he could look into her eyes. "Why such a strong reaction, Roxy? Are you trying to figure out if Graylord felt love when he made love to you?"

"Of course not." Roxy jerked her head away. "Later events told me clearly what he was feeling. Lust, lust, lust."

"I think you're wrong, honey," Ace began gently, but the rest of his words died on his lips. Roxy was walking away from him. He shook his head sadly as she went through the side door that would take her to Belle's house.

Belle was picking a bouquet from her flower garden when Roxy opened the gate and stepped inside. She lifted her perspiring face and it broke into a wide smile when she saw who her visitor was. A small frown creased her forehead though when Roxy came closer.

"You don't look at all well, honey," Belle said after kissing Roxy on the cheek. "Your face is all flushed and you have shadows under your eyes. Have you been ailing?"

"I'm fine, Belle. I didn't sleep well last night, and just had a heated debate with Ace."

"Come on inside," Belle said, picking up the basket that held the flowers she had cut. "We'll have a bottle of sarsaparilla while you tell me all about it."

The big house was cool and smelled faintly of the roses sitting in a pretty vase on the table. As Roxy sat down, Belle tossed her wide-brimmed straw hat on a chair and plunged the flowers into a pail of water. "I'll arrange them in vases later," she said, smiling at Roxy.

When the madam had washed her hands and placed two opened bottles of a soft drink on the pink flowered tablecloth, she sat down opposite Roxy and said, "What's bothering you, honey?"

"It may sound silly to you, but Ace and I were

arguing about the difference between love and lust. He said they were the same thing if you loved the person you were with. I said if you loved someone, lust didn't enter into it. Which of us is right?"

"Well"—Belle picked up a rose petal that had fallen to the table and rubbed it between her fingers—"I hate taking sides, but I think Ace is right."

When Roxy looked at her in disbelief, Belle continued. "I loved once, Roxy, and the man loved me back. We went to bed with love in our hearts, but before the night was over, pure lust for each other crept into bed with us. So you see, there are two kinds of lust. Love lust and plain old horny lust." She looked at Roxy, who sat staring down at her clasped hands. "Did I help clear anything up for you?"

"Yes, you did." Roxy blinked her eyes, leaving a few teardrops on her lashes. "A lot of things are clear to me now."

"Now look here, Roxy." Belle leaned forward and said impatiently, "If you're thinking that Tanner didn't love you when you made love, you're a foolish young woman. I know that man loved you. He was crazy about you. Why he went away, I don't know, but it wouldn't surprise me if he still loves you."

There was sadness and anger in Roxy's voice when she looked at Belle and asked, "You know that Tanner has asked Julia to marry him?"

"Yes," Belle answered reluctantly.

"Then I would say that he loves her, wouldn't you?"

"I guess it looks that way."

"Answer me this then, was it love or was it lust when he made love to me last night?"

Belle stared at Roxy in dismay, struggling to speak.

"You don't have an answer, do you, Belle?" Roxy stood up and walked toward the door.

When she was about to step outside, Belle roused herself to call out, "Roxy, honey, be careful. He'll get you with child again."

Chapter Twenty-five

Roxy rode several lengths behind Jory. Her son was eager to get back to the ranch. She was not. A dread of seeing Tanner again hung over her head like a throbbing toothache. She wished she hadn't given in to Jory's tears.

All the time she'd worked at bringing the books up to date, going for the usual Saturday ride with Christy, talking and smiling at people, in the back of her mind was a persistent question: how was she going to make herself go on living under the same roof with Tanner? After her discussion with Ace and Belle about lust and love, she knew now that Tanner didn't even have respect for her. It was Julia he respected and it was Julia he would marry.

But how long before the marriage? she wondered. She wished it would happen this week. Jory wouldn't want to stay on at the ranch when Julia moved in. Like it or not, he'd have to move back to town.

Roxy silently cursed herself for ever taking the job as housekeeper for Tanner. If she hadn't, she wouldn't have discovered that she still loved the no-good wolf; she wouldn't have made a fool of herself by making love with him.

It was twilight when the light from the cook house appeared in the distance. Roxy could make out the dim figures of the cowhands trailing into the building. Good, we're in time for supper, she thought. She had forgone the evening meal back in town. Ace had gone on and on about how he had finally broken Michelle down and when he finally finished there wasn't time to eat.

"Ma," Jory called, "I'm going to ride on ahead." She nodded and he sent his little pinto racing toward the barn.

"Huh," Roxy grumbled. "He can't wait to see that long-legged idol of his, silly child."

Tanner sat on the porch, hidden in the evening gloom. He had been there just before the sun started going down, his eyes glued to the narrow, dusty road leading from town.

A frown was beginning to form on his forehead. Roxy and Jory should have been home by now. It was nearly dark. Critters would start roaming around before long.

But what if she wasn't coming back? Maybe she had changed her mind after spending a weekend with the gambler. After the way he had spoken to her, he couldn't blame her if she didn't return.

Tanner stood up and moved from behind the climbing morning glory vine that reached to the top of the porch roof. If she and the boy didn't show up soon, he would wait until all the men were in the cook house, then he was going to ride into town and find out why she had broken her word to Jory.

He moved to the end of the porch and watched as the door closed behind the last cowhand. He started down the steps, then paused, peering through the darkening twilight. A lone rider was galloping his horse up the road. Peering, he made out a small figure in the saddle. Jory. Where was Roxy? Had the boy run away?

He saw Roxy then, riding the mare at a walk. He jumped off the porch and faded into the darkness at the side of the house. He didn't want her to catch him waiting for her like some anxious teenager.

When Roxy entered the house, she found that with the exception of Tanner's room, the house was exactly as she had left it. She had only to do a little dusting tomorrow.

Tanner's room, however, would need a thorough going over. Lying on the floor where he had discarded them were shirts, Levi's, underwear and socks. A dusty pair of boots lay on the floor, one beside the bed, the other a few feet away as though he had tossed it there. As for the bed, she could only shake her head. It was plain he hadn't even made an effort to smooth the covers. They were in a tangled wad in the middle of the bed. Had he purposely let his room get into that condition? she wondered as she stepped out onto the porch and called to Jory to come wash his hands before supper.

Jory came tearing up the gravel path, all smiles. "I just washed up with Tanner in the bunkhouse," he explained, then added, "Boy, it's good to be back."

"I'm glad you think so," Roxy muttered to herself and went back inside to freshen up.

The men were gone and Roxy was sitting at one end of the long table when Tanner and Jory walked into the cook house. Jory sat down opposite her as usual, and when Tanner took his place at the head of the table, he gave her a quick glance and a slight nod of his head in greeting. She didn't acknowledge him, only silently helped herself from the platter of fried chicken.

"Did you see Sonny while we were gone?" Jory asked as he helped himself to mashed potatoes.

"No, he wasn't around," Tanner answered. "Busy helping his mother, I expect."

"I can't wait to go to the farm tomorrow," Jory said, biting into a crispy fried chicken leg.

"How'd you find things in town, Roxy?" Pee Wee asked as he poured coffee, then sat down beside her.

Roxy was about to say that it was hot and dusty and that she couldn't wait to get back to the ranch, when from the corner of her eye she saw that Tanner was waiting for her answer.

"Everything was fine, as usual," she lied. "The saloon is busy as ever. I visited with friends, took a ride with Christy, and"—she dimpled at him as she lied again—"I bought a new dress and bonnet. I had a really good weekend."

She shot Tanner another quick glance and rejoiced inside at the sour look on his face. He didn't like the idea that she had enjoyed herself away from his precious ranch.

"I've been thinkin' about goin' to the Lady Chance to sit in on a poker game at that Ace's table," Pee Wee said. "I've heard tell that a man always gets a fair deal with him. It's said that he's never been known to cheat a man."

"No, nor will you ever hear that he has," Roxy said proudly. "Ace is an honest dealer."

"I wonder why it is he most always wins," Tanner said gruffly.

"He wins because he's good at cards," Roxy said, quick to defend her cousin. "He keeps his mind on the game and reads faces and mannerisms. He can tell when a man is bluffing and when one is holding a good hand."

"I've been trying to get him to teach me how to play poker," Jory put in, "but he always says no, that he doesn't want me to grow up to be a gambler. He says he wants better things for me. I told Uncle Ace yesterday that I wanted to be a cowboy."

"I can imagine what he said to that," Tanner said, a sneering tone in his voice.

"He said that would be an honorable job, but that a fellow never got rich punching cows. He said I should work at being a rancher. He said there was big money in cattle if a man worked hard at raising them. So I expect I'll do that." He smiled at Tanner. "I'll be rich, just like you."

There was soft laughter from the adults, then Pee Wee said, "Your uncle is right, boy, and Tanner can teach you the ropes." The cook looked at Tanner for confirmation.

Tanner's answer was a grunt. He pushed away from the table and stalked outside. Jory scrambled out of his chair and hurried after him.

"That boy sure does admire the boss." Pee Wee grinned. "And I think the feelin' is mutual. Tanner always seems lost on the weekends without him at his heels, talkin' a hundred miles a minute."

"My son is going to miss him when Tanner brings his bride here," Roxy said, bringing a cup of coffee to her lips.

"You know, Roxy, it seems to me that Tanner and Miss Bradford have a strange relationship. Iffen I was engaged to a woman, I would want to be with her all the time. Tanner hardly ever sees Miss Bradford."

"Did he see her over the weekend?"

Pee Wee shook his head in the negative. "He didn't leave the ranch at all, and she didn't come here."

When Roxy went outside to call Jory in, she was pondering the relationship between Tanner and the woman he had asked to marry him. Perhaps, she thought, when two people really loved each other, and hot desire didn't enter into it, they didn't have to see each other so often. Still, that didn't seem logical to her.

When Jory came running up from the barn, she told herself that she was weary of thinking about Tanner and Miss Bradford.

When Roxy awakened in the early morning several weeks later, she had a nagging headache. August had arrived, hot and close, and she couldn't remember the heat ever affecting her the way it had recently. She was edgy, quick-tempered, even impatient with Jory. She knew he was confused by her mood swings but she couldn't seem to help herself.

Tanner stayed out of her way, sending her puzzled looks. She was thankful for that. At least he wasn't making snide remarks every time she turned around.

She even picked on poor Pee Wee. One afternoon she had complained that the steaks he was preparing for supper smelled spoiled. Even though he vehemently denied that there was anything wrong with the meat, she still thought she had been right. The odor of frying meat made her stomach feel uneasy.

With a tired sigh, Roxy sat up and swung her feet to the floor. She didn't look forward to the long, hot day ahead, but she had to get through it. If only it would rain and cool off the air.

It was a little after ten when Jory came storming into the house. I hope nobody saw him, Roxy thought, a little alarmed. He looks exactly like Tanner when he's in a rage.

"What's wrong, honey?" She motioned him to sit down beside her.

"It's that Bradford woman," he said, flinging himself down on the sofa. "Me and Tanner were grooming our horses when she rode up. I don't think he was glad to see her, but"—Jory paused a second and there was a catch in his voice when he continued—"when she told me to go away, he didn't tell me not to."

"Jory," Roxy said gently, "you must accept the fact that Tanner is going to marry Miss Bradford. Also, when they do wed, she will be coming here to live."

Jory swallowed hard, then said, "I wouldn't want to live here then. I hate her."

"That's a harsh word, honey."

"I don't care. It's true."

"Maybe it won't happen for a while," Roxy suggested, trying to console him. "We'll deal with it when we have to."

268

"It will happen soon, Ma. I know it will." Jory's voice rose in a loud wail.

"Hush now." Roxy leaned forward to sit on the edge of her seat. "I see her coming toward the house. Do you want to slip out the front door?"

The words were barely out of Roxy's mouth before Jory was gone, slamming the door behind him. She stood up and was smoothing her hair when Julia walked into the kitchen without knocking.

"Roxy," she called in her sharp voice, "where are you? I'd like to speak to you a minute."

"I'm in the parlor," Roxy called back.

"Won't you sit down," Roxy invited when Julia swept into the room.

"No, thank you. I haven't got time. Anyway, it's not a social call. I just want to tell you something that Tanner hasn't got the nerve to tell you."

"And what is that?"

"He wants you and your . . . boy out of here."

"Why doesn't he tell me himself?"

"He doesn't want to hurt the boy's feelings. For some reason, he has tender feelings for him," Julia said with a curl of her lips.

"I see. And when does he want us out of here?" Roxy fought to control the painful lurching of her heart.

"He's going to Utah at the end of the week to buy a new breed of cattle. I imagine he would like for you to be gone by the time he returns."

"We'll be gone," Roxy said. Then, walking to the front door and holding it open, she dismissed the other woman with a cool, "Thank you for being Tanner's messenger."

Julia's face grew fiery red. With her chin in the

269

air, she stamped past Roxy without a word of goodbye.

Roxy slammed the door behind her, then sank weakly onto the sofa. "I should have seen this coming." Her hands gripped each other. Tanner's attitude toward her had grown steadily colder. Looking back, she realized he had begun ignoring her after the night they had spent in bed together.

It came to Roxy in a blinding flash that he had made love to her to prove that he could have her anytime he wanted to. And that done, he now wanted to be rid of her. And what more insulting way to do it than by sending haughty Julia to tell her it was time she moved on!

She stood up and began pacing the floor, thinking how she dreaded telling Jory that they must leave the ranch for good at the end of the week. He wouldn't understand why, because Tanner wasn't married yet, and would ask a dozen questions. He wouldn't understand her answers if she told him the truth.

Dizzy with all that was rushing through her mind, Roxy started to sit down. The next thing she knew, she lay stretched out on the sofa with someone rubbing her wrists and calling her name. She opened her heavy lids and stared blankly at the woman who did the washing for her.

"What happened to me, Martha?" she asked, trying to sit up. "Why am I lying here?"

"You fainted, Roxy," the big farm woman answered. "Lie still now and rest."

"But I have never fainted in my life," Roxy protested. "It has to do with Pee Wee's spoiled steaks. I probably have some kind of food poisoning."

"Has your stomach been bothering you lately?"

"A little, off and on. Especially when Pee Wee is frying something."

Martha, the mother of four sons, hesitated before asking gently, "Is it possible, Roxy, that you are in a family way?"

Roxy started to deny such a possibility, then tried to recall her last menses. She realized with a sickening lurch of her stomach that she hadn't had her woman's time since she and Tanner made love. Belle's warning had come too late. Even as the madam's words were spoken, Tanner's seed was growing in her body.

With firm determination Roxy fought back the hopeless, bitter tears that fought to wash down her cheeks. Tanner mustn't learn of her pregnancy until it could no longer be hidden. He must never suspect that the child she carried was his. Let him think that Ace had fathered it.

She looked up at Martha and with a smile shook her head. "I'm not expecting, but I'm going to tell Pee Wee to throw away that beef he has in the cellar room."

"That's a good idea, and I think you should take a physic; purge your stomach of any poison that may still be in it."

"I intend to. I'll just lie here a minute longer before I take something."

Martha went out to start the washing and Roxy was left alone with the latest dilemma she found herself in. She asked herself if she could bear to face the women of Denver, expecting again, and still with no husband. Would Christy still be her staunch friend? Roxy Bartel was no longer a teenager, a young girl who had made a mistake. She was a grown woman now, and had no excuse for bringing another fatherless child into the world.

271

How would Ace take it? she wondered. Would he be her bulwark of strength a second time or would he turn his back on her for being so foolish?

A long sigh escaped her. The only one she could depend on was Belle.

When her brain could take no more, Roxy sought oblivion in sleep. When she awakened, dusk was setting in and she could hear the ranch hands talking as they stood around outside the cook house waiting to be called for supper. She rose, washed her face, exchanged her rumpled dress for a fresh one and brushed her hair. She walked out onto the porch and sat in one of the rockers until it was time for her to join Jory and Tanner for supper. It was the last meal she would ever eat here.

Chapter Twenty-six

Roxy sat up in bed, groggy eyed but alert. Today she would leave the ranch for good. That thought had been on her mind when she went to bed last night, and consequently she had tossed and turned most of the eight hours.

But out of her restlessness had come an unexpected decision. She'd had a splinter of a dream. A dream of old Elisha Roundtree, the man she had grubstaked. His words still seemed to ring in her ears:

"Come to Cripple Creek and have a look at our diggings."

And that was where she and Jory would go to wait out the birth of her baby. The excitement of panning for gold would help ease Jory's pain at leaving Tanner and the ranch.

As Roxy got dressed for the day in a split riding

skirt and shirt, she saw Tanner and Jory pass the kitchen window on their way to breakfast. She had told Jory last night that they would be spending some time in town while Tanner was gone. She would tell him later that they wouldn't be coming back. She didn't want him crying in front of Tanner.

Roxy waited until Jory and Tanner left the cook house, then set about gathering up her and Jory's clothes.

By the time she had everything packed, she could tell by the noise down at the barn that Tanner and his three chosen men were ready to start the trek to Utah. She heard Jory calling goodbye and thought, *Another chapter of my life is ending. Pray God the next one will be better.* She couldn't see how it would be, though.

Roxy's body gave a startled jerk when the kitchen door opened and the jingle of spurs came toward her. She straightened up from strapping shut one of the bags and looked at Tanner standing in the doorway, Jory beside him.

"Tanner came to say goodbye, Ma." Jory beamed at her.

Roxy shifted her eyes to Tanner and waited for him to speak.

He held her gaze for a moment, his face unreadable. He looked away then, but quickly sought her eyes again. He shifted his feet, wet his lips, then said quite pleasantly, if a little hesitantly, "Jory tells me that the two of you will be staying in town while I'm gone."

So, she thought, the coward is going to play along with that story. For two cents she would come right out and tell Jory the truth, that they wouldn't ever be coming back. That Tanner wanted it that way.

But she knew that she wouldn't when she looked at her son and saw how happy he was in his ignorance.

Her only answer was a cool look before she bent to fasten the last bag. What she would have liked to do was fly at Tanner and scratch his face bloody.

When Roxy went about carrying the bags to the door and setting them on the floor to be loaded on their horses later, ignoring Tanner all the while, he watched her a moment, then said gruffly, "I guess I'd better get going. The men are waiting for me."

Jory gave his mother a reproachful look and followed his hero out the door.

With his men riding behind him, Tanner cut across country, his face reflecting his disappointment. He had hoped to get a kinder reception from Roxy, not the look of an icy blizzard blowing across the range. She seemed colder and more remote than she ever had before.

"Why in hell should I care what her attitude is?" he burst out, muttering. She had played him false eight years before. Why should she be any different now?

For a while he had hoped that because she let him make love to her, she still had some feelings for him. But the way he'd acted afterwards had probably killed any soft feelings she might have had for him. He didn't know what had gotten into him. He just couldn't let the past alone. He kept feeding his wounds with bitterness and bile, keeping them alive. They would never die as long as he

275

kept nourishing them. He would never find any peace until he let go of the past.

When Tanner and his men disappeared over a knoll, Roxy smiled at Jory and said, "Let's get going. I'd like to reach town before it gets hot." When he dragged his heels, Roxy snapped, "And stop your pouting."

"You could have been friendlier to Tanner. After all, he came to tell you goodbye."

"That was big of him, considering he hasn't said a dozen words to me the past few days."

When the stable hand began saddling the mare and pinto, Jory asked, "Why don't you like Tanner, Ma? He's awfully nice."

"He's nice to you, but—"

Their conversation was interrupted when Rock walked up to them, a large box in his hands. He rested it on the top rail of the corral and said, "Jory tells me you'll be spending time in town while Tanner is gone."

Roxy nodded, then asked, "What have you got in the box?"

"Well"—Rock looked a little embarrassed—"when Tanner first came home, mad at the world, and you, he told the cleaning woman to throw away all the things you had put there to pretty up the place. I got to thinking that he might want them back someday, so I put them in this box. I'm sure he would like for you to put them in his new house now. Seeing as how you are friendly with each other again."

Roxy sensed that Jory was watching her, listening for what she would say. So instead of saying what she would like to—"Throw them away"— she said, "I haven't got time to take care of them now. Why don't you put them on the porch for the time being?"

Evidently her answer had pleased Jory, for as they rode toward town he was once again his usual cheerful, talkative self.

It was just the opposite with Roxy, however. She answered his chatter in monosyllables or not at all. She was thinking with dread of facing Ace and telling him she had acted a fool again. She didn't want to see his face when she told him she was expecting again and that she was moving to Cripple Creek. He would probably be glad about the latter. He would be so disgusted with her he wouldn't care where she went, or what she did. He would be glad to see the back of her.

Roxy's nerves were at the breaking point when Denver came in sight. She and Jory had just dismounted at the livery when Zack appeared from one of the stalls, leading his saddled horse. She remembered that the piano player went for a ride every day.

His eyes lit up when he saw them, and looping the reins over a post, he walked over to them, a wide smile on his face. "I didn't expect to see you back so early in the week."

"We'll be here until Tanner returns from Utah," Jory answered as he untied the two bags on his pinto.

"That's great," Zack said and loosened the bags on the mare. As they walked toward the Lady Chance, he said, "Will you go to the town picnic with me this Sunday, Roxy?"

Roxy knew it would be cruel of her to let Zack feel that there was a future for him with her. She would not string him along as Tanner had her. So she shook her head and said gently, "I don't think that would be a good idea, Zack. People might start getting the wrong idea about us if we're seen together too often."

"Would it be a wrong idea, Roxy?"

"Yes, Zack, I'm sorry, but it would. I could never be more than a friend to you. You see, I love someone else."

Zack was silent a moment, then he said, "Ace is not worthy of you, Roxy. Since you've been out at Graylord's ranch, he's been chasing Michelle something shameful."

"I know"—Roxy made herself look sad—"but we can't help whom we love."

"Ma," Jory called from the saloon porch, "aren't you coming?"

"I'm sorry, Zack," Roxy said gently again and walked away from him.

She found Ace in the kitchen, eating lunch. He gave her a surprised smile and said, "You're in town early. Have some shopping to do?"

"No. My job as housekeeper is over."

"Oh?" Ace raised an eyebrow. "I take it you've had enough of Graylord's arrogance."

"Something like that. When you've finished eating, I'd like to talk to you in your rooms."

"Sounds serious." Ace pushed away from the table. "Let's go."

Roxy led the way into her cousin's neat quarters and with a sigh sat down on the brown leather couch. How she dreaded the next few minutes.

"All right," Ace said, sitting down beside her. "Out with it. Did you have a big row with Graylord?"

"No, worse than that," Roxy answered in a small voice.

"What can be worse than that?" Ace's brows

drew together. "He didn't strike you, did he?"

"Oh, no." Roxy shook her head. Then, with her hands clasped in her lap, she looked away from her cousin and said in a voice so low he could barely hear her, "I went to bed with him."

"What!" Ace leaned forward and stared at her in disbelief. "Are you crazy? Why in the hell did you do that?"

"I couldn't help myself," Roxy wailed and broke into a fit of crying.

Ace put his arms around her shaking shoulders. "I'm sorry I yelled at you. Don't cry, little cousin." He pulled her to him. "No harm done. Just don't let it happen again. Come on, dry your eyes." He pushed a handkerchief into her hand.

"But there has been harm done," Roxy sobbed into the square piece of linen.

Ace's body stiffened. "I hope you're not hinting at what I think you are."

Roxy's wail rose higher.

"You little fool. I could slap you silly. When are you going to learn not to trust that man?" Ace jumped to his feet and began to pace the floor.

Roxy's answer was to cry harder.

After a while Ace sat back down and pulled her into his arms again. "Stop crying now," he said softly. "Tears aren't going to solve anything. You're going to have another baby, so make up your mind that once again you'll be the talk of Denver."

"Not this time, Ace." Roxy drew away from him and dried her eyes. "I'm taking Jory and moving to Cripple Creek."

"Cripple Creek?" Ace almost shouted the words. "Where did that harebrained idea come from? That's no more than a rough mining camp."

"I know that. I've got a half interest in a claim there. It's the ideal place for me to have my baby."

"What do you mean, you have a half interest in a claim there? How could that be?"

"I grubstaked Elisha Roundtree and he insisted that I have half his claim."

"Old man Roundtree," Ace snorted. "That old windbag is always about to strike it rich, to hear him tell it."

"Well, I have faith in the old fellow. He may never become wealthy, but I have a feeling he'll get lucky and find enough gold to take care of himself in his old age."

"Old age, hell. He must be a hundred already."

"I don't care how old he is. He's going to be my haven until next spring."

"Roxy, you haven't thought this thing through. The logical thing to do is to tell Graylord that you are expecting his child, and demand that he marry you."

Roxy gave a bitter little laugh. "As if he would believe that he's the father. He'd think the baby was yours, just like he thinks Jory is yours. So you see, he would laugh at me if I demanded he marry me. Besides, you seem to forget that he's going to marry Julia Bradford."

"He has no right to marry any woman except the one who is carrying his child. I'm going to ride out there and give him a few home truths. If he dares to laugh at me, I'll knock it back in his throat. I've been wanting to smash his handsome face for a long time."

"He's not there," Roxy said. "He's on his way to Utah to buy some special cattle. I don't know when he'll be back."

"I'll just wait him out, then."

"No, you won't. I'd rather die than force him to marry me."

"Let's be reasonable about this, Roxy. You don't even know where Cripple Creek is."

"Yes, I do. It's about a hundred miles from Denver. Elisha drew me a map. It shows how to get there and where his claim is."

"Have you considered that you'd have to camp out for close to a week? You've never done that in your life, and to try it with a child is crazy. What would you do if you ran into a bear, a pack of hungry wolves, or God forbid, some renegade Indians?"

Roxy hesitated briefly, then with a crooked smile said, "I was hoping that you would take us."

"Forget that," Ace said brusquely. "I'm not taking you to a place where you'll freeze to death when winter sets in."

"Then don't." Roxy stood up and rushed to the door. "We'll go by ourselves."

"What does Jory think about going to live in a rough mining camp for seven or eight months?" Ace called after her. When she didn't answer, he asked, "He doesn't know anything about it, does he? He'll not want to leave Tanner, you know."

"Sooner or later he's going to have to face the fact that eventually Tanner will have no part in his life. Miss Julia will see to that, so he might as well get used to it now."

Before Ace could argue further, Roxy was out the door and slamming it behind her.

But as she climbed the stairs to her room, there was a little feeling of hope in her heart. Ace was weakening. He would take her to Cripple Creek.

Chapter Twenty-seven

Roxy felt a little less desperate than before as she changed from her dusty riding habit into a cool blue sprigged muslin. Ace hadn't said so, but she felt sure he would ride with her and Jory to Cripple Creek. She had counted on his not wanting her to make the trip alone.

As she brushed her hair, preparing to visit Belle, she worried some about what Jory's reaction would be to spending several months in a mining camp. It could go one of three ways: he might like the excitement of panning for gold; he might miss playing with Sonny; or he might resent her for taking him away from Tanner.

She laid the brush down and tied her long hair back with a blue satin ribbon. It had to be done, she told herself, and her son would just have to accept the move.

Her mind made up, Roxy hurried down the stairs. At the bottom step she gave a start and stopped short. Standing at the bar, talking to Ace, was old man Roundtree. What was he doing here so soon since his last visit? Had he struck it rich? Or, God forbid, had the gold in his claim died out?

Fearing the worst, she walked toward the two men. "Elisha," she said, clapping Roundtree on the shoulder. "What brings you back to Denver so soon? Did you have a big strike?"

"I wish you was right, girl." Elisha looked at Roxy, his eyes full of failure. "My claim petered out on me. Ain't seen no color in two weeks. Some of the fellers gave up a month ago and moved on. Me and a couple other men stayed on until last week, but the stream didn't show any color."

Roxy slumped against the bar, only vaguely hearing Ace ask, "Where will you go now?" and hearing the old man answer that he figured to go to California.

What was she to do now? she cried inside. Where could she go? The two questions kept running through her mind. Should she sell the Lady Chance? With the realization that she was pregnant, her whole life had turned upside down. She couldn't think straight.

When Roundtree took her hand and said, "I'm awfully sorry, Roxy, that the claim didn't pan out," she forced herself to smile and shake his hand.

"Keep your spirits up, old friend," she said. "You'll hit it one of these days."

"I know I will, and I'll be payin' you back for grubstakin' me."

The old man shook hands with Ace and left them standing at the bar. Roxy gave Ace a defeated look and broke out crying.

283

*   *   *

Tanner was tired and thoughtful as he sat in front of the dying campfire. It was their first night camp on the way to Utah for his special cattle.

He had felt an uneasiness in his mind ever since riding away from the ranch this morning. Something was up with Roxy. She had seemed different somehow. Not that she was ever overfriendly with him, but she was unusually distant when he stopped by to have a last few words with her before leaving. He had got the feeling that she wouldn't be coming back to live at the ranch, and it had grown stronger with every mile he rode. He hadn't liked the way she looked, either. Her face was pale and strained looking, and there were shadows under her eyes. Was the gambler nagging her to come back to him and the saloon? Something had certainly happened that had caused her to go into a deep freeze.

One of the burning pieces of wood slid off the coals, making a sharp cracking sound. Tanner roused from his worrisome thoughts and rising, kicked dirt on the fire until it was out. He removed his boots and gunbelt, but when he stretched out on his bedroll, he kept the Colt within easy reach. The three men he had taken with him had been snoring for over an hour.

The gray of daylight was showing through the aspens when Tanner awoke. As he pulled on his boots and strapped on the Colt, he watched lightning flash across the shallow valley below and heard thunder grumbling in the distance. Good, he thought as he shook his men awake. A good storm would drive away the unbearable heat and cool the air.

While the men yawned and scratched them-

selves, then walked back among the trees to answer nature's call, Tanner built a fire. He put a pot
of coffee to brewing, then with his knife opened
two cans of beans. He emptied them into a battered pan and set them on the fire to heat.

When later they were eating, he spoke of the
decision he had come to before falling asleep the
night before. "Men, I've decided to ride back to
the ranch and send Rock to take you on to Utah.
You can stay here and wait for him or ride on at
a walk so that he can catch up with you."

The men didn't question him. They had learned
a long time ago never to do that.

The men were still lolling around the fire when
he saddled Brave and rode away.

The storm held off for an hour or so, the lightning zigzagging more fiercely across the sky and
the thunder louder and nearer. Shortly there came
the moan of wind, then a pattering of rain. Tanner
took his rolled-up slicker from behind the cantle
and shrugged into it. In moments it shone black
and wet.

As he rode on, the slanting sheets of rain striking the side of his face, Tanner smiled. Already the
heat was disappearing. By late afternoon when he
arrived at the ranch, the air was almost cold. The
storm had broken the back of the heat wave.

The rain had slowed to a drizzle when he rode
up to the barn. He was climbing stiffly from the
saddle when Rock opened one half of the big double doors and stepped outside.

"Hey, Tanner," Rock called, splashing through
the mud and puddles of water, "what brings you
back? You run into trouble?"

"No, I just decided I didn't feel like making the
trip. I'd like you to make it for me, if you don't

mind. If you start early tomorrow morning you can catch up with the men by late afternoon."

Normally, Rock wouldn't have had any reservations about questioning Tanner, but something told him that his young friend's decision not to make the trip had to do with Roxy. Consequently, he wouldn't get the truth from him, so he might as well save his breath.

All he did was nod and say, "You'd better get on up to the house and get out of them wet clothes."

As Tanner hopped up on the porch he saw the box sitting by the door. After he removed his spurs he picked it up and carried it into the parlor and placed it on the floor next to the chair he always sat in.

In his bedroom he hung his soaked hat on a peg and dropped his gunbelt over a bed post. He grimaced as he tugged off his boots, afraid that they were ruined. It took some effort to peel off the wet Levi's, taking his socks with them. His shirt came off next, then his underwear. There was quite a pile of wet clothes on the floor when he went to his chest of drawers and started taking clothing from it. When he had pulled on a pair of dry boots, he walked over to the dresser and looked at his whisker-stubbled face in the mirror. He needed a shave, he thought, then dismissed the idea.

Roxy wasn't here to see him and his men didn't care what he looked like. On his way out of the house he almost walked past the box in the parlor. He picked it up and carried it to the kitchen. He might as well see what was in it before he went to supper.

On opening it, the first things he saw were the two pot holders that Roxy had hung beside the stove in the little house he had built for her.

A softness came over his face and he dug eagerly into the box, much as old Roundtree would do when panning for gold.

All the well-remembered little treasures that Roxy had placed around his first home were there. He spent the next half hour lovingly placing the little knickknacks around the room and hanging pictures and pot holders. When he had finished, there was an expression of satisfaction on his face. Roxy's personal stamp was on his home now.

When he stepped out on the porch, the happy whistle on his lips died. Julia Bradford was in the middle of climbing off her horse. All his pleasure drained away. What was she doing here? As far as she knew, he was well on his way to Utah and would be gone for weeks.

A startled look came over Julia's face. "Why, Tanner, I . . . I thought . . . I thought you had left on your trip," she stammered.

"I changed my mind. I'm not going. Why did you ride out here in this wet weather? Who did you want to see?"

"Well, I thought I'd visit with Roxy." Julia looked away from Tanner, visibly uncomfortable.

Tanner thought it was most unlikely that Julia had come to visit Roxy. The two women didn't like each other at all.

It came to him in a flash why Roxy had been so cold to him yesterday morning. This bitch had said something to Roxy that had upset her. He studied the haughty woman from under his lashes. It was time their farce of an engagement was ended.

Forcing a bright smile to his lips, Tanner said lightly, "Roxy isn't here, but come on in and visit with me for a while."

"Where is she?" Julia lingered at the foot of the steps.

"She and the boy have gone into Denver for a visit."

"Only a visit?" Julia frowned as she took the hand Tanner held down to her. "I thought . . . I understood Roxy to say that they were leaving here permanently."

"Oh, no." Tanner pulled her beside him. "They were only to stay as long as I was away. They'll probably be back tomorrow. I hope so. I miss Jory."

"I don't understand this affection you have for the boy," Julia said crossly. "A person would think he was your son."

"He'll do until you give me a son." Tanner put his arm around Julia's waist and led her inside. When she tried to pull away from him, he tightened his hold and asked softly, "You will give me sons, won't you, Julia? I'd like at least four."

As Julia stared up at him in horror, Tanner pulled her up tight against his body. When she gasped in startled surprise, he lowered his mouth to give her a hard kiss, at the same time raising a hand to cup her breast. He nearly laughed aloud at her fierce struggle to free herself.

He finally released her so that she could breathe and said with pretended hurt, "Don't pull away from me, honey. We'll be much more intimate when I take you to bed on our wedding night. I'm going to strip off all your clothes, then kiss every inch of your body." While Julia stared at him in anger and disgust, he added, "And then I'll expect you to do the same thing to me. Just think what fun we're going to have making those sons for me."

"You loathsome brute!" Julia sprang away from him. "You sicken me with your pawing, you repulsive man!"

"Aw, Julia, honey"—Tanner reached a hand out to her. "Don't say you've changed your mind about marrying me. I promise I'll only bed you three times a week if you'll marry me. That wouldn't be too often, would it?"

"Oh, you vile creature!" Julia's voice shook with anger. "Never, ever would I marry you. There's not enough money in this world to make me do so."

She turned and dashed out of the house as if the devil were breathing down her neck. She scrambled into the saddle and jabbed the horse with her spurs. As the animal lunged away, Tanner roared with laughter. His hunch had been right. The woman couldn't stand to have a man's hands on her.

He stopped laughing on his way to the cook house. He was remembering how she had yelled that there wasn't enough money in the world to make her marry him. That angry outburst could only mean one thing: the banker was pressuring her to marry him. He wondered what the crooked banker had been up to.

Once again, Julia laid her riding crop on the beautiful white stallion. She couldn't get away from that dreadful man fast enough. She shuddered, remembering his hand on her breast.

The horse was heaving by the time it arrived at the big house at the edge of town. Julia slid out of the saddle and half ran into the home that had turned into a prison for her.

As she sped down the great tiled hall, she glimpsed the day's mail on the side table. She was about to walk on past the scattering of magazines and envelopes when she saw that one was addressed to her. Her heart skipped a beat as she recognized the handwriting. Jenny!

She was ripping the white square open as she entered her bedroom and closed the door behind her.

When she unfolded the sheet of paper, several bills of a large denomination slid to her lap. With trembling hands she began to read the letter.

"My darling Julia," the letter began. "I miss you so much and I think it is dreadful of your father not to let you return to New York. If it is a question of money, I have sent you fare for the train or however you can travel from that terrible small town. If you are unable to wire me that you are coming, don't worry. I will wait two weeks, then I will know that you're not coming and I will sail for Europe alone. Please don't disappoint me. Love as ever, Jenny."

"I will not disappoint you, darling Jenny," Julia whispered as she returned the letter and money to the envelope. She strode out of the house then and turned left to walk the two blocks to her father's bank.

As she entered Enos's office a well-dressed rancher was just leaving. His face was grim, and when she looked at her father he wore a sick look. She didn't wonder why his face was pale or care that there was desperation in his eyes. She came straight to the point of her visit.

Bracing her hands on the edge of the desk, and leaning across it, she said coldly, "I will not marry Tanner Graylord under any circumstances. He grossly insulted me today."

"What did he say to you, honey?" Bradford's face had gone whiter.

"It wasn't so much what he said, but he laid his hands on me."

"He hit you? I can't believe that."

"No, he didn't hit me, you old fool. He fondled my breasts."

"Is that so bad? A man—"

"It made me sick," Julia interrupted and straightened up. "You might as well know I'm taking the late morning train to New York."

"But Julia"—Bradford lunged to his feet, reaching a pleading hand toward her—"you know the trouble I'm in. Can't you put up with him a little longer? Just don't rock the boat. I desperately need the money he'll be depositing after the fall trail drive. That man that just left wanted to withdraw a large sum of money. I stalled, but if he and a few other customers demand their money, I'll be ruined."

"I'm sorry, Father, but you got yourself into this fix and you're going to have to get yourself out of it."

With that, Julia wheeled and strode out of the room.

Chapter Twenty-eight

It was late morning when Roxy stepped out of the Lady Chance and sat down in one of the four chairs on the porch.

Ever since she got out of bed this morning she had moved around in dragging despair. She had wracked her brain for a solution to her dilemma and hadn't come up with anything. She was tired of looking at Jory's sullen face and listening to him badgering her to return to the ranch. "I hate it here," he whined. "There's nothing to do here."

I hate it too, Roxy thought as she listlessly watched passengers disembark from the puffing train that had pulled in a few minutes before she walked outside, but I'm not going back there.

A deep sigh escaped her. She couldn't tell Jory that Tanner didn't want them in his home. It would break his heart. But it would also break his heart when she could no longer hide her pregnancy and he heard still worse taunts from his peers. He would lose his respect for her, maybe even grow to hate her.

"What grim thoughts are going through your mind now?" Ace asked, coming from the saloon and taking a chair beside her.

"No thoughts," she lied, "just watching the people get off the train."

"Anybody you know?"

"No. They're mostly men. Salesmen and such."

When the last passenger stepped off the train and went to claim his luggage, those who were waiting to board the long, dusty car surged forward. Ace suddenly sat forward and, squinting his eyes, said in some surprise, "Is that Julia Bradford the conductor is helping onto the little step?"

Roxy sat forward also and peered at the people lined up to board the train. "It's her," she said. "I wonder where she's going."

"Let's hope she's going to New York, and that she stays there." Roxy silently agreed.

There were only six fares and soon the train was chugging out of town.

When its thick, rolling black smoke disappeared around a bend in the rails, Roxy stood up. She would go back inside and work on the books again. She had taken one step when a shot rang out from down the street.

"That sounds like it came from the bank," Ace exclaimed. "Do you suppose it's being held up?" He jumped to his feet and went down the two steps. When Roxy would have followed him, he ordered, "You stay here. There may be stray bullets flying."

Roxy sat back down, and as she watched men

hurrying down the street, she worried where Jory was.

She relaxed a little when no more shots were fired, but she watched to see if any men came running out with guns drawn.

No one came out and the men milled around in the street for several minutes before the tall, thin teller stepped outside. She couldn't hear what he was saying, but she could read the stunned expressions on the waiting people's faces.

A short time later she saw Ace separate himself from the crowd and walk toward the saloon.

"What was the shot about?" she asked, walking to the edge of the porch to meet him.

Ace looked up at her and said in a stunned voice, "Enos Bradford just blew his brains out."

"Oh, dear Lord." Roxy sat down. "Do you suppose he did it because Julia left him?"

"We don't know if she's left for good. It's something deeper than that. It's my guess people are going to start making a run on the bank to draw out their money and there won't be enough to go around."

"Oh my goodness, Ace, what if you are right? Do we have much in there?"

"Not enough to ruin us if we lose it. I haven't made any deposits in three weeks. Thank God."

"But there will be some depositers who will be badly hurt," Roxy said with concern. "Old people who trusted him with their life savings.

"Yes, it's a shame if that happens. Let's hope I am wrong."

But an hour later there was a line of worried-looking people in front of the now locked door. Ace walked down to the big brick building again to see what he could discover. A half hour later he was back, a solemn look on his face.

"The bank ran out of money within fifteen minutes. The sheriff has come, and those poor people still waiting outside will get nothing. The undertaker took Bradford's body out through the back door. The people are so angry and upset, the sheriff was afraid they might attack the banker even though he's dead."

Roxy made no response. She was worrying how hard hit Tanner would be.

Tanner was one of the lucky ones. When Julia had raced away from the ranch he'd felt a warning niggle in his mind. Even though he needn't worry about her chasing him anymore, he still had his suspicions about Enos. He'd bet his life that the old reprobate had financial problems and badly needed a wealthy son-in-law.

He snatched up his hat and hurried to the barn. All hell was going to bust loose when Julia told her father she had broken her engagement and something warned Tanner to draw his money out of the bank before it closed its doors for good.

Tanner kept Brave at a mile-eating pace and arrived at the bank just as Julia went storming into her father's office. When he entered the building he could hear her angry voice and Enos's placating one. He couldn't make out the words, only the tone, but that was enough. Old Enos was getting both barrels from his daughter.

The bank was empty of customers and Tanner went straight to the teller, who stared owlishly at him through the thick lenses of his glasses. The young man looked nervous when Tanner told him he was closing his account and wanted his money.

He sent a worried look toward his boss's office. He started toward it, then paused. The angry shouting going on inside warned him that this wasn't a good time to interrupt his boss.

With his forehead beaded with sweat, he unlocked the heavy safe and spent several minutes counting out Tanner's money. When he carried it over to his cage, Tanner pushed his saddlebag through the small opening and the thick packets of greenbacks were transferred into it.

Tanner said, "Thank you," and turned to leave just as Julia strode out of the office. She didn't even see him in her mad rush to leave the bank. As he rode down the street, he missed seeing Roxy step out onto the porch by about two minutes. He was almost at the edge of town when the train gave a blast of its whistle, signaling that it was pulling out. He had reached the end of the street and was about to head out to the open range when a shot rang out.

He reined Brave in. Should he ride back and see what it was all about? He remembered the large amount of money in his saddlebag and decided the smart thing to do was to get it home as soon as possible. Some of his men would be going into town tonight and they would learn what had happened.

By late afternoon everyone in Denver knew that Enos Bradford had shot himself because he had embezzled close to a million dollars from the people who had entrusted him with their money. Elderly people wept at losing their life savings and ranchers and businessmen swore bitterly at what they had lost. Some said that they were wiped out for good, while others complained that they would have to start all over again. There were very few citizens who hadn't been touched by Bradford's perfidy. Belts would be tightened in the months to come.

There was also talk of how the engagement between Graylord and Julia Bradford had been broken, and how Julia had left town shortly before her father took his life. Was there a connection? people wondered.

Tanner got the news from his friend John Allen. After the evening meal, some of his men were about to ride into town when John arrived.

"Howdy, John," Tanner called from his lounging stance against the corral. "What brings you out here at this hour? Is everything all right with Christy?"

"She's fine. I rode out to ask if you lost any money when the bank closed its doors this morning."

"The bank is closed? You mean for good?"

"Yeah. The sheriff locked it up soon after Bradford shot himself in the head and the bank ran out of money. There was a big run on it when people learned what Bradford had done. Only a handful got their money. What about you? Did you lose much?"

Tanner shook his head, stunned that Bradford had taken his life. "I was in earlier and drew all mine out. What about you? Did you lose much?"

"Are you joshing me?" John laughed. "I didn't have any money in the old bastard's bank. As to that, I haven't got any money anywhere. Well, except for maybe a hundred dollars or so in an old cracked teapot. What made you go in and draw out your money? Did Julia hint that her old man was in trouble?"

Tanner gave a short laugh. "You must be joshin'

me now. That would be the last thing she would do."

Without going into too many details, Tanner told his friend how the banker had instigated the odd courtship between him and Julia. "A blind man could see that her heart wasn't in it, so it didn't take me long to wonder why she was pretending that it was. When the old devil took it upon himself to announce our engagement at a party, I knew he was desperate for us to get married.

"It was pretty obvious he was in financial trouble up to his neck. When Julia rode out here this morning, I decided it was time to end our so-called romance. Neither one of us cared a whit for the other. It was very simple to end it. All I had to do was kiss her and touch her breast. She jerked away from me like a scalded cat, calling me every name in the book. She broke the engagement on the spot. I knew she would tell her father that it was all off between us, so I rode as fast as Brave could take me to draw out all my money."

"I wonder how Julia is taking all of this."

"She probably doesn't know anything about it. She had already boarded the train when Enos put the gun to his head." Tanner was silent a minute, then said, "I wonder if Roxy lost much money."

"I don't know. The gambler was there with the others standing in front of the bank. He didn't look worried." After a moment John asked, "Is Roxy still keeping house for you?"

"I think so. But before my aborted trip to Utah, I believe Julia said something to her that upset her. In any case, she was acting strange the last time I saw her. I guess I'll know Sunday afternoon if she's coming back."

"I've wondered how it was working out with you two living under the same roof. I know there's a lot of resentment on both sides. It just seems very strange to me and Christy. We know how it used to be between you two."

Tanner stared out into the gathering darkness for a while before answering. "We don't say much to each other. The only reason Roxy agreed to take the job was to get Jory out of town. I guess he gets a lot of razzing from the town boys. Especially from one bully."

"That's a shame. He seems like a fine little fellow."

"He is. Smart as a whip, too," Tanner said proudly, causing John to give him a curious look. "Loves ranch life."

"Do you think we'll ever have sons of our own, Tanner?" John asked, yearning in his voice. "Me and Christy have about given up hope of ever having children."

"It looks like my chances of ever having a son are slim, too." Tanner gave a short, barking laugh. "I can't even find a wife."

John Allen was tempted to say, *You only have to look past your stubborn nose to find a mate. The perfect woman for you is living under your roof.* Instead, he changed the subject.

"I don't expect you'll be going to the old bastard's funeral."

"It's no more likely than that I'll be going to the moon." Tanner laughed.

"You and everybody else in town, I expect." John Allen laughed, too. He straightened away from the corral, stretched, then said, "I'd better be getting home. Stop by some day."

"I'll do that," Tanner answered and continued leaning on the horse pen, staring out into the darkness.

After the rain, the air had cooled considerably. When Roxy walked across the alley and passed through Belle's gate, she wore a light shawl over her shoulders.

She had two reasons for visiting her friend. Number one, she wanted to learn if Belle had lost any money in the bank closing, and two, she wanted to discuss with her the fact that Tanner and Julia were no longer engaged. That being the case, perhaps she could continue housekeeping for Tanner.

She hadn't told Belle that she was expecting Tanner's baby. She was too ashamed to tell her how foolish she had been.

Belle was sitting outside enjoying the cool evening as Roxy walked up the flower-bordered path. She gave Roxy her usual warm smile. "Should we sit outside, honey?" She patted the chair next to her. "It's been so long since we've had an evening like this."

"Yes, let's do," Roxy said and sat down. She came straight to the point then. "I've been wondering if you and the girls lost much money when the sheriff put a lock on the bank door."

"More than I'd like," Belle sighed. "I feel sorry for my girls. They work hard for their money," she said wryly. "But they're taking it in pretty good spirits. What about you? Did you lose a lot?"

"I lost a few hundred dollars. Luckily Ace hadn't

made any deposits for the past three weeks. Otherwise we'd have been hurt badly."

"I never did trust that old bastard," Belle said. "He had shifty eyes. Never looked at a person straight on. The girls never liked him either. He always made sure he got his money's worth from them."

"What do you think about Tanner and Julia breaking up?"

"Hah," Belle snorted. "It didn't surprise me at all. That engagement took place for two reasons. Julia was pressured into it by Enos, and Tanner went along with it hoping to make you jealous."

"Make me jealous, that's a laugh! I'm sure he doesn't care what I think about anything."

"Well, you know Tanner would never marry a cold, selfish woman like Julia Bradford."

"He told me that he wanted a lady to be mistress of his big fancy house."

"A lot he knows about ladies if he thinks that one is a lady. She only knows how to be a mean, hateful snob."

The stars were beginning to come out and Roxy gazed up at their twinkling brightness for a while before speaking again. "I hadn't intended to go back to the ranch. Julia told me that Tanner didn't want me there anymore, that he wanted her to tell me so. I don't know if he still feels the same."

"The thing for you to do is to go back there and let him tell you that you're fired. It's my opinion that he didn't tell the bitch any such thing. She was the one who didn't want you there."

"I don't know," Roxy said thoughtfully. "I usually return to the ranch on Sunday. Maybe I'll wait until Monday, see if he comes looking for me."

"I think that's a good idea. You'll know for sure

then whether or not he wants you there."

Roxy said good night shortly after that. She was relieved that she had come to a decision. How it would work out, she had no idea.

Chapter Twenty-nine

Night had fallen and Tanner still sat on in the cook house, idly stirring a spoon in his second cup of coffee.

It was Sunday and Roxy and Jory should have been home hours ago.

When had he started thinking of the ranch as being home for Roxy and her son? he asked himself.

Since the first night she slept under my roof, he realized. *But maybe she doesn't think of it as home. The Lady Chance has been her home almost all her life. And the gambler is there.*

"Shouldn't Roxy and the button have been here by now?" Pee Wee asked as he dried the last pot and took off his apron. "She's always been back before dark."

"I've been thinking that, too." Tanner pushed

away the cup of coffee, which had grown cold. "But her plans had been to stay in town while I was gone to buy new cattle. Maybe she doesn't know that I'm back."

"I think that's unlikely, considering all the talk that's been going on about your breakup with the Bradford woman. She's bound to know that you're home."

"I guess so," Tanner said glumly, remembering Roxy's strange behavior the morning he had ridden out. "I wonder if I should take a ride, look for them. They might have run into trouble. One of the horses might have thrown a shoe."

"If anything had happened to them, the cowhands who rode into town would have come upon them and brought them to the ranch."

That was logical, Tanner admitted to himself. Then he had to come to the conclusion that Roxy wouldn't be arriving at the ranch that night.

But would he see her tomorrow? he wondered, worry shadowing his gray eyes. Had he carried his gruffness and coldness too far? Had she finally gotten fed up with him and decided not to come back?

Tanner knew that was possible, but he still had his suspicion that Julia had said something to Roxy, told her some lie.

"I gotta tell you, boss"—Pee Wee sat down at the table—"me and the men are mighty glad you ain't marryin' that Julia Bradford. We all agree that she's the coldest woman we ever saw. The men made jokes about how she'd never let you get between her bony legs, that you'd have to go to Belle's place if you wanted to wrinkle the sheets."

"They were probably right." A small smile hovered around Tanner's lips. "Julia is not overly fond of men. Fact is, I never had any intention of marrying the woman. Nor did she ever aim to marry me, although she didn't know that I was aware of it. It amused me to lead Enos Bradford on. He was the one who wanted the marriage."

"I'm glad to hear you wasn't foolish enough to want to marry that one. You know," Pee Wee continued, "that Roxy girl would make a fine wife for a feller. She's warm and caring and very beautiful. A man couldn't go wrong, making her his wife. Don't you agree?"

"You forget she's already taken," Tanner replied.

"You mean the gambler. If she'd wanted to marry him, she could have done that a long time ago."

"Don't you think she should have? She would have saved her son being called a bastard."

"It's too bad about the boy, but maybe she doesn't love Ace Brandon. There's nothing worse than being trapped in a loveless marriage."

"What do you know about a loveless marriage?" Tanner grinned as he asked the question. "I didn't know you had ever been married."

"Well, I have. I married me a whore once. It was the worst mistake I ever made. I thought she loved me, but it turned out she only wanted to get out of the business.

"After our wedding night I was lucky if I got to sleep with her once a month. And that was only if I bought her a new dress or fancy hat. The onliest good thing I could say about her, she sure kept a clean house. She wouldn't even let me smoke in it. Said it smelled up her curtains.

"Yeah, that little house I bought her was her

pride and joy. And when she kicked me out, she kept the place."

"Why did you let her get away with that?"

" 'Cause she had took up with the blacksmith there in Trail Town, and he was three times my size and had fists the size of hams. If I'd said a word, he'd have beaten me to a pulp. I've got my divorce papers around here someplace. I heard she married that big brute and that they're living in the house that I paid for."

Pee Wee gave a sad shake of his head. "A man can't be too careful about who he gives his heart to. Some women are straight out of hell. They'll lead you on, then stomp your heart to smithereens."

Tanner knew too well what his cook was talking about. Standing up, he said, "Good night, Pee Wee," and walked out into the night.

Roxy had dithered back and forth all day. What should she do? She had been asking that question since she'd been awakened this morning by the ringing of the church bells summoning the parishioners to Sunday services. One minute she thought she would return to the ranch, and the next, she would not. She would stick to her decision and wait to see if Tanner came looking for her.

Jory hadn't helped any when around five o'clock he began badgering her that it was time they started back to the ranch.

"But our plans were to stay in town for the length of time Tanner would be gone," she had pointed out.

"He turned back, though; he's home. There's no reason for us to stay here," Jory insisted.

Around six o'clock she had stopped seesawing and told Jory firmly that they wouldn't be returning to the ranch today, that there was a chance they might never live there again.

He had thrown a tantrum, jumping up and down, demanding why not. She had answered that it was her business and he'd just have to live with it.

Roxy heaved a deep sigh. He was pouting in his room now, refusing to come down for supper, but she knew she hadn't heard the last from him.

Tanner stepped out of the dim interior of the barn and blinked against the brightness of the morning. He looked up at the sun and noted that it was high noon.

And Roxy hadn't put in an appearance yet.

What should he do? Go after her or wait her out? Those questions had kept him awake half the night.

Tanner started toward the cook house to grab a sandwich when the rattle of wagon wheels turned him around. Bertha Sheldon was handling the reins of the two work horses. Sonny and Sissy sat beside her on the high seat. The farm woman halted the wagon alongside the cook house and jumped to the ground.

"Good afternoon, Tanner," she called, dropping the tailgate and pulling forward bushels of vegetable produce. "A very nice day, isn't it?"

"Yes, it is." Tanner walked up to the wagon and ruffled Sonny's hair as the boy helped his young sister to the ground.

"Where's Jory?" Sonny looked around the yard, searching for his friend.

"He's not here yet, son," Tanner answered, then

at the disappointment that came over young Sheldon's face, he added, "Maybe he'll be here later."

Bertha gave Tanner a curious look, then turned her attention to Pee Wee as the cook stepped outside. "What do you need today, Pee Wee?" she asked, smiling at the little man.

Tanner stood by and watched his cook choose what produce he wanted, then helped him carry it inside. When Pee Wee settled up with Bertha, Tanner invited her to have a cup of coffee with him. "Give your team a rest."

"They'll appreciate that. Ben has been working them hard, planting winter rye and hauling in the corn. Before we know it, winter will be upon us."

"I'm afraid so," Tanner agreed. "We're into the last week of August."

"I dread winter." Bertha shivered. "That awful cold, merciless air hanging over the land. And the long nights when no sound breaks the silence, except for the lonesome yowl of wolves. It near drives me crazy."

"I guess it is hard on a woman," Tanner sympathized. "Penned up in the house for months with few visits from your neighbors."

As Pee Wee poured coffee, Tanner wondered how Roxy would feel about spending a winter at the ranch.

Bertha watched Tanner closely as she asked, "Has Roxy decided that she doesn't like ranch life? Has she gone back to town for good?"

"Not that I'm aware of. I figure something came up at the saloon that kept her in town. I may ride in later to see what's keeping her."

"She didn't look too good when I was here last week. Kinda pale and peaked-like. Maybe she's come down with something."

"I hadn't noticed." Concern leapt into Tanner's eyes.

But how would he know what she looked like when he only gave her fleeting glances, he reproached himself.

"She's a lovely young woman," Bertha said, bringing her cup to her mouth, "and raising Jory all by herself. I admire her a lot."

She set her cup down and continued in her outspoken way, "I was awfully pleased when I heard that you're not marrying that Bradford woman. You two would never have gotten along. She doesn't like children, you know. She never would have given you any sons."

"I suspected that." Tanner smiled, amused, thinking that Bertha and his cook had probably discussed his engagement with Julia. Neither had anything good to say about his supposed intended.

"For a man and woman to have a good marriage, they ought to have several younguns if they're able to." Bertha grinned wryly. "A husband and wife get close to each other when they have to band together to keep their children from taking over the place."

"I never thought about that, but it makes sense."

"That's because you ain't experienced it yet." Bertha drained her coffee and rose to her feet. "I've got to get on home. Ben will be waiting to use the horses. He plans on hauling in some hay from the field so that our livestock can eat this winter." She bustled out the door, calling for her children.

Tanner finished his coffee and, no longer hungry, left the table. He was going to ride into town and see what was up with Roxy. This waiting, not knowing what Roxy had in mind, had to cease.

Roxy had spent the first half of the morning in her office, hiding from Jory. She had just finished her book work when there was a loud knock on the door, followed by "I know you're in there, Ma. Open the door."

She sighed. The little imp had tracked her down. "What is it, Jory?" she asked impatiently, letting him in.

"You know what it is." Jory stared belligerently at her. "I want to go back to the ranch."

"I thought we settled that last night."

"You thought wrong, then. If you don't go with me, I'll go alone."

"Don't talk nonsense, Jory. I would come and get you."

"No, you wouldn't. I know every inch of the ranch and a good part of the mountains. I'll hide somewhere that you'll never find me."

"Oh? And how would you live? What will you eat? Wild berries and roots?"

"Don't worry about that," Jory said, a stubborn tilt to his chin. "I'll get along fine. I've got friends, you know."

Roxy knew he was referring to Sonny. She also knew that the Sheldon boy would sneak food to him. Her big fear was the bears, wolves and mountain lions that roamed the mountains. It was no place for a young boy to be wandering about.

When Jory's face crumpled and he melted into tears, Roxy began to weaken. When he sobbed, "I hate it so here in town, I can hardly bear it," she knew she was lost. She knew what her son was experiencing.

She put her arms around his narrow, shaking shoulders and said quietly, "Stop crying now and go get your clothes together. We'll be leaving in fifteen minutes."

"Oh, thank you, Ma." Jory hugged her around the waist so hard, she grunted. He flew out of the room then, a wide smile on his face even as he knuckled the tears out of his eyes.

Chapter Thirty

Roxy only half listened to Jory's excited chatter as they rode out of town and took the dusty, narrow road to Tanner's ranch.

She felt no excitement, only dread. It was against her better judgment, returning to the ranch. Nothing had changed between her and Tanner. Just because he and Julia were no longer engaged didn't necessarily mean he would want her to continue keeping house for him. It wouldn't surprise her if he told her he no longer needed her services.

At any rate, sooner or later the time would come when she and Jory must return to town and stay there until she could think of someplace for them to go. A place where they could start a new life along with the baby she carried. Roxy was thinking that there must be somewhere they could go when Jory gave a whoop and urged his little pinto into a full gallop. Coming back to the present, she saw Tanner riding toward them.

This is it, she thought, a coldness coming over her. He will either greet us pleasantly, or tell us to turn back.

At least he's happy to see Jory, she thought, watching the smiles on both their faces. And he knows that I'm part of the package.

"Ma," Jory exclaimed as she rode up to them, "Tanner says that Sonny was over at the ranch this morning looking for me. Can I ride to the farm now?"

Roxy directed a cool look at Tanner and thought for a moment she saw a softness in his eyes. But the usual coolness settled over his face so swiftly, she decided that she had imagined that tenderness in his gray eyes.

Tanner touched the brim of his hat and said, "Good morning, Roxy. Ride on in, I have some business to take care of in town." She nodded. Touching his hat brim again, he rode off.

"Can I go see Sonny now, Ma?" Jory broke in on Roxy's confused thoughts.

"Go on," she answered absentmindedly, and added out of habit, "Be careful, and mind Bertha."

As the pinto went racing toward the Sheldon farm, Roxy continued to try to figure out just what had passed between her and Tanner. He had acted as though he was expecting her to return. If so, had Julia lied to her about him wanting her and Jory to leave? It was something his scheming fiancee would do.

What had caused the breakup of their engagement? she wondered. Surely she had had nothing to do with it.

Pee Wee was emptying a basin of dishwater behind the cook house when Roxy rode in. A wide, pleased smile lit up his wrinkled features. "I knew you would come back," he said, grinning up at her.

"Who doubted that I would?" Roxy asked, dismounting.

"For some reason, the boss thought you might not."

"I wonder why he thought that," Roxy muttered sourly. "He must have thought I'd grown tired of his pleasant disposition."

"Yeah," Pee Wee laughed, catching her sarcasm. "The boss doesn't have the best temperament in the world, does he? He's the moodiest man I ever saw. But I reckon you can handle it, huh?"

"Only to a degree, Pee Wee. I have my limit," Roxy answered, and when a stable hand came up and led the mare away, she walked into the house.

The first thing that caught her eye when she entered the kitchen was her pot holders hanging beside the big black stove. When had Tanner hung them there, and why?

She walked on into the parlor and spotted the other little things she had put around the small room in the cabin. A softness came into her eyes as she picked up each little piece and stroked a finger over it before setting it back down. She walked over to where her pictures of western landscapes had been hung, noting that they needed a good dusting.

Those had been such happy days when she had worked at making the cabin pretty and comfortable. She'd had such big plans for the little place that she thought would be her home someday.

With a sigh she walked down the hall to Tanner's room and was surprised to find that everything was neat and tidy; even the bed was made up. Not the way she would have done it, but he had at least made an effort. There were no dirty clothes scattered about as there usually were when she returned from town. There were no boots lying around on the floor.

This gave her something to ponder. Had Tanner kept his room orderly to please her, or because he didn't think she was coming back?

"I understand that Bradford will be buried today," Tanner said as he passed Roxy a platter of bacon and eggs. "I suppose you will be attending the funeral." His crooked grin took away the seriousness of his remark.

"Yes, indeed. I figure we could go there together," Roxy joked back, helping herself to an egg, then passing the platter to Jory. "Do you think anyone will show up to see him laid to rest?"

"I doubt it," Tanner answered as the breakfast fare was returned to him. Then, amusement in his eyes, he said, "Unless maybe that timid teller of his shows up. That poor fellow was so afraid of Bradford he'll probably pay his respects out of fear Bradford might rise out of his coffin to chew him out for not being there."

Roxy smiled at Tanner's wry humor. Then it grew silent at the table as the three of them began to eat the morning meal, each engrossed in his own thoughts. Roxy was thinking that when she and Jory had joined Tanner in the cook house, he had greeted Jory with a wide smile, then said pleasantly enough, "Good morning, Roxy."

For a moment she hadn't responded. She hadn't expected him to look at her, much less speak. If

Norah Hess

only they could continue like this, she thought.

Tanner was thinking that he had made a little headway with Roxy. At least they'd exchanged some light conversation. He hadn't felt so hopeful of mending things between them for a long time. He was going to do everything in his power to make it so.

And Jory was planning what he and Sonny would do today.

Breakfast had been eaten and Pee Wee was pouring coffee when Sonny came walking down the path he and Jory had made as they went back and forth between the ranch and farm. He carried a fishing pole in one hand and a can of bait in the other.

"May I be excused, Ma?" Jory asked eagerly. "Me and Sonny are going fishing."

"Oh but, Jory . . ." Roxy began, a frown gathering between her eyes.

"He'll be all right," Tanner said, cutting her off. "Jory can swim like a fish, if you're afraid he'll fall into the river."

Anger sparked in Roxy's eyes, and she gave him a cold, reproachful look as though to say, *Don't interfere with how I raise my son.*

The hardness came back into Tanner's eyes and he snapped, "If you had your way, the boy will still be tied to your apron strings when he's thirty years old." He picked his hat off the floor, slapped it on his head and strode toward the door, his spurs jangling angrily.

Roxy sighed and said wearily, "Go along, Jory. Just be careful."

When the screen door slammed the second time, Pee Wee came and sat down beside Roxy. "Don't be too hard on the boss," he said. "He

316

doesn't take into consideration that there hasn't been a man around to guide you a great deal in how to raise a young boy. You've had it all on your shoulders and you've been like a mother hen with one chick. Always clucking around, afraid some thing will happen to him."

"Maybe you're right, Pee Wee," Roxy reluctantly agreed. "But I live in dread of something happening to Jory."

"He'll not run into any more danger here on the ranch than he would in town. He could be run down by some drunken cowboy racing down the street. Here at the ranch, Tanner has taught him what dangers to be on the lookout for and what to stay away from. The kid knows he's never to go farther away than a mile from the ranch. Tanner would like to get him a rifle, teach him how to shoot it, for added protection." He grinned at Roxy, "But he knows you would never allow it."

"I should say I wouldn't." Roxy looked appalled at the idea.

"There you go. If Jory had a father, you wouldn't have much to say about it."

"The hell I wouldn't." Roxy lunged to her feet and slammed out of the cook house. Pee Wee grinned after her, shaking his head.

As Tanner cantered the stallion down the river road, he had no destination in mind. He only knew that he had to get away from Roxy before they got into a royal battle over Jory. A battle he would lose, because he had no right to interfere with how she was raising her son. And the last thing he wanted to do was to exchange harsh words with her.

She had softened a little toward him this morning, and he, dumb bastard that he was, had ruined it by sticking his nose in where it didn't belong. She would be freezing him with her cold looks again.

Tanner was startled a moment when he realized that a short distance up ahead lay Denver. Brave had taken the path there on his own. As he rode on, he saw to his right the cemetery. A hearse was pulled up to a freshly dug grave, and Bradford's very plain coffin was being carried from it. As he and Roxy had joked, only the lone figure of the timid teller stood to one side, watching his boss being lowered into the ground.

"I wonder what God will have to say to you, Bradford?" Tanner said as he rode on into town, and on to the Red Dog.

Roxy had spent an hour dusting furniture and had just finished the last piece in the parlor when she saw through the window her friend Christy Allen riding up to the house.

She looks awfully happy about something, she thought, stepping out onto the porch.

"Hey, Christy," she called as her young neighbor climbed out of the saddle and threw the reins over the hitching post. "This is a pleasant surprise. Come on in."

"It's such a glorious day I felt like taking a ride. Am I interrupting you at anything?"

"Not at all. I just finished polishing the furniture and was wondering what to do with the rest of the day."

"Tanner's home is so beautiful, but don't you get bored with ranch life sometimes?" Christy asked as she settled herself into a comfortable chair.

"No, not at all. If I find time hanging on my

hands I take long rides, or go pester Pee Wee. He's very interesting to talk to. And sometimes I ride over to the Sheldon farm and help Bertha make jelly or can fruit and vegetables for the winter."

"Your new acquaintances are certainly diffcrent from those you've known all your life. Don't you find the new ones a little dull?"

Roxy shook her head. "They are warm and caring people. People I can trust and depend on. Besides, Jory is so happy living out here, it makes me content to be here also."

"But how long do you plan on living here? Don't you find it a little uncomfortable living in the same house with Tanner, considering how things used to be between you and him? Don't old memories crop up sometimes? Tanner is a handsome brute, and I'd think that seeing him all the time would stir your pulses a little."

"If that should happen, all I'd have to do is recall how he rode away without a word, and stayed away for eight years."

"I expect that would do it," Christy agreed, "but I still can't see any future for you, living here. The next time Tanner gets engaged, it might stick. Then what would you do? You couldn't think of Jory's happiness then. You'd have to go back to town."

"I guess I'll wait until that time comes. I've got nothing better to do." She didn't add that she would be leaving the ranch anyway when her pregnancy began to show.

"You could be concentrating on finding a good man and marrying him. Maybe a rancher. Then you could have the kind of life you seem to like so much. You could have more children, brothers and sisters for Jory."

A sharp pain clutched at Roxy's chest. She wanted to yell, *Shut up, Christy*, even though she knew that what her friend had said was true, that she should have done it years ago. She realized now that unconsciously she had been waiting for Tanner to return. Well, he had come back, and all she had received for her waiting was another child that he had planted in her body.

She managed to control herself and say quietly, "You're probably right. I'll give your suggestion some thought."

"Good girl. Now that that is settled, I've got some wonderful news to tell you."

"I knew you were bursting with something when you rode up. What is it?"

"You won't believe this, Roxy. I can hardly believe it myself. But after all these years, I'm going to have a baby."

"Oh, Christy, I'm so happy for you!" Roxy exclaimed. "When will the baby arrive?"

"Sometime in mid-March. I can't wait, Roxy. John and I had given up hope of ever having a family. He's so excited he's still going around in a daze."

Mid-March. The words stuck in Roxy's mind. The same time her baby would arrive. How very different would be the worlds the two babies would be born into. The Allen infant would have two adoring parents, a warm, loving home to grow up in. Her poor little one would have only a mother and a bastard brother to care for it. And where that home would be, she had no idea.

When Christy asked, "Will that be all right with you?" Roxy looked at her blankly. "I'm sorry, Christy, I didn't hear you. I'm still taking in your good news."

"I said that John and I want you and Tanner to be godparents to the baby."

"Wonderful. I feel honored," Roxy smilingly agreed even as she knew she couldn't keep the promise. She wouldn't be around when Christy's baby was baptized.

When Christy finally left, it was the first time in their friendship that Roxy was glad to see her leave. She couldn't have taken much more of Christy's happy chatter about her coming baby.

After waving goodbye to her friend she went to her room and, throwing herself on the bed, wept bitter tears until she was exhausted. Her last thought before she fell asleep was, "Damn you, Tanner Graylord."

Chapter Thirty-one

It was the first week in September and there was a crisp coolness in the evening air as Tanner sat on the front porch staring out at the open range. The days were getting shorter and there was color in the aspens. In the mornings everything was gray with frost. By the end of the month they would have their first light snowfall, Tanner thought.

Would that chase Roxy back to town? he wondered. It would give her a good excuse to get away from him. He had lost what little headway he had made with her by interfering the day she was leary about Jory going fishing.

But dammit, he couldn't help putting his two cents in. She would make a sissy out of the boy if she kept it up.

It is no affair of mine how she raises her son, he

told himself. *If he was my son it would be different. I would have some say about him then.*

The porch slowly became shrouded in darkness. When the air turned nippy, Tanner rose and entering the house, walked into a heated argument between Roxy and her son. He paused just inside the door. He had planned to sit awhile with mother and son, and talk with Jory at least. He realized now that wouldn't be wise, considering the crackling atmosphere in the room. The two were arguing over school starting next week, and he might not be able to prevent himself from giving his opinion on the topic.

He walked on into his room and closed the door.

Roxy sat in her favorite chair, a pencil positioned over a pad of paper. She had been there close to an hour, most of the time chewing thoughtfully on the pencil. On one side of the paper was a list of names she had written down in her neat hand, and on the other side, a list of foods, drinks and other provisions for a party.

Cousin Ace was getting married.

She was still stunned. It had happened so fast. A month ago, when Michelle moved in with her cousin, Roxy was sure the romance was doomed. Now that Ace had bedded the singer, he would soon lose interest in her and move on to the next female who caught his fancy. Ace had always enjoyed the chase more than the capture.

This time it appeared that Michelle had done the luring and the gambler was solidly hooked. Last Friday when Roxy had returned to the Lady Chance for the weekend, the first thing out of Ace's mouth was, "Michelle and I are getting married next Saturday."

"You . . . you are?" was all she could stammer.

"That's right. And we want you and Zack to stand up with us." He gave her a smug look and added, "We're getting married in church. I've made the arrangements with Father O'Donnell. The ceremony will take place at ten in the morning."

She had finally been able to smile and say "Congratulations, Cousin," even as the thought went through her mind that Ace probably hadn't seen the inside of a church since his mother used to take him to Mass.

"I want to throw a big to-do that evening, so I'd like for you to take charge of seeing to everything. It will be here in the saloon, of course, with invited guests only. The doors will be closed to the public. Here's a list of people I'd like to invite."

With a wry smile Roxy had noted Miss Aggie Newheart's name. She seriously doubted that the old-maid dressmaker would show up. She had never set foot in a saloon in her life. If everybody who was invited attended, it was going to be an unlikely group of people. They would range from Belle and her girls to the wealthiest businessmen in town. She must tell Belle to warn her girls against letting on that they knew those important men. It wouldn't do to shame their wives.

Roxy stretched her cramped fingers. She couldn't imagine how she could get everything done with only Friday afternoon to do it in. She would have to go to town Thursday whether Tanner liked it or not. If he refused to let her go a day early, she would go anyway. It would be just fine with her if he fired her. It would settle the running argument she'd been having with Jory.

Next week school would resume, and she had

learned from Bertha that in the dead of winter her children missed as much as a month of school because of heavy snows that sometimes drifted to eight feet. Feeling that was unacceptable, Roxy had told her son that they would be moving back to town before winter set in.

Roxy heard the kitchen door slam and steeled herself for another onslaught of arguments from her son.

"I've been thinking, Ma," Jory said as soon as he came into the room and plopped down in a chair. "Tanner wouldn't mind taking me to school when the weather gets real bad."

"You are being very selfish, Jory," Roxy said with frowning disapproval. "Do you realize what you are suggesting? Would you really have the nerve to ask him to accompany you to school every morning, then ride back to town in the afternoon to bring you home?"

"I guess not," Jory answered with a long face. "I still don't understand why Mrs. Sheldon isn't concerned that Sonny and his brothers are going to miss so much schooling, and you're so insistent that I don't miss one day."

"Because, young man, the Sheldon boys don't need as much education as you do. They will be farmers like their father, which is very good, but you don't have a father to pass anything on to you. You will go to college, where you will get advanced schooling enabling you to have a profession of some sort. Maybe a doctor or a lawyer. I have no intention of you running a saloon when you grow up."

"But what if I don't want to go to college?" Jory yelled, his face flushed with anger. "I want to be a rancher."

325

"Well, whatever you turn out to be"—Roxy slapped the pencil and pad down on the table—"we're moving into town when winter sets in and you'll be going to school from there."

"I won't! I won't!" Jory jumped to his feet. "I hate you!"

Roxy shot to her feet also. "Go to your room," she grated out. "Right now before I slap your face."

Jory stared at his mother. Never before had she threatened to strike him. But he knew from the glitter in her eyes that she would do so now if he didn't do as she ordered.

It was around noon the next day when Tanner saw a cloud of dust rolling toward the ranch. His eyes lit up. Rock and the men were returning, bringing with them the Herefords. He swung onto Brave's back and raced him to meet the new herd.

Rock's dust-encrusted face cracked into a grin when Tanner rode up to him.

"They look good," Tanner called over the noise of bawling cattle as he peered at the animals through the kicked-up dirt. "Did you lose any?"

"Only one." Rock took off his black hat, now gray from dust, and wiped his sweating face with the red bandana tied across his mouth. "Rattle-snake bit her the third day we were on the trail. We didn't know it until it was too late. Had to shoot the poor thing to put her out of her misery. How's things at the ranch? Roxy and the button all right?"

"Yeah, they're fine."

Rock gave his friend a sidelong look at his terse answer and speculated that nothing had changed between him and Roxy.

326

When the Herefords had been driven into the pen that was waiting especially for them, Tanner and Rock leaned on the top wooden rail of the corral, looking them over.

"They seem to be in good condition," Tanner said, running his gaze over the solidly built cows.

"We brought them in slow, doing only ten miles a day. There was plenty of water and grass along the way. The majority of them have come into heat. I'd say let them rest a couple days, then put them to the steers you've picked to breed them with."

"It will be interesting to see the calves they drop next spring," Tanner said thoughtfully.

Rock dropped his foot off the bottom rail. "I'm gonna get cleaned up and ride into town with the men. They're hankerin' for some whiskey to cut the dirt in their throats." Rock grinned. "And dally awhile with Belle's girls."

"What about you, are you going to do any dallying?" Tanner asked slyly.

"Could be," Rock laughed and walked toward the bunkhouse.

Tanner watched his friend disappear into the long building, wondering if he should go with his men. Maybe if he wrinkled the sheets with one of Belle's girls, he wouldn't have Roxy on his mind so much. It was hell every night to lie in his bed knowing that only a wall separated them.

As he climbed into the saddle and headed Brave in the direction of the Sheldon farm, he knew he wouldn't be going to Belle's place. Even if he could perform, which he had doubts about, when he left the pleasure house he'd still have the same empty feeling he'd been carrying around ever since coming home.

It was around ten o'clock that night and Tanner was sitting on the front porch having a cigarette before retiring when Rock and his men returned from town. They look like a sorry bunch, he thought, seeing them clearly in the moonlight. They looked half drunk and half worn out from making pigs of themselves with Belle's girls.

He peered more closely when Rock separated himself from the others and walked toward the house. His cigarette made a red arch across the yard as he flipped it into the darkness.

Whiskey was strong on Rock's breath as he stepped up on the porch and sat down beside Tanner. "I heard a puzzling thing in town tonight. I think it might interest you."

"And what is that? Is there going to be a new whorehouse opening up?" Tanner joked.

"No, dammit, this is serious."

"What is it then?"

"The gambler, Ace Brandon, is gonna marry that singer next Saturday. He's doing it up all fancy-like. Gettin' married in church, then havin' a big blow-out party at the Lady Chance that night. All private-like. A feller can't get into the saloon unless he's got an invite."

A murderous heat ran through Tanner's veins. The bastard! How could he marry another woman after fathering a child on Roxy, keeping her waiting all these years for him to marry her?

As Tanner continued to sit silently, his body stiff and his fists clenching and unclenching, Rock asked cautiously, "Don't that make you a little mad, Tanner? You know, Jory and all."

"Yes, I'm mad. I'm damned mad. That low-down timber wolf ought to be shot."

"I agree that he ought to be done away with, but

don't insult the wolf. He's a noble animal, the un-rivaled ruler of the range and mountains."

When Tanner made no response, Rock asked, "What are you gonna do about it?"

Tanner gave a short, bitter laugh. "What can I do? Hold a gun to the bastard's head and make him marry Roxy?"

"I guess you're right. It's a shame, though. Roxy is such a nice woman. Life ain't been good to her for a long time." Rock stood up, teetered a bit, then said, "I'm off to bed. I just thought you ought to know what's going on."

I didn't need to know it now, Tanner thought darkly. It was doubtful if he'd close his eyes tonight.

Wednesday morning, when Tanner joined Roxy and Jory for breakfast, his eyes were red-rimmed. When Jory chattered away in his usual fashion, he responded mechanically.

What was stuck in his craw? Roxy wondered. It was obvious that he hadn't slept much last night. Had he gone to town after she and Jory retired?

A soft breath feathered through her lips. He was upset about something and his bad mood wasn't going to help her case when she asked to take Thursday off.

When breakfast was finished, with Tanner eating very little, he cleared his throat and said, "Go on outside, Jory. I want to talk to your mother."

Even as a shudder of alarm swept over Roxy at the serious note in Tanner's voice, she couldn't help noticing that Jory didn't give Tanner an argument, but rose immediately to his feet and left the room. Had she given him that same order, he would have dawdled, asking her what she wanted to talk about.

There was no doubt about it. Her son was getting out of hand. For the first time, she admitted to herself that he needed a father to keep him in line.

When Tanner looked out the window, watching if Jory was going to the barn, Roxy brought his attention back to her by asking, "What did you want to talk to me about?"

Tanner looked at her, then back to the window. "I heard last night that the gambler is getting married Saturday."

"He's got a name, Tanner. Ace Brandon. And yes, he is getting married Saturday."

"You don't act like you're upset about it." Tanner looked at her, surprise on his face.

"I'm not bothered by it in the least. I wish him and Michelle all the happiness in the world. It's way past time that Ace settled down and raised a family."

"But what about your wasted years? And Jory?"

"None of that is any fault of Ace's."

"Are you saying it is all your fault that he didn't marry you years ago?"

"No, I'm not saying that. I'm saying don't put the blame on Ace for my unmarried state."

"Isn't it the same thing?" Tanner asked impatiently, running his fingers through his hair.

Roxy sighed in frustration. She was being backed into a corner. The only way to get out of it was to tell Tanner the truth about Ace.

She settled her clasped hands on the table and began slowly, "I'm going to tell you something that only Belle and I know. Ace got into trouble in Utah over eight years ago and when he came here my father gave him a job. Ace is my first cousin on my mother's side."

Tanner stared at her, his mind racing, trying to take in the importance of Roxy's statement. Since it wasn't Brandon who had fathered Jory, who then? The question showed in his eyes and he opened his mouth to pose it to Roxy.

"Don't ask, Tanner." Roxy held up her hand, stopping the question on his lips. "I will never tell you."

"Why not?" Tanner's hard gaze bored into her eyes. "What is so secret about it? Is the man married?" he asked as an afterthought.

"I'm not saying anything further about it, so let's drop the subject," Roxy said firmly.

"How long do you plan on letting Jory go along without his father's name?" Tanner asked heatedly.

"As long as it takes. Maybe forever. What do you care?"

"I care because he's a fine little fellow that any man should be proud to call son."

A thought hit Tanner. He leaned forward and said in a voice that was rough, yet soft, "Marry *me*, Roxy. Let me be Jory's father."

Roxy blinked at him, unable to speak for a moment. She burst out laughing then. "That's got to be the most romantic proposal a woman ever received."

"If you had your son's interests at heart, you wouldn't think of yourself and you'd jump at the chance that he would be given everything, including my love. Also, you'd be a respectable married woman."

Roxy knew she had better control her anger or she would recklessly fling the truth of Jory's parenthood in Tanner's face, and that would never do. She shook her head and said after a long breath, "Jory is a very intelligent child. It wouldn't get past him that his mother and new father had no affection for each other. When he grew older, he'd have no respect for either one of us. He and I will carry on as usual for the time being."

Before Tanner could speak, Roxy said, "This isn't the best time, but I need to ask you to let me take Thursday off. I'm in charge of preparing a wedding party for Ace and Michelle Saturday night. I need more than one day to get everything ready."

Tanner stared out the cook-house window a moment, then said in clipped tones, "I expect you'll have a fine time in the company of the man you've longed for all these years."

"He won't be there," Roxy said dully, and left him sitting alone at the table.

Chapter Thirty-two

"I don't want to go to the wedding," Jory complained to Tanner as they perched on the top rail of the cattle pen Thursday morning. "I'll have to get all dressed up and stand around being polite."

"Is it hard for you to be polite?" Tanner grinned down at the deeply tanned boy so close to his heart.

Jory shrugged. "I guess not. That is, unless I have to do it too long." He sighed. "Grownups expect a lot from a kid."

"I expect we do sometimes, but it's always in your best interest." He ruffled Jory's dark curls. "You know your Uncle Ace will expect you to see him get married, and his feelings will be hurt if you're not in church to see it happen."

"Yes, he would be," Jory agreed after a thoughtful moment. "He's an awfully good uncle. Besides you and Ma, I love him best. Sometimes he takes my side against Ma. He tells her to loosen up on me, that I'm not a baby anymore."

Tanner found himself changing his opinion of the gambler. Evidently he had tried to take part in raising Jory, but Roxy wouldn't let him do anything she didn't approve of. And she approved of very little when it came to what she thought best for the boy.

"I think you should go to the wedding, son. It will please your ma and make your uncle proud."

"Yeah, I guess so," Jory agreed reluctantly. "I wish you were coming, too."

"I don't know Mr. Brandon very well and I haven't been invited." All the same, Tanner wished that he was going to the reception. He could watch Roxy interact with the men there, see whom she spent the most time with. That might give him a clue as to who Jory's father was.

They both looked toward the house when they heard the door slam. As usual, Tanner's heart skipped a beat as he watched Roxy come toward them, her long legs striding gracefully, her breasts bobbling a bit. He took a long breath, wishing that he could cup them in his hands, feel their firm silkiness in his palms.

He fought back the stirring in his loins and cautioned, "Now be pleasant to your ma, Jory, and don't go pouting all the way to town. Your ma has enough on her mind planning your uncle's reception."

When Jory jumped off the corral and came running to join her where she stood between the two saddled horses, Roxy smiled. The glowering frown was gone from her son's face. Tanner, watching, nodded his approval at Jory when he helped his mother to mount her mare. Jory mounted his pinto then and as he rode off, leading the way, he flashed Tanner a big grin.

The rancher watched the swing of Roxy's slender back until they rode out of sight.

"Will Uncle Ace keep living at the Lady Chance after he's married?" Jory asked when Roxy rode up beside him.

"I don't know. He's never said what his plans are. I'm sure he and Michelle have discussed it, though."

"It will seem strange, him being married. Do you think he'll still have time for me?"

"Of course he will. But I must say you haven't had much time for him lately. He's missed you a lot now that you're spending so much time at the ranch. But you'll see more of him when we move back to town this winter."

Jory didn't want to talk about that and said no more as they rode along.

Roxy was silent also. She was thinking about an idea she'd had concerning her cousin and his bride. She would put it to them today.

Judging by the height of the sun, it was near nine o'clock when Roxy and Jory rode into town. Roxy dismounted in front of the saloon and Jory took the reins of the mare and led her away to the livery.

"Come right back," Roxy called after him. "I'm going to need your help."

Jory started to grumble, then remembered what Tanner had said. "Okay, Ma," he called back. When he thought it over, he felt quite pleased and grown up that his mother needed him to organize his uncle's big to-do. His chin came up and his narrow shoulders squared proudly.

Roxy found Ace and Michelle in the saloon kitchen. They sat at Skinny's well-scrubbed table, their heads together as they studied the list of invited guests, as well as the list of what foods and drinks would be served to those who would attend the wedding party.

"Don't you dare add anything to either of those lists," Roxy commanded by way of greeting, only half joking. "As it is, I'm going to be run half ragged getting everything together. Thanks, Skinny." She smiled up at her cook when he placed a cup of coffee in front of her. "Do you two have everything under control on your side?" She looked at Ace and Michelle.

"I think so," Michelle answered. "Miss Newheart finished my dress yesterday, and the bag and shoes I ordered by mail came in Monday. Are you all prepared, Ace?"

"I think so. I've got the ring." He took Michelle's left hand in his and stroked the slim finger next to the little one. "It's the most important part of the whole affair."

"Hardly the most important, Cousin," Roxy said, giving him a crooked smile. "Your wedding vows are number one, don't you think?"

"Of course." Ace's handsome face became very serious looking. "When I say 'I do,' they will be the most sincere and heartfelt words I've ever uttered. Michelle and I are going to grow old together right here in the Lady Chance."

"Amen to that." Roxy gripped a hand of each. "May you live to a happy old age. Now, do you plan to continue living here in the saloon?"

"I think so," Michelle answered. "I have plans to pretty up Ace's quarters. Right now they're too masculine to suit me."

"I have an idea that might suit you better," Roxy said. "What about exchanging your rooms for mine and Jory's? It will be fun for me to fix up his place."

"Are you sure?" Ace and Michelle asked in unison. "Your apartment is so beautiful," Michelle added.

"I'm sure. Ace's rooms are more convenient to my office, and I can keep a closer eye on Jory's coming and going. There's no back door for him to sneak out of," she ended with a small laugh.

"I hope the little cuss came in with you." Ace looked at Roxy, doubt in his eyes.

"Of course he did. He wouldn't miss seeing his uncle get married," Roxy said, not entirely truthfully. She remembered how at first Jory hadn't wanted to attend the ceremony, then an hour later seemed to be looking forward to it. She had a sneaky feeling that Tanner had something to do with her son's change of heart.

"I'd better get started organizing things." Roxy carried her empty cup to the big galvanized sink. "The first thing I'm going to do is go see if Miss Newheart has my dress ready for the big day."

Miss Aggie Newheart was alone when Roxy walked into her neat little shop.

This pleased her. During the time she'd been at the ranch she had forgotten the pain of receiving cold looks and being snubbed by the elite female citizens of Denver. She hoped to have a friendly chat with Aggie, to try on her dress, then go about her business.

"Good morning, Roxy," said Miss Newheart, a welcoming smile on her lips as she parted the heavy drapes that separated the store from her living quarters. "Let me put my Closed sign in the window and we'll have a cup of tea I just brewed. After we drink it, you can try on your dress."

Roxy followed the trim little figure of the old maid into her attractive parlor. Steam rose from a flower-painted teapot that had been placed beside a dainty cup and saucer that matched it. A matching sugar bowl had been placed in the middle of the linen tablecloth.

"Sit down, Roxy." Aggie motioned to a dainty-looking chair pulled up to the table. "Let me get you a tea setting and we can chat awhile before trying on your dress.

"Now," the little dressmaker said when she had drawn up a chair and filled their cups, "Are Ace and Michelle all set for their big day?"

"I believe so." Roxy gave a light laugh. "They're both a little nervous. It's the first time for both of them, you know."

"I know that it's Ace's first time. He used to joke with me, claiming that he and I were too smart to tie ourselves down to a mate. He'd laugh and say that we liked our freedom too much to give it up. But I wasn't sure about Michelle."

"She's never taken that step before either. She's always been too busy with her singing career."

"She's lucky to have found such a fine man to marry, after having waited so long." There was a hint of yearning in Aggie's voice. Roxy wondered if there had been a man in Miss Newheart's past.

When both their cups were empty, Aggie asked, "Will you have more tea before I bring out your dress?"

"No, I'm fine. I'm anxious to see the dress."

Roxy had chosen material of thin blue wool. The pattern she had picked from Aggie's ample supply was a modestly cut gown with a square neckline, a snug-fitting bodice, a full skirt and long, tight sleeves.

When Aggie brought out the finished creation, Roxy exclaimed her pleasure. "It's lovely, Miss Newheart. I love the narrow ecru lace you've sewn on the neckline and cuffs." She stood up and hurried out of her riding skirt and shirt.

"It fits you perfectly, Roxy." Aggie beamed as she smoothed out the skirt.

"I can't wait to see," Roxy exclaimed as she finished doing up the pearl buttons on the bodice.

"Take a look then." The dressmaker led her to a long mirror fastened to a wall.

"I love it, Miss Newheart." Roxy's eyes gleamed. "It hangs beautifully." She grinned wryly. "And it will fall even better when I'm wearing slippers instead of boots."

"I made you a little matching wrist purse. It's lace trimmed and has a satin ribbon gathering its top. And I held back for you a hat from my fall collection. It will look lovely with your dress."

Aggie picked a round box off the floor and lifted from it a dark blue felt creation with a narrow, rolled brim. When she placed it on Roxy's head, the soft, jaunty point lay in the middle of her smooth brow. A dark brown feather flowed from a nosegay of yellow silk roses.

"Oh, Miss Aggie," Roxy cried woefully, "I'm going to outshine the bride. I mustn't do that."

"Nonsense, honey," Aggie scolded. "You'd outshine any woman there even if you had a burlap bag tied around your head."

Excited voices and the impatient rattling of the doorknob made Aggie sigh and smile at the same time. "That's Belle's girls come to try on their dresses. They are so excited to be attending Ace's wedding and reception. When they walk into church in a group, the bright colors they have chosen will blind anyone within three rows of them. I near went blind sewing them," Aggie laughed.

Roxy changed back into her riding clothes, then carried her new dress into the store for Aggie to box up.

"Let's see your new dress, Roxy," one of Belle's girls said as all five of them gathered round her.

When Roxy had unfolded the blue woolen on the counter and stepped aside so the young prostitutes could view it, they exclaimed in disappointment. "It's so plain, Roxy," one of the youngest cried.

"Maybe if you pinned a big, bright flower on one shoulder and one at your waist, the dress might perk up some," another advised.

"I'll take that into consideration," Roxy said, trying to keep a straight face. She glanced at Aggie and saw by the twitching of her lips that she was having the same problem.

"I'll see you later, girls." Roxy picked up the package the dressmaker shoved across the counter.

"Don't forget the flowers," she was reminded as she left the shop.

As Roxy headed down the street, walking toward the Lady Chance, she caught a glimpse of a familiar-looking man turning onto a side street. It looked like Tanner, but when she came to the end of the block and glanced down the side street, there was no one in sight.

She dismissed the thought and walked on. Every tall, broad-shouldered man she saw reminded her of the rancher. Anyway, Tanner was

too busy at the ranch with his new breed of cattle
to have come into town.

Tanner had tried to keep his mind on the stocky
Herefords as they had begun settling in at the
ranch, but his thoughts kept wandering. He could
only think of Roxy and the big wedding party she
would be attending, and the men who would hold
her in their arms as they danced together. Especially one man, whoever he was.

It had frustrated him that his one chance to discover Jory's father was being denied him. Of
course he could ride into town that night and
stand across the street watching to catch sight of
Roxy and her dance partners, but he was damned
if he'd do that. Only green teenagers would stoop
to that.

If only he could attend the reception, but he
knew he would not be welcome there. If the gambler didn't throw him out, Roxy would order him
to leave. Then a brilliant idea had hit him. What
if he showed up with someone who had been invited, as their guest?

But he didn't know anyone well enough who
was going except John and Christy Allen. He
couldn't impose on them. They knew how things
were between him and Roxy. Then Tanner's eyes
had lit up. The perfect person had come to mind.
He'd ridden to town now to arrange it.

His step was light as he hurried down the side
street.

Chapter Thirty-three

Roxy sat up in bed, stretched and yawned, then became fully alert. It was Saturday, Ace's wedding day. She could tell by the light coming through the curtains that it was still early in the morning. She scooted out of bed and drew on her robe. She needed to get downstairs and remind the swamper not to open the saloon doors today. The Lady Chance would be closed until Sunday noon. She had a lot of last-minute things to do: direct the setting up of long tables to hold the food and drink, make sure the extra chairs she was renting from the church arrived, as well as plates and flatware and napkins Father O'Donnell said she could use from his banquet hall. Then there was seeing that her cousin and his intended got to the church on time. There had been a small celebration with a few close friends last night after the saloon was closed. It had lasted until four in the morning and the couple wouldn't have gotten much sleep.

But Jory was up. She could hear him moving around in his room, probably wishing that he was back at the ranch.

Surprisingly, he had been a big help to her the last two days. He had done a lot of errands that had saved her time. And he hadn't complained once. There was no doubt about it, Tanner had a good influence on his son.

On her way downstairs Roxy rapped on Jory's door and called, "Honey, I would like for you to run one more errand for me. I promise it's the last one."

Jory opened the door, a slight frown on his face. "What is it?"

"Miss Newheart forgot to put the little matching bag to my dress in the package. I'd really appreciate it if you'd go get it."

Roxy kissed the top of his head when he said, "All right, Ma, I'll pick it up."

When she opened the kitchen door she found Skinny removing pies from the big oven. He carried them to a long worktable and placed them with ten others he had baked, some yesterday and the others this morning. Bertha Sheldon had provided apples and peaches and two jars of canned strawberries. She had also baked the three-tier wedding cake, iced with white frosting, and three other cakes that sat with the pies. The white three-layer confection, however, sat proudly on its own small table.

"It smells like a bakery shop in here, Skinny," she said, smiling at him and pouring herself a cup of coffee. "The aroma is simply delicious."

"It gets sickening after a while, though."Skinny

343

wiped the hem of his apron across his sweaty brow. "I'm giving you warning now, when this shindig is over I'm not baking any sweets for a month."

"I don't blame you, but I must tell you that Ace appreciates your hard work very much."

"I know he does. That's why I don't mind doing it." Skinny looked up at the big wooden, smoke-stained clock over the door and said, "He and Michelle should be getting up. They have to be at the church in another hour and a half."

"Yes," Roxy agreed, then chuckled. "Don't you know Father O'Donnell got his ears roasted yesterday when Ace went to confession. The poor man is probably still reeling."

"I don't doubt that. Ace has been a bounder all right. He seems to be settling down now, though."

"He's marrying a young woman who will see to it." Roxy heard a wagon pull into the alley and jumped to her feet. "That will be the tables and chairs. I've got to get dressed."

On her way up the stairs she met Jory coming down. "Be polite to Miss Newheart," she said in passing.

An hour later everything was in readiness, even to the big sign over the bar that said "Congratulations Ace and Michelle." Roxy cast an anxious glance at the happy couple. "Where is Jory?" She frowned. "He should have returned from Aggie's shop half an hour ago."

As if in answer to her question, the saloon door was flung open and a disheveled Jory stood there, a small package clutched in his hand. His face was dirt smeared, his nose bloodied, and his right eye was swollen and beginning to turn black.

"Oh, Jory, who did this to you?" Roxy ran to him.

"The same bunch as always." Jory swiped the back of his dirty hand across the blood trickling out of his nose.

"Oh, honey, I'm sorry I sent you for that foolish purse." Roxy pressed his sweaty head to her breast.

"It's all right, Ma." Jory looked up at her with a grin. "I got in a few good licks. Tanner has been showing me how to hit where it hurts. I'm not the only one who has a bloody nose."

Ace lifted Jory's chin and examined his eye. "After you've washed up, hold a wet cloth to that bruise. It will take down some of the swelling."

"Thanks, Uncle Ace. You always tell me to do that."

"And it works, too, doesn't it?" Ace gave him a soft clip on the jaw.

Tears welled in Jory's eyes, and before anyone could stop him, he threw his arms around Ace's waist, his dirty clothes rubbing up against the gambler's spotless gray suit. When Roxy would have pulled the boy away, Ace held up a hand, stopping her. He hugged the boy back, saying softly, "I'll always be here for you, son."

Jory nodded and pulled away.

Roxy looked at Ace's soiled suit with alarm. When she started toward her cousin, he said gently, his eyes damp, "You and the button had better get ready for church."

With her arm around Jory's shoulder, they mounted the steps. Her eyes were damp also. She hadn't realized how Jory had worried about Ace getting married, that maybe he would no longer be a part of their lives. After all, Ace was the only father figure her son had ever known . . . until recently.

When the five of them had gathered on the saloon porch, preparing to walk to church, Roxy ran a glance over everyone. Ace and Zack looked so handsome in their vested suits and highly polished boots. Ace looked almost naked without his Colt strapped around his waist. And Michelle looked lovely in her simple ecru woolen dress, a small matching hat and veil on top of the curls she had pinned up on her head. She is so nervous, Roxy thought, seeing the slight trembling of her hands.

Roxy looked next at her son and a soft smile curved her lips. His suit was a replica of his uncle's, and she had managed to brush and tame his unruly curls for the time being. She hoped they would stay that way until after the ceremony at least. She quelled the desire to stroke her fingers over his swollen and bruised eye.

"Well, we'd better get to church," Ace said, returning his silver watch to a vest pocket.

The small church was packed. As she walked down the aisle and took a seat in the first pew, Roxy thought that most of Denver had turned out to see the popular gambler get married. She scooted over to make room for Jory and Zack to sit beside her, then sat quietly, waiting for Father O'Donnell to make his appearance.

Two young altar boys came through a side door and Zack nudged Roxy in the side and whispered, "That taller one has a shiner that matches Jory's." She glanced at her son and he wore a pleased smile as he stared at his handiwork.

The gray-haired priest followed the boys when they had taken their places, his long robe flapping around his legs. He motioned Ace and Michelle forward, and when they rose, Roxy and Zack followed them to the altar.

"Dearly beloved, we are gathered here," he began, and in twenty minutes Ace and Michelle were husband and wife.

Everyone stood around in the churchyard, waiting to congratulate the happy couple. With tears of happiness brimming in her eyes, Roxy kissed her cousin, and then his bride.

When Roxy left the gathering, Belle's girls swooped down on her, demanding to know why she hadn't fancied up her dress. "I'm sorry, girls, but I was so busy getting everyone else ready, I didn't have time to pin on the flowers," she lied prettily and walked on.

As Roxy neared the Lady Chance she saw the old miner Elisha Roundtree sitting on the porch. Had he heard about Ace's wedding and come to help celebrate the affair? she asked herself as she crossed the street.

The old man stood up as she climbed the steps. "I guess you're surprised to see me again so soon." He gave her a wide smile.

"Yes, kind of. Did you come to join the festivities tonight?"

"No." Elisha shook his head. "What festivities are you talkin' about?"

"Ace and Michelle just got married," she said, unlocking the saloon door.

"Well, I'll be jiggered." Elisha grinned. "I never thought that gambler would give up his freedom," he said, following Roxy inside.

Roxy was ready for the old fellow to ask her to stake him again to another search for gold. Instead, he thumped a small leather pouch on the bar and pushed it toward Roxy. "Here's payment for grubstaking me."

"You don't have to repay me, old friend." Roxy pushed the bag back to him. "Keep it. You may need it later."

Elisha shook his head. "After spending most of my life lookin' for that yellow stuff, I finally found me a decent claim. It ain't the richest in the world, but I can pan enough out of it to take care of me when rheumatiz cripples me up so I can't work the streams anymore."

"I'm truly happy for you, Elisha. Whereabouts is your claim?" Roxy asked as she walked behind the bar and set a bottle and glass in front of the old miner.

"Well, it's the dangdest thing," Elisha began, watching the amber liquor flow from the bottle into his glass. "Every time I thought about where to go next to try my luck, something inside me said I should go back to Cripple Creek and try again. So I did. I found a shady little spot at the bend in the river that no one else wanted because they thought the water was too swift to ever drop any gold. But I had a feelin' about the spot, so I pitched my tent and staked my claim. It was dark by then and I had to wait for the next mornin' before I started panning. By the end of the next day I had washed out almost an ounce of gold flecks.

"Every once in a while I'd find a small nugget in my pan. I brought them to you in that pouch. You've got to come visit my little camp, Roxy. It's a delightful place."

"I don't know if I could get away any time soon," Roxy began, then was interrupted by Jory coming through the door asking if he could change his clothes. "Some of them bullies followed me here and I don't want my new suit dirtied up when they pounce on me."

Roxy looked into her son's eyes, saw the dread in them, the one that was still swollen and black. In that instant she knew that she and her son would go to Cripple Creek, not for a visit, but to stay until she had her baby. While awaiting its arrival she would have time to figure out where to go afterward.

"Elisha," she said, "tell Jory about your claim."

As the old man talked in glowing terms of the gold dust he panned out of the river, Jory's eyes shone with the same excitement as Roundtree's.

"Roxy, I'd like to do that," he exclaimed when Elisha wound down.

"Maybe you can," Roxy said, smiling at him. "How would you like to spend some time there, helping Elisha?"

"Oh, Ma, could I?"

"I think so. That is, if you promise to study your books with me a couple hours a day. We mustn't forget your schooling."

"I will, Ma, I promise." Jory's eyes gleamed. "I'll study harder than I ever did at school."

"Don't say a word to anyone about this, Jory," Roxy cautioned. "I mean don't speak of it to anyone, especially Tanner. Go change your clothes now, and why don't you stay inside and talk to Elisha about his claim?"

When Jory had left them, Elisha looked at Roxy and said, "It sounds like you mean to stay awhile with me."

"If that's all right with you, I'd like to."

"You're more than welcome, Roxy, you know that. You can stay as long as you like. But I'm pull-

349

ing out tomorrow morning before daybreak."

"That's fine, Jory and I will be ready. Where will we meet you?"

"Down at the livery around four o'clock." Elisha finished his whiskey, drawing the back of his hand across his lips. Then he grinned and said, "I'd better get goin'. I'll need to lay in some extra supplies."

"Take back your pouch to pay Jory's and my way."

"Go on, girl, I'm rich now," Elisha joked. "It won't be no hardship to buy you and your youngun grub."

"Thank you, old friend." Roxy squeezed his gnarled fingers. "And Elisha, as I told Jory, please don't say anything to anybody about our leaving with you."

"You have my word, Roxy. I'll see you in the morning at four sharp."

Roxy watched him go, a relief coming over her that she hadn't felt in a long time. She would have a respite from worry for a few months.

The wedding party was in full swing; laughter and the chattering of the guests filled the long room. Some of the merrymakers danced to the music of a fiddle, banjo and guitar that Ace had hired so that Zack would be free to join in the festivities. Her mind free of worry, Roxy was enjoying herself, and was laughing gaily as Zack swung her around the floor to a rollicking tune played by the three musicians.

She stopped suddenly, stepping on Zack's toes when Belle came through the door, followed by Tanner. What was he doing here? He certainly hadn't been invited. Just wait until she got Belle alone.

All levity left her as Zack continued to whirl her around the floor, unaware that she no longer found anything amusing. Luckily the set ended soon and she made her way straight to Belle, who now stood with her girls. A fast glance showed Roxy that, to her amazement, Tanner was talking to Ace and Michelle, and all three of them were smiling. What was the sly devil up to now? She ground her teeth together.

Belle saw her coming and a sheepish look crossed her face. "Now, Roxy," she said when Roxy stood before her, "I can explain."

"Well, it had better be good." Roxy glared at her friend.

"Tanner came to me Thursday morning and practically begged me to bring him to the reception. Said that he had figured Ace wrong and wanted to make amends, congratulate Ace and his bride. I didn't think it was the thing to do, but I did think it was wise for Tanner to mend fences with Ace. So I agreed. He won't start trouble, if that's what you're worried about."

"I don't think that, but his presence will ruin the rest of the party for me."

"I'm sorry, honey." Belle held out a placating hand to her. "Maybe he won't stay long."

"I hope not," Roxy said, somewhat mollified by Belle's sincere apology. "Let's go get something to eat while the band takes a rest."

Before they could make their way to the table that practically groaned under the weight of all the food, Zack met them with two plates of food in his hands. "I hope you like what I chose for you, Roxy," he said, smiling at her.

"Thank you, Zack, but Belle was going to eat with me."

"That's fine. Let's find a table; then I'll go back and get something for Belle."

Roxy looked at Belle and raised an eyebrow helplessly. "Thank you so much, Zack." Belle smiled at the eager piano player and led the way to an empty table.

Roxy smiled to herself when Bertha Sheldon and her husband joined them shortly after Zack returned; then Skinny came over to the table and sat down beside Belle. The meal wasn't turning out the way Zack had planned.

As she chatted with Bertha, Roxy could hear Belle and Skinny talking and laughing together. Every time she looked at her cook, she was amazed at how different he looked dressed in a black suit and white shirt, his hair combed neatly. Nothing about him looked like the cook she knew, with his wrinkled trousers and big stained apron. She could tell that Belle was taking a second look at the big man, too.

Roxy pushed the tender ham and potato salad around on her plate, her appetite gone. She was very conscious of Tanner's gaze drifting toward her every few minutes, his eyes hard and cold when they rested on Zack. If she didn't know better, she'd think he was jealous of the piano player.

When the music started up again, Zack rose and reached for her and Belle's plates. "I'd like the next dance after I take these back to the table," he said.

Roxy reluctantly nodded while wishing she could go to her apartment. She had packing to do.

"May I have this dance, Roxy?" a familiar voice asked. Roxy looked up, a dumbfounded look on her face. Tanner was bending over her, a hand reaching out to help her rise.

She was about to refuse coldly when she saw that everyone at the table was watching them. There was nothing gracious about her demeanor when she rose and went into his strong arms.

The first dance of the new set was a slow one and Tanner's arm tightened around her waist, drawing her close to his lean body. As they circled the floor, Roxy remembered how they had danced together before, how attuned they had been to each other's steps. Tanner's whip-lean body was as graceful as one of the cats that roamed the mountains.

She was relaxing and enjoying herself when she became aware of the hard arousal pressing against her. She looked up at Tanner, indignation in her eyes. His only response was to smile lazily down at her, pull her closer and give her a little buck of his hips. Blushing, she glanced around to see if anyone had seen his action. Nobody but Ace had seemed to see it. He gave her a knowing look and a wicked wink.

She wanted to stop right there and stamp her foot. But the arm around her waist propelled her along.

Roxy's face was beet red when the number finally finished. She was ready to jerk free of Tanner, but he held her long enough to growl, "Think of our dance when you join your fancy man." He left her then, striding to the door and disappearing into the darkness.

From the corner of her eye Roxy saw Zack approaching her. She went in the other direction, circling the room until she came to Ace and Michelle. "I'm going to turn in now," she said after hugging them both. "I'm beat."

"So are we," Michelle said. "I have a pounding headache."

Roxy slipped unnoticed up the stairs and entered her apartment. On her way to her desk she peeked in Jory's room and saw that he was sound asleep, a smile on his face. She shook her head in amusement, guessing that Cripple Creek had been the last thing on his mind before he nodded off.

She opened the desk drawer, looking for a pad of paper, and found that she had none left. Irritation formed a frown between her brows. She didn't want to go downstairs and chance running into Zack again, but she had to write Ace a note. She remembered having her father's desk moved into Jory's room for him to do his schoolwork on. There was bound to be paper in it.

She slipped silently into the room and began quietly to open drawers. There was nothing in the long top drawer but Jory's books and pencils. In the next drawer down on the left-hand side she found only odds and ends a boy would collect. In the next drawer she found papers of her father's, and toward the back a sheaf of paper. When she pulled it toward her, an envelope came sliding out with it. She turned the white square over and gave a little cry of dismay. It was addressed to Tanner in her handwriting. Her father had never mailed it as he had promised he would. It was still sealed.

"Oh, Pa," she silently wailed, "why did you lie to me?"

She laid the letter on top of the paper and carried them into the parlor, where she sat down at her desk. She would never know now whether or not the letter would have made any difference, even if Tanner had received it. Maybe it was a blessing that the letter never got to its destination. Considering Tanner's affection for Jory, he would have taken him away from her as soon as he returned home from the wars he had been fighting.

With a sigh she put her mind on writing the note to Ace.

"Dear Ace," she wrote, "Jory and I will be gone when you read this. We are in good hands, so don't worry about us. If you don't know where we've gone, you won't have to lie if somebody comes looking for us. As soon as we're settled, I'll write to you and let you know where we are. Kiss Michelle goodbye for me. I trust you to take care of things at the Lady Chance. Your loving cousin, Roxy."

Chapter Thirty-four

The stars were beginning to fade when Roxy shook Jory awake. Her sleep had been light. She had been afraid she might not waken in time to meet Elisha at the livery. Jory gave her a groggy look, then sat up, excitement in his eyes.

"I've got my clothes laid out, Ma. I'll be with you in a jiffy."

As Roxy hurried to her room to get into her riding clothes, she found herself caught up in the spirit of the great adventure they were about to embark upon. She couldn't wait to leave Denver behind: the cruel snobbery of its women, her fear of Tanner discovering he had fathered Jory.

This is only the first step in eliminating him from my life, she told herself. Sooner or later word will drift back that I'm living with the old miner.

But at least she would have breathing space where she could make further plans.

Roxy barely had time to wash her face, brush her hair and get into her riding skirt before Jory was knocking on her door. "I'm ready, Ma," he whispered loudly.

"I'll be right out," she whispered back, trying to tug together the two sides of the skirt. No matter how she pulled and tugged, they would not meet. It seemed that overnight the baby inside her had grown. She smiled wryly. It had grown enough that the unfastened waistband wouldn't fall below her hips. Luckily her flannel shirt and lightweight jacket would cover the decided roundness of her stomach. But with each inch her waistline expanded, so too did her love for the little being that was growing inside her. How could she ever have thought that she didn't want it?

Roxy threw her brush and soap into the open saddlebag, buckled it up, checked that her note to Ace still lay on the desk where he would find it, then walked into the parlor. Jory took the bag from her, and quietly they descended the back stairs.

Elisha was waiting for them in the shadow of the livery. He had the mare and pinto saddled, ready to be mounted. "Let's get goin'," he said. "Light is comin' fast."

He led off then, leading his packhorse. Roxy and Jory grinned at each other and followed him.

The morning was cool and their breath hung on the air in small white clouds as they left Denver behind them. They were several miles out of town when daylight arrived, pinkening the eastern horizon. Birds awakened and their songs rang out as they flew about looking for bugs to eat for breakfast.

Elisha kept his horse in a straight line for an hour or so, then turned right, taking a dim trail that would lead them to Cripple Creek and his claim.

Time passed swiftly for Roxy as her gaze took in the country they traveled through. This land is so beautiful, she thought, drawing in deep breaths of the pure, fresh air.

It was around noon when Elisha drew rein in a grove of willows at the edge of a small stream. "We'll have us a bite to eat," he said, climbing out of the saddle. He grinned at Jory and said, "I'll bet you're hungry, young feller."

"I sure am," Jory smilingly answered as he helped his mother to dismount. Something else he'd learned from Tanner, she thought. Her son had never been so attentive to her before.

"You go fetch some wood, Jory, while I go through my grub bag," Elisha ordered. "Then while I'm makin' us some lunch you can lead the animals to water."

Roxy walked stiffly to a large aspen that stood alone a few yards from the willows. As she sat down in the grass and leaned against its trunk, she was thankful Elisha hadn't given her a task. "I don't think I'd have been up to it," she muttered as she nodded off to sleep.

She awoke a short time later to the delicious aroma of cooking food and her son's hand shaking her shoulder. "Grub's ready, Ma. Come on, let's eat. I'm starved."

So am I, Roxy thought as Jory tugged her to her feet.

The meal was plain—fried salt pork and beans—

but she was sure she had never eaten anything so tasty. The cup of strong, black coffee Elisha poured her was invigorating, bringing back her energy. She sat and sipped contentedly at it while Elisha entertained Jory with tales of the places he had panned for gold.

Elisha was announcing it was time to get going then, and they broke camp.

Tanner got out of bed just as the sun was rising. His face was haggard looking and his eyes bloodshot. He had hardly slept all night. Every time he fell asleep, an hour later he would jerk awake, his brow bathed in sweat. He had the distinct feeling that all was not well with Roxy.

Over and over in his sleep he had seen the dim figures of Roxy and Jory riding through fog, following a male figure also on horseback. Who was the man? Tanner had only seen the back of him.

He sat on the edge of the bed staring out the window, going over in his mind the wedding party, how the piano player seemed to be always at Roxy's side. He thought then of the one dance he'd had with her, how he had become aroused, how it had angered her.

She had felt so good in his arms, he couldn't help growing hard.

"Can't you get it through your hard head that she wants nothing to do with you, that you might as well forget her?" he muttered angrily as he stood up and rummaged through his chest of drawers for clean underclothing. Clothes that she had washed and laid in the chest, he remembered. "Forget that," he ordered himself. "Another housekeeper will do the same thing."

But as Pee Wee served Tanner his breakfast,

Roxy was still on his mind. He didn't want any other housekeeper. He liked the way she ran his home just fine. He liked having the kid around all the time.

As he ate the bacon and eggs placed before him, he thought of ways to soften Roxy's attitude toward him. He knew how to arouse her, to get her in bed. But after their fiery coming together, they went straight back to the same old coldness between them.

He knew now that possessing Roxy's body wasn't enough. He wanted her love, her respect. He wanted her to like him as well.

Tanner pushed away his half-eaten breakfast, his appetite gone. As he drank his coffee, he pondered what else he could do to make her realize that he loved her.

It came to him in a blinding flash what he hadn't done. He hadn't told her that he loved her and that he wanted to spend the rest of his life with her.

He jumped to his feet and left in such a rush, Pee Wee stared after him. "A bee must have stung him in the rump," he muttered as he picked up Tanner's plate and coffee cup.

Tanner had never before made the trip to Denver so fast. When he pulled rein in front of the Lady Chance, the old swamper was just opening its doors. As he walked into the dim interior, he saw Ace standing at the bar talking with his cook.

"Good morning, Tanner," the handsome gambler said, giving him a genial smile. "What brings you to town so early in the day?"

"I want to talk to Roxy. Is she up?"

"I haven't seen her this morning. She's probably sleeping late because of the shindig last night. I'll go upstairs and see if she's awake."

"Will you have a cup of coffee while you're waiting, Tanner?" Skinny asked.

"No thanks, Skinny. Roxy will probably be down in a minute."

Only Ace descended the stairs a minute later, his face as white as the paper he held in his hand.

As he walked toward Tanner, he folded the paper and shoved it into his vest pocket. "Well?" Tanner said, dread in his eyes.

"She's gone." Ace shook his head as if in a daze.

"What do you mean, she's gone? Gone where?"

"I don't know. She only wrote that she and Jory were going away, and they were in good hands and for me not to worry."

"She left with that damn piano player!" Tanner's fists clenched at his sides.

Ace shook his head. "Roxy would never take off with him. She leans more toward the strong type of man."

"Who then?" A wildness had come into Tanner's eyes.

"I have no idea, Graylord." Ace gave Tanner a close look. "Would I be out of line if I asked you why you want to see her?"

Tanner gave a short, sardonic laugh. "I was going to ask her to marry me. Isn't that a laugh?"

"Not at all. You should have done it as soon as you came home from fighting the Indians." Tanner made no response to Ace's remark, but the defeated look on his face told the gambler that he was thinking the same thing.

"I'm going to go talk to Belle," Tanner decided. "She might know something."

"That's a good idea. If Roxy confided in anyone, it would be her old friend."

"Good morning, Tanner," Belle said when she

answered his knock on her kitchen door. As she swung the door open for him to pass through, she added sharply, "Roxy was real put out at me for bringing you to the reception last night."

"Roxy is the reason I'm here." Tanner sat down at the kitchen table. "She's gone."

"Gone? Gone where?"

"I don't know. Neither does Ace. I just came from the Lady Chance. She left him a note saying that she and Jory were in good hands and not to worry about her."

"That foolish girl. Why would she do a thing like that?" Belle sat down, bewilderment on her face.

"I don't know. I thought maybe you might know something about it."

When Belle shook her head, he asked, "Does Roxy have a man friend she might have left with?"

"None that I know of. I think she would have told me if there was a special man in her life. She told me once that Jory was enough for her, that she didn't need any other male."

Tanner heaved himself up from the table, his face weary and frustrated. "I'd better get on back to the ranch," he muttered and left Belle sitting at the table staring blindly out the window.

It was a week later when Elisha pulled in his horse and pointed a knobby finger. "There she is— Cripple Creek."

Roxy gazed down at a mixture of tents and shacks, some in good repair, others just thrown together. There were a few women moving about, hanging up wash, busy at a cookfire, or just standing around talking to each other. Off by themselves, sitting in front of a tent somewhat larger than the others, were five other women.

When Elisha saw Roxy looking at the scantily clad women, he spit and said contemptuously, "Them there is camp followers, if you know what I mean."

"I think I do." Amusement shimmered in her eyes.

"Yeah, they're makin' more money than some of their customers do diggin' for gold. The damn fools. Now here is what I'm gonna put out about you, Roxy. You're my niece, a widder woman with a boy. Most of these folks will respect that you recently lost your husband to a rattlesnake bite. But there will be some men who ain't got respect for nothin', man or woman. I'm gonna give you a gun to strap around your waist, and you wear it in plain view all the time. And if need be, don't hesitate to use it."

"Don't worry, I won't. And I'm a fair shot. A long time ago a friend taught me how to shoot his Colt."

Lisha lifted the reins and said, "Let's get on down there. I'm anxious to show you and the kid my shack and my claim."

Roxy and Jory kept their horses close behind Elisha's horse and pack animal as he led the way around tents and shacks. Some of the women nodded and smiled at Roxy, while others sent her lowering looks. She shot a look at Jory, and though there was uneasiness on his face, his eyes glittered with excitement.

They left the mishmash of homes behind and several yards ahead lay the river. All up and down the wide, shallow stream men worked, panning for the elusive gold. Some looked curiously at them, some called a greeting to Elisha.

Elisha led them upstream about a quarter mile,

then reined up in front of a neat little shack made with pieces of scrap wood the old man had taken from other shacks that had been deserted when the owners decided that they weren't going to get rich and had pulled out.

A smoke stack came up through the tar-papered roof. There was one large window and a sturdy door that didn't hang just right. I'll not be picky, Roxy thought. As humble as it is, it will be my haven until my baby is born.

When Roxy had complimented the old miner on his home, he led them behind the building and swung out of the saddle. "This is where I keep my tools." He pointed to a shed attached to the shack. Roxy noted that it had a large, strong lock on the door. "And here is where I keep my animals." He led his horse to a pen built out of slender poles tightly lashed together. He opened a gate and led his mount inside, and Roxy and Jory followed him.

When Roxy stepped inside the shack, she was surprised and relieved to see how neat and clean the little place was. She had been afraid it would be a regular pig sty. In the center of an outside wall sat a small black cooking stove, with a wood-box beside it. There were two long shelves above it, holding a few tin plates and cups, two frying pans, a bean pot and two long-handled pans. On the stove's other side was a rudely constructed table with a bench on either side. Attached to the wall was a small mirror hanging beside the window. The rest of the room held two rickety looking rockers and one straight chair. Placed in front of the chairs was a big woven rug Elisha had found somewhere. In the center of the room was a door.

"This leads to my bedroom," Elisha said proudly

and swung the door open. "Take a look."

There was no window on this side of the shack, but Roxy could make out a narrow bed, neatly made up, an old trunk sitting against a wall and an up-ended apple crate sitting beside the bed and holding a kerosene lamp. Elisha's clothes hung neatly from pegs driven into the wall.

"Where will Ma and I sleep?" Jory asked.

"Well now, that is a poser." Elisha scratched his head. "I reckon me and you had better get busy and build a couple bunk beds in my livin' room."

Roxy shook her head warningly at Jory when she saw him begin to grin at Elisha's referring to the small room behind them as his living room. The old man was proud of his home and had every right to feel so. If he wanted to say he had a living room, so be it.

"When we've knocked them together, I've got some grub sacks that you can sew together, Roxy, and there's an old farmer a mile or so back who will give me straw to stuff inside them. We'll be real comfortable on them, Jory."

"Then Ma gets the bedroom all to herself?"

"That's right. A woman needs her privacy," Elisha said, and taking Jory by the arm, he added, "Let's get busy cutting down some good-sized saplings."

Roxy could hear the chopping of the axe as she unpacked her and Jory's clothes. Since there was nowhere to put them, she stacked them on top of the trunk. She walked back into the other room and looked at the bags of supplies Elisha and Jory had brought in. Should she stow them away? she wondered. Not seeing any place she could put them, she went outside.

Elisha's shack was only feet away from the bend

in the river, with gravel in front and willows crowding its back and sides. A beautiful setting for the little rustic shack, she thought.

The gravel crunched under her feet as Roxy walked down to the water's edge. The river wound between wooded banks. It flowed in shallow ripples over gravel bars as it moved out of sight. She was bending over, peering into the water, when Elisha and Jory appeared, dragging long poles behind them.

"You're not going to find any gold that way," Elisha laughed.

"I thought I might," Roxy laughed back.

"I'll show you and the boy how to pan for it tomorrow."

Chapter Thirty-five

Tanner escaped his doldrums for most of the morning as he and Rock drove his prize herd to mingle with the steers he had chosen to breed with the cows. Most of the Herefords were in heat and the longhorns lost no time in mounting them.

As he and Rock stood outside the pen watching, Rock grinned and said, "Them bulls are like children turned loose in a candy shop. Makin' real pigs of themselves, ain't they?"

Tanner grinned as he watched a bull leave one cow and go after another. "They mean to please, I guess."

"What are you gonna do with the rest of the day?" Rock asked as they left the pen and walked toward the barn.

"I thought maybe I'd ride into town for a bit."

Rock glanced at Tanner from the corner of his

eye, saw the lines of worry on his face and thought, Poor devil, he's eating his heart out over Roxy.

"I don't suppose Ace has heard anything from Roxy," he said.

"No, nothing. It's like she and the boy vanished into thin air."

They arrived at the barn and no more was said as Tanner went about the business of saddling Brave.

Ace sat in Roxy's office trying to catch up on the book work. "Dammit, Roxy," he muttered as he wrote down three bottles of whiskey in the wrong column, "I wish you'd get your rump back here where it belongs. I'm going crazy trying to take care of the business end of the saloon besides worrying about your welfare and where in the hell you are."

Belle's laughter rang out from the kitchen, mingling with Skinny's. Ace sat back, a wry smile on his face as he flexed his cramped fingers. The madam had been over to check whether he had heard from Roxy every morning since his wedding reception. He knew that she was worried about her young friend, but he was also wise to the fact that his cook was a big attraction. He hadn't missed how well they had gotten along the night of his wedding party. Was there a romance budding there? As far as he knew, Belle hadn't been interested in a man in years.

He was about to go back to the big ledger when through his open door he saw Tanner enter the saloon. A heavy sigh escaped him. He wished he had some news to give the big man, but he hadn't heard a word from his cousin.

He left the office and waited at the end of the bar for Tanner to join him. "Well," Tanner said, "I can tell by your face you haven't heard anything from her."

"Sorry, but not a word. I've wracked my brains as to where she could have gone. Nothing comes to mind."

"She has to be in some town. Jory has to go to school. She's real strict about him getting an education."

"I thought of that, too, and I hired a Pinkerton man to hunt for her. As of yesterday he hadn't found a trace of her."

His shoulders sagging, Tanner said, "I'd better get back to the ranch." He turned and left the saloon.

Ace watched him climb onto his stallion and ride away, feeling sorry for the other man. But, he thought, he had some of his pain coming to him for the mean way he treated Roxy.

Ace was about to go back to his books when the old swamper came through the bat-wing doors and laid the mail on the bar. Ace riffled hurriedly through the envelopes, hoping to find one from Roxy.

On the very bottom was a dirt-smudged envelope. He recognized Roxy's handwriting from seeing it so often in the ledger. He took it to his room and tore it open.

"Dear Cousin Ace," the letter began. "You will be surprised where Jory and I have settled in. Cripple Creek. Elisha showed up at the saloon on the eve of your reception, all excited about coming back here and staking a claim again. It is paying off for him. Not in a big way, but well enough for his needs and his retirement. I decided that Jory

369

and I would return with him to Cripple Creek.

"Jory and I have been having a fine time panning for gold, too. We are well and I have found contentment. Please don't give away my whereabouts. I will write you again next month. Give my regards to Michelle. Love, Roxy."

Ace immediately wanted to go after Tanner, to tell him the good news. But on the heels of that thought came the realization that he must bend to Roxy's wishes. Tanner was the one she was hiding from. Ace folded the single sheet of paper and returned it to the much-handled white square. Then holding it over a cuspidor he struck a match and set fire to it. When it burned to within an inch of his thumb and finger, he dropped the black and curling letter into the spittoon. He didn't even want Michelle to see it. She might accidentally let something drop that would lead Tanner to Cripple Creek.

He went back to his book work with a much lighter heart. Old Roundtree would take good care of Roxy and Jory.

Roxy shivered as she waded out into the middle of the river, and gravel and cold mud squeezed up between her bare toes. She didn't pay it too much mind, however. She was well on the way to getting gold fever. The little leather pouch that Elisha had given her was beginning to have some weight to it, and yesterday she had found a small nugget in the bottom of her pan. If her luck continued, she would have a sufficient sum for her and Jory to travel to California after the baby came.

As she dipped the pan into the water, scooping up gravel and sand, then swishing it around to reveal what might lie at the bottom, she thought of Ace, and wondered if he had received her letter yet, and how he was doing, managing the Lady Chance. She thought of Tanner then and wondered how he had taken her and Jory's disappearance. She had thought a couple of times that she should have taken up his offer of marriage. But each time, she knew why she hadn't. His offer had come because of Jory. And because of Jory she had refused. Sooner or later Tanner would be bound to discover that Jory was his son and he would divorce her so fast she wouldn't know what was happening. And he would take Jory from her, of course.

He'd probably let her take the baby. She could swear on her mother's grave that the little one was his and he'd never believe her.

Jory called to her that lunch was ready and Roxy waded to the bank, ready to eat. Although she was barely showing, she had a ravenous appetite. Elisha teased that he would have to go to the general store a man had set up under a large tent to buy more grub. No one bought anything from the tall, bearded man unless he absolutely had to. The fellow charged three times the money that a store in town would.

"Have you noticed that the wind has changed?" Elisha asked as they ate cold beef sandwiches from the roast he had baked for supper the night before in the outside oven he had erected from rocks and mud. "I'm afraid we're gonna have an early winter. It wouldn't surprise me if we get a little snow soon. I was talkin' to an old Indian yesterday, and he said that for sure cold weather was coming soon. He pointed out to me that the wild ducks have left the river, and that he has seen many geese flying south."

"How long do you pan after winter comes?" Jory asked.

"Some of the younger, hardier men keep at it until ice skims the water. Us older folks don't. The freezing water is too hard on the rheumatiz in our old bodies. We like to hug the fire then until spring comes."

When they left the shack later to resume panning, Roxy thought to herself that she wouldn't mind hugging the stove once winter arrived.

She thought so again when the wind picked up that night and she edged closer and closer to the little stove. The wind whistled around the shack, rattled the window frame and buffeted the door. She got very little sleep as the wind found every little crevice in the shack and blew over the sleeping bodies. And though Elisha had dragged out every blanket he owned and kept the stove going all night, she had never felt so cold in her life.

The wind died down around midnight, but when Roxy awakened the next morning and walked into the kitchen area, she saw through the window that an inch of snow lay on the ground. Elisha was putting crispy fried salt pork on the table but he still only wore his red woolen underwear. She smiled at Jory, who stood as close as possible to the heat of the stove.

"Why aren't you dressed, Elisha?" she asked as she sat down at the table. "You're going to get a late start panning."

Elisha lifted his attention from his plate and stared at Roxy as if he couldn't believe what she had said. "We'll do no more panning until next spring, girl. I've got to hustle to get you and Jory out of here before we get snowed in. Most everybody will be pullin' up stakes."

372

Roxy gaped at the old man as if she couldn't believe what he had said. "I thought we would be spending the winter here," she wailed. "I don't want to go back to Denver."

"I don't either," Jory said, joining his mother's cry of disbelief. "I like it here."

"You wouldn't like it, son, when the snow piled up as high as six feet, practically covering the shack."

"But there's no ice on the river," Roxy pointed out.

"There will be by tomorrow morning. I stepped outside before and took a look at the sky. It's all black to the north. There's bad weather on the way. Some of the longtime miners are taking down their tents already. So, as soon as we finish breakfast, we're gonna pack up and head out of here."

"Do we have to, Elisha?" Roxy begged, her eyes shimmering with unshed tears.

"Yes, Roxy girl, we have to. It would mean sure death if we stayed."

In her heart Roxy knew the old man was right. Nevertheless, she felt despondent as she gathered her and Jory's clothes and shoved them into her saddlebag. She was being forced back to the place she had fled. Was it her destiny always to live in shame and heartache? she asked herself as she tossed in her little pouch of gold flakes. She pulled on the heavy jacket she had brought with her for the winter weather, and tying a scarf around her head, she walked outside without a look at the two little rooms where she had found contentment for a short time.

Elisha and Jory waited for her, the horses and pack animal standing by. Jory, bundled up in his heavy jacket, had tears in his eyes as he took the saddlebag from her and positioned it on his pinto. "We'll be back in the spring, Ma," he tried to console her. "We can make it in town for another winter."

If only you knew how hard it is going to be for me, she thought as her son helped her to mount.

Ace had made numerous trips to the big glass window of the Lady Chance, watching the snow fall. A good eight inches of the white stuff had been trampled into mud by horse hooves and wagon tracks. By the blackness of the sky, there would be more, much more, by the end of the day.

Was it snowing in Cripple Creek? he worried. Was Roundtree bringing Roxy and Jory out? If so, what kind of weather were they traveling through?

He came to a decision about the question he had been asking himself: Should he break faith with Roxy and let Tanner know where she was? He wheeled from the window and hurried into his quarters.

Michelle was still asleep as he dressed in heavy clothing and walked out of the saloon. Bending his head against the sharp wind, he made his way to the livery and ordered the teenager there to saddle his stallion.

"It's not a very good day to go horseback riding, Mr. Brandon," the young man cautioned as he brought the saddled roan out to Ace. "Nobody is out today unless he has to be."

"I know," Ace said as he swung into the saddle. "That's why I'm taking a ride. I need to."

* * *

374

Tanner and Rock had spent the morning separating the Herefords from the steers and driving them back to the pen behind the barn. There they could be fed and watched over. Tanner had no idea how the Hereford cows would fare in a Colorado winter. The special steers were turned loose to join the other ones. The Sheldon brothers had worked all morning bringing wagonloads of dry grass to be strewn around for the cattle to eat. They wouldn't get fat on the diet, but they would be kept alive.

When the last cow was in the pen, Tanner closed and fastened the pole gate. "I'm ready for a glass of whiskey and a cup of coffee. What about you?" He grinned at the snow-covered Rock.

"You damn betcha." Rock nodded. "I'd like to set down in a tub of Pee Wee's hot coffee. I'm froze to the bone. I think we've brought the cows in just in time. From the looks of them clouds, we're in for a real norther."

The little cook had seen them coming, their heads bent against the stinging snow, and when they came in he had coffee poured and the whiskey bottle on the table.

Tanner and Rock stamped the snow off their boots, removed their jackets, shook the snow off them, then reached for the bottle.

"We're in for a bad one, ain't we?" Pee Wee said as he set two glasses on the table. "And ain't it unusual to get a storm so early in the season?"

"Yes, it is," Tanner said as he filled his glass. "But not that uncommon really. We had a blizzard around this time five years ago."

"I pity any poor devil caught out in it," Pee Wee said as he added more wood to the cookstove.

375

"I agree," Rock said as he lifted his glass to his mouth.

Tanner and Rock were thawing out and drinking their coffee when the cook-house door slammed open and a man completely covered with snow stumbled into the room. Tanner and Rock jumped to their feet and caught him just as he was about to fall. As they sat him in a chair, Pee Wee hurried over, bringing another glass.

"What the hell," Tanner swore when he wiped the snow off their unexpected guest and recognized the gambler. "What are you doing out in weather like this?" he asked, then hope flared inside him. "You've heard from Roxy, haven't you?"

"Yes," Ace panted, then paused. He didn't dare tell the rancher when he had heard from Roxy. The man would probably take his fists to him.

"Where is she?" Tanner shook his shoulder.

"Let's help him out of his jacket and get some whiskey inside him before you fire more questions at him," Rock said as he splashed the golden liquid into a glass.

Tanner nodded reluctantly and helped Ace out of his snow-encrusted mackinaw. When Ace had taken a long swallow of whiskey, Tanner looked at him expectantly.

"She and Jory are in Cripple Creek with the old miner Elisha Roundtree. A couple miners came in this morning from there. They said the weather is bad, and they think that Roundtree was pulling out."

He looked at Tanner, whose face had gone white, and said, "I'm afraid they're caught in this storm."

Tanner lunged to his feet, knocking over his coffee. As he jerked on his jacket, he ordered, "Pack

376

me some grub, Pee Wee, and put a bottle of whiskey in it. Rock, bring it to me while I saddle up Brave."

Elisha, Roxy and the boy had fared fairly well since leaving Cripple Creek. They had spent two days and a night on the trail, spending the night in a cluster of pines, sleeping close to a fire that Elisha kept going all night. Roxy and Jory had shared the same bedroll, the extra blankets piled on top of them. Elisha had high hopes that they would reach Denver in good shape.

They were a day away from Denver when the wind picked up and roared from the north, whispering the promise of death to anyone caught in its path.

Elisha was thankful that the wind was at their backs when the pellets of snow began flying. As it was, they could scarcely distinguish each other as they urged their horses on.

After an hour of the extreme cold, the horses began to tire and could only plod along in the foot-high snow.

"I'm plumb beat, too," Elisha muttered to himself as he looked back at his companions. Roxy had put Jory between them, protecting him as much as she could. "And I'm lost besides." He hung his head in despair.

He was berating himself for bringing Roxy and her son to Cripple Creek. It was the pride of his claim that had made him throw caution away. Now there was danger that this lovely young woman and her son might freeze to death.

As well as himself, he was thinking when suddenly, just feet away, he saw through the falling snow the dim bulk of a building. Maybe God is looking after us, he thought and called to Roxy to look ahead.

The cabin was old and deserted, probably owned by a trapper at one time. Elisha saw that the roof was still intact, that the door was still hung and that the window in front had been boarded up. *I guess it would be asking too much to find a supply of wood inside,* Elisha thought as he climbed stiffly to the ground. At least we'll be out of the wind and this infernal snow.

The wind almost jerked the warped door out of Lisha's hands as he opened it. He managed to hold it open until Roxy and Jory more or less fell into the little building. They stood in the center of the room waiting for their eyes to get used to the dimness. "It's got a fireplace," Roxy exclaimed when objects became visible.

"And thank the dear Lord, there is a good supply of wood stacked near it," Elisha said, feeling in his pocket for matches as he walked toward the fireplace.

The wood was old and dry and caught fire right away. Jory and Roxy gathered around the old man, their hands outstretched to the flames.

Elisha stood up and walked through a door leading into another room. He came back shortly and said, "I hope nobody minds if I bring the horses in out of the storm. There's plenty of room back there, and we can keep the door closed."

"By all means, bring them in," Roxy said immediately. "I'm sure they are just as cold as we are, and entirely spent."

Before Elisha went after the horses, he dragged a straw-filled mattress from the room and laid it close to the fire. "No use leaving it in there for the horses. They sleep standing up." He laughed lightly.

Roxy sat down on the moldy-smelling mattress while Elisha and Jory led the horses in, the clomping of their hooves shaking the wooden floor. As the heat reached out to her, she grew warm enough to remove the scarf that had covered all but her eyes in the blowing snow, and to unbutton her jacket. She became aware then of how hungry she was. There had been no stops to build a fire and make a meal.

When Elisha and Jory came back into the room, closing the door behind them, Elisha wore a worried look as he put the grub bag on the floor. "Something is bothering you, Elisha. What is it?" Roxy asked in anxious tones.

"Well, I'll tell you the whole biscuit." Elisha sat down beside her. "The storm don't seem to be letting up. It could carry on for two or three days, and we don't have that much grub." He took a deep sigh and added, "I hate to tell you this, but we're lost. I got turned around in the snow and I don't know where we are."

Roxy's first instinctive act was to put a protective arm around Jory, who sat on the other side of her. Was her son going to die without knowing who his father was? she wondered. And Tanner would never know about his son.

"What are we going to do, Elisha?" she asked, near tears.

"The onliest thing I can think of, girl, is try to wait out the storm. If this infernal snow ever stops, I can get my bearings and set out in the right direction. We'll have to ration our grub."

"Do you think the horses can make it if the snow piles up much higher?"

"We may have to leave the animals and walk in. There's several pair of snowshoes in the room yonder. Unless I really got off the track, we're only about half a day from Denver.

"For now I'm gonna make us a bite to eat and brew a pot of coffee," he said, dumping the contents of the grub sack out onto the rude, narrow hearth. He dug the battered coffee pot from among the skillet and two pans and, looking at Jory, said, "Son, will you go out and fill this with snow? Pack it down tight so that when it melts we'll have enough to make each of us a couple cups of coffee."

In half an hour they were eating fried salt pork and beans. Each mouthful was washed down with strong, hot coffee. The little room had warmed up enough for them to shed their jackets and the garments now were spread out in front of the fire to dry.

With food in their bellies the storm didn't seem so bad, even though the wind still whipped around the cabin, screaming over the chimney.

The wind that Elisha had been thankful was at his back now blew full force against Tanner's face and body. The snow had coated his shoulders and the crown of his hat, which he kept fastened on his head by a scarf tied under his chin. Every once in a while he had to draw a gloved hand across his eyebrows to clear the snow from his eyes.

Roxy and Jory seldom left Tanner's mind as Brave lunged through snow past his fetlocks. Were they still in the mining camp, safe and warm, or had old Roundtree decided to bring them out?

It was shortly after the noon hour that Tanner

came upon the tracks of four horses. He reined Brave in and sat studying them. Why had they veered off to the east? he asked himself, a troubled look in his eyes. And were they made by Elisha's and Roxy's and Jory's horses? Maybe the tracks were made by some miners who were headed for warmer quarters.

Should he follow the tracks, he debated, or go on to the mining area? Instinct told him to go east.

He followed the wandering tracks, going first one way and then the other. With his head bent to ward off some of the wind and keep the tracks in sight, he was almost upon the little cabin before seeing it.

His heart leapt and beat fast when he saw two sets of small boot prints, almost filled in with snow. Surely they'd been made by Roxy and Jory.

As he swiftly swung from the saddle, he wondered where the horses were. Then he spotted their tracks leading right up to the door and then disappearing. A wry smile twisted his lips. The old man had brought the animals into the cabin.

Tanner gave one loud knock on the door, then pushed it open. Three pairs of eyes stared at him. Then with a glad cry Jory was up and rushing toward him. "I knew you would come looking for us!" He threw his arms around Tanner's waist.

Tanner held him, pressing Jory's face to his chest as his eyes went to Roxy who still sat on the old mattress staring at him. Was she glad to see him too? he asked himself. He couldn't tell by her expression.

But Elisha was very happy to see another man, who would know what to do. "I'm sure glad to see you, Tanner." His relief showed on his wrinkled face. "I'm afraid I got lost in the storm and things were lookin' pretty scary for us. Come sit down and have a cup of coffee while you warm up by the fire."

"It will have to be a fast one," Tanner said as he walked to the fire and sat down beside Roxy. "We've got to get out of here while we can. This storm isn't going to let up for some time."

While Jory poured him a cup of coffee, Tanner looked at Roxy and asked, "Are you all right? No frozen fingers or toes?"

"No, they're fine." She laughed lightly. "There were a few times when I was sure they were frozen." When Jory handed the coffee to Tanner, she said softly, "I'm awfully glad you're here, Tanner. I was afraid Jory and I might die in this old cabin."

"Don't say that." His voice was harsh as a shiver ran through his body. He knew that could have very well happened.

"Get the horses saddled, Elisha. We'll leave as soon as I swallow this coffee. Time is precious."

While Elisha and Jory put on their coats, then went to prepare the horses, Tanner helped Roxy gather up the gear, tossing the unwashed skillet and pan in the sack. In two minutes flat Tanner was leading them in the right direction, three happy people following him.

The snow hadn't slackened and the wind was as fierce as ever. Brave was tiring because he was breaking the trail that the others followed. Tanner didn't urge the big horse to go faster, but let him take his own pace. Roxy rode behind him and he looked back often to see how she was faring. Not too well, he knew, by the way her body drooped and the way she leaned forward in the saddle. He would like to take her up with him, hold her, shield her from the wind. But it would be too hard on Brave to carry them both.

It was nearing an early dusk when Tanner saw, with thanksgiving, the large shape of his barn through the heavy curtain of swirling snow. Tanner stepped out of the saddle and hurried to Roxy's mount, which stood with drooping head. He reached his arms up to Roxy and she practically fell into them. Jory hurried alongside him as he carried her up to the house.

The big parlor was warm, thanks to Rock, Tanner imagined. Rock would have thought ahead, expecting him to arrive with Roxy and Jory.

As he laid Roxy's limp body on the sofa and took the shawl from her head and shoulders, then started undoing the jacket buttons, he looked up at Jory's anxious face and said, "Son, go turn down the covers in your ma's room."

Rock and Pee Wee rushed into the house as he was pulling Roxy's boots off. "Is she all right?" Rock asked, kneeling down and pulling a woolen sock off Roxy's slender foot.

"It's pink." He smiled at Tanner who watched anxiously. "I think she's just wore out. Get her to bed and try to get some whiskey into her."

"Ma doesn't drink," Jory protested. "She won't like it."

"It will be like medicine for her, son," Tanner said as he lifted Roxy into his arms and started for the hall that led to the bedrooms.

When he had laid Roxy down on her bed, he knelt to pull off her other boot and sock. When he would have pulled her riding skirt off, Jory pushed him aside, saying firmly, "You can leave now. I'll get her ready for bed."

Tanner's face took on a red flush even as amusement shimmered in his eyes. The boy was very protective about his mother. Of course he wouldn't want a man's hands on her.

"You're right, Jory," he said quietly, "but I didn't mean any disrespect to your ma."

"I know that, Tanner, but you're not married to her."

"No, I'm not," Tanner said, and as he left the room he doubted that he ever would be.

He was outside in the hall, leaning against a wall, when Jory opened his mother's door and said with a smile, "I got her in bed. You can come in now."

Tanner straightened up, took one step and was almost knocked over by Rock as he entered Roxy's room, a cup of coffee in his hand. Tanner frowned and was about to take another step when Elisha, hard on the heels of Rock, bumped into him.

"Hell's fire," Tanner swore. "Where's Pee Wee? Doesn't he want to get in on this parade?"

He stood in the doorway watching the two men fuss over Roxy. Rock was helping her sit up and Elisha was propping the pillows behind her back. When she was settled to their satisfaction, the covers smoothed neatly over her lap, Rock handed her the coffee, saying anxiously, "I hope it's the way you like it."

Tanner thought to himself with disgust that the two idiots looked like minions serving a queen. But who could blame them? She looked so fragile, so lovely in the flannel gown that Jory had buttoned up to her chin.

He stepped into the room and approached the bed. "Roundtree," he said gruffly, "don't you want to get over to the cook house and eat something?" Elisha mumbled that he was a little hungry, and after patting Roxy on the head, he stumped out of the room.

Tanner looked at Rock next. "Shouldn't you be checking on the Herefords?"

"Yeah, I should," Rock agreed, knowing that he was being dismissed. He smiled down at Roxy and said, "I'll see you tomorrow. Have a good night's rest."

Tanner and Roxy were alone in the room then. Tanner pulled a chair up beside the bed and looking steadily at Roxy, asked, "Why did you run away to a wild mining camp? Why did you feel that you had to hide from everybody?"

"I wasn't hiding from anyone," Roxy answered sharply, not quite meeting his eyes. "I just wanted to be alone for a while, to make some important decisions."

"And you couldn't do that here?"

"No, damn you, I couldn't." Anger was sharp in her voice.

Tanner leaned forward and, his eyes darkening with a glimmer of hope, said as if to himself, "You were running from me. Why, Roxy?"

"I don't know." Roxy stirred uneasily. "You keep me so confused. Most times you look at me contemptuously, then other times you want to make love to me. What am I to think?"

"I know, and I don't blame you." Tanner rose and paced about. "I hated you when I first came home. It tore me apart to find you had a son and no husband. I felt sure the gambler had fathered Jory and I wanted to shoot him. Then I met Jory and fell in love with the little tyke. He was such a brave little fellow. He had been fighting with a boy much older and bigger than him. He had gotten the worst of the scrap, his nose was bleeding and

385

his eye was swelling. I knew he wanted to cry, but he was holding his tears back.

"It was later, when I found out he was your son, that I began to really hate you and feel contempt for you. The old Roxy that I had known would never let her child be called a bastard.

"But even as I despised you, I wanted you so badly it was a pain in my gut. It took me a long time to realize that—"

"I'm going to bed now, Ma." Jory walked into the room, dressed in his nightshirt. "Are you feeling all right?"

"Yes, honey, I feel fine." Roxy smiled up at him. "What about you?"

"I'm fine, too." Jory put his arm around Tanner's waist. "Isn't it good to be home again? Safe and warm. I don't want to ever leave here again."

"Those are my sentiments, too, son." Tanner pressed the curly dark head to his waist. "I went through hell when your ma took you away."

"You won't do it again, will you, Ma?" Jory looked at her confidently.

"You'd better get to bed now," Roxy said, not answering his question. "You've had a long, hard day and must get some rest."

Tanner watched the boy leave, and the little hope he'd had died inside him. He knew that Roxy would run again. Withholding a sigh, he sat back down and looked at her with despairing eyes.

"Well," she said, "what was it you came to realize?"

Tanner didn't answer, only stared at the floor. Would she laugh at him when he told her how he felt about her? Would she finally say the name of the man she was waiting to marry someday?

When Roxy said impatiently, "Well, I'm waiting," he threw all caution away. He was tired of waiting, hoping.

"I realized that I love you, that I want to marry you, to be the father of your children and that includes Jory."

Tanner waited for Roxy to burst out laughing, to ridicule his words of love. He couldn't bear to look at her and stood up and paced about once more.

There was a long stretch of silence, then Roxy said softly, "I've waited a long time to hear you say that, Tanner."

When Tanner turned around and looked at Roxy, wondering what her words meant, she held her arms out to him. "I love you, too, Tanner, and I'll be happy to marry you."

"Oh, Lord, Roxy, do you mean it?" Tanner threw himself down beside her and went into her arms.

"I mean it, my love, with all my heart. If you only knew—" Her words were cut off by Tanner's lips descending hungrily on hers.

All his waiting, the years of despair, the longing for her with every breath he took, was in his kiss.

Roxy returned the pressure of his lips with equal fervor. At long last her cowboy had come home.

She purred her pleasure when he left her lips to place scorching kisses along her jaw, down her throat. All the time, he had been undoing the buttons Jory had so carefully done up. When he spread the edges apart, he encountered more clothing. He chuckled softly. Her son, the little gentleman, hadn't even let his own eyes see his mother's bare body. He had pulled the gown down over her camisole, and probably her underwear, too.

A small giggle escaped Roxy at her son's tact, and she sat up and pulled the flannel over her head and tossed it on the floor. She lay back down then, letting her lover remove the camisole.

Tanner's hands trembled as he removed the camisole and bared Roxy's breasts. His gaze was hot as it moved over them. He lifted his hand and trailed a finger around each nipple, saying huskily, "They seem to be larger than I remembered." He laid a palm over one and added, "They spill over my hand now."

With a lazy smile he lowered his head, murmuring, "I bet they taste as good as ever, though."

He swirled his tongue around one nipple and when Roxy gasped her delight, he drew the pebble-hard nub into his mouth, nibbled gently on it a moment, then began to suck.

Roxy moaned his name and trailed her finger around his working mouth. That fired Tanner into leaving her breast and trailing kisses down her smooth stomach, stopping only when he came to the barrier of her underclothes. Undoing a button, he hooked his thumbs in the waistband and, sliding them over her hips and legs, tossed them to lie on the floor with her other clothes.

When Roxy gazed up at him, her eyes heavy with desire, he tore off his clothes and climbed between her welcoming legs.

As he bent his head to kiss her again, Roxy could feel the pounding of his heart against her breast. She remembered then the baby that lay beneath *her* heart. Tanner didn't know about it yet, and in his desire to possess her, he might drive too hard, maybe hurt them both. And she wasn't ready yet to tell him he was going to be a father for the second time. Let him first learn about Jory.

She reached down between their hot bodies and, taking his large, engorged member in her hand, she guided its tip inside her. "Let's go slow," she whispered, "savor it to its fullest."

When Tanner began to slide slowly back and forth inside her, she felt she had never had him so tender before. Nor had she ever enjoyed lovemaking more when the climax burst upon her.

It was only moments later that Tanner's body stiffened and he called her name as he strained and jerked.

When Tanner's breathing had returned to almost normal, he lifted his head from Roxy's breast, rolled over on his back and pulled her over to rest her head on his shoulder. With his arm wrapped around her and his hand stroking her breast, he asked, "When can we get married? I don't want to be waiting every night for Jory to fall asleep before I can sneak into your bed and make love to you. I want the right to have you in my bed, to make love to you until we're both worn out."

Roxy leaned over the bed and picked up her gown. To Tanner's disappointment, she pulled it over her head and said, "Pull on your trousers. I want to show you something."

"Show me what? Where?" Tanner asked, buttoning up his Levi's.

"You'll see. It's in Jory's room."

"Light the lamp," Roxy whispered when they entered the bedroom next to hers.

"Won't the light wake him up?"

"No. I've seen him sleep through thunderstorms."

Jory didn't stir as Roxy pulled the covers down to his knees. He lay on his left side, his hands curled under his chin. Tanner looked at Roxy, his eyes questioning her action as she pulled the boy's nightshirt up past his hip.

"What do you see?" she asked.

"I see his bare rump," Tanner began, then leaned closer, his eyes fastened on a small heart-shaped mark high on the boyish hip. "I don't understand." He looked up at Roxy in confusion. "I have that same mark on my hip. So did my father, and his father. It's a mark that runs in our family."

"That's right." Roxy put her arm around Tanner's waist and leaned her head on his shoulder. "It runs in the family."

Tanner looked down at her, wonderment and fear of hoping warring in his eyes. "Roxy, are you saying that—"

"I'm saying that Jory is your son, Tanner." She answered, happy tears glimmering in her eyes. "At long last you know."

A coldness replaced the joy on Tanner's face. "Why did you keep this from me all this time?" he grated out. "You know how I love the lad."

"I wrote to you as soon as I knew I was expecting. When you didn't answer, I figured you didn't care. That you didn't want to become a family man."

"I never got any letter from you."

"I know. I found out why just a short time ago. Let's go back to my room. I have something else to show you."

Tanner pulled the covers back over Jory and lovingly tucked them around his shoulders. "My son," he murmured, letting his hand lie on the dark curls a moment before following Roxy through the door.

"Light the lamp, please," Roxy said as she

picked up her saddlebag, which had been set down at the foot of the bed.

When he had struck a match to the wick and light flared up, Tanner sat down on the bed and watched Roxy unstrap the heavy leather. She rummaged beneath the clothing and brought out the envelope she had found in her father's desk.

"Here." She handed it to Tanner. "It's finally being delivered. As you can see, it has never been opened."

Tanner tore its end off and withdrew the single sheet of paper. His eyes skimmed over the letter; then it was dropped to the floor as Tanner reached for Roxy and drew her down to sit on his knees.

"Oh, Roxy," he groaned, pressing her head into his shoulder. "How we have suffered all this time."

"And all because of my father's meanness," Roxy said sadly. "I gave the letter to him, but he never posted it."

"Let's don't look back, Roxy." Tanner held her away from him and looked deeply into her eyes. "The three of us will finally be a family. I can't wait to tell Jory that his favorite cowboy is really his father."

"I'm going to let you explain that to him." Roxy straightened up and slid her arms around his neck. "Now, do you think you can stand one more shock?"

Tanner looked at her, a wary look coming into his eyes. "I hope it's nothing that is going to spoil my happiness."

"I'm hoping that it will add to your happiness."

"Well, what is it?"

Roxy laid a hand on her stomach. "I'm going to have another baby."

Tanner looked at her, his eyes widening.

"Tanner Graylord, don't you dare ask who the father is." Roxy gave his hair a yank.

"I wasn't about to, you minx. I just can't take it all in." He looked at her and grinned. "That's why you wanted me to love you gentle, wasn't it?" When Roxy nodded, he asked, "Do you think it would be all right if I was gentle with you again tonight?"

The wind died down and the storm moved out as twice more they made slow, leisurely love.

Epilogue

The morning April sun shone brightly on the three people leaning against the cow pen. "What a little beauty," Roxy exclaimed, watching the two-hour-old white-faced calf wobble around its mother's legs.

Tanner smiled, well pleased with the first calf dropped from breeding his longhorns to the short-legged Herefords.

"Can I keep it for a pet, Pa?" Jory looked pleadingly at Tanner.

Tanner thought a moment, then tousling his son's hair, said, "Why not? It's a little heifer and she will make a good start toward a herd of your own."

"I'll name her Sunshine," Jory said excitedly as he climbed over the pen and rubbed the baby's head.

Roxy and Tanner smiled at each other, then with their arms around each other's waists, they walked toward the house. Baby Belle would be hungry around this time, and her doting parents had their own hungers to satisfy once she'd been nursed to sleep.

NORAH HESS *Wildfire*

Bestselling Author Of *Storm*

"A grand and beautiful love story....Never a dull moment! A masterpiece about the American spirit."
—*Affaire de Coeur*

The Yankees killed her sweetheart, imprisoned her brother, and drove her from her home, but beautiful, golden-haired Serena Bain faces the future boldly as the wagon trains roll out. Ahead lie countless dangers. But all the perils in the world won't change her bitter resentment of the darkly handsome Yankee wagon master, Josh Quade.

Soon, however, her heart betrays her will. Serena cannot resist her own mounting desire for the rough trapper from Michigan. His strong, rippling, buckskin-clad body sets her senses on fire. But pride and fate continue to tear them apart as the wagon trains roll west—until one night, in the soft, secret darkness of a bordello, Serena and Josh unleash their wildest passions and open their souls to the sweetest raptures of love.

_51988-7 $4.99 US/$5.99 CAN

Lacey

NORAH HESS

Norah Hess's historical romances are "delightful, tender and heartwarming reads from a special storyteller!"

—*Romantic Times*

Stranded on the Western frontier, Lacey Stewart suddenly has to depend on the kindness of strangers. And no one shows her more generosity than the rancher who offers to marry her. But shortly after Trey Saunders and Lacey are pronounced husband and wife, he is off to a cattle drive—and another woman's bed. Shocked to discover that the dashing groom wants her to be a pawn in a vicious game of revenge, the young firebrand refuses to obey her vows. Only when Trey proves that he loves, honors, and cherishes his blushing bride will Lacey forsake all others and unite with him in wedded bliss.

_3941-9 $5.99 US/$7.99 CAN

WINTER LOVE

NORAH HESS

"Norah Hess overwhelms you with characters who seem to be breathing right next to you!"
—*Romantic Times*

Winter Love. As fresh and enchanting as a new snowfall, Laura has always adored Fletcher Thomas. Yet she fears she will never win the trapper's heart—until one passion-filled night in his father's barn. Lost in his heated caresses, the innocent beauty succumbs to a desire as strong and unpredictable as a Michigan blizzard. But Laura barely clears her head of Fletch's musky scent and the sweet smell of hay before circumstances separate them and threaten to end their winter love.

_3864-1 $5.99 US/$7.99 CAN

Fancy

NORAH HESS

After her father's accidental death, it is up to young Fancy Cranson to keep her small family together. But to survive in the pristine woodlands of the Pacific Northwest, she has to use her brains or her body. With no other choice, Fancy vows she'll work herself to the bone before selling herself to any timberman—even one as handsome, virile, and arrogant as Chance Dawson.

From the moment Chance Dawson lays eyes on Fancy, he wants to claim her for himself. But the mighty woodsman has felled forests less stubborn than the beautiful orphan. To win her hand he has to trade his roughhewn ways for tender caresses, and brazen curses for soft words of desire. Only then will he be able to share with her a love that unites them in passionate splendor.

_3783-1 $5.99 US/$6.99 CAN

Storm
NORAH HESS

"Norah Hess not only overwhelms you with characters who seem to be breathing right next to you, she transports you into their world!"
—*Romantic Times*

Wade Magallen leads the life of a devil-may-care bachelor until Storm Roemer tames his wild heart and calms his hotheaded ways. But a devastating secret makes him send away the most breathtaking girl in Wyoming—and with her, his one chance at happiness.

As gentle as a breeze, yet as strong willed a gale, Storm returns to Laramie after years of trying to forget Wade. One look at the handsome cowboy unleashes a torrent of longing she can't deny, no matter what obstacle stands between them. Storm only has to decide if she'll win Wade back with a love as sweet as summer rain—or a whirlwind of passion that will leave him begging for more.

_3672-X $4.99 US/$5.99 CAN